SKAVENSLAYER

'BEWARE! SKAVEN!' Felix shouted and saw them all reach for their weapons. In moments, swords glittered in the half-light of the burning city. From inside the tavern a number of armoured figures spilled out into the gloom. Felix was relieved to see the massive squat figure of Gotrek among them. There was something enormously reassuring about the immense axe clutched in the dwarf's hands.

'I see you found our scuttling little friends, manling,' Gotrek said, running his thumb along the blade of his axe until a bright red bead of blood appeared.

'Yes,' Felix gasped, struggling to get his breath back before the combat began.

'Good. Let's get killing then!'

A WARHAMMER NOVEL

Gotrek and Felix

SKAVENSLAYER

By William King

A BLACK LIBRARY PUBLICATION

First published in Great Britain in 1999 by
Games Workshop Publishing
Willow Road, Lenton,
Nottingham, NG7 2WS, UK

10 9 8 7 6 5 4 3

Cover illustration by John Gravato

A CIP record for this book
is available from the British Library

ISBN 1 84154 102 8

Set in ITC Giovanni

Printed and bound in Great Britain by
Caledonian International Book Manufacturing Ltd., Glasgow

See the Black Library on the Internet at
http://www.blacklibrary.co.uk

Find out more about Games Workshop
and the world of Warhammer at
http://www.games-workshop.com

CONTENTS

SKAVEN'S CLAW

'I would like to forget the long hard trudge through the winter woods which followed our encounter with the children of Ulric. And it pains me to this day to think of the punishment we meted out to the girl, Magdalena, but my companion was unrelenting, and no evil we encountered was ever spared if that could be avoided. In this case it could not be. With a heavy heart, we entered the forest once more and set off northwards.

'At long last we found ourselves in the great Elector city of Nuln, a place of refinement, sophistication, wealth and great learning – and a city in which my family had long had business dealings. At that time, the Countess Emmanuelle was at the height of her fame, power and beauty and her city attracted the wealthy, the aristocratic and the famous like a candle flame attracts moths. Nuln was one of the most beautiful cities in all the Empire.

'Of course, our own entry into the life of the city was made at a level far lower on the social scale. Short of cash, hungry and weary from our long journey, we were forced to take employment in what was possibly the very worst occupation we were to pursue in our long wanderings. And during that period we encountered a fiend who was to bedevil our paths for long years to come.'

— From *My Travels With Gotrek, Vol. III*,
by Herr Felix Jaeger (Altdorf Press, 2505)

'STUCK IN A SEWER, hunting goblins. What a life,' Felix Jaeger muttered with feeling. He cursed all the gods roundly. In his time he had come to consider himself something of an expert on unprepossessing surroundings but this must surely take the prize. Twenty feet overhead, the population of the city of Nuln went about its lawful daily business. And here he was, in the dark, creeping along narrow walkways where a single slip could put him over his head in reeking foulness. His back ached from stooping for hours on end. Truly, in all of his long association with the Trollslayer, Gotrek Gurnisson, he had never before plumbed such depths.

'Stop moaning, manling. It's a job, isn't it?' Gotrek said cheerfully, paying not the slightest heed to the smell or the narrowness of the ledge or the closeness of the bubbling broth of excrement the sewerjacks called 'the stew'.

The Slayer looked right at home in the endless maze of brickwork and channels. Gotrek's squat muscular form was far better adapted to the work than Felix's own. The dwarf picked his way along the ledges as sure-footed as a cat. In the two weeks they had been part of the sewer watch, Gotrek had become far more adroit at the job than ten year veterans of the service. But then he was a dwarf; his people were reared in the lightless places far beneath the Old World.

It probably helped that he could see in the dark, Felix thought, and did not have to depend on the flickering light of the watchmen's lanterns. That still did not explain how he endured the stink, though. Felix doubted whether even the dwarfholds smelled quite so bad. The stench down here was exquisitely vile. His head swam from the fumes.

The Trollslayer looked peculiar without his usual weapon. Felix had come to think of the battle-axe as being grafted to his hand. Now the dwarf had his huge starmetal axe strapped across his back. There was not enough space to swing it in most areas of the sewer. Felix had tried to get Gotrek to leave the weapon in the watch armoury alongside his own magical sword but had failed. Not even the prospect of its weight dragging him below the sewage if he fell in could cause the Slayer to part with his beloved heirloom. So Gotrek carried a throwing hatchet in his right hand and a huge military pick in the other. Felix shuddered when he imagined the latter being used. It resembled a large hammer with a cruel hooked spike on one side. Driven by the dwarf's awesome strength he did not doubt that it could shatter bone and tear through muscle with ease.

Felix tightened his grip on his own short stabbing sword and wished that he still carried the Templar Aldred's dragon-hilted mageblade. The prospect of facing goblins in the dark made him long for the reassurance of using his familiar weapon. Perhaps Gotrek was right to keep his axe so close.

In the gloom of the lantern light, his fellow sewerjacks were ominous shadowy figures. They wore no uniform save the ubiquitous scarves wrapped round their heads like Araby turbans, with a long fold obscuring their mouths. Over the last two weeks, though, Felix had become familiar enough with them to recognise their silhouettes.

There was tall, spare Gant whose scarf concealed a face turned into a moonscape by pockmarks and whose neck was a volcanic archipelago of erupting boils. If ever there was a good advertisement for not staying a sewerjack for twenty years Gant was it. The thought of his toothless smile, bad breath and worse jokes made Felix want to cringe. Not that he had ever pointed this out to Gant's face. The sergeant had hinted that he had killed many a man for it.

There was the squat, ape-like giant Rudi, with his massive barrel chest and hands almost as big as Gotrek's. He and the Trollslayer often arm-wrestled in the tavern after work. Despite straining until the sweat ran down his bald pate, Rudi had never beaten the dwarf, although he had come closer than any man Felix had ever seen.

Then there were Hef and Spider, the new boys as Gant liked to call them, because they had only been with the sewer watch for seven years. They were identical twins who lived with the same woman on the surface and who had the habit of finishing each other's sentences. So strange were their long, lantern-jawed faces and their fish-like staring eyes, that Felix suspected that in-breeding or mutation was part of their heritage. He did not doubt their deadliness in hand-to-hand combat, though, or their dedication to each other and their girl, Gilda. He had seen them do terrible things with their long hook-bladed knives to a pimp who had insulted her one night.

Along with the burly, one-eyed dwarf, these were the men he worked with, as desperate a crew as he had ever known. They were vicious men who couldn't find work that suited them anywhere else and who had finally found an employer who asked no questions.

There were times when Felix felt like going along to the office of his father's company and begging for money so he could leave this place. He knew they would give him it. He was still the son of Gustav Jaeger, one of the Empire's wealthiest merchants. But he also knew that word of his capitulation would get back to his family. They would know that he had come crawling back to them, after all his fine boasts. They would know he had taken the money he had affected to so despise. Of course, it had been easy to despise money on the day he had stormed from their house, because he had never known the lack of it. His father's threat to disown him was meaningless because he simply had not understood it. He had grown up rich. The poor were a different species: sad, sickly things that begged on street corners and obstructed the path of one's coach. He had learned since that day. He had endured hardship and he thought he could take it.

But this was very nearly the last straw: being forced to become a sewerjack, the lowest of the low amongst the hired bravoes of Nuln. But there had simply been nothing else for it. Since their arrival no one else would hire two such down-at-heel rogues as himself and Gotrek. It pained Felix to think of how he must have looked, seeking work in his tattered britches and patched cloak. He had always been such a fine dresser.

Now they needed the money, any money. Their long trek through the land of the Border Princes had yielded no reward. They had found the lost treasure of Karak Eight Peaks but they had left it to the ghosts of its owners. It had been a case of find work, steal or starve – and both he and the Trollslayer were too proud to steal or beg. So here they were in the sewers below the

Empire's second greatest city, crawling beneath a seat of learning that Felix had once dreamed of attending, haunting slimy tunnels below the home of the Elector Countess Emmanuelle, most famous beauty of the nation.

It was not to be borne. Felix wondered constantly what ill-omened star had marked his birth. He consoled himself with the thought that at least things were quiet. It might be dirty work but so far it had not proved dangerous.

'Tracks!' he heard Gant shout. 'Ha! Ha! We've found some of the little buggers. Prepare for action, lads.'

'Good,' Gotrek rumbled.

'Damn!' Felix muttered. Even as inexperienced a sewerjack as Felix could spot these tracks.

'Skaven,' Gotrek hawked and spat a huge gob of phlegm out into the main channel of the sewer. It glistened atop a patch of phosphorescent algae. 'Rat-men, spawn of Chaos.'

Felix cursed. On the job only two weeks and already he was about to meet some of the creatures of the depths. He had almost been able to dismiss Gant's stories as simply the imaginings of a man who had nothing better with which to fill his long tedious hours.

Felix had long wondered if there really could be a whole demented subworld beneath the city as Gant had hinted. Were there colonies of outcast mutants who sought refuge in the warm darkness and crept out at night to raid the market for scraps? Could there actually be cellars where forbidden cults held ghastly rituals and offered up human sacrifices to the Ruinous Powers? Was it possible that immense rats which mocked the form of man really scuttled through the depths? Looking at those tracks it suddenly seemed all too possible.

Felix stood frozen in thought, remembering Gotrek's tales of the skaven and their continent-spanning webwork of tunnels. Gant tugged his sleeve.

'Well let's get on with it,' the sergeant said. 'We ain't got all day.'

'NEVER BEEN HERE before,' Hef whispered, his voice echoing away down the long stretch of corridor.

'Never want to come here again,' Spider added, rubbing the blue arachnid tattoo on his cheek. For once Felix was forced to agree with them. Even by the standards of Nuln sewers, this was a dismal place. The walls had a crumbled, rotten look to them. The little gargoyles on the support arches had been blurred by age until their features were no longer visible. The stew bubbled and tiny wisps of vapour rose when the bubbles burst. The air was close, fetid and hot.

And there was something else – the place had an even more oppressive atmosphere than usual. The hair on the back of Felix's neck prickled, as it sometimes did when he sensed the undercurrents of sorcery nearby.

'Doesn't look safe,' Rudi said, looking at a support arch dubiously. Gotrek's face twisted as if this were a personal insult.

'Nonsense,' he said. 'These tunnels were dwarf-built a thousand years ago. This is Khazalid workmanship. It'll last an eternity.'

To prove his point he banged the arch with his fist. Perhaps it was just bad luck but the gargoyle chose that moment to fall forward from its perch. The Slayer had to leap to one side to avoid being hit on the head and narrowly avoided skidding into the stew.

'Of course,' Gotrek added, 'Some of the labour was done by human artisans. That gargoyle for instance – typical shoddy manling workmanship.'

No one laughed. Only Felix dared even smile. Gant stared up at the ceiling. The lamp set down at his feet underlit his face making him look eerie and daemonic.

'We must be below the Old Quarter,' he said wistfully. Felix could see he was contemplating the district of palaces. A strange melancholy expression transfigured his gaunt, bony features. Felix wondered whether he was pondering the difference between his life and the gilded existence of those above, contemplating the splendours he would never know and the opportunities he would never have. Momentarily he felt a certain sympathy for the man.

'There must be a fortune up there,' Gant said. 'Wish I could climb up and get it. Well, no sense in wasting time. Let's get on with it.'

'What was that?' Gotrek asked suddenly. The others looked around, startled.

'What was what?' Hef asked.

'And where was what?' added Spider.

'I heard something. Down that way.' All their gazes followed the direction indicated by the Trollslayer's pointing finger.

'You're imagining things,' Rudi said.

'Dwarfs don't imagine things.'

'Aw sarge, do we have to look into this?' Rudi whined. 'I want to get home.'

Gant rubbed his left eye with the knuckles of his right fist. He seemed to be concentrating. Felix could see he was wavering. He wanted to leave and be off to the tavern just as quickly as the rest of them, but this was his responsibility. If something was wrong beneath the palaces and anyone found out they had been there and done nothing about it, then it was his neck for the block.

'We'd better look into it.' he said eventually, ignoring the groans of his fellow sewerjacks.

'It shouldn't take long. I'll lay odds it's nothing anyway.'

Knowing his luck, Felix decided, that was a bet he wouldn't take.

WATER DRIPPED DOWN from the arch of the tunnel. Gant had narrowed the aperture of his lantern so that only the faintest glimmering of light was visible. From ahead came the sound of voices. Even Felix could hear them now.

One of the voices was human, with an aristocratic accent. It was impossible to believe the other belonged to a man. It was high-pitched, eerie and chittering. If a rat had been given the voice of a human being it would have sounded like this.

Gant stopped and turned to look back at his men, his face pale and worried. He obviously didn't want to go on. Glancing round the faces of his fellow sewerjacks, Felix knew they all felt the same. It was the end of the day. They were all tired and scared and up ahead was something they didn't want to meet. But they were sewerjacks; men whose only virtue was courage and the willingness to face what others would not, in a place where others would not go. They had a certain pride.

Gotrek tossed the hatchet into the air. It spun upward, blade catching a little of the light. With no apparent effort the Trollslayer caught it by the haft as it fell. Spider pulled his long-bladed knife from its sheath and shrugged. Hef gave a feral smile. Rudi looked down at his shortsword and nodded. Gant grinned. The Trollslayer looked pleased. He was in the company of the sort of maniacs he could understand.

Gant gestured softly and they shuffled forward, picking their way carefully and quietly along the slimy ledge. As they turned the bend he opened up his lantern to illuminate their prey.

'Your payment, a token of my esteem. Something for your own personal use,' Felix heard the aristocratic voice say. Two figures stood frozen like trolls in a fairy tale, petrified by the sudden bright light. One was a tall man, garbed in a long black robe like a monk's. His face was patrician: fine-boned, cold and aloof. His black hair was cut short, ending in a widow's peak above his forehead. He was reaching forward to hand the other figure something that glowed eerily.

Felix recognised it. He had seen the substance before, in the abandoned dwarf fortress of Karak Eight Peaks. It was a ball of warpstone. The recipient was short and inhuman. Its fur was grey, its eyes pink; its long hairless tail reminded Felix of a great worm. As the thing turned to squint at the light, the tail lashed. It reached inside its long, patchwork robes and clutched something in its taloned paws. From its belt hung an unscabbarded rusty, saw-toothed blade.

'Skaven!' Gotrek roared. 'Prepare to die!'

'Fool-fool, you said you were not followed,' the thing chittered at its human companion. 'You said no one knew.'

'Stay where you are!' Gant said. 'Whoever you are, you're under arrest on suspicion of witchcraft, treason and unnatural practices with animals.'

The sergeant's confidence had been restored by the fact there were only two of them. Even the fact that one of the perpetrators was a monster seemed to leave him undaunted.

'Hef, Spider, take them and bind them.' The rat-thing suddenly threw the sphere it had withdrawn from its clothing.

'Die-die, foolish manthings.'

'Hold your breath!' Gotrek shouted. His hatchet hurtled forward simultaneously.

The skaven's sphere tinkled and shattered like glass and an unhealthy looking green cloud billowed outward. As he shoved Felix back down the corridor, Gotrek grabbed Rudi and pulled him with them. From inside the gas-cloud came the sound of gurgling and choking. Felix felt his eyes begin to water.

Everything went dark as the lantern went out. It was like being caught in a nightmare. He couldn't see, he was afraid to take a breath, he was stuck in a narrow corridor underground and somewhere out there was a monster armed with deadly, incomprehensible weapons.

Felix felt the slick slime of the stone under his hands. As he fumbled he suddenly felt nothing. His hand was over the stew. He felt unbalanced and afraid to move, as if he could suddenly topple in any direction and plunge into the sewage. He closed his eyes to keep them from stinging and forced himself to move on. His heart pounded. His lungs felt as if they were about burst. The flesh between his shoulder blades crawled.

He expected a saw-toothed blade to be plunged into his back at any moment. He could hear someone trying to scream behind him and failing. They gurgled and gasped and their breathing sounded terribly laboured as if their lungs had filled with fluid.

It was the gas. Felix realised. Gotrek had told him of the foul weapons which the skaven used, the products of a Chaos-inspired alchemy allied to a warped and inhuman imagination. He knew that to take one breath of that foul smelling air was to die. He also knew that he could not keep from breathing indefinitely.

Think, he told himself. Find a place where the air is clear. Keep moving. Get away from the killing cloud. Don't panic. Don't think about the huge rat-like shape creeping ever closer in the dark with its blade bared. As long as you keep calm you'll be safe. Slowly, inch by torturous inch, his lungs screaming for air, he forced himself to crawl towards safety.

Then the weight fell on him. Silver stars flickered before his eyes and all the air was driven from his lungs. Before he could stop himself he took in a mouthful of the foul air. He lay in the dark gasping and slowly it dawned on him that he wasn't dead. He wasn't choking. No knife had been driven into his back. He forced himself to try and move. He couldn't. It was as if a great weight lay across him. Terror flashed through his mind. Maybe his back was broken. Maybe he was a cripple.

'Is that you, Felix?' he heard Rudi whisper. Felix almost laughed with relief. His burden was his huge fellow sewerjack.

'Yes... where are the others?'

'I'm all right,' he heard Hef say.

'Me too, brother.' That was Spider.

'Gotrek, where are you?' No answer. Had the gas got him? It seemed impossible. The Trollslayer couldn't be dead.

Nothing as insidious as gas could have killed him. It wouldn't be fair.

'Where's the sarge?'

'Anybody got some light?'

Flint sparked. A lantern flickered to life. Felix saw that something large shuffling towards them along the shadows of the ledge. Instinctively his hand reached for his sword. It wasn't there. He had dropped it when he fell. The others stood poised and waiting.

'It's me,' said the Trollslayer. 'Bloody human got away. His legs were longer.'

'Where's Gant?' Felix asked.

'Look for yourself, manling.'

Felix squeezed past and went to do so. The gas had vanished as quickly as it appeared. But it had done its work on Sergeant Gant. He lay in a pool of blood. His eyes were wide and staring. Trickles of red emerged from his nostrils and mouth.

Felix checked the body. It was already cooling and there was no pulse. There was no wound on the corpse.

'How did he die, Gotrek?' Felix knew about magic but the fact that a man could be killed and have no mark left on him made his mind reel.

'He drowned, manling. He drowned in his own blood.' The Slayer's voice was cold and furious.

Was that how he dealt with fear, Felix wondered? By turning it into anger. Only after the dwarf went over and started kicking the corpse did he notice the dead skaven. Its skull had been split by the thrown hatchet.

WEARILY FELIX LAY on his pallet of straw and stared at the cracked ceiling, too tired even to sleep. From below came the sound of shouting as Lisabette argued with one of her seemingly interminable stream of customers.

Felix felt like banging on the floor and telling them to either shut up or get out, but he knew that it would only cause more trouble than it would solve. As he did every night, he resolved that he would begin looking for another rooming house tomorrow. He knew that tomorrow night he would be too tired to start.

Ideas chased each other like frolicking rats inside the cavern of his brain. He was at that stage where weariness made his thoughts strange even to himself. Odd conjunctions of images and maze-like chains of reasoning came from nowhere and went nowhere in his mind. He was too tired even to be angry about the fate of Sergeant Gant, killed in the line of duty and destined for a pauper's grave on the fringes of the Gardens of Morr. A watch captain too bored to pay much attention to reports of monsters in the sewers. No family to mourn him, no friends save his fellow sewerjacks, who were even now toasting his memory in the Drunken Guardsman.

Gant was a cold corpse now. And the same thing could so easily have happened to me, Felix thought. If he had been in the wrong place when the globe exploded. If Gotrek had not told us to hold our breath. If the Slayer had not pushed him away from the gas. If. If. If. So many ifs.

What was he doing anyway? Was this how he intended to spend the rest of his days; chasing monsters in the dark. His life seemed to have no reason to it any more. It merely moved from one violent episode to the next.

He thought of the alternatives. Where would he have been now if he had not killed Wolfgang Krassner in that duel, if he had not been expelled from university, if he had not been disinherited by his father? Would he be like his brothers working in the family business: married, secure, settled? Or would something else have gone wrong? Who could tell?

A small black rat scuttled across the rafters of the room. When he had first viewed this attic with its one small window, he had imagined that it would be at least be free from the rats which infested all of the buildings in the New Quarter. He had deluded himself with the thought that the rodents would have heart attacks from the effort of climbing all those stairs. He had been wrong. The rats of the New Quarter were bold and adventurous and looked better fed than many of the humans. He had seen some of the larger ones chasing a cat.

Felix shuddered. Now he wished he had not started thinking about rats – it made him think of the mysterious aristocrat and the skaven in the sewers. What had been the purpose of that clandestine meeting? What profit could any man find in dealing with such alien monstrosities? And how could it be that folk could roister and whore through the teeming streets of Nuln and be unaware of the fact that evil things burrowed and crawled and nested not six yards beneath their feet? Perhaps they just didn't want to know. Perhaps it was true, as some philosophers claimed, that the end of the world was coming and it was best to simply lose oneself in whatever pleasures one could find.

Footsteps approached on the stairs. He could hear the old rickety boards creak under the weight. He had been going to complain that the whole place was a firetrap but Frau Zorin had always seemed too pitiful and poor to bother.

The footsteps did not stop on the landing below but continued to come closer. Felix reached beneath his pillow for his knife. He could think of no one who would be visiting him at this time of night and Frau Zorin's was right in the roughest part of the New Quarter.

Noiselessly he rose and padded on bare feet to the door. He stifled a curse as a splinter embedded itself in the sole of his foot. There was a knock on the door.

'Who is it?' Felix asked, although he already knew the answer. He recognised the old widow woman's wheezing breath even through the thin wood.

'It's me,' Frau Zorin shrieked. 'You have visitors, Herr Jaeger.'

Cautiously Felix opened the door. Outside stood two huge burly men. They carried clubs in their hands and looked as if they knew how to use them. It was the man they flanked that interested Felix. He was handing the landlady a gold coin, which she took with an ingratiating smile. As the man turned to look at the door Felix recognised him. It was his brother, Otto.

'Come in,' Felix said, holding the door open. Otto stood, staring at him for a long time, as if he couldn't quite recognise his younger brother. Then he strode into the room.

'Franz, Karl, remain outside,' he said quietly. His voice carried an authority that Felix had not heard in it before, an echo of their father's calm, curt manner.

Felix was suddenly acutely aware of the poverty of his surroundings: the uncarpeted floor, the straw pallet the bare walls, the hole in the sloping roof. He saw the whole scene through his brother's eyes and wasn't at all impressed.

'What do you want, Otto?' he asked brusquely.

'Your taste in accommodation hasn't changed much, has it? Still slumming.'

'You haven't come all the way from Altdorf to discuss my domestic arrangements. What do you want?'

'Do you have to hold that knife so ready. I'm not going to rob you. If I was, I would have brought Karl and Franz in.'

Felix slid the knife back into its scabbard. 'Maybe I would surprise Karl and Franz.'

Otto tilted his head to one side and studied Felix's face. 'Maybe you would at that. You've changed, little brother.'

'So have you.' It was true. Otto was still the same height as Felix but he was far broader. He had put on weight. His chest had thickened and his hips broadened. His large soft belly strained against his broad leather belt. Felix guessed that his thick blond beard hid several chins. His cheeks were fatter and seemed padded. His hair was thinner and there were bags under his eyes. His head jutted forward aggressively. He had grown to resemble the old man. 'You look more like father.'

Otto smiled wryly. 'Sad but true. Too much good living, I'm afraid. You look like you could use some yourself. You've become very skinny.'

'How did you find me?'

'Come on, Felix. How do you think I found you? We have our agents and we wanted to find you. How many tall blonde men travelling in the company of dwarf Slayers do you think there are in the Empire? When the report came into my office about two mercenaries answering the description I thought I'd better investigate.'

'Your office?'

'I run the business in Nuln now.'

'What happened to Schaffer?'

'Vanished.'

'With money?'

'Apparently not. We think he was deemed politically undesirable. The Countess has a very efficient secret police. Things happen in Nuln these days.'

'Not Schaffer! There was never a more loyal citizen in the Empire. He thought the sun shone out of the Emperor's fundament.'

'Nuln is only just part of the Empire, brother. Countess Emmanuelle rules here.'

'But she's the most flighty woman in the Empire, or so they say.'

'Von Halstadt, her Chief Magistrate is very efficient. He's the real ruler of Nuln. He hates mutants. And rumour has it that Schaffer had begun to show stigmata.'

'Never.'

'That's what I said. But believe this, little brother: Nuln is no place to come under suspicion of being a mutant. Such people vanish.'

'But it's the most liberal city of the Empire.'

'Not any more.' Otto looked around fearfully as if realising that he had said too much. Felix shook his head ruefully. 'Don't worry, brother. No spies here.'

'Don't be too sure about that, Felix,' he said quietly. 'In these days, in this city, walls have ears.' When he spoke again his voice was loud and held a note of false heartiness. 'Anyway I came around to ask if you'd like to dine with me tomorrow. We can eat out if you'd like.'

Felix half-wanted to refuse and half-wanted to talk to his brother some more. There was much family news to catch up on and perhaps the possibility of returning to the fold. That thought alone frightened him as well as intrigued him.

'Yes, I'd like that.'

'Good. I'll have my coach collect you from here.'

'After I've finished work.' Otto shook his head slowly. 'Of course, Felix. Of course.'

They said their goodbyes. It was only after his brother had left that Felix began to wonder what could so frighten a man of Otto's power and influence that he would worry about eaves-droppers in a place like Frau Zorin's.

FRITZ VON HALSTADT, head of the secret police of Nuln, sat among his files and brooded. That damned dwarf had come within an inch of catching him. He had actually tried to lay his filthy hands on him. He had come so near to undoing all his good work. One blow would have been enough. It would have brought Chaos and darkness to the city von Halstadt was sworn to protect.

Von Halstadt reached out and raised his cut glass pitcher. The water was still warm. Good, the servants had boiled it for exactly eleven minutes as he commanded. He was to be com-mended. Von Halstadt poured some into a glass and inspected it. He raised the glass to the light and checked it for sediment, for stuff floating in it. There was none. No contamination. Good.

Chaos could come so easily. It was everywhere. The wise knew that and used it to their advantage. Chaos could take many forms; some were worse than others. There were relatively benign forms, like the skaven – and there was the festering evil of mutation.

Von Halstadt knew that the rat-men just wanted to be left alone, to rule their underground kingdom and pursue their own form of civilisation. They were intelligent and sophisticated and they could be dealt with. If you had what they wanted, they would make and keep bargains. Certainly they had their own plans but that made them comprehensible, controllable. They were not like mutants: vile, insidious, evil things that lurked everywhere, that hid in secret and manipulated the world.

We could all so easily be puppets on the end of the mutant's foul strings, he thought. That is why we must be vigilant. The enemy are everywhere, and more and more are spawned all the time. The commoners were the worst for it, spawning an endless string of slovenly, lazy, good-for-nothings. Most mutants were born among the herd. It made a sick kind of sense. There were more of them and they were notoriously immoral and lewd and licentious.

The thought made him rigid with horror. He knew that the mutants took advantage of the commoners' stupidity. They were so clever. They used the ill-educated, lazy oafs: filled their heads with seditious nonsense, fed their envious anger of their betters, whipped them up to riot and loot and destroy. Look at how they had ruined his poor father, burned the estate to the ground in one of their brutish uprisings. And his father had been the kindest and gentlest man who had ever lived.

Well, Fritz von Halstadt would not make that mistake. He was too clever and too strong. He knew how to deal with revolutionaries and upstarts. He would stand guard and protect mankind from the menace of the mutant. He would fight them with their own weapons; terror, cunning and ruthless violence.

That was why he kept his files, even though his beloved ruler Emmanuelle laughed at them, calling them his secret pornography. Within these lovingly detailed and carefully cross-indexed records was a kind of power. Information was power. He knew who all the potential revolutionaries were. His web of spies and agents kept him informed. He knew which nobles secretly belonged to the Dark Cults and had them watched at all times. He had sources that could penetrate any meeting place, and who no one ever suspected.

That was part of his bargain with the skaven. They knew many things and could find out many more. Their little spies were everywhere, unsuspected. He used their dark wisdom and dealt with the lesser of two evils to keep the greater anarchy at bay.

He picked up the small framed portrait Emmanuelle had given him and licked his thin lips. He thought about her choice of words for his files: 'pornography'. He was shocked that she had used such a word, even knew what it meant. It must be that brother of hers! Leos was a bad influence. Emmanuelle was too good, too pure, too unsullied to have learned such a word herself. Perhaps he should put his spies on her, just to watch out for–

No, she was his ruler! He did this all for her. Though the countess could not see its worth now, one day she would. Spying on her would be crossing a line he had set for himself. Besides, sometimes he suspected that the lies which he heard about her might just conceivably contain a kernel of truth, and finding out that would be too painful.

He put the picture back down on his desk. He had been allowing himself to drift from the main problem. The dwarf and the sewerjacks. Could they have recognised him? And what would he do about it if they had? They were simple men doing their simple job. Like him, they were struggling to keep Chaos at bay. But would they understand the necessity of what he did? If they did not, perhaps they would understand that it was necessary to ensure their silence forever.

SLOWLY THE HUNGOVER sewerjacks lowered themselves into the depths. One by one they clambered down the ladders lowered through the access ports. Rudi, now acting sergeant, lit the lantern and illuminated the tunnel.

The stink hit Felix like a hammer even as he carefully stepped from the ladder onto the ledge. This was the trickiest part of the operation. There was only about one foot clearance between the ladder and the edge of the walkway. A misstep had carried many a still-drunk sewerjack into the stew.

'You missed yourself last night, young Felix,' Hef said.

'We gave the sarge a fine send-off,' Spider added.

'Gotrek downed seven jacks of ale one after the other and wasn't even sick. We took a week's wages off the first watch.'

'I'm very pleased for you,' Felix said. Gotrek looked none the worse for his exploits. Of all the sewerjacks he was the only one who didn't appear ill. The rest were ghastly, pale, and walked with the shuffling gait of old men.

'Ah, there's nothing like the smell of the stew to clear your head in the morning,' Hef said, proceeding to stick his head out over the edge of the walkway and be violently sick.

'Fair clears the head it does,' Rudi added, with no trace of irony.

'I can see that,' Felix said.

'We're going to sweep through the area where the sarge got taken,' Rudi said. ' We decided it last night. We want to see if we can find the scumbag who deals with the skaven. And maybe if we can't find him we'll find some of his pink-tailed little friends.'

'And what if they've got more of those gas bombs?' Felix asked.

'Not to worry. Gotrek's an old tunnel fighter. He explained how to deal with it.'

'Oh, did he? '

'Yes. We soak our scarves in piss and breathe through them. That cuts out the gas.'

'I knew it would be something like that,' Felix said, glaring at the Trollslayer, wondering if the others were really convinced by Gotrek's claims or whether they were simply humouring him. One look at their haggard, determined faces convinced him that it was the former.

'It's true, manling. My ancestors fought the skaven at Karak Eight Peaks and it worked for them.'

'If you say so,' Felix said. He could tell it was going to be a long day.

THEY FOLLOWED THE route of the previous day towards the area beneath the Old Quarter. As they went, Felix had time to reflect on how strange his life was. His brother's house was somewhere above his head and he had not known it. He had not even known Otto was in the city. The fact that his brother had found him was certainly a testimony to the efficiency of his spy network.

Felix suspected that such things were necessary to anyone who wanted to do business in Nuln nowadays. What Otto had said about Schaffer and the countess's secret police was worrying too. Felix was sorry for the old man but he was more worried about himself. Both he and the Trollslayer were wanted by the law for their part in the great Window Tax riots in Altdorf. If the secret police were so efficient here and he and Gotrek were really so recognisable then they too might vanish. He consoled himself with the thought that the capital was a long way away and that the local authorities would probably not be interested in what happened outside their jurisdiction.

In a way it was even more reassuring that they were part of the sewer watch. It was tacitly understood that the watch did not look too closely into the backgrounds of those who volunteered for it. Indeed it was said to be a sure way of having them ignore your previous crimes. All of the others had been involved in acts of criminal violence at some point in their lives, or so they claimed. No, there wasn't too much to worry about. He hoped.

More immediately worrying was the prospect that they might actually come across some skaven. He did not fancy facing such vicious foes in their own environment. Frantically he tried to recall what Gotrek had told him of the rat-men, hoping to remember something that would give him an edge if it came to a fight. He knew that they were a race of vicious mutant rats, products of warpstone in ancient times. They were said to inhabit a great polluted city called Skavenblight, the location of which nobody knew. Rumour had it that they were divided up into clans, each of which had their own function: the practice of sorcery, the making of war, the breeding of monsters and so forth. They were lighter than a man but faster and more vicious, and possessed of a feral intelligence which made them deadly enemies.

He could recall one book he had read about the battles of the ancients that described their few interventions on surface battlefields: their terrifying charges in great, chittering hordes, their twisted evil and their penchant for torturing their prisoners. It had been a skaven horde which had undermined the walls of Castle Siegfried and broke the siege after two years of

trying. Legend said that Prince Karsten had paid a terrible price
for the service of his allies. Sigmar himself destroyed an army
of them before his ascension to the heavens. It had been one of
his less well-known exploits.

Felix himself had seen some evidence of the skaven's handiwork
in Karak Eight Peaks. The thought of the warpstone-polluted wells
and the great mutated troll gave him the chills even after all this
time. He hoped that he would not have to face any more of their
monstrous creations in his lifetime. Looking at the others he could
tell that they did not share his hope.

UNTIL YESTERDAY, Felix had never given a second thought to the
number of rats in the sewers. Now he saw that they were everywhere. They scuttled away from the lights as the watchmen
approached and he could hear the pitter-patter of their feet
behind them after they had gone. Their eyes caught the reflection of the lantern and glittered like tiny stars far off in the
darkness of the undercity.

He found himself wondering now if there was any connection between the rats and the skaven. He started to imagine the
little ones as spies for their larger brethren. It was a madman's
fantasy, he knew, one straight out of the tales of sorcery he had
read as a boy, but the more he thought of it the more terrifying
the prospect became. Rats were everywhere in the great cities of
man, living amid the garbage and refuse of civilisation. They
could see much and overhear much and go, if not unnoticed,
at least unsuspected.

He began to feel their cold eyes staring malevolently at him
even as he walked. The walls of the sewer seemed to close in
about him threateningly and he imagined himself caught in a
vast warren. Thinking of the skaven out there, it suddenly
seemed possible to him that he was in a vast burrow, that he
and the others had been shrunk to the size of mice and that the
skaven were ordinary rats, walking upright and dressed in a
fashion that aped man.

The fantasy became so vivid and compelling that he began to
wonder whether the fumes of the stew were going to his head
or whether the scent deadening narcotics prescribed by the city
alchemists had hallucinatory side-effects.

'Steady, manling,' he heard Gotrek say. 'You're looking very
pale there.'

'I was just thinking about the rats.'

'In the tunnels your mind creates its own foes. It's the first thing a tunnel fighter learns to guard against.'

'You've done this sort of thing before then,' Felix said half sarcastically.

'Yes, manling. I was fighting in the depths before ever your father was born. The ways around the Everpeak are never free of foes and all the citizens of the King's Council do their share of military service in the depths. More young dwarfs die that way than any other.'

Gotrek was being unusually forthright, as he sometimes was before moments of great peril. Danger made him garrulous, as if he wanted to communicate with others only when he realised he might never get another chance. Or perhaps he was simply still drunk from the night before. Felix realised he would never know. Fathoming the dwarf's alien mind was nearly as far beyond him as was understanding a skaven.

'I can remember my first time in the tunnels. Everything seemed cramped. Every sound was the tread of some secret enemy. If you listen with fearful ears you are soon surrounded by foes. When the true foe comes you have no idea from which quarter. Stay calm, manling. You'll live longer.'

'Easy for you to stay,' Felix muttered as the hefty Slayer shoved past. All the same he was reassured by Gotrek's presence.

WITH SOME TREPIDATION they approached the place where Gant had been killed. Mist rose from the surface of the stew and in places a slow current was evident in the sludge. The area of the fight looked very much the same as Felix remembered it, except that the body was gone. The area where the corpse had lain was disturbed.

There was a trail in the slime that suddenly ended at the ledgeside, as if the body had been dragged a short way then dumped. He knew they should have shifted it yesterday, when they had the chance, but they had been too shaken, disturbed and excited by what had happened to do so. No one had wanted to carry the mangy, rat-man body. Now it wasn't there.

'Someone took it,' Hef said.

'Wonder who?' Spider said.

Gotrek scanned the ledge where the body had been. He bent down and peered closely at the tracks, then rubbed his eye-patch with his right fist. The hatchet which had killed the skaven came dangerously close to his tattooed scalp.

'Wasn't a man anyway. That's for sure.'

'All sorts of scavengers in the sewers,' Rudi said. He voiced the common belief of all sewerjacks. 'There are things you would-n't believe living in the stew.'

'I don't think it was any scavenging animal,' Gotrek said.

'Skaven,' Felix said, voicing their unspoken thoughts.

' Too big. One of them was anyway. The other tracks might be skaven.' Felix peered out into the gloom; it suddenly appeared even more menacing.

' How big?' He cursed himself for taking on the same mono-syllabic way of speaking as the others. 'How large exactly was this creature you referred to, Gotrek.'

'Perhaps taller than you, manling. Perhaps heavier than Rudi.'

'Could it be one of the mutants you say the skaven breed? A hybrid of some sort?'

'Yes.'

'But how can all those prints simply vanish?' Felix asked. 'They can't all have thrown themselves in the stew, can they?'

'Sorcery,' Hef said.

'Of the blackest sort,' Spider added.

Gotrek looked down at the ledge and cursed in his native tongue. He was angry and his beard bristled. The light of mad violence shone in his one good eye. 'They can't just disappear,' he said. 'It's not possible.'

'Could they have used a boat?' Felix asked. The idea had just struck him. The others looked at him incredulously.

'Use a boat?' Hef said.

'In the stew,' Spider said.

'Don't be stupid,' Rudi said. Felix flushed.

'I'm not being stupid. Look the tracks end here. It would be quite simple for someone to step down from the ledge into a small skiff.'

'That's the daftest thing I've ever heard,' Rudi said. 'You've got some imagination, young Felix. Who'd ever have thought of using a boat down here?'

'There's a lot of things you'd never think of,' Felix snapped. 'But then thinking's not your strong suit, is it?' He looked at the other sewerjacks and shook his head. 'You're right – a boat doesn't make sense. Much better to believe they vanished by magic. Maybe a cloud of pixies wafted in and carried them away.'

'That's right, a cloud of pixies. That's more like it,' Rudi said.

'He's being sarcastic, Rudi,' Spider said.

'A very sarcastic fellow, young Felix,' added Hef.

' Probably right though,' Gotrek said. 'A boat wouldn't be too hard to come by. The sewers flow into the Reik, don't they? Easy to steal a small boat.'

'But the outflows into the river all have bars,' Rudi said. 'To stop vagrants getting in.'

'And what's our job, if not hunting down those self-same vagrants when they file through the bars?' Felix asked. He could see the idea was starting to filter into even Rudi's thick skull.

'But why, manling? Why use boats.' Felix felt briefly elated. It wasn't often that Gotrek admitted that Felix might know more than him. He considered the matter rapidly.

'Well for a start, they don't leave tracks. And they might be connected with a smuggling operation. Suppose someone was bringing warpstone in by river, for instance. Our noble skulker yesterday seemed to be paying the rat-man off with it.'

'Boats make me sick. The only thing I hate more than boats is elves,' Gotrek said as they set off again.

They searched for the rest of the day and found no trace of any skaven, although they did find that the bars had been sawn away on one of the outflows to the Reik.

FELIX STEPPED OUT of the street and into the Golden Hammer. He stepped from reality into a dream. The doorman held the great oak door for him. Servile waiters ushered him away from the squalor of the streets into a vast dining hall.

Richly clad people sat at well-filled tables, and dined and talked by the light that sparkled from huge crystal chandeliers. Portraits of great Imperial heroes watched the diners sternly from the walls. Felix recognised Sigmar and Magnus and Frederick the Bold. The style of the brushwork was Vespasian's, the most famous Nulner painter of the past three centuries. The far wall was dominated by a portrait of the Elector Emmanuelle, a ravishing raven-haired beauty garbed in a less than modest ball gown.

Felix wished his borrowed clothing fitted him better. He was wearing some of his brother's old garments. Once he and Otto had been of the same size and build, but in the years of his wandering Felix had grown thinner and Otto more stout. The linen shirt felt baggy and the velvet vest felt loose. The trousers had been cinched with a leather belt tightened to its last notch. The boots were a comfortable fit, though, as was the cap. He had tilted it to a rakish angle to show off the peacock feather in the band. He let his hand toy idly with the golden pomander that dangled from a chain round his neck. The smell of fine Bretonnian perfume wafted up from it. It was nice to smell something other than the sewers.

The servant led him to a booth in the corner in which Otto sat. He had a leather-bound accounts book in front of him and was ticking entries off in it with a quill pen. As Felix approached he looked up and smiled. 'Welcome, little brother. You're looking much better for a bath and a change of clothes.'

Having studied himself in the great silvered mirror in Otto's townhouse earlier, Felix was forced to agree. A warm bath, scented oil and a change of clothing had made him feel like a new man. In the looking glass he had seen the foppish young dandy he once had been, albeit with more lines round the eyes and a firmer, narrower set to the mouth.

'This is a very charming establishment,' he said.

'You could dine here every evening if you wished.'

'What do you mean, brother?'

'Simply that there is a place for you in the family business.'

Felix looked around to see if they were being overheard. 'You know I'm still a wanted man in Altdorf because of the Window Tax business?'

'You exaggerate your notoriety, little brother. No one knows who the leaders of that riot were. Altdorf isn't Nuln you know.'

'You've said yourself Gotrek is a very easily recognisable figure.'

'We're not offering the Trollslayer employment. We're offering you your birthright.' And there it was; what Felix had half-hoped for and half-feared. His family would take him back. He could give up the restless uncomfortable life of the adventurer and return once more to Altdorf and his books. It would mean a life chained to the ledgers and the warehouses, but it would be safe. And one day he would be rich.

It was a tempting prospect. No more crawling around in sewers. No more beatings at the hands of thugs. No more catching strange illnesses in terrible, out of the way places. No more muscle-searing treks through wild, savage lands. No more descents into darkness. No more confrontations with the Chaos-worshipping minions of obscure cults. No more adventures.

He wouldn't have to put up with Gotrek's sullenness or his whims any more. He could forget his oath to follow the Trollslayer and record his doom in an epic poem. The promise had been made when he was drunk; surely it didn't count? He would be his own master. And yet, something held him back.

'I'll have to think about it,' he said.

'What is there to think about, man? You can't actually tell me that you prefer being a sewerjack to being a merchant, can you? Most people would kill to be given this opportunity.'

'I said, I'll think about it.'

They ate on in uncomfortable silence. After some minutes, the door to the great room opened and a tall man was led in by the servant. He was clad in black and his monkish robes made him seem out of place in his opulent setting. His face was thin and ascetic, and his black hair ended above his forehead in a widow's peak.

As he crossed the room, silence spread in his wake. Felix saw that the wealthy diners were afraid of him. As he passed close to the table Felix was shocked to recognise him: it was unquestionably the man he had seen in the sewers with the skaven. His mind reeled. He had assumed that the man was some kind of sorcerer or renegade. He pictured a cultist or a desperado. He had not expected to see him here in the haunts of Nuln's wealthiest and most respectable citizens.

'What's the matter, brother. You look like you've seen a ghost.'

'Who– who is that man?'

Otto let out a long sigh. 'You don't want to know. He's not a man that you ask questions about. He asks them about you.'

'Who is he, Otto? Do I have to go over and ask him?' Felix saw a look of alarm and admiration pass across his brother's face.

'I do believe you would too, Felix,' he whispered. 'Very well. That is Chief Magistrate Fritz von Halstadt, the head of Countess Emmanuelle's secret police.'

'Tell me about him.'

'There are those who see him as the enemy of corruption everywhere. He is hard working and no one doubts his sincerity. He sincerely hates mutants and for that reason he has the backing of the Temple of Ulric. His home is guarded by their Templars.'

'I thought the Temple of Ulric had no power here, that the countess disliked it.'

'That was before von Halstadt's rise to power. He came from being a minor court functionary to the most powerful man in the city-state very quickly. Some say it was by blackmail; some say his enemies have a habit of being found dead under mysterious circumstances. He's risen far for a man whose father was a minor nobleman in an out of the way province. A callous cunning old swine by all accounts.

'Von Halstadt is cold, cruel and dangerous, not just because of his influence. He has a deadly blade. He's killed several people because they've insulted the honour of the countess.'

'I would have thought her brother, Leos, did enough of that without him having to.'

'Leos is not always about and rumour has it that our chief magistrate would be prepared to fight him over the countess. Apparently he's got it hard for her.'

'Then he's mad. Leos is the deadliest blade in the Empire and Emmanuelle's not worth fighting over.'

Otto shrugged. Felix stared at von Halstadt, wondering what the connection between the skaven and the head of the countess's secret police could be. And hoping against hope that the man did not recognise him.

VON HALSTADT WAS TIRED. Not even his usual excellent supper could cheer him. His mind was filled with worry and the cares of high office. He looked around at his fellow diners and returned their smiles, but in his heart of hearts he despised them. Shallow, indolent cattle. Garbed liked nobles but with the hearts of shopkeepers. He knew that they needed him. They needed him to keep Chaos at bay. They needed him to do the work they were too soft to do themselves. They were barely worth his contempt.

It had been a trying day. Young Helmut Slazinger had failed to confess, despite von Halstadt himself supervising the torture

implements. It was strange how some of them maintained their
innocence even unto the grave. Even when they knew that he
knew they were guilty. His secret sources had told him that
Slazinger belonged to a clandestine cell of Slaanesh-worship-
ping cultists. The jailers had been unable to find any of the
usual tattoos that marked coven members but that meant nothing. His most trusted informants, the skaven, had let him in on
the secret. That in fear of his ruthless crusade, his hidden enemies had taken to using sorcerous tattoos visible only to fellow
coven members.

Gods, how insidious the mutant fiends were! Now they
could be everywhere; they could be sitting right in this very
room, their initiation tattoos plain to each other on their faces
and he would not know. They could be sitting there right now
mocking him and there was nothing he could do about it. That
lanky young fellow in the ill-fitting clothes could be one. He
was certainly studying von Halstadt intently enough. And
come to think of it, there was something quite sinister about
him. Perhaps he should be the next subject of an official investigation.

No, get a grip on yourself, von Halstadt told himself. They
cannot hide forever. The blinding light of logic can pierce the
deepest darkness of falsity. So his father had always told him
before yet another beating for his sins, real or imagined. No,
his father had been correct. Von Halstadt had done wrong.
Even if he could not work out exactly what. The beatings had
been for his own good, to drive out sin. His father had been a
good man, doing the work of the righteous. That was why he
smiled as he punished him. He didn't enjoy it. He told him
that often and often. It was for his own good. In a way it had
been a great lesson. He had learned that it was often necessary
to do painful, bad things for the greater good.

It had made him hard. It enabled him to do what he had to
today, free from the weakness of lesser men. It enabled him to
stand up for right. It had made him into a man his father could
be proud of and he should be grateful. He was strong without
being malicious. He was like his father.

He had taken no pleasure in the torture of young Slazinger.
He had taken no pleasure in the skaven report that the nobleman was a Slaaneshi cultist. Although he had to admit that it
was a fortunate coincidence, given the rumours concerning

Slazinger and Emmanuelle. More malicious lies: someone as pure as the countess would not, could not, have anything to do with the likes of Slazinger. The worm was a notorious rake, the sort of handsome young dandy who thought it witty to speak out against the lawful servants of the state, to criticise the harsh measures needed to maintain law and order in this festering sink of iniquity and sin.

He pushed Slazinger from his mind and gave his thoughts over to other matters. His agent in the watch house had brought him the report on the Gant incident. No action was being taken. It would cost too much to make a full sweep through the sewers beneath the Old Quarter and that would cut into the take the watch captain got from his station's financial allocation. Well, even corruption sometimes has its uses, thought von Halstadt.

His spy had brought him word that Gant's patrol had been nosing around in the area of his death though, which was more worrying. They might accidentally come across some more skaven going about their business. They might even discover the skiffs that ran from the docks to van Niek's Emporium. He doubted, though, that they could ever discover that the shop was simply a government front which channelled warpstone from outside the city to the skaven in payment for their services. He smiled.

It was an arrangement with a certain pleasing symmetry. He paid the skaven in the currency they wanted. They did not seem to realise it was both useless and dangerous. Warpstone actually caused mutation. The skaven claimed to use it as food. Well, it was a relatively harmless way of disposing of an incredibly dangerous substance and it provided him with a fine source of information at the same time.

Yes, a pleasing symmetry indeed. In a way, it was a pity that he could not make known the service he was doing the Empire by disposing of the evil stuff in a safe way. It had been a lucky day for all mankind when von Halstadt had got lost in the sewers and stumbled across the skaven. It was fortunate they had recognised him as a man with whom they could do business.

He must get some more. This very evening he must contact another skaven agent and see to it that the watchmen met with an accident. He was sorry to have to do that to men who were only doing their duty, but his security must come first.

He was the only man who understood the real dangers threatening Nuln and he was the only man who could save the city. He knew this wasn't simply vanity; it was the truth. Tonight he would contact the new skaven leader, Grey Seer Thanquol and order him to eliminate his enemies. The thought of this secret use of his power made him shiver. He told himself it was not with pleasure.

'I'M TELLING YOU I saw him last night,' Felix insisted. The other sewerjacks stared at him out of the gloom. Overhead he heard the thunder of wheels as a cart passed over a manhole cover. 'At the Golden Hammer. He was standing not twenty feet away from me. His name is Fritz von Halstadt and he's the man we saw dealing with the skaven.'

'Sure,' Rudi said, glancing back worriedly. 'And he was having dinner with the Countess Emmanuelle and the enchanter Drachenfels. What were you doing in the Golden Hammer anyway? It's where nobs go. They wouldn't let a sewerjack in if his clothes were made of spun gold. You don't expect us to believe you were there.'

'My brother took me. He's merchant. And I'm telling you that's where I saw our man, von Halstadt.'

'You're not from Nuln, are you, young Felix?' Hef spoke calmly and helpfully, as if he were genuinely concerned with clearing up any misapprehension the young sewerjack might have. 'Do you know who Fritz von Halstadt is?'

'The head of the Nuln secret police, is who he is. The scourge of mutant scum in this city,' Spider said. A tic moved somewhere far back in the twin's jaw. Felix had not realised the twins were such great admirers of von Halstadt's. 'And the head of the secret police don't go about consorting with rat-men.'

'Why not?'

'Because he's the head of the secret police and the head of the secret police wouldn't do that sort of thing. It stands to reason, don't it.'

'Well, that is irrefutable logic, Rudi. But I'm telling you I saw him with my own eyes. It was the man from the sewers.'

'Are you sure you're not mistaken, manling? It was very dark down there and human eyesight is not good in the dark.'

'I'm certain,' said Felix. 'I've never been more certain of anything in my life.'

'Well, young Felix, even if you're right, and I'm not saying that you are mind, what can we do about it? We can hardly go marching up to the Countess Emmanuelle and say "By the way your majesty, did you know your most trusted advisor has been sneaking around the sewers below your palace in the company of giant talking rats?"' Hef didn't even smile as he said this.

'She'd ask you how much weirdroot you'd been chewing and order her Kislevite lover to throw you in the cells,' Spider said.

Felix could see their point. What could they do? They were just ordinary watchmen and the man he was talking about was the most powerful person in the city. Perhaps it would be best just to forget the whole thing. He was seeing Otto again this evening, was going to have a fine meal in his townhouse. Soon he could be far from here and it wasn't his problem.

But the thought nagged at him. What was the terrible and feared master of the countess's secret police doing in the company of skaven? What hold could they possibly have over him?

'Right, lads enough of this,' Rudi said. 'Back to work.'

HOSTLEADER TZARKUAL SKAB looked back at his stormvermin. They filled this tunnel chamber and the smell of their musk was sweet. His heart swelled with something akin to pride. These were big, burly skaven and their black fur was sleek and well-groomed. It matched their fine lacquered black armour and their rune-encrusted helms of black iron. They were elite: well-fed, well turned out, disciplined, as far above the lowly clanrats and slaves as he was above them. He commanded two dozen of the finest warriors his clan could field. In the coming war this would be swelled to two hundred or more.

He did not need the full force for this mission; this was simple. The elimination of some pink flesh manthings. Easy. Grey Seer Thanquol had made it plain it would be so. Even though he didn't like Skrequal's replacement, he agreed. He doubted he would even need four claws of stormvermin to deal with some lowly manthing warriors. Behind him Thanquol gave a discreet little bark of impatience. The rat-ogre which accompanied the sorcerer rumbled angrily.

A little shimmer of fear passed through Tzarkual when he contemplated the giant hybrid's formidable muscles and claws. He would not want to face it in battle. It must have cost the grey seer a fair stash of warpstone to purchase from the packmasters of Clan Moulder, and from what Tzarkual had heard it would prove worth every ounce.

Yet he would not let himself be hurried. There were certain proprieties to be observed. He must keep face in front of his troops. He allowed none of his anxiety to show in his bearing and he controlled the urge to squirt the musk of fear.

He twitched his nose authoritatively and then lashed his tail to get their attention. Two dozen pairs of alert pink eyes turned to look at him. 'We go to the bigstink below the mancity,' he told them. 'We go to kill five manthings who guard the tunnels. They are enemies of our clanlord and have killed-dead a clanbrother, yes. Vengeance and manblood will be ours. Fight well and more breeders and more warptokens will be yours. Fight badly and I will chew your guts with my own fangs.'

'We hear, hostleader,' they squeaked thunderously. 'Glory to the clan. Vengeance for our clanbrother!'

'Yes-yes, blood-vengeance for our clanbrother!' Tzerkual smiled, revealing row on row of sharp serrated teeth. In skaven it was a gesture of menace and his followers fell silent. He was pleased by the fear he had imposed on them.

Yes, he wanted vengeance for Skrequal. They had belonged to the same birthing, had fought their way to the top of their clan together. Had connived and killed and assassinated their way to power. He understood his brother's ambitions and insofar as he trusted anybody he had trusted Skrequal. He wanted the blood of his killers. It would in some way make up for the inconvenience of having to find another ally in the great game of clan politics.

Perhaps Thanquol might do, if the grey seer didn't attempt to slip a saw-knife into his back first. Well, only the future would tell.

He covered his teeth once more and the stormvermin relaxed. He was looking forward to visiting the undercity once more. He liked slinking through the vast stinking maze that reminded him of Skavenblight. It made a change from this hideously barren outpost of the Underway he had been forced to occupy since Warlord Skab dispatched him here. He was glad the stupid manthing had enough sense to contact them about his problem. The guards were potentially a threat to the great plan. Nothing must menace their pawn before they took over the city.

He wasn't sure what the great plan was but that didn't matter. He was a simple and vicious soldier. It was not his place to philosophise on the ways the Thirteen Lords of Decay chose to order the Universe. It was his task simply to kill the enemies of Clan Skab. That was what he intended to do.

FELIX WAS WORRIED. It wasn't just the number of rats he had seen, it was the way they followed him that was worrying. He told himself not to be stupid. The rats weren't following him. They were just there, like they always were in the sewers. His imagination was playing tricks on him, as it always did.

He gazed round what the other sewerjacks called 'the cathedral'. It was a major confluence of several of the city's greatest sewerways. It had been designed in a style he thought he recognised from the halls of Karak Eight Peaks. He called it Dwarf Imperial. The dwarfs who had built these sewers were refugees, he knew. They had fled from the World's Edge Mountains when their lands had become too dangerous. They had come to the human lands bringing a great store of engineering knowledge and a tremendous nostalgia for their ancestral homes under the mountains.

The then-Elector of Nuln had been an enlightened man. He put their knowledge and skills to good use, improving the sanitation of his fast-growing city. They had responded to the challenge by creating places that resembled great temples rather than sewers. Mighty arches supported masonry that had lasted nearly a thousand years. Intricate carved stonework adorned the arches, revealing the traditional dwarf hammer and shield designs. The work had been made beautiful in its way, as well as functional. Of course time had eroded much of it. Coarse patchworks of plaster and brick filled gaps where human repair teams less skilled than the original builders had been at work. But this place almost directly below the elector's palace was a sewer fit for an emperor.

Then suddenly Felix saw it. He saw how vulnerable those ancient master builders had made the city. He remembered Gotrek's tale of how the skaven had attacked Karak Eight Peaks from the direction least expected: from below.

The sewers provided a means of access to below any place of importance in the city. Teams of assassins or shock troops could be moved through them by a foe adapted to the darkness. They

were a perfect highway for a skaven invasion. The great walls of
Nuln would prove no barrier to them. The watchers on the roof
of the temple of Myrmidia would notice nothing.

The peril to the city was even greater if its own chief magistrate were in league with the rat-men! The pieces clicked. He
knew how Von Halstadt's foes disappeared. They were dragged
down into the depths by the skaven. He would bet anything
that a web of access tunnels existed which gave access to the
palaces and walled houses above. If nothing else, a small
enough assassin could gain access through the sewage channels, gross as that thought was.

The question now was why? Why was von Halstadt doing it?
What did he stand to gain? The demise of his enemies? Perhaps
he was a mutant in league with the forces of darkness. Perhaps
he was mad. Felix asked himself whether he could walk away
now, knowing what he did. Could he take the offer of a safe job
along side his brothers and leave the second greatest city of the
Empire in the hands of its enemies?

It was infuriating; there was nothing he could do. No one
would believe him if he accused the chief magistrate. The word
of a sewerjack against that of the most influential man in the
city? And if he revealed who he really was, that would only get
him into deeper trouble. He was a known revolutionary and an
associate of the dwarf who had slaughtered ten of the
Emperor's own elite household cavalry. No one would be too
bothered if the pair of them disappeared. Perhaps it would be
best to let things be. It was only then, as he came to his decision, that he noticed that the rats had vanished and the sound
of soft padding could be heard behind him.

'We're being followed, manling,' Gotrek said quietly. 'Several
groups. One behind. Two taking tunnels parallel to us. There's
more up ahead.'

'Followed? By what?' Felix had to force his words out. His
throat felt constricted and his voice was barely louder than a
whisper. 'Skaven?'

'Yes. We're going to be ambushed. Our scuttling little friends
should be quieter. Dwarf ears are keen.'

'What can we do?'

'Fight bravely and, if need be, die heroically, manling.'

' That's all very well for you – you're a Slayer. The rest of us
aren't quite so keen to get ourselves killed.'

Gotrek glared at him contemptuously. Felix felt the need to find an excuse for his fear. 'What if it's an invasion? Someone has to warn the city. It's our duty. Remember the oath we swore when we joined the watch.'

He could see this made an impression on the Trollslayer. Dwarfs were always impressed by talk of duty and of oaths.

'You have a point, manling. At least one of us should get away and warn the city. Best talk with the others and make up a plan.'

TZARKUAL SAW THAT his prey had stopped. They were huddling together in the passage and talking in low tones. He knew they were afraid. It had finally dawned on even their dim manbrains that they were being followed. He knew the righteous fear that the true skaven warrior inspired in most humans. He had seen the look of cringing horror in many a human eye. The awful majesty and dignity of the skaven form filled the manthings with awe.

He stood taller and preened his fur with his tongue. At times, looking in the polished mirror of his shield, he almost understood their feelings. There was no denying he cut an impressive figure even among the regal forms of his fellow high ranking skaven. It was only proper that manthings should be suitably impressed by the master race.

He gestured for his stormvermin to halt. He would allow his victims a minute's grace to fully savour their fear. He wanted them to understand the hopelessness of their position. Perhaps he might even allow them to beg for their lives. Some victims did. He knew it was a tribute to the impressive bearing he mustered.

'Hostleader. Should we not attack now? Maimslay the manthings while they are in confusion?' Clawleader Gazat asked.

Tzarkual shook his head. Gazat had showed his true lack of understanding of the finer points of strategy. He thought it better to simply attack rather than wait for the correct moment when their foes were paralysed with fear.

The hostleader twitched his tail indulgently. 'No-no. Let them know fear. When they spray musk and know hopelessness then we shall charge-charge.'

Tzarkual could see that Gazat was dubious. Well, let him be. Soon he would see the superiority of his leader's tactical knowledge for himself.

'Hostleader! They come back to our path.'

'Doubtless they flee in panicked terror. Prepare to meet them with fixed weapons.' The ledge here was wide enough for two skaven abreast. The stormvermin took up position, their pole-arms braced to meet the charge. Tzarkual waited expectantly.

Triumph filled his heart as the terror-struck manthings confronted his elite warriors. So full of fear were they that they did not even stop their headlong rush. Blind panic drove them to throw themselves onto the blades.

Surely it was only luck that allowed the sweep of the dwarf's hatchet to chop though both weapons. Yes, he could see more clearly now. The dwarf was so scared that he frothed at the mouth like a clanrat with rabies. He howled fearful prayers to whatever gods he worshipped. He knew he was doomed.

Still, in his terror he was doing terrible damage, as panic-stricken brutes often did. One blind swing clove the head of a trooper. The frantic thrashing of his axe knocked two trusty stormvermin into the channel of the sewer.

If Tzarkual had not known better he would have sworn that the skaven had leapt into the filth to avoid the blade. Surely not! A tall blond-tufted manthing had joined the dwarf. He fought with a certain precision. A thrust from his shortsword took another skaven in the throat.

No! This wasn't happening. Four of his best warriors had gone down and the manthings had not even taken a casualty. The furless ones had been lucky. He was filled with pride as more brave stormvermin leapt into the fray.

Now, he felt certain that victory would be his. The manthings just didn't know it. They kept coming. More worthless vermin fell before their weapons. Tzarkual knew that he had been betrayed! Instead of elite stormvermin, he had been sent useless clanrats. Some cunning enemy back in Skavenblight must have arranged it to discredit him.

It was only explanation of how two puny surface-dwellers could chop through half a dozen skaven so-called warriors without taking a cut. Tzarkual steeled himself to face the foe. He, at least, was not afraid to face the dwarf's hatchet or the man's sword. He was a hostleader. He knew no fear.

It was simply excitement that made his tail twitch and his muskglands swell as the dwarf painted the sewer wall with blood with a flick of the small axe. Tzarkual knew he could take any manthing, but he decided to hang back as Clawleader Gazat tackled the dwarf. He wanted to study his foe's fighting style to best advantage.

It was certainly impressive the way that the dwarf caught the flying skaven by the throat and dashed his brains out against the ledge floor.

It definitely wasn't terror that made Tzarkual fling himself into the sewage when he confronted the foaming mouthed berserker. It was just that he knew that this was not the correct time to fight. It would be more elegant to take the foe off guard, by surprise, say when they were asleep. Less wasteful of skaven lives too. He would tell Thanquol this as soon as he had finished his swim.

'THEY WERE AFTER us weren't they?' Felix said, glancing around worriedly. He dabbed at some of the blood on his face and inspected the tips of his fingers distastefully. He was not surprised to learn that skaven blood was black.

'Don't be foolish, manling. Why would they be after us?'

Felix was getting annoyed at people telling him not to be foolish. 'Well, doesn't it seem odd that we managed to go for two weeks without meeting a single thing down here, then barely two days after you kill that skaven we're ambushed? Come to think of it, it's only one day after I saw von Halstadt at the Golden Hammer. Perhaps he recognised me.'

Gotrek flicked his hatchet forward. Black blood speckled the ledge where the droplets fell. 'Manling, he couldn't recognise you. For a start you were dressed differently. And you were behind the lantern that Gant shone on him – all he could make out would be your outline. That's if he saw anything at all. Most likely he was too busy running.'

It slowly sank in what Gotrek had said. Or rather what he hadn't said. He hadn't questioned the fact that Felix had seen von Halstadt at the Golden Hammer.

The other sewerjacks back from inspecting the bodies. 'Good work, you two,' said Hef. 'You can certainly fight.'

'Might have left us some though? I though there was some coming up behind us but they seemed to stop when you two got stuck in.'

'Probably scared them away.'

'Well let's take a body and show it to the watch captain. Maybe they'll believe us this time.'

'Right-o, young Felix. You going to carry it?'

Felix kept his mouth shut as he bent to lift the smelly furry carcass. Even amid the stink of the sewers the smell of the corpse was offensive. Felix was quite pleased when, halfway back to the watch station exit, Hef offered to take a turn carrying it.

'AND YOU SAY that there are rat-men below the city, brother? In the sewers even?'

Looking around the dining chamber of Otto's house, Felix found it easy to understand his brother's incredulity. Everything here seemed solid and safe and unthreatening. The expensive brocade curtains shut out the night just as effectively as the high walls enclosing the garden shut out the city. The solid teak furniture spoke of wealth based on a firm foundation of prosperity. The silver cutlery, different for each course, reflected an ordered world where everything had its place. Here in his brother's stone-walled house it was hard to recall details of the nightmare battle he had fought that morning.

'Oh yes,' as he said it he saw again the snarling feral rat-face of the skaven he had killed. He remembered the bubbles of bloody froth blowing from its lips. He felt its stinking weight press against his body as it fell. He forced the memory back and concentrated on the goblet of fine Parravonian wine his brother had placed before him.

'It seems almost impossible to believe. Even though you do hear rumours.'

'Rumours, Otto?'

The merchant looked around. He got up and walked around the chamber, making sure each of the doors was securely closed. His Bretonnian wife, Annabella, had retired to her chambers, leaving the two men to talk business in private. Otto returned to his seat. His face was flushed from the wine. Candlelight flickered off little beads of sweat on his face.

'They say that there are mutants in the sewers and goblins and other monsters.' Felix smiled at his brother's seriousness. Otto was telling this to a sewerjack as if it were a great secret. 'You may smile, Felix, but I've talked to folk who swear it's true.'

'Really?' It was hard to keep a note of irony from his voice. Otto didn't notice it.

'Oh yes, the same folk who swear that there's a great mutant undertown called the Night Market. They say it's on the edge of the city. In an abandoned graveyard. It's frequented by followers of certain depraved cults.'

'Slaanesh worshippers, you mean?'

Otto pursed his lips primly. 'Don't use that word in my home. It's cursed unlucky and I don't want to attract the attention of the Dark Powers. Or their followers.'

'Unlucky or not, these things exist.'

'Enough, brother.'

At first Felix found it hard to believe his brother was serious. He wondered what Otto would say if he told him that he had once witnessed a Slaaneshi orgy on Geheimnisnacht. Best not to, he decided. Seeing his brother's serious, fear-filled face he realised quite how large the gap between them had grown.

Could he really once have been as sheltered as his elder brother, shivering and fearful at the mention of a dark power about which he knew not the slightest thing? He had to admit that it was perhaps possible. He began to understand how the cultists got away with it. There was a veil of secrecy drawn over the whole subject in polite society; it wasn't mentioned or discussed. People preferred to believe or pretend to believe that such things as Chaos cults couldn't exist. If they were mentioned, they didn't want to talk about them. Everyone abhorred mutants and talked about that widely.

That was fine. It was easy to pick on visible targets, they provided a focus on which to vent deep seated unease. But bring up the fact that normal, supposedly sane folk might be interested in the worship of the dark ones and a door was slammed in your face.

The playwright Detlef Sierck had been right when he wrote: 'Ours is a land chained by silence; ours is a time when the truth goes unspoken.' People just didn't want to know.

Why? Felix did not understand. Did they honestly think that pretending a problem did not exist would make it go away? The watch captain today had looked at the body and could not deny its existence, even though he had obviously wanted to. He was forced to report the matter to higher authority.

A sudden chill ran through Felix when he recalled who had come to collect the corpse for examination. They were men from the office of Chief Magistrate von Halstadt. Felix wondered if the body of the dead skaven would ever be seen again.

'Tell me more about von Halstadt,' Felix asked. 'Where does he live?'

Otto seemed glad to change the subject. 'His father was a minor noble, killed in one of the peasant uprisings in the early seventies. He studied for the Sigmarite priesthood, but was never ordained. There were hints of a scandal, something to do with spying on the nunnery. He is efficient. He's said to keep files on everyone. And his enemies disappear mysteriously.'

Felix fell silent. A pattern had emerged. He believed he understood what had happened. It would take a little checking though. He would make a start early tomorrow. 'You say he lives nearby.'

'Two streets away. Near the palace, on Emmanuelleplatz.'

'Well, well.' Felix leant back in his chair and yawned expansively. 'Well, brother, it's late and I really must go. I have work tomorrow.'

'Very well.' Otto rang the small bell that sat beside his plate. 'I'll have Franz bring your cloak.'

'I TOLD YOUR predecessor never to come here,' von Halstadt said, staring at the skaven with barely concealed distaste. He hated it when anyone else but him entered his filing chamber. 'The servants might see you.'

The rat-man met his gaze levelly. There was something about this one that made von Halstadt nervous. Perhaps it was the greyish fur or perhaps it was the strange blind-seeming eyes, but there was something different about this one. Something scary, almost.

'This one is not as the other, manthing. Grey seer this one is. Magelord in the service of the Thirteen. Contracted to the clan but not of it. Important I see you. Things went badly with the guards. Many skaven dead.'

'But my servants–'

'Worry not, foolish manthing – they snoresleep. A simple spell.'

Von Halstadt laid down his file. He marked the place with a uninked quill and closed it gently. He let his hand fall near the hilt of his blade. The touch of it reassured him somewhat. He met the skaven's stare and dared it to look away. 'I'm unused to being called "foolish". Do not do so again.'

The skaven smiled. It was not calming. For a second the magistrate felt as if it might leap forward and bite him. He kept his hand on his weapon. With an almost imperceptible shake of its head the skaven stopped smiling. It twitched its tail.

'Of course. So-sorry. Many apologies, yes. Grieve for the loss of kin. Cost many warptokens to replace.'

'I accept your apology.' Von Halstadt was reassured. It was obscurely pleasing that even so monstrous seeming a creature as the rat-man felt a sense of loss at the death of its relatives. Still he found himself longing for the day when he would no longer have to deal with the skaven and could have them destroyed. He picked up the file and returned it to its precise place in the proper cabinet.

'The manthings are dangerous to our association. Know your appearance and can pickchoose you from others. They must not be allowed to threaten you or us.'

'True.' The thought was worrying. Von Halstadt's enemies were legion and the slightest hint of scandal would be used against him. The treacherous sewerjacks would sell that information to the highest bidder he felt sure. Their lack of loyalty to the cause of humanity sickened him. They deserved to die. And to think he had once felt sorry for them. 'They must die.'

'Yes-yes, and you must show us where to find them.'

'That is straightforward enough. I had their watch captain interviewed today.' he opened a new cabinet and pulled out a slim dossier. 'Here is my file on them.'

'Good-good. Soon they will all die-die.'

ONCE SAFELY BACK in the sewer, Grey Seer Thanquol cursed to himself. He was tired of dealing with morons like Tzarkual and the manthing von Halstadt. He would have preferred to have been back home in his warm burrow in Skavenblight, surrounded by his breeders and with a few captive humans to run through his maze. He missed the beautiful rotting aroma of the swamps and he was worried about the intrigues which might be taking place against him in his absence. He hated working with the idiot Tzarkual, who could not even carry out the simple assassination of five manthings properly.

The thought of the hostleader's chittering excuses made Thanquol want to bite his own tail with anger. By the Thirteen, it was true! If you wanted a bone gnawed properly you had to gnaw it yourself. No sense entrusting vital tasks to the likes of the useless hostleader.

Still, his masters had assigned him to Tzarkual's clan and he was obliged by the binding oaths of his order to implement and expedite their plans. And this one was sound. It resounded to Clan Skab's credit in the Great Game being played back in Skavenblight. He could see that, foolish though he was, von Halstadt represented a valuable agent to have in place. Of all the humans he had ever met, the spymaster thought most like a skaven – a very stupid skaven, admittedly, but still a skaven. He was easy to manipulate due to his strange jealousy of and attraction to the breeder Emmanuelle, prepared to believe anything so long as it was connected to her. Imagine thinking that the skaven use the city's rats as spies, foolish manthing!

However, von Halstadt had proven useful in removing those who might prove to be a threat to the long term plans of the Thirteen and he was an adroit and effective collector of the warpstone so necessary for the continued research plans of the seers.

Yes-yes, it would be wise to resist the urge to slay the manthing. He was more useful alive than dead, at least until the Great Day came and humanity writhed beneath the talons of the skaven once more.

Thanquol easily deciphered the strange scratchmarks humans called writing. He had trained all his life for this. The study of mankind and its arts were his particular forte. Von Halstadt had thoughtfully attached the maps showing the closest sewers to the victim's dwellings. The manthing was not entirely incompetent. How convenient! Two of the manthings dwelled together in an easily accessible place. He would start with them.

'Come-come, Boneripper. I have work for you this night,' Thanquol squeaked.

The rat-ogre growled its assent from the shadows. Enormous claws slid smoothly from their sheaths at the prospect of food.

HEF WAS LURCHING drunkenly down the muddy side-street when he heard the sounds of a struggle coming from the hovel which he shared with Gilda and his brother. He knew he shouldn't have stayed in the tavern for that last pint with Gotrek. If Big Jax and his men had returned for vengeance while he was away, he would never forgive himself.

The hook knife felt cool and reassuring in his hand. He wished he were more sober but that was not to be helped. He broke into a trot and almost immediately tripped over a pile of rotting garbage in the path. At night, without street lighting the New Quarter was a death-trap.

He picked himself up and set off more carefully along the lane. As he recalled there was an open sewer near here and it wouldn't do to fall in. He heard Gilda scream and all thought of caution vanished when the scream ended in a moan of pain. He ran, scrabbling over the garbage, knocking over a pile of muck. He knew that no one else but him would answer a scream for help in Cheap Street. It was that sort of area.

Flames started to leap skyward over the hovel. Someone must have knocked over a lamp in the struggle. He heard a feral snarl from within the hut. Maybe Jax had brought his tame war-dogs, as he had threatened. Hef covered the open ground near the entrance in one final spurt. By the light of the flames flickering within he could see that the door had been ripped off its hinges.

Something moved within. His brother met him at the door. Spider opened his mouth and tried to speak. Blood gushed forth. Hef caught him as he fell forward. As his arms met round his brother's back, he felt the hole and the great soft mass of the lungs pumping though it. Spider moaned and was still.

It was a nightmare. He had returned home and his home was in flames. His brother was dead. No, that could not be. He and Spider had been inseparable since they could walk. They had served on the same fishing boat, stolen the same money, ran off together to the same city, lived with the same girl. They had the same life. If Spider was dead, then…

Hef stood absolutely still. Tears streamed down his face as the monstrous shape emerged from the ruins of the burning hut and loomed over him. The last thing he heard was the sound of chittering from behind him.

FELIX WAS UP bright and early. He made his way down the muddy streets of the New Quarter, ignoring the pall of smoke that rose from the shantytown near Cheap Street. Another fire, he supposed. Well, he had been lucky, the wind had not fanned the flames in the direction of Frau Zorin's tenement. If they had, he might have died in his sleep. And he couldn't afford to die just now. He still had things to do.

He turned left down Rotten Row and hit the cobbled streets of Commercial Way. Coaches clattered past as merchants made their way to the coffee houses before starting business for the day. He found his way to the Hall of Archives and made his way to the division of the planning office with responsibility for sewers.

He knew he would find what he needed there. Three quarters of an hour, much browsing through ancient, dust-covered files and plans, two threats and one bribe later, he had proven himself to be correct. Pleased with himself, Felix made his way to the watch house.

THEY WERE INSTANTLY assigned to help out the rest of the watch in the area that had burned: burying the dead, searching the rubble for the living. They marched up to shantytown to take a look. The fire had ripped through many hovels, burned and the disfigured dead were everywhere. A little boy, his face blackened by soot sat near an old woman who whimpered quietly to herself.

'What happened here, son,' Felix asked.

'It was the rat-daemon what did it,' the boy said. 'I saw it myself. It killed the men who lived there and carried them below to feast. Ma says it'll come for me next if I don't behave.'

Felix exchanged looks with Gotrek. Savage interest was evident in the Trollslayer's one good eye.

'There's no such thing as rat-daemons, lad. Don't lie to us – we're with the watch.'

'There is too. I saw it with my own eyes. It was taller than you and heavier than that big one-eyed dwarf. It was led by a smaller rat-man with grey skin and horns on its head.'

'Did anyone else see it?'

'Don't know. I hid. I thought they might take me too.'

Felix shook his head and went to check the ruins of Hef and Spider's hut. There was little left of the pitiful building save the burned out remains and the charred corpse of a woman.

'No sign of Hef or Spider?'

Gotrek shook his head and pointed with his toe to something grey and sharp lying in the ashes. 'That's Hef's knife.'

Felix bent and picked it up. the metal was still warm from lying in the embers. Felix looked at the corpse. The smell of burnt meat filled his nostrils.

'Gilda?' said Felix.

Felix shook his head. Sorrow and rage filled him. He had liked the brothers. They had been good men. Now he wanted vengeance.

'You were an engineer once, Gotrek. Tell me what these mean.'

Felix ignored the Trollslayer's incredulous look. He cleared a space on the table in the watchroom and spread out the charts. Rudi watched curiously as he smoothed the cracked old parchment flat and weighed down each corner with an empty tea mug.

The Slayer gave his attention back to the papers. 'These are charts of the sewers, manling. Dwarf-made plans of the Old Quarter.'

'That's correct. They show the area beneath Chief Magistrate von Halstadt's mansion. If you look closely, you'll discover that it's not too far from the place where Gant was killed. I'd also bet if we looked we'd find a way up from the sewers to his house.'

A frown creased Rudi's low brow. 'You're suggesting that we break into Fritz von Halstadt's house! We'll be hung if we're caught. We might even lose our jobs!'

'That would be a pity. What do you say, are you in? Rudi?'

'I don't know...'

'Gotrek?'

'Yes, manling – with one provision.'

'What's that?'

'If von Halstadt is the Chaos worshipping, skaven-loving, snotling-fondler we saw in the sewer then we kill him.'

An appalled silence hung over the chamber. The import of the Trollslayer's words sunk into their brains. Felix felt his mouth go dry. What the dwarf was suggesting was murder, pure and simple.

No he decided, thinking of Gant, and the dead in the New Quarter, it wasn't murder, it was justice. He'd go along with that. 'Fine.'

'There's no backing out then. Rudi?' The bald-headed man looked shocked. His face was pale and fear was in his eyes.

'You don't know what you're suggesting. /

'Are you coming with us or not?' Rudi didn't answer for a second. 'Yes,' he said at last. 'I'll come. I just hope you're wrong, that's all.'

'I'm not,' Felix said.

'That's what I'm afraid of.'

THE SEWERS HAD never seemed so ominous to Felix. Shadows danced away from the lantern light. Every time he heard Rudi's heavy tread behind him, he had to fight the urge to look around. The sound of the Slayer continually tapping the walls with his hatchet blade was getting on his nerves. He knew that Gotrek was only doing it to see if he could find a hollow area but that did not make it any easier to take.

Something was out there. He knew that now. Something had killed Hef and Spider, and their girl too, and it would surely kill the rest of them if they let it. It was the not knowing that was so terrifying. Not knowing what it was that hunted them. Not really knowing why. Not knowing how many skaven might appear, nor what daemonic henchmen they might have. The brothers had been formidable fighters and they were gone.

Worse, half of the Cheap Street shanty town had gone with them. Whatever dark thing sought them it had no qualms about killing a lot of people to get the ones it wanted. He asked himself why he had not simply fled the city-state.

He could be on the road even now, not creeping about in this dark, smelly stinkhole. Why did he have to be cursed with this urge to interfere in what was really none of his business?

He already knew the answer. He had to take a stand somewhere, for something. Because if he did not, he would be exactly like his brother, Otto, and all the others like him, pretending that he did not know what was going on; making deals with the Darkness so that it would leave him alone; pretending all was right with the world when he knew that it wasn't.

Knowing that something was wrong meant that he had to do something about it, even if the only reason for doing it was to keep his self-image intact and allow him to feel superior to those he despised. And if that made him feel a little more like the heroes he used to read about when he was young, well, so much the better.

Thinking about his reasons kept his mind occupied and allowed him to forget his fears. He made himself concentrate on what he knew. The only real lead he had was that he knew that the head of the city's secret police was in league with the skaven. He had seen it with his own eyes. He did not know why such a thing should be; he only knew that it was so. And that it should be stopped.

'Stop daydreaming, manling. We've been down here for hours and we still haven't found this secret entrance of yours. It'll soon be dark up above and we're still no further forward.' Felix gave his attention back to scanning the walls. From up ahead the sound of Gotrek tapping the brickwork with the blade of his hatchet continued.

THANQUOL STARED AROUND the darkened room. He felt exposed here in the surface world, so high above the ground. He gazed out through the single window and then looked at the straw pallet. Boneripper stood hunched near the doorway, flexing his great claws.

They had stood here in the dark for nearly two hours and still there was no sign of their prey. He lashed his tail in frustration. Where was the stupid manthing? Why wasn't he home in bed where he should be? They were all the same, frittering away their time in drunkenness and debauchery. They deserved to be replaced by the Master Race. He swore that he would make this particular manthing pay for wasting a grey seer's valuable time.

He didn't have any more time to waste. He had to meet with von Halstadt and check on the arrangements that had been made for the countess's homecoming ball. Soon it would be time to reveal to him that Emmanuelle's guest, the Emperor's own brother-in-law was secretly a mutant and worse yet, the countess's latest lover.

The fact that neither of these things were true was not in the slightest bit important. What was important was that when von Halstadt had the graf kidnapped and tortured, word of it would be released. War would come between Nuln and the rest of the Empire. The Emperor could not stand for the insult of his own brother-in-law being tortured by the Elector's secret police. Civil war would erupt. The greatest kingdom of mankind would be thrown into anarchy. The power of the skaven would grow. The thought so excited Thanquol that he had to take some powdered warpstone snuff to calm his nerves. The drug bubbled into his brain and filled him with delightful visions of torture, bloodshed and agony.

The sound of footsteps coming up the stairs brought him out of his reverie. He nodded to Boneripper. There was a tentative knock on the door. 'Herr Jaeger, it's me, Frau Zorin. Rent time!'

Before Thanquol could countermand him, Boneripper threw open the door and dragged the old woman inside.

'Herr Jaeger, there's no need to be so rough!' They were Frau Zorin's last words before Boneripper tore her throat out.

Well, at least he wouldn't have to feed the rat-ogre for another three hours, thought the grey seer. He waited for Boneripper to finish his meal.

'Come-come, we have business elsewhere,' he told him. They headed for the sewers and their meeting with von Halstadt.

'SUCCESS, MANLING!' Gotrek exclaimed, and tapped again to make sure. He nodded his head smugly. 'I've found the passage or my mother was a troll!'

I wouldn't bet against that, thought Felix, but kept the thought to himself. He watched as the Slayer set down his hatchet and began to run his fingers around the brickwork. 'Nice bit of work this. Well concealed. Probably dwarf, I'd say. No wonder I missed it the other day. The git must have paid a dwarf crew to dig his bolt-tunnel and then sworn them to secrecy. Now if I'm right there should be–'

His stubby powerful fingers pushed against a single brick. It sank into the wall. There came a quiet grinding sound, as of perfectly balanced counterweights shifting. A section of the wall slid back. Felix saw a small vestibule and a metal ladder leading up. Gotrek turned and smiled, revealing his missing teeth. He looked genuinely pleased. 'Very nice work indeed. Bugger must have outdistanced me, turned that corner and ducked in. No wonder I couldn't find him. My eyes were still stinging from the gas too.'

'There's no need to made excuses, Gotrek,' Felix said.

'No excuse, manling. I just want–'

'Are we going to stand here all night, young Felix, or are you going to go up and take a look around?' Rudi interrupted.

'Me?'

'Well, all this was your idea.' Felix saw the unease written on Rudi's face. The big man was scared by the prospect of burgling so important a citizen's home. Not surprisingly, thought Felix. He's a watchman. He's spent the last ten years catching criminals, not being one.

'Are you going to do it, manling, or should I?' The thought of the Trollslayer clumping around upstairs galvanised Felix into action. He remembered Otto's words about there being Templars of the White Wolf on guard above. He didn't relish the prospect of being discovered by them.

'I'll take a look first,' he said, 'and I'll let you know if it's safe.'

FELIX HELD HIS breath and glanced around. The ladder emerged in another small chamber with a single door. This led out into a large wine cellar.

Looking back, Felix saw that the door was attached to a wine rack, so that when it was closed it was virtually invisible. Felix checked a label on one of the bottles. He blew away dust to reveal the emblem of one of the best Parravonian vineyards, Desghulles.

'Someone has expensive tastes,' he told himself. He turned swiftly reaching for his sword when he heard the ladder creak behind him. Gotrek's head poked round the edge of the doorway.

'Don't wet yourself manling, it's me,' he said. Rudi emerged from behind him. 'Right, let's check the house and see if we can find our friend, the chief magistrate.'

'Not much noise above. The place sounds empty.'

'Let's hope so.'

'I'll stay here,' Rudi said. 'And make sure your line of retreat is covered.'

Felix shrugged. It was probably better than having the big man blundering about up above. 'You do that.'

FELIX MADE HIS way cautiously to the foot of the stairs, keeping his lantern to the narrowest aperture so that only the faintest glimmer of light showed.

'I told you so: the house is empty,' Gotrek said.

Felix had to admit it looked like the dwarf was right. Where were the White Wolf guards? Where were the servants?

'Guards are most likely at the gatehouse. But where are the servants? A place this size should have some.'

'You'd know about that, I suppose.'

'Yes.'

Felix gently put his foot on the stairs. A shiver ran down his spine as it creaked under his weight. He paused and held his breath. No one came to investigate.

'Why are you being so quiet, manling. There's no one here.'

'I don't know. Maybe it's just because it's not my house. I feel like a criminal. Why are you whispering?'

'You are being a criminal. So am I. Let's search this place and see what we can find. You take upstairs. I'll take below.'

It was only after he padded off near silently that Felix noticed that Gotrek was moving stealthily too. Felix moved on up the stairs, hoping that they would not creak.

IN THE BEDROOM, Felix closed the aperture of his lantern completely before sliding aside a curtain and looking outside. He glanced down into a large walled courtyard and he could see over the high walls into the street beyond. A large gate opened into the courtyard. On the left of the square was a stable and coach-house; on the right was a small barracks and a privy for the servants. Old oak trees lined the square. There were sentries: tall blond men in full armour, white wolf pelts draped round their shoulders. One paced from the gatehouse across the courtyard.

For a moment Felix feared that the man might be coming inside, but he soon turned off and headed towards a small barracks next to the stables. Slowly Felix let the curtain slide back into place and then he allowed himself to exhale.

No, it wouldn't do to get caught here. The White Wolves had a reputation for ferocity that equalled that of a Slayer, and there was at least half a dozen of them out there.

THE MOST APPROPRIATE thing to do when he found the locked door was to force it. He jimmied it open with the blade of his shortsword and went in. He found himself in a place that reminded him of the ledger hall in his father's warehouse back in Altdorf.

It was a big room dominated by an oak desk large enough to hold a party on. The walls were lined with filing boxes, hundreds and hundreds of them. He opened one at random and pulled out a thick sheaf of papers written in a precise hand.

Glancing through it, he came upon the names of the countess and notes referring to several of her better-known lovers.

There was an extensive section dealing with suspected mutation in her family. Many sources were quoted.

What drew Felix's attention were the references to 'our most special source' and 'our friends down below'. He picked up another file and went through it. There were similar notes. One referred to the need for a certain Slazinger to disappear. The files were sorted alphabetically. He couldn't resist it. He sought out the one on the Jaeger family. After finding one concerning a family of bakers on Cake Street who shared the same name, he got his own family file on the second try.

Felix felt his stomach lurch when he came across references to the merchant house of Jaeger and Sons. The file remarked on how amenable his brother Otto was and noted that he was a sound man who gave generously to the elector's fund for the maintenance of civil order. As he flipped the page he saw his own name mentioned. He read on.

THANQUOL NOTICED THAT the secret entrance to von Halstadt's had been disturbed almost as soon as he entered. There was a strange manscent in the air of the chamber at the foot of the ladder. Several manscents in fact, and something that smelled like dwarf.

Fool-fool! he cursed inside, gnawing at the tip of his tail. The spymaster had been discovered. It didn't take the application of a mind as clever as Thanquol's to work out by whom. He had two manthings and a dwarf left to kill.

Well, the manthings had saved him the bother of tracking them down. Their desire to meddle in business that was not theirs would prove to be their undoing.

He nodded to Boneripper and chittered his instructions. The ladder groaned under the weight of the rat-ogre. It swarmed up the rungs, as agile as an ape.

FELIX SHOOK HIS HEAD. He was referred to as a spendthrift younger son who had vanished under mysterious circumstances. There was a line devoted to his duel with Krassner and a hastily scribbled memo in pencil to the effect that a further investigation should be conducted.

Well, perhaps there were worse things to be than the black sheep of the Jaeger family. Perhaps he should show Gotrek. Maybe there was something in the files about the Slayer too.

He was just about to look when he heard the door open down below.

Damn, he thought, closing the chamber door. He'd have to wait.

VON HALSTADT KNEW he was running late. He hoped the skaven was too. He deplored giving the wrong impression even to a brute like the skaven. But Emmanuelle was due back tomorrow and he wanted every little detail of her household to be perfect.

He imagined the smile with which she would reward his diligence and knew that all his care had been worthwhile. Even if he had been forced to waste fifteen minutes punishing that young footman for his clumsiness in setting the paintings. The flogging had left the magistrate tired and sweaty, and in need of a bath.

He picked up a house lantern and lit it. The gloom rushed away from him. Von Halstadt was going to call a servant to draw some water when he recalled that he had given them all the night off because the skaven was coming. He would have to forego the pleasure of a wash till later. The skaven's tidings were more important.

Before departing last night he had intimated that his agents were about to ferret out a particularly important mutant plot. Von Halstadt had to admit he was far more concerned with the assassination attempt on the sewerjacks. He knew that Hef and Spider were dead. His agents had reported on the fire in Cheap Street.

That had been a neat bit of work, disposing of two traitors and half a hundred riffraff at the same time. Come to think of it, perhaps the rat-man had inadvertently provided a solution to another problem. Perhaps he could have fires set across the New Quarter. That would certainly cut down on the numbers of mutant-worshipping scum who dwelled there.

The thought of burning the dregs of society out of their festering sinkhole of vice warmed the cockles of his heart. He took the stairs two at a time and rushed down the corridor to his filing room. But his heart sank when he saw the door had been forced. Anger filled him. Someone had desecrated his sanctum. After Emmanuelle, his beloved files were the most important thing in his life. If someone had harmed a page of them... He drew his sword and pushed the door open with his foot. A lantern shone in his face.

'Good evening, von Halstadt,' a cultured voice said. 'I think you and I have some business.'

As the chief magistrate's eyes grew accustomed to the illumination he recognised the face of the young man he had seen with Otto Jaeger the other night. 'Who are you, whelp?' he asked.

'My name is Felix Jaeger. I am the man who is going to kill you.'

RUDI HAD NEVER seen so much wine before. It was everywhere in the cellar: old bottles covered in a thick layer of dust and cobwebs, newer ones with only the slightest gilding of dirt. There was so much of it he wondered how any one man could drink it all. Maybe if he had plenty of guests, he supposed.

What was that noise? Probably nothing. It would be best to pretend there was nothing there.

Ever since they had found the rat-man in the sewers, nothing had gone right. Perhaps he could hide. But there was no place into which he could squeeze his large frame.

He should go back to the top of the ladder and take a look. He was sure he had heard the rungs of the metal ladder creak. Yes, he should.

He swallowed and tried to make himself move back to the hidden niche. His limbs responded slowly. It was as if all strength had been drained out of them. His heart beat sounded loud in his ears. It raced like he had just run a mile.

He realised that he had been holding his breath, and let it out in a long sigh. The sound seemed unnaturally loud in the silence. He wished Gotrek or even that cocky young snob Felix would come back. He didn't like being here on his own, in the basement of a powerful noble whose wealth and influence he could hardly imagine.

It was ridiculous, he told himself. He'd spent nearly fifteen years, man and boy, in the sewers, hunting mutants and monsters in the dark. He shouldn't be frightened. Ah, but it had been different then. He had been younger and he'd been with friends and comrades, Gant and the brothers and the others now dead or gone.

The last few days had truly shaken him. The solid foundations of his life had vanished. He was alone: no wife, no children. His last friends had vanished or died. And if young

Felix was right, the order that he had sworn to protect, the city's rulers who he was pledged to defend against all enemies, were the enemy. Life didn't make sense any more.

Wait! There was definitely something moving inside the niche. Something heavy had stealthily pulled itself over the lip of the sinkhole. It was here in the cellar.

'Who's there?' Rudi asked. His voice sounded weak and strange to him. It was the voice of a stranger. The soft padding footfalls came closer.

His lantern revealed the shape as it emerged into the wine cellar. It was huge, a head taller than him and perhaps twice as heavy. Great muscles bulged under its ruddy fur; long claws slid from the sheaths in its fingertips. Its face was a mixture of rat and wolf. A chilling, malign intelligence burned in its pink, beady little eyes.

Rudi raised his club to defend himself, but it was on him with one leap, startlingly swift for so large a creature. Pain flared through Rudi's weapon arm as its great claws bit into the flesh of his wrist. He opened his mouth to scream. He looked up into the pink eyes of death. He felt the breath of the monster on him. It smelled of blood and fresh meat.

'DON'T BE FOOLISH, young man,' Fritz von Halstadt said. As he spoke, he put his hand on the hilt of his longsword. He was confident. He was a formidable swordsman and his opponent had only a short stabbing blade. 'One shout and I'll have six Knights of the White Wolf in here. They'll hand me your head.'

'Perhaps they'll be interested in the fact that you consort with skaven and keep a ledger of your dealings with them.'

Felix's words chilled von Halstadt to the bone. He didn't know whether the grey seer was in the house already or about to arrive. He couldn't risk summoning the knights if that was the case. They were reassuringly anti-mutant but their zeal also extended to dealing with the likes of the skaven.

'You don't know what you're talking about, boy!' the magistrate spat. His blade rung as he pulled it from the scabbard.

'I'm afraid I do. You see, I saw you in the sewers the other day. I saw you with my own eyes. I nearly didn't believe them when I saw you again in the Golden Hammer.'

The young man seemed certain. There would be no reasoning with him, he would have to die. Von Halstadt let his blade point to the floor as he moved closer. He let his shoulders slump in defeat.

'How did you know?'

'I'm a sewerjack.'

'You can't be. Sewerjacks don't eat at the Golden Hammer. Not in the company of Otto Jaeg…' As he spoke the words, realisation dawned on von Halstadt. Felix Jaeger, Otto Jaeger. The family black sheep. He knew that had been worth looking into.

'What do you want, boy? Money? Preferment? I can arrange for either but it will take time.' He edged ever closer. The young man had relaxed a little, seeing how cowed he had become. Soon it would be time to strike.

'No, I think I want your head.'

Even as Felix spoke, von Halstadt struck, serpent-swift. To his surprise the young man parried his blow. Steel sparked where the blades met. Felix lashed out with his foot catching von Halstadt on the shin. Pain flared in his leg. He only just managed to leap back out of the way as the younger man thrust. He knew he had to keep his distance, to use his longer blade to advantage.

They circled and wheeled, moving with the precision of masters as they sought out openings. Blades wheeled and glittered in the shadows of the two lanterns. They moved too fast for the eye to follow, danced with a life of their own, seeking holes in the other's defences. Von Halstadt allowed himself a snarl of satisfaction as he pinked Jaeger's arm. It turned into a smile as he cut open a nasty gash above the young man's eye.

Soon blood would drip down blinding him. Both breathed hard now. But Fritz von Halstadt knew that he would win this duel. He could sense it. He would fight defensively for the moment. It was simply a matter of waiting.

THANQUOL HEARD THE noise upstairs. It sounded like a dance was taking place. Heavy boots slammed into the stone floor. Well-well, he thought, it was fortunate that he had arrived when he did. It would seem that von Halstadt's enemies had tracked him to his lair. and were even now in the process of assassinating him.

Assassination had a long and honourable history in skaven politics and Thanquol was tempted to let things run their course.

It would gratify his sense of petty malice to let the manthing die. Pleasing though the thought was he couldn't allow himself the pleasure. It would interfere too much with the great plan.

He kicked Boneripper. The rat-ogre raised its bloody muzzle from the remnants of its meal. It growled at him. Thanquol glared at it, letting his slave feel his will. Slowly the rat-ogre rose. They climbed the stairs out of the cellar towards the battle above.

FELIX WAS FORCED to admit that perhaps this had not been such a good idea after all. He blamed too much watching the plays of Detlef Sierck as a youth. He had always wanted to play out one of those melodramatic scenes where the hero confronts the scheming villain.

Unfortunately things weren't quite going according to script. It was the story of his life. His arms burned with fatigue and the pain of the wound von Halstadt had inflicted. He jerked his head quickly to one side to shake off the blood running down his forehead, a risky move against a swordsman as skilled as his opponent.

Red droplets splattered onto the desktop. Felix was relieved that von Halstadt hadn't been quite swift enough to take advantage of the opening. His breathing was coming swift and laboured. It sounded like a bellows. Pain interfered with the smooth flow of his movements.

Von Halstadt's long blade seemed to be everywhere. It was the sword that made the difference. Felix believed that had the blades been of equal length he would just have been the nobleman's superior. But they were not and it was killing him.

'HURRY-HURRY!' Thanquol ordered Boneripper as they ran towards the bottom of the stairs. The fight above was still going on but now that he had decided to save his pawn he didn't want to take the chance of fate intervening.

An accident at this stage would be most annoying. Boneripper let out a little moan and stopped so suddenly that Thanquol ran into the solid wall of his back and bounced. The pain in his snout was considerable. The grey seer glanced around his pet. He saw why Boneripper had halted.

A dwarf stood there, blocking the way to the stairs. He was massive and his fur was strangely crested. In one hand he held

an enormous battle-axe. He, too, looked as if he had been racing to get up the steps and intervene in the ongoing fight. He,
too, looked astonished to discover there was another in the
house.

'Bloody palaces!' he grumbled. 'You never know who you'll
meet in them.'

'Die-die, foolish dwarfthing,' chittered Thanquol. 'Boneripper! Kill! Kill!'

Boneripper surged forward, claws extended. He loomed up
over the dwarf, a terrifying daemonic apparition, a living tribute to the fearsome imaginations of the sorcerer-scientists of
Clan Moulder. It would not have surprised Thanquol if the
dwarf too was paralysed with fear by the very sight of him, as
the others had been.

'Chew on this,' the dwarf said.

Brains splattered everywhere as the axe clove Boneripper's
head in two. Thanquol found himself confronting an irate
Trollslayer.

The musk of fear sprayed as he reached into his pouch for a
weapon. Then, deciding discretion was the better part of valour,
he turned and scuttled off. To his relief the dwarf did not follow
but raced up the staircase. Thanquol headed for the sewers,
swearing that if it took him a lifetime, he'd make that dwarf pay.

BOTH MEN HEARD the noise from below. It sounded like an
immense tree had crashed to the ground. Felix saw von
Halstadt's eyes flicker to the window. He knew this would be
his only chance. Throwing caution to the wind he dived
straight at the nobleman, all defences down. Momentarily he
expected to feel von Halstadt's blade bite into his chest. The
split-second of distraction proved almost enough. Too late, his
opponent tried to bring his blade round. Felix was already
within the sweep. It bit into his side as his own shortsword tore
up through von Halstadt's stomach, under his ribs and into the
heart. With a gurgle the chief magistrate died. Agony seared
Felix's brain and he fell.

'WAKE UP, MANLING. This is no time to be lying around.'

Felix felt water splash over his face. He coughed and spluttered and shook his head.

'What the–'

'We'd better get out of here before the White Wolves arrive.'

'Leave me alone.' Felix just wanted to lie there. 'You go and fight them. You always wanted to die heroically.' Gotrek shuffled his feet and looked embarrassed. 'I can't, manling. I'm a Slayer. I'm supposed to die honourably. If we're caught now folk might think we were committing a burglary.'

'So?'

'Theft brings disgrace. I'm trying to atone for my disgrace.'

'I can imagine some worse crimes, like drowning a dying man, for instance.'

'You're not dying, manling. That's barely a scratch.'

'Well, if we must.' Felix pulled himself to his feet. He looked around at the files. It occurred to him that the information here would be worth a fortune to the right person. Even a small selection of what was here would be invaluable. The possibilities for blackmail and extortion were endless.

He looked at the Slayer and remembered what he had said of theft. Gotrek wouldn't condone him taking the papers. Even if he would Felix decided he could not take them. It was corrupt, the life work of a maniac like von Halstadt. Contained in those papers were things that could ruin men's lives. There were too many secrets already in Nuln. These represented too much power to fall into anybody's hands. He took the lanterns and poured their oil over the filing cases. Then he set them alight.

Running downstairs with the smell of burning paper filling his nostrils, Felix felt oddly free. He realised that he would not be going to work with Otto after all, and that pleased him tremendously.

GUTTER RUNNERS

'Needless to say, we could not tell the authorities the whole truth of our encounter with the skaven, for in doing so we would implicate ourselves in the murder of a high official of the court of the Countess Emmanuelle. And murder, no matter how deserving the victim, is a capital crime.

'We were dismissed from service and forced to seek alternate employment. As luck would have it, during a drunken spree in one of the less salubrious quarters of the city, we happened upon a tavern, the owner of which had been a companion of the Slayer's in his mercenary days. We were employed to eject undesirables from the bar, and believe me when I tell you that people had to be very undesirable indeed to warrant being thrown out of the Blind Pig.

'The work was hard, violent and unrewarding but at least I thought we were safe from the skaven. Of course, as was so often the case, I was wrong. For it seemed that one of them at least had not forgotten us and was plotting revenge...'

— From *My Travels With Gotrek, Vol. III*,
by Herr Felix Jaeger (Altdorf Press, 2505)

FELIX JAEGER DUCKED the drunken mercenary's punch. The brass-knuckled fist hurtled by his ear and hit the doorjamb, sending splinters of wood flying. Felix jabbed forward with his knee, catching the mercenary in the groin. The man moaned in pain and bent over, Felix caught him around the neck and tugged him towards the swing doors. The drunk barely resisted. He was too busy throwing up stale wine. Felix booted the door open then pushed the mercenary out, propelling him on his way with a hard kick to the backside. The mercenary rolled in the dirt of Commerce Street, clutching his groin, tears dribbling from his eyes, his mouth open in a rictus of pain.

Felix rubbed his hands together ostentatiously before turning to go back into the bar. He was all too aware of the eyes watching him from beyond every pool of torchlight. At this time of night, Commerce Street was full of bravos, street-girls and hired muscle. Keeping up his reputation for toughness was plain common sense. It reduced his chances of taking a knife in the back when he wandered the streets at night.

What a life, he thought. If anybody had told him a year ago that he would be working as a bouncer in the roughest bar in Nuln, he would have laughed at them. He would have said he was a scholar, a poet and a gentleman, not some barroom brawler. He would have almost preferred being back in the sewer watch to this.

Things change, he told himself, pushing his way back into the crowded bar. Things certainly change.

The stink of stale sweat and cheap perfume slapped him in the face. His squinted as his vision adjusted to the gloomy, lantern-lit interior of the Blind Pig. For a moment he was aware that all the eyes in the place were on him. He scowled, in what he hoped was a fearsome manner, glaring around in exactly the fashion Gotrek did. From behind the bar, big Heinz, the tavern owner, gave a wink of approval for the way in which Felix had dealt with the drunk, then returned to working the pumps.

Felix liked Heinz. He was grateful to him as well. The big man was a former comrade from Gotrek's mercenary days. He was the only man in Nuln who had offered them a job after they had been dishonourably discharged from the sewer watch.

Now that was a new low, Felix thought. He and Gotrek were the only two warriors ever to be kicked out of the sewer watch in all its long and sordid history. In fact they had been lucky to escape a stretch in the Iron Tower, Countess Emmanuelle's infamous prison. Gotrek had called the watch captain a corrupt, incompetent snotling fondler when the man had refused to take their report of skaven in the sewers seriously. To make matters worse, the dwarf had broken the man's jaw when he had ordered the pair of them horsewhipped.

Felix winced. He still had some half-faded bruises from the ensuing brawl. They had fought against half of the watch station before being bludgeoned unconscious. He remembered waking up in the squalid cell the morning after. It was just as well his brother Otto had got them out, wishing to hush up any possible scandal that might blacken the Jaeger family name.

Otto had wanted the pair of them to leave town but Gotrek insisted that they stay. He was not going to be run out of town like some common criminal, particularly not when a skaven wizard was still at large and doubtless plotting some terrible crime. The Trollslayer sensed an opportunity to confront the forces of darkness in all their evil splendour and he was not going to be robbed of his chance of a mighty death in battle against them. And bound by his old oath, Felix had to remain with the dwarf and record that doom for posterity.

Some mighty death, Felix thought sourly. He could see Gotrek now, huddled in a corner with a group of dwarfish warriors, waiting to start his shift. His enormous crest of dyed orange hair rose over the crowd. His enormously muscular figure hunched forward over the table. The dwarfs slugged back their beer from huge tankards, growling and tugging at their beards, and muttering something in their harsh, flinty tongue. Doubtless they were remembering some old slight to their people or working through the long list of the grudges they had to avenge. Or maybe they were just remembering the good old days when beer was a copper piece a flagon, and men showed the Elder Races proper respect.

Felix shook his head. Whatever the conversation was about, the Trollslayer was thoroughly engrossed. He had not even noticed the fight. That in itself was unusual, for the dwarf lived to fight as other folk lived to eat or sleep.

Felix continued his circuit of the tavern, taking in every table with a casual sidelong glance. The long, low hall was packed. Every beer-stained table was crowded. On one, a semi-naked Estalian dancing girl whirled and pranced while a group of drunken halberdiers threw silver and encouraged her to remove the rest of her clothes. Street-girls led staggering soldiers to dark alcoves in the far wall. The commotion from the bar drowned out the gasps and moans and the clink of gold changing hands.

One whole long table was taken up by a group of Kislevite horse archers, guards for some incoming caravan from the north. They roared out drinking songs concerning nothing but horses and women, and sometimes an obscene combination of both, while downing huge quantities of Heinz's home-distilled potato vodka.

There was something about them that made Felix uneasy. The Kislevites were men apart, bred under a colder sun in a harsher land, born only to ride and fight. When one of them rose from the table to go to the privy, his rolling, bow-legged walk told Felix that here was a horseman born. The warrior kept his hand near his long-bladed knife – for at no time was a man more vulnerable than when standing outside in the dim moonlight, relieving himself of half a pint of potato vodka.

Felix grimaced. Half of the thieves, bravos and muscle boys in Nuln congregated in the Blind Pig. They came to mingle with newly arrived caravan guards and mercenaries. He knew more than half of them by name; Heinz had pointed them out to him on his first night here.

At the corner table sat Murdo Mac Laghlan, the Burglar King who claimed to be an exiled prince of Albion. He wore the tartan britches and long moustaches of one of that distant, almost mythical island's hill-warriors. His muscular arms were tattooed in wood elf patterns. He sat surrounded by a bevy of adoring women, regaling them with tales of his beautiful mountainous homeland. Felix knew that Murdo's real name was Heinrik Schmidt and he had never left Nuln in all his life.

Two tall hook-nosed men of Araby, Tarik and Hakim, sat at their permanently reserved table. Gold rings glittered on their fingers. Gold earrings shone in their earlobes. Their black leather jerkins glistened in the torchlight. Long curved swords hung over the back of their chairs. Every now and again, strangers – sometimes street urchins, sometimes nobles – would come in and take a seat. Haggling would start, money would change hands and just as suddenly and mysteriously the visitors would up and leave. A day later someone would be found floating face down in the Reik. Rumour had it that the two were the best assassins in Nuln.

Over by the roaring fire at a table all by himself sat Franz Beckenhof, who some said was a necromancer and who others claimed was a charlatan. No one had ever found the courage to sit next to the skull-faced man and ask, despite the fact that there were always seats free at his table. He sat there every night, with a leather bound book in front of him, husbanding his single glass of wine. Old Heinz never asked him to move along either, even though he took up space that other, more free-spending customers might use. It never pays to upset a magician, was Heinz's motto.

Here and there, as out of place as peacocks in a rookery sat gilded, slumming nobles, their laughter loud and uneasy. They were easy to spot by their beautiful clothing and their firm, soft flesh; upper-class fops out to see their city's dark underbelly. Their bodyguards – generally large, quiet, watchful men with well-used weapons – were there to see that their masters came to no harm during their nocturnal adventures. As Heinz always said, no sense in antagonising the nobs. They could have his tavern shut and his staff inside the Iron Tower with a whisper in the right ear. Best to toady to them, look out for them and to put up with their obnoxious ways.

By the fire, near to the supposed necromancer, was the decadent Bretonnian poet, Armand le Fevre, son of the famous admiral and heir to the le Fevre fortune. He sat alone, drinking absinthe, his eyes fixed at some point in the mid-distance, a slight trickle of drool leaking from the corner of his mouth. Every night, at midnight, he would lurch to his feet and announce that the end of the world was coming, then two hooded and cloaked servants would enter and carry him to his waiting palanquin and then home to compose one of his blasphemous poems. Felix shuddered, for there was something about the young man which reminded him of Manfred von Diehl, another sinister writer of Felix's acquaintance, and one which he would rather forget.

As well as the exotic and the debauched, there were the usual raucous youths from the student fraternities, who had come here to the roughest part of town to prove their manhood to themselves and to their friends. They were always the worst troublemakers, spoiled, rich young men who had to show how tough they were for all to see. They hunted in packs and were as capable of drunken viciousness as the lowest dockside cutthroat. Maybe they were worse, for they considered themselves above the law and their victims less than vermin.

From where he stood, Felix could see a bunch of jaded young dandies tugging at the dress of a struggling serving-wench. They were demanding a kiss. The girl, a pretty newcomer called Elissa, fresh from the country and unused to this sort of behaviour, was resisting hard. Her struggles just seemed to encourage the rowdies. Two of them had got to their feet and began to drag the struggling girl towards the alcoves. One had clamped a hand over her mouth so that her shrieks would not be heard. Another brandished a huge blutwurst sausage obscenely.

Felix moved to interpose himself between the young men and the alcoves.

'No need for that,' he said quietly.

The older of the two youths grinned nastily. Before speaking he took a huge bite of the blutwurst and swallowed it. His face was flushed and sweat glistened on his brow and cheeks. 'She's a feisty wench – maybe she'd enjoy a taste of a prime Nuln sausage.'

The dandies laughed uproariously at this fine jest. Encouraged he waved the sausage in the air like a general rallying his troops.

'I don't think so,' Felix said, trying hard to keep his temper. He hated these spoiled young aristocrats with a passion, had done ever since his time at the University of Altdorf where he had been surrounded by their sort.

'Our friend here thinks he's tough, Dieter,' said the younger of the two, a crop-headed giant larger than Felix. He sported the scarred face of a student duellist, one who fought to gain scars and so enhance his prestige.

Felix looked around for some help. The other bouncers were trying to calm down a brawl between the Kislevites and the halberdiers. Felix could see Gotrek's crest of dyed hair rising above the scrum. No help from that quarter, then.

Felix shrugged. Better make the best of a bad situation, he thought. He looked straight into the duellist's eye.

'Just let the girl be,' he said with exaggerated mildness – then some devil lurking at the back of his mind prompted him to add, 'and I promise not to hurt you.'

'You promise not to hurt us?' The duellist seemed a little confused. Felix could see that he was trying to work out whether this lowly bouncer could possibly be mocking him. The student's friends were starting to gather around, keen to start some trouble.

'I think we should teach this scumbag a lesson, Rupert,' Dieter said. 'I think we should show him he's not as tough as he thinks he is.'

Elissa chose this moment to bite Dieter's hand. He shrieked with pain and cuffed the girl almost casually. Elissa dropped as if pole-axed. 'Bitch took a chunk out of my hand!'

Suddenly Felix had just plain had enough. He had travelled hundreds of leagues, fought against beasts, monsters and men. He had seen the dead rise from their graves and slain evil cultists on Geheimnisnacht. He had killed the city of Nuln's own chief of secret police for being in league with the wretched skaven. He didn't have to take cheek from these spoiled whelps, and he certainly didn't need to watch them beat up an innocent girl.

Felix grabbed Rupert by the lapels and swung his forehead forward, butting the duellist on the nose. There was a sickening crunch and the big youth toppled backward, clutching his face. Felix grabbed Dieter by the throat and slapped him a couple of times just for show, then slammed the student's face into the heavy tabletop. There was another crunch. Steins toppled.

The spectators pushed their chairs backwards to avoid being soaked. Felix kicked Dieter's legs out from under him and then, after he hit the ground, kicked him in the head a couple of times. There was nothing pretty or elegant about it, but Felix was not in the mood to put up with these people any more. Suddenly they sickened him and he was glad of the chance to vent his anger.

As Dieter's friends surged forward, Felix ripped his sword from its scabbard. The razor-sharp blade glittered in the torch-light. The angry students froze as if they had heard the hissing of a deadly serpent.

Suddenly it was all deathly quiet. Felix put the blade down against the side of Dieter's head. 'One more step and I'll take his ear off. Then I'll make the rest of you eat it.'

'He means it,' one of the students muttered, Suddenly they did not look so very threatening any more, just a scared and drunken bunch of young idiots who had bought into much more trouble than they had bargained for. Felix twisted the blade so that it bit into Dieter's ear, drawing blood. The young man groaned and squirmed under Felix's boot.

Rupert whimpered and clutched his nose with one meaty hand. A river of red streamed over his fingers. 'You broke my node,' he said in a tone of piteous accusation. He sounded like he couldn't believe anyone would do anything so horribly cruel.

'One more word out of you and I'll break your fingers too,' Felix said. He hoped nobody tried to work out how he was going to do that. He wasn't quite sure himself, but he needn't have worried. Everybody took him absolutely seriously. 'The rest of you pick your friends up and get out of here, before I really lose my temper.'

He stepped away from Dieter's recumbent form, keeping his blade between himself and the students. They hurried forward, helped their injured friends to their feet, and hurried towards the door. A few kept terrified eyes on Felix as they went.

He walked over to Elissa and helped her to her feet.

'You all right?' he asked.

'Fine enough. Thanks,' she said. She looked up at him grate-fully. Not for the first time Felix noticed how pretty she was. She smiled up at him. Her tight black ringlets framed her round face. Her lips pouted. He reached down and tucked one of her jet-black curls behind her ear.

'Best go and have a word with Heinz. Tell him what happened.'

The girl hurried off.

'You're learning, manling,' the Trollslayer's voice said from behind him.

Felix looked around and was surprised to see Gotrek grin-ning malevolently up at him. 'I suppose so,' he said, although right at this moment he felt a little shaky. It was time for a drink.

GREY SEER THANQUOL perched on the three-legged bone stool in front of the farsqueaker and bit his tail. He was angry, as angry as he could ever remember being. He doubted he had been so angry even on the day he had made his first kill, and then he had been very, very angry indeed. He dug his canines into his tail until the sensation made his pink eyes water. Then he let go. He was sick of inflicting pain on himself. He felt like making someone else suffer.

'Hurry-fast! Scuttle-quick or I will the flesh flay from your most unworthy bones,' he shrieked, lashing out with the whip he carried for just such occasions as this.

The skaven slaves squeaked in dismay and scuttled faster on the lurching treadmill attached to the huge mechanisms of the farsqueaker. As they did so, the powerglobes began to glow slightly. Their flickering light illumined the long musty chamber. The shadows of the warp engineers of Clan Skryre danced across the walls as they made adjustments to the delicate machine by banging it lightly with sledgehammers. A faint tang of warpstone and ozone became perceptible in the air.

'Quick! Quick! Or I will feed you to the rat-ogres.'

A chance would be a fine thing, Thanquol thought. If only he had a rat-ogre to feed these slaves too. What a disappointment Boneripper had proved to be – that cursed dwarf had slain him as easily as Thanquol would slaughter a blind puppy. Just the thought of that hairless dwarf upstart made Thanquol want to squirt the musk of fear. At the same time, hatred bit at Thanquol's bowels and stayed there, gnawing as fiercely as a newly born runt chomping on a bone.

By the Horned Rat's fetid breath, he wanted revenge on the Trollslayer and his henchman! Not only had they slain Boneripper and cost Thanquol a lot of precious warptokens, they had also killed von Halstadt and thus disrupted the grey seer's master plan for throwing Nuln and the Empire into chaos.

True, Thanquol had other agents on the surface but none so highly placed or so malleable as the former head of Nuln's secret police. Thanquol wasn't looking forward to reporting the failure of this part of the scheme to his masters back in

Skavenblight. In fact, he had put off making his report for as long as he decently could. Now he had no option but to talk to the Seerlord and report how things stood. Warily he looked up at the huge mirror on top of the farsqueaker, as he waited for a vision of his master to take form.

The skaven slaves scuttled faster now. The light in the warp-globes became brighter. Thanquol felt his fur lift and a shiver run down his spine to the tip of his tail as sparks leapt from the globes at either end of the treadmill, flickering upwards towards the huge mirror at the top of the apparatus. One of the warp engineers rushed over to the control panel and wrenched down two massive copper switches. Forked lightning flickered between the warpglobes. The viewing mirror began to glow with a greenish light. Little flywheels began to buzz. Huge pistons rose and fell impressively.

Briefly Thanquol felt a surge of pride at this awesome triumph of skaven engineering, a device which made communication over all the long leagues between Nuln and Skavenblight not only possible but instantaneous.

Truly, no other race could match the inventive genius of the skaven. This machine was just one more proof, if any was needed, of skaven superiority to all other so-called sentient races. The skaven deserved to rule the world – which was doubtless why the Horned Rat had given it into their keeping.

A picture took shape in the mirror. A towering figure glared down at him. Thanquol shivered again, this time with uncontrollable fear. He knew he was looking on the features of one of the Council of Thirteen in distant Skavenblight. In truth, he could not tell which, since the picture was a little fuzzy. Maybe it was not even Seerlord Tisqueek. Swirls and patterns of interference danced across the mirror's shimmering surface. Perhaps, Thanquol should suggest that the engineers of Clan Skryre make a few adjustments to their device. Now, however, hardly seemed the time.

'What have... to... report... Seer Thanq...' The majestic voice of the council member emerged from the machine's squeaking trumpet as a high-pitched buzzing. Thanquol had to strain to make out the words. With his outstretched paw he snatched up the mouthpiece, carved from human thighbone and connected to the machine by a cable of purest copper. He struggled hard to avoid gabbling his words.

'Great triumphs, lordly one, and some minor setbacks,' Thanquol squeaked. His musk glands felt tight. He fought to keep from baring his teeth nervously.

'Spea… up… Grey… I… hardly hear you… and…'

Thanquol decided there were definitely a few problems with the farsqueaking machine. Many of the Seerlord's words were being lost, and doubtless his superior was only catching a few of Thanquol's own words in return. Perhaps, thought the grey seer, this could be made to work to his advantage. He must consider his options.

'Many triumphs, lordly one, and a few minor setbacks!' Thanquol bellowed as loud as he could. His roaring startled the slaves and they stopped running. As the treadmill slowed, the picture started to flicker and fade. The long tongues of lightning dimmed. 'Faster, you fools! Don't stop!'

Thanquol encouraged the slaves with a flick of his lash. Slowly the picture returned until the dim outline of the gigantic skaven lord was visible once more. A cloud of foul-smelling smoke was starting to emerge from the farsqueaker. It smelled like something within the machine was burning. Two warp engineers stood by with buckets of foul water drawn directly from the nearby sewers.

'…setbacks, Grey …eer Thanquol?'

If ever there was time for the machine's slight irregularities to prove useful, now was that time, thought Thanquol. 'Yes, master. Many triumphs! Even as we speak our warriors scout beneath the man-city. Soon we will have all information we need for our inevitable triumph!'

'I said… setbacks… Seer Thanquol.'

'It would not wise be to send them back, great one. We need every able-bodied skaven warrior to map the city.'

The councillor leaned forward and fiddled with a knob. The picture flickered and became slightly clearer. Thanquol could now see that the speaker's head was obscured by a great cowl which hid his features. The members of the Council of Thirteen often did that. It made them seem more mysterious and threatening. Thanquol could see that he was turning and saying something to someone just out of sight. The grey seer assumed his superior was berating one of the engineers of Clan Skryre.

'…and how is… agent von Halstadt…'

'Indisposed,' Thanquol replied, a little too hastily for his own liking. Somehow it sounded better than saying he was dead. He decided to change the subject quickly. He knew that he had better do something to save the situation and fast.

No matter how cunningly he stalled his masters on the farsqueaker, he knew that word of Fritz von Halstadt's death would get back to them eventually. Every skaven force was full of spies and snitches. It was only a matter of time before the news of his scheme's failure reached Skavenblight. By then Thanquol knew he had better have some concrete successes to report.

'We have news... change of plans... we send army to Nuln... when ready... ttack city...' The Seerlord's words made Thanquol ears rise with pleasure. If an army was being dispatched to Nuln, he would command it. Taking the city would increase his status immeasurably.

'Warlord Vermek Skab will command... render him all... sible assistance...'

Thanquol bared his teeth with disappointment. He was being replaced in command of this army. He sniffed as he considered the matter. Maybe not. Vermek Skab might have an accident. Then Grey Seer Thanquol could rise majestically to claim his full and rightful share of the glory!

Thanquol's nose twitched. The billowing cloud of smoke from the machine almost filled the chamber now, and Thanquol was pretty sure that the device was not supposed to be emitting great showers of sparks like that. The fact that two of the warp engineers were running for the door wasn't a good sign either. He considered following them.

'I have foreseen the presence... ill-omened elements in your future, Than... I predict disaster for you unless... do something about them.'

Suddenly Thanquol was rooted to the spot, torn between his desire to flee and his desire to hear more. He almost squirted the musk of fear. If the seerlord prophesied something then it had almost as good as happened. Unless, of course, his superior was lying to him for purposes of his own. That happened all too often, as Thanquol knew only too well.

'Disaster, lordly one?'

'Yes... see a dwarf and a human... destinies are intertwined with yours... you do not slay them then...'

There was a very loud and final bang. Thanquol threw himself off his stool and cowered on the floor. An acrid taste filled his mouth. Slowly the smoke cleared and he saw the fused and melted remains of the farsqueaking machine. Several dead skavenslaves lay in its midst, their fur all charred and their whiskers burned away. In one corner a warp engineer lay curled up in a ball, mewling and writhing in a state of shock. Thanquol was unconcerned about their fate. The Seerlord's words filled him with a great fear. He wished he had been able to speak with his superior a little longer but alas he had not that option. He raised his little bronze bell and tinkled it.

Slowly members of his bodyguard entered the chamber. Clawleader Gazat looked almost disappointed to see him alive, Thanquol thought. Briefly the idea that the warrior might have sabotaged the farsqueaker crossed Thanquol's mind. He dismissed it – Gazat did not have the imagination. Anyway, the Grey Seer had more important things to worry about.

'Summon the gutter runners!' Thanquol squeaked in his most authoritative tone. 'I have work for them.'

For a moment silence fell over the chamber. A foul smell made Thanquol's whiskers twitch. Just the mere mention of the dreaded assassins of Clan Eshin had caused Clawleader Gazat to squirt the musk of fear.

'Quick! Quick!' Thanquol added.

'Instantly, master,' Gazat said sadly and scuttled off into the labyrinth of sewers.

Thanquol rubbed his paws in glee. The gutter runners would not fail, of that he was assured.

FELIX UNLOCKED THE door of his chamber and entered his room. He yawned widely. He wanted for nothing more than to lie down on his pallet and sleep. He had been working for more than twelve hours. He put the lantern down beside the straw-filled mattress and unlaced his jerkin. He tried to give his surroundings as little attention as was possible, but it was difficult to ignore the loud moans of passion coming from the next room and the singing of the drinkers downstairs.

The chamber wasn't good enough for paying guests but it suited him well enough. He had occupied better, but this one had the great virtue of being free. It came with the job. Like a minority of old Heinz's staff, Felix chose to live on the premises.

Felix's little pile of possessions stood in one corner, under the barred window. There was his chainmail jerkin and a little rucksack which contained a few odds and ends such as his fire-making kit.

Felix threw himself down on the bed and pulled his old, tattered woollen cloak over himself. He made sure his sword was within easy reach. His hard life on the road had made him wary even in seemingly safe places, and the thought that the skaven they had recently encountered might still be about filled him with dread.

He recalled only too well the huge corpse of the slain rat-ogre lying at the foot of the stairs in von Halstadt's mansion. It had not been a reassuring sight. Somehow he was unsurprised that he had heard nothing at all about the fire at von Halstadt's mansion. Perhaps the authorities had not found the skaven bodies, or perhaps there was a cover-up. Right now, Felix didn't even want to consider it.

Felix wondered how men could ignore the tales of the skaven. Even as a student he had come across scholarly tomes proving that they didn't exist, or that if they had ever existed they were now extinct. He had come across a few references to them in connection with the Great Plague of 1111 and of course the Emperor of that period was known as Mandred Skavenslayer. Yet that was all. There were innumerable books written about elves and dwarfs and orcs, yet knowledge of the rat-men was rare. He could almost have suspected an organised conspiracy to cloak them in secrecy but that thought was too disturbing, so he pushed it aside.

There was a soft knock at the door. Felix lay still and tried to ignore. Probably just one of the drunken patrons lost and looking for his room again, he told himself.

The knock came again, more urgently and insistently this time. Felix rose from the bed and snatched up his sword.

A man could never be too careful in these dark times. Perhaps some bravo lurked out there, and thought a sleep-fuddled Felix would prove easy prey. Only two months ago Heinz had found a murdered couple lying on bloodstained sheets a mere three doors away. The man had been a prominent wine merchant, the girl his teenage mistress. Heinz suspected that the merchant had been slain by assassins on order of his harridan of a wife, but claimed also that it was none of his business. Felix had got his new tunic all covered in blood when he dumped the bodies in the river. He hadn't been too thrilled about having to use the secret route through the sewers either.

The knocking came a third time, and he heard a woman's voice whisper, 'Felix.'

Felix eased his blade from its scabbard. Just because he heard a girl's voice didn't mean that there was only a girl waiting for him out there. She might have brought a few burly friends who would set about him as soon as he opened the door.

Briefly he considered not opening the door at all, of simply waiting till the girl and her friends tried to batter the door down then he realised quite how paranoid he had become. He shrugged. Since the deaths of Hef and Spider and the rest of the sewer watch he had every reason to be paranoid. Still, was he going to wait here all night? He slipped the bolts and opened the door. Elissa was waiting there.

She looked up at him nervously, brushing a curl from her forehead. She was very short but really very pretty indeed, Felix decided.

'I... I wanted to thank you for helping me earlier,' she said eventually.

Felix thought that it was a bit late for that. Couldn't she have waited till the morning? Slowly, though, realisation dawned on him. 'It was nothing,' he muttered, feeling his face flush.

Elissa glanced quickly left and right down the corridor. 'Aren't you going to invite me in, I wanted to thank you properly.'

She had to stand on her tiptoes to kiss his lips. He stood there dumbfounded for a second then pulled her into the room and slammed the door, slipping the lock into place.

As HIS HENCHLING Queg reached twelve in his muttered count, Chang Squik of Clan Eshin twitched his nose and sampled the smells of the night.

Strange, he thought; so like the stinks of the man-cities of Far Cathay and yet so unlike. Here he could smell beef and turnip and roast pig. In the east it would have been pickled cabbage and rice and chicken. The food smelled different but everything else was the same. There was the same scent of overflowing sewers, of many humans living in close proximity, of incense and perfume.

He opened his ears as his master had trained him as well. He heard temple bells tolling and the rattle of carriage wheels on cobbles. He heard the singing of drunks and the call of the night watchmen as they shouted the hour. It did not trouble him. He could not be distracted. He could, if he so wished, tune out all extraneous sound and pick out one voice in a crowd.

The skaven squinted out into the darkness. His night-vision was keen. Down there were the shadowy shapes of men and women leaving the taverns arm in arm, heading for brief liaisons in back alleys and squalid rooming houses. Chang did not care about them at all. His two targets were in the building that humans called a tavern.

He did not know why the honourable grey seer had selected these two, out of all the inferior souls in this city, for inevitable death. He merely knew it was his task to ease the passing of their souls into the maw of the Horned Rat. He had already offered up two sticks of narcotic incense and pledged their immortal essence for his dark god's feast. He could almost, but not quite, feel sorry for the doomed ones.

They were there in that tavern, under the sign of the Blind Pig, and they did not know that certain doom approached. Nor would they, for Chang Squik had trained for years in the delivery of silent death. Long before he had left the warm jungles of his eastern homeland to serve the Council of Thirteen in these cold western climes, he had been schooled to perfection in his clan's ancient art of stealthy assassination. While still a runt, he had been made to run bare-pawed through beds of white hot coals, and snatch coins from the bowls of blind beggars in human cities. Even at that early age he had learned that the beggars were often far from blind, and often viciously proficient in the martial arts.

By the time of his initiation he had become proficient in all forms of unarmed combat. He was a third degree adept in the way of the Crimson Talon and held a black belt in the Path of the Deadly Paw. He had spent twelve long months being trained in silent infiltration in the jungles, and a month in fasting and meditation high atop Mount Yellowfang with only his own droppings for food.

Since that time he had killed and killed again in the name of the Council of Thirteen. He had slain Lord Khijaw of Clan Gulcher when that mighty warlord had plotted the downfall of Throt the Unclean. He had served as personal assistant to Snikch when the great assassin had killed Frederick Hasselhoffen and his entire household, and he had been rewarded with one-on-one instruction by the Deathmaster himself.

Chang Quik's list of triumphs was long, and tonight he would add another to it. It was his task to slay the dwarf, Gotrek Gurnisson, and his human henchling, Felix Jaeger. He did not see how he could fail.

What chance had a one-eyed dwarf and his stupid human friend against a mighty skaven trained in every art of death-dealing? Chang Squik felt confident that he could take the pair himself. He had been almost insulted by Grey Seer Thanquol's insistence that he take his full pack of gutter runners.

Surely the dire rumours of this dwarf were exaggerated. The Trollslayer could not possibly have slaughtered a unit of stormvermin single-handed. And it seemed well nigh unbelievable that he could have slain the rat-ogre, Boneripper, without the aid of an entire company of mercenaries. And, of course, it was impossible that this could be the same dwarf who five years ago had slain Warlord Makrik of Clan Gowjyer at the Battle of the Third Door.

Chang exhaled in one long controlled breath. Perhaps the grey seer was right. He had often proved to be so in the past. It was simple prudence to assign the task of slaying the dwarf to Slitha. Chang would slay the human, and if there were any difficulties he would race to the assistance of his henchling's squad. Not that there would be any difficulties.

Queg stopped counting at one hundred and tapped his superior on the arm. Chang lashed his tail once to show that he understood. Slitha and his team, with the clockwork precision which characterised all skaven operations, would be in position at the secret entrance to the tavern by now. It was time to proceed.

He loosened his swords in their scabbards, checked to make sure that his blowpipe and throwing stars were ready at paw, and whistled the signal to advance.

Like a dark wave, the pack of gutter runners surged forward over the rooftop. Their blackened weapons were visible only as shadowy outlines in the moons' light. Not a weapon clinked. Not an outline was visible. Well, almost.

HEINZ MADE HIS last rounds of the night, checking the doors and windows of the lower floor to make sure they were securely barred. It was amazing how often thieves tried to break in to the Blind Pig and steal from its cellars. Not even the reputation for ferocity of Heinz's bouncers could keep the desperately poor and alcoholic denizens of the New Quarter from making the attempt. It was quite pathetic really.

He made his way down into the cellars, shining his light into the dark corners between the great ale barrels, and wine racks. He could have sworn he heard a strange scuttling noise down here.

Just his imagination, he told himself.

He was getting old, starting to hear things. Even so, he went over and checked the secret door that led down into the sewers. It was hard to tell in this light but it looked undisturbed. He doubted anybody had used it since he and Felix had dumped those bodies two months back and saved everybody quite a scandal. Yes, he was just getting old, that was all.

He turned and limped back to the stairwell. His bad leg was playing up tonight. It always did when there was going to be rain. Heinz smiled grimly, remembering how he'd got the old war wound. It had been stamped on by a Bretonnian charger at the Battle of Red Orc Pass. Clean break. He remembered lying there in the bloody dirt and thinking it was probably a just payback for spiking the horse's owner on his halberd. That had been a bad time, one of the worst he had faced in all his years of soldiering. He'd learned a lot about pain that day. Still there had been good times as well as bad during his career as a mercenary, he was forced to admit that.

There were occasions when Heinz wondered whether he had made the right decision, giving up the free-spirited life of the mercenary companies for the life of a tavern keeper. On nights like this he missed the camaraderie of his old unit, the drinking round the campfires, the swapping of stories and recounting of tales of heroism.

Heinz had spent ten years as a halberdier, and had seen service on half the battlefields of the Empire, first as a lowly trooper and later as a sergeant. He had risen to captain during

Emperor Karl Franz's campaigns against the orc hordes in the east. During the last Bretonnian scrap he had made enough in plunder to buy the Blind Pig. He had finally given in to old Lotte's promptings to settle down and make a life for the two of them. His old comrades had laughed when he had actually married a camp follower. They had insisted she would run off with all his money. Instead the two of them had been blissfully happy for five years before old Lotte had to spoil it all by going and dying of the Wasting Sickness. He still missed her. He wondered if there was anything to stay here in Nuln for now. His family were all dead. Lotte was gone.

As he reached the head of the stair, Heinz thought he heard the scuttling sound again. There was definitely something moving down there.

Briefly he considered calling Gotrek or some of the other lads, and getting them to investigate, then he spread his huge hands wide in a gesture of disgust. He really was getting old if he would let the noise of some rats scrabbling round in his cellar upset him. He could just imagine what the others would say if he told them he was scared to go down there himself. They would laugh like drains.

He drew the thick cosh from his waistband and turned to go back down. Now he really was uneasy. He would never have drawn the weapon normally. He was too calm and easy tempered. Something definitely did have him spooked. His old soldier's instincts were aroused, and they had saved him on more than one occasion.

He could still remember that night along the Kislevite border when he had somehow been unable to get to sleep, filled with a terrible sense of foreboding. He had risen from his bed and gone to replace the sentry, only to find the man dead at his post. He had only just roused the camp before the foul beastmen attacked. He had a similar feeling in the pit of his stomach now. He hesitated at the top of the stair.

Best go get Gotrek, he thought. Only the real hardcore drinkers were still in the tavern by now. The rest were asleep, under the tables, in the alcoves, in the private rooms, or else gone home.

There it was again, that skittering sound, like the soft scrabble of padded claws on the stone stairs. Heinz was definitely worried now. He pulled the door closed and turned, almost running down the corridor until he came out in the main bar area. A handful of the bouncers chattered idly with a few of the barmaids.

'Where's Gotrek?' Heinz asked. A burly lad, Helmut, jerked his thumb in the direction of the privies.

SLITHA REACHED THE head of the staircase and flung the door open. So far, so good. All was going like a typically well-oiled Clan Skryre machine. Everything according to plan. They had entered the tavern undetected; now it was simply a case of searching the place until they came upon the dwarf and killed him. And furthermore killed anything else that got in their way, of course.

Slitha felt a little irritated. It was typical of his superior to take the easy task. They had already found out where the human Jaeger slept, and their leader had taken the task of killing him for himself. Surely that was the only explanation. It could not be that the great Chang Squik was afraid of an encounter with the Trollslayer. Not that Slitha cared. When he dispatched the feared dwarf it would simply reflect all the more to his credit. He gestured for his fellows to go in first.

'Quick! Quick!' he chittered. 'All night we haven't got!' The gutter runners moved quickly into the corridor.

FELIX AND ELISSA lay on his palette, kissing deeply, when suddenly Felix shifted uneasily. He thought he heard the faintest of scrabbling sounds from outside the window.

He gently untangled Elissa's arms from around him, and was suddenly aware of the area of heat and sweat where their bodies met. He looked down on the serving girl's face. Her face was a little puffed on the left side from where the student had hit her but she really was very pretty.

'What is it?' she asked, looking up at him with wide, trusting eyes. He listened for a moment and heard nothing.

'Nothing,' he said and began kissing her again.

SLITHA BOUNDED DOWN the corridor. He smelled dwarf. He followed the scent, whistling commands to his fellows in the fore. Surprised by skaven stealth, speed and savagery their weak foe would swiftly be dragged down. What chance would a mere dwarf have against the deadliest warriors of the master race?

Slitha almost felt sorry that he was in the rear, the traditional position of honour any skaven leader adopted whenever possible. He would have liked a chance to be the first to sink his blade into the dwarf and offer up his soul to the Horned Rat.

They reached the end of the corridor. The stench of dwarf intensified. He must be very close now. Slitha's heart rate accelerated dramatically. Blood raced through his veins. His tail stiffened and lashed. The claws in his feet extruded instinctively. As he made ready for combat, he bared his fangs in a snarl. The scent was very strong: they must be almost on top of the Trollslayer. His warriors lashed their tails proudly, ready to overwhelm their opponent with their numbers and savagery.

Suddenly a red mist filled Slitha's eyes. It looked as if a huge axe had cut Klisqueek in half but that could not be. They could not have been detected. It was impossible that a mere dwarf would have the cunning to ambush a pack of skaven gutter runners.

Yet suddenly Hrishak was squeaking in pain and terror. A huge fist had caught him by the throat. The butt of a monstrous axe cracked his skull. The thick, cloying scent of the musk of fear filled the air now. Klisqueek's body had already started to dissolve into a puddle of black slime, as the Clan Eshin decomposition spells took effect.

Slitha looked out into a swirling melee where half a dozen of his finest gutter runners were attempting to swarm over a massive dwarfish form. His pale hairless flesh was emphasised by the black of the skaven's cloaks. Slitha saw the huge axe swing around in a deadly arc. He heard bones crunch and brains splatter.

'Try and sneak up on me, would you,' muttered the dwarf in Reikspiel. He added a guttural curse in Dwarfish as he clove a path of red ruin through the skaven assassins. The dwarf bellowed and chanted a strange war-cry as he fought.

Slitha shuddered. The noise was enough to awaken the dead, or at least any sleeping human guards. He felt the advantage of stealth and surprise slipping away. His eyes widened with terror as he watched the dwarf complete his bloody work, cutting down Snikkit and Blodge with one stroke. Suddenly Slitha realised that he was alone, facing one very angry and very dangerous dwarf.

It was impossible to believe but the dwarf had killed most of his brethren in a matter of seconds. Nothing in all the world, not even an assassin of Clan Eshin, could conceivably be so deadly. Slitha turned to flee but a hob-nailed boot descended on his tail pinning him in place. Tears of pain filled Slitha's eyes. The musk of fear voided from his glands.

The last thing he heard was the whoosh of a huge axe coming closer.

DESPITE HIMSELF, Felix untangled himself from Elissa again and looked around. What was that noise? It sounded like fighting downstairs. He was sure he could recognise Gotrek's deep-throated battle-cry. The girl was looking up at him, puzzled, wondering why he had stopped kissing her. She opened her mouth to speak. Felix placed a hand gently over her lips. He leaned forward until his mouth was over her ear.

'Be very quiet,' he whispered. A cold trickle of fear ran through him. He could definitely hear a strange scrabbling sound coming from over by the window. Felix lifted himself off the recumbent girl and reached for his dragon-hilted sword. He slipped backwards off the straw pallet and fell into a half crouch.

Placing one finger against his lips to indicate she should be quiet, he gestured for the woman to get up off the bed. She stared at him uncertainly then followed his gaze over to the window.

That was when she screamed.

CHANG SQUIK WATCHED as Noi swung down on the rope. He felt almost proud of his pupil. Noi had fixed the grapnel in the guttering perfectly then abseiled down the side of the tavern like a great spider. He had sprayed the metal bars covering the window with acid, then filed through the weakened iron like a master burglar. He reached up and gestured to the rest of the squad on the tavern roof. They fixed their ropes in position and made ready to follow Noi. Chang would be last in, as befitted the glorious strike leader. Noi kicked himself back from the wall, swinging out into space, gaining momentum to crash through the window.

THE WINDOW CAVED IN and a black-clad skaven crashed through it. It hit the floor rolling and emerged into a fighting crouch, tail lashing, a long curved blade glinting evilly in each claw. Felix didn't wait for it to get time to orientate itself. He lashed forward with his own blade, almost catching the thing by surprise. Sparks flashed as the creature parried, deflecting Felix's blade so that it only seared along its cheek.

'Run, Elissa!' Felix shouted. 'Get out!'

For a moment, he thought the girl was too shocked to move. She lay on the straw pallet, her eyes wide with horror, then suddenly she sprang up. The distraction almost killed Felix. The moment he took to look at her was a moment he did not look at his opponent. Only the deadly whine of the skaven's blade as it darted towards his skull warned him. He ducked his head, and the sword passed over him, coming close enough to shave a lock off his hair. Felix lashed back instinctively. The skaven sprang away.

'Felix!' Elissa shouted.

'Run! Get help!' Over the skaven's shoulder, he could see other feral forms crowding round the window. They seemed to be struggling to force a way in, each getting in the other's way. The window was packed with mangy scarred skaven faces. Things did not look good.

'Die! Die! Foolish man-thing,' the skaven chittered, bounding forward. It feinted a stroke with its right blade, then lashed out with its left. Felix caught its hand just above the wrist and immobilised it. The thing's tail snaked obscenely round his leg and tried to trip him. Felix brought the pommel of his sword down behind the skaven's ear. It fell forward but even as it did so it struck with its blade, forcing Felix to jump away. He bounded back across the room and skewered the skaven as it started to rise. Blood frothed from the foul thing's lips as it died. A strange reeking stink filled the air. The skaven's flesh started to bubble and rot.

Felix heard Elissa throw the door bolts. He risked a glance at her. She had turned and was looking at him in a mixture of horror and confusion, as if she did not know whether to leave him or to stay.

'Go!' he shouted. 'Get help. There's nothing you can do here.'

She vanished through the doorway leaving Felix feeling obscurely relieved. At least now he wasn't responsible for her safety. As he turned to look back he saw that the skaven he had killed was gone. It had left behind only a pool of black slime

and its rotting clothing. Felix wondered what deadly sorcery
was at work.

A hiss of displaced air warned him of another threat. From
the corner of his eye, he caught sight of several glittering objects
hurtling towards him. He dived forward, aiming for the bed,
hoping it would break his fall. His mouth filled with straw
from the mattress as he landed. He fumbled with his left hand
for his old red cloak and pulled its wadded mass up in his left
fist. He was just in time. More shining objects spun through the
air towards him. He brought the cloak up and they impacted in
the roll of thick wool. Something sharp penetrated the cloth
just between his fingers. Felix looked down. He saw a throwing
star, smeared with some foul reddish substance, doubtless poison.

Two more skaven had extricated themselves from the mass
outside the window and dropped into the room. They scuttled
towards him with eye-blinding speed, evil shadows of man-
sized rats, their yellow fangs glistening in the lantern-light. He
knew better now than to even glance at the doorway. There was
no way he could reach it without taking a blade in his back.

Why me, he asked himself? Why am I standing here half-
naked and alone, facing a pack of skaven assassins? Why do
these things always happen to me? This sort of thing never happened to Sigmar in the legends!

He threw the cloak over the head of the oncoming skaven. It
writhed in the tangle of woollen folds. Felix ran his blade
through it. His razor-sharp sword cut through flesh like butter.
Black blood soiled the garment. Felix struggled to pull the
blade free. The second rat-thing took advantage of his preoccu-
pation and sprang forward, both blades held high, swinging
downwards like butcher's cleavers. Felix threw himself backwards; the blade came free with an awful sucking sound. He
landed flat on his back, his sword clutched in his hand. He
raised its point and the flying skaven impaled itself on it. As it
fell, its weight pulled the blade free from Felix's grasp.

Damn, he thought, rising to his feet. Weaponless. The point
of his blade was visible, protruding from the skaven's back. He
was reluctant to touch the foul beast with his naked flesh but
he had no choice if he wanted the blade. His cloak was already
starting to flatten as the skaven decomposed with terrifying
rapidity.

Too late! More skaven leapt in through the window. There was no time for any qualms. He picked up the skaven sword and charged. The sheer fury of his rush took the skaven by surprise. He cleaved one's skull before it could react and disembowelled another with his return stroke. It fell, trying to hold in its ropy guts with one claw, even as it attempted to strike Felix with the other.

Felix hacked at it again, severing the limb. He cut around him in blind fury, feeling the terrible shock of impact run up his arm from every blow. Slowly, though, more and more skaven pressed into the room, and remorselessly, defending himself as best he could every step of the way, he was pressed back towards the wall.

HEINZ LOOKED UP in surprise as Gotrek stomped into the bar. In one hand he held his blood-smeared axe. His other huge fist clutched a dead skaven by the scruff of the neck. The thing was decomposing at a frightening rate, seemingly undergoing weeks of decomposition in moments. Gotrek glared around at the surprised bouncers with his one good eye and dropped the body. It squelched and formed a puddle at his feet.

'Bloody skaven,' he muttered. 'Whole bunch of them lurking just outside the privy. Too stupid to know dwarfs have good ears.'

Heinz moved over to stand by the Trollslayer. He looked down at the pool of rot with a peculiar mixture of fascination and distaste written on his features.

'That's a skaven alright.'

Gotrek looked up at him in surprise. 'Of course, it was a bloody skaven! I've killed enough of them in my time to know what they look like by now.'

Heinz shrugged apologetically. Then he swivelled on his heels as a scream emerged from the top of the stairwell. Heinz looked up in surprise as the partially clad form of Elissa appearing at the head of the stairs. The girl looked pale with terror.

'Felix!' she shouted.

'What has Felix done, girl?' he asked soothingly. She threw herself at him. He enfolded her shivering form with his brawny arms.

'No. They're trying to kill him. Monsters are trying to kill Felix. They're in his room!'

'Has that girl been taking weirdroot?' a bouncer asked placidly.

Heinz looked over at Gotrek and the rest of the bouncers. All his earlier forebodings returned. He remembered the scrabbling in the cellars. He could see that the dwarf was having the same thought as he was.

'What are we doing standing here?' Heinz roared. 'Follow me, lads!'

This was better. This was more like the old days.

FELIX KNEW THAT he was doomed. There was no way he could fight all these skaven. There were too many of them and they were too fast. If he had been wearing his chainmail shirt perhaps he would have some chance of surviving all those stabbing blades. But he wasn't.

His foes sensed victory and advanced. Felix danced in the centre of a whirlwind of stabbing blades. Somehow he managed to survive with only a few nicks and scratches. He found himself standing beside his bed. Thinking quickly, he kicked the lantern over. Oil spilled out onto the straw and lit it. In an instant, a wall of flame separated him from the rat-men. He reached out and grabbed the nearest one, hurling it into the flames. The skaven shrieked in agony as its fur caught fire. It began to roll around on the floor, howling and squeaking. Its fellows leapt back to avoid its blazing form.

Felix knew he had bought himself only a moment's breathing space. He knew now there was only once chance. Doing what the skaven least expected, he dived directly through the flames. Heat scorched his flesh. He smelled the stink of his own singed hair. He saw a gap in the skaven line near the door and dived through it, almost slamming into the corridor wall. Heart pounding, breath rasping in his lungs, blood pouring from a dozen nicks, he raced for the head of the stairs, as if all the hounds of Chaos were at his heels.

A head poked out from the room next door. He recognised the bald pate and lambchop whiskers of Baron Josef Mann, one of the Blind Pig's most dedicated customers.

'What the hell is going on out there?' the old nobleman shouted. 'Sounds like you're performing unnatural acts with animals.'

'Something like that,' Felix retorted as he sprinted past. The old man saw what was following him. His eyes went wide. He clutched his chest and fell.

CHANG SQUIK GLANCED out round the doorway and gnawed the tip of his tail in frustration. It was all going wrong. It had all started going wrong from the moment that fool Noi had swung in through the window. In their enthusiasm to be part of the kill, the rest of the pack had all tried to get in behind him at once, all eager to claim their share of the glory. Of course their lines had become entangled, and they had all ended up clutching the window sill and each other and frantically trying to scuttle into the room. Several of the idiots had fallen to their deaths on the hard ground below. Serves the fools right too.

It was ever the fate of great skaven captains to be let down by incompetent underlings, he thought philosophically. Not even the most brilliant plan could survive being executed by witless cretins. It was starting to look like his entire command consisted of those. They could not even kill a single feeble manling, even with all the advantages of surprise, numbers and superior skaven armament. It made him want to spit with frustration. Personally he suspected treachery. Perhaps rivals in the clan had sent him a bunch of ill-trained louts in order to discredit him. All in all, that seemed the most likely explanation.

Briefly Chang considered taking a hand in the fray himself but only briefly. It was glaringly obvious to his superior intellect what was going to happen next. The entire tavern would be roused and his underlings would soon encounter stiff, and very likely fatal, resistance.

Let them get on with it, Chang thought. They deserve whatever fate befalls them.

He slid back into the room, petulantly threw some of the manling's clothing on the fire to add to the blaze, and then leapt out the window. He caught the climbing line easily in one hand and swarmed up the side of the building to safety.

Already he was considering what would be the best way to report this minor setback to Grey Seer Thanquol.

HEINZ GRUNTED AS something slammed into him. He almost toppled backwards as the weight hit him.

'Sorry,' said a polite voice that Heinz recognised as belonging to Felix Jaeger. 'I was having a little trouble back there.'

Throwing stars whizzed past Heinz's ear. The smell of burning filled his nostrils. He looked down a corridor crowded with scurrying rat-men. A cold fury filled him. Those cursed skaven were trying to burn down the Blind Pig and rob him of his livelihood! He pulled out his cosh and made to rush forward. He need not have bothered. Gotrek pushed him to one side and charged headlong into the throng. The rest of the bouncers advanced cautiously behind him. From the far end of the corridor, various nobles and their bodyguards emerged and slammed into the skaven from the rear. Terrible carnage began.

It was all over very soon.

FELIX SAT IN FRONT of the fire, wrapped in a blanket and shivering. He looked across at Elissa. The girl smiled back at him wanly. All around, the bouncers hurried upstairs with buckets of water, making sure that the fire did not spread from Felix's room.

'I thought you were very brave,' Elissa said. There was a look of complete doting admiration in her eye. 'Just like a hero in one of those Detlef Sierck dramas.'

Felix shrugged. He was tired. He was riddled with dozens of cuts and bruises. And he knew now that the skaven were definitely trying to kill him. He didn't feel very heroic. Still, he thought, things could be worse. He reached out and put an arm around Elissa's shoulder and drew her to him. She snuggled in close.

'Thank you,' he said, and for a moment the girl's smile made everything feel more worthwhile.

NIGHT RAID

'It is a frightening thing to be sought by enemies unknown, invisible and untraceable, who can strike at you when they will without fear of vengeance or punishment. At least, I found it to be so. If my companion shared these feelings, he never gave any sign of it to me. Indeed he seemed rather to enjoy the situation – which I suppose was natural enough, given that his avowed purpose in life was to seek a violent death. Yet I was worried. The attack on the alehouse had left me shaken, and the knowledge that somewhere out in the night an implacable foe was lurking did nothing to calm my fraught nerves. But it seemed that we had allies as well, who were determined to aid us for their own unguessable purposes.'

— From *My Travels With Gotrek, Vol. III*,
by Herr Felix Jaeger (Altdorf Press, 2505)

'WHAT ARE YOU doing there, young Felix?' A shadow fell on Felix Jaeger. Startled, he reached for the hilt of his sword. The

book fell from his lap, almost landing in the fire, as he started
to rise from the overstuffed leather armchair. Looking up he
saw that it was only old Heinz, the owner of the Blind Pig tavern, standing over him, polishing a tankard that he held in
one huge meaty fist. Felix let out a long sigh, suddenly all too
aware of how tightly wound he was. He sank back into the
chair, forcing his hand to release its tight grip on the weapon
hilt.

'You're a little tense this evening,' Heinz said plainly.

'A little,' Felix agreed. A quick glance around told him that
the old ex-mercenary wasn't going to hassle him to start working. His services as a bouncer were not needed just yet. It was
early evening and few patrons were about. Normally the tavern
didn't really start jumping until well after dark. On the other
hand, for the first time, Felix noticed that the Pig was much
quieter than usual. Custom had definitely dropped off since
last week's skaven attack, an event which had not improved the
Blind Pig's already dire reputation.

Felix reached down and picked up his book, a cheap printed
manuscript of one of Detlef Sierck's more melodramatic plays.
It had served the purpose of distracting his thoughts from the
fact that the rat-men were apparently out to get him.

'It will be a quiet night tonight, Felix,' Heinz said.

'You think?'

'I know.' Heinz held the tankard up to the light, making sure
he had removed every last speck of dust from the thing. He set
it down on the mantelpiece. Felix noticed the way the light
gleamed on the old mercenary's bald head. Felix sighed and
laid his book down on the chair arm. Heinz was a sociable sort
and he just naturally liked to chat. Besides, maybe Heinz was
just as nervous as himself. The tavern keeper had every reason
to be. He had almost lost his livelihood to ferocious Chaos-
worshipping monsters. It was only in the last few days that all
the damage the rat-men had done had been repaired.

'Business has been bad since the skaven attack,' Felix said.

'Business will pick up again. Same thing happened after that
murder a couple of months back. The nobs will stay away for a
bit but then they'll come back. They like a sense of danger
when they drink. It's what they come here for. But we'll see
nobody this evening, if I'm not mistaken.'

'Why's that?'

'The Feast of Verena. It's a special night here in Nuln. Most folk will be at home, praying and fasting, making sure everything's spick and span. She's the patron of this city, as well as of you bookish folk, and this is her special night.'

'There has to be someone wanting a drink.'

'The only folk that will be having any fun are the Guild of Mechanics and their apprentices. Verena's their patron too. The countess has a big feast for them tonight in her palace. Nothing but the best for them.'

'Why does the countess feel compelled to give a feast for commoners?' Felix was curious. Countess Emmanuelle was not famed for her generosity. 'She's not normally so fond of us.'

Heinz laughed. 'Aye but these are special commoners. They run her new College of Engineering for her. They're making steam-tanks and organ guns and all sorts of other special weapons for her forces, same as the Imperial College does for the Emperor. She can afford to give them a nice dinner once a year if it keeps them happy.'

'I'll wager she can.'

'I thought maybe you might like to take the night off and be with Elissa. I know it's her day off. I did notice you've been seeing a lot of each other recently.'

Felix looked up. 'You disapprove?'

'Nothing wrong with a man and a maid being together, I always say. Just making an observation.'

'She's gone back to her village for the day. One of her relatives is sick. She should be back tomorrow.'

'Sorry to hear that. There's a lot of sickness about. Folk are starting to mutter about the plague. Well, I'll let you get back to your book then.'

Felix opened the book once more but didn't turn the page. He was amazed that Heinz could be so sanguine just a few days after the attack. Felix was jumping at shadows but he was happily polishing his tankards. Maybe all those years of being a mercenary had given the old warrior nerves of steel. Felix wished he had them too. Right now he could not help but wonder what the skaven were up to. He was sure it was nothing good.

GREY SEER THANQUOL leaned against the huge bulk of the Screaming Bell. He gazed malevolently around the vast chamber and out at the teeming sea of ratty skaven faces. All around him Thanquol sensed the surge of activity, smelled the packed mass of the assembling skaven troops in the surrounding tunnels. All the warriors of Clan Skab were here, reinforced by contingents from all the great and powerful factions in skavendom. It was good to be away from the sewers, to be back here in the Underways, the subterranean highways linking all the cities of the Under-Empire. It was good – but right now he could take no pleasure from it. He was too angry.

He fought the feeling, reminding himself that somewhere, far overhead, the humans went about their business, ploughing their fields, chopping their forests unsuspecting, not knowing their days of dominance were nearly done, that soon their city and then their Empire would fall beneath the iron paw of skaven military genius. Not even these thoughts cheered him up or helped dispel his rage.

He ran a talon over the bell, drawing forth a slight ringing tone, still seeking to control his anger. The bell swung slightly at the grey seer's touch, and the carriage on which the ancient artefact sat groaned as it moved. The seething magical energies within the bell comforted Thanquol a little. Soon, he told himself, he would unleash these enormous forces against his enemies. Very soon, he hoped, but right now he was filled with a terrible, all consuming rage and he needed to find someone to vent it upon.

Chang Squik grovelled in the dirt before him, waiting for the grey seer to decide his fate. It had taken nearly a week for Thanquol to locate him. The would-be assassin sprawled face down in the shadow of the great bell. His tail lay flat. His whiskers drooped despondently. The leader of the gutter runners continued to mutter pathetic excuses about how he had been betrayed, about how the targets had been warned of his otherwise irresistible attack, of how they had used vile sorcery to slay his warriors – above all, about how it had not been his fault. Near the assassin stood Thanquol's lieutenants, hiding their mouths with their paws to cover the sound of their mirth.

Thousands of faces peered up at Thanquol, eager to know what he would do next. It was not often that they got to see one of the mighty abase himself. Thanquol let his glance rest on each of the warleaders. They squirmed under his inspection. Their tittering stopped. None of them wanted to be the focus of his anger – which was unfortunate for them, because one of them was going to be.

The grey seer looked at the representatives of Clan Moulder, Clan Eshin, Clan Skryre and Clan Pestilens. All of them were his to order about, at least until his replacement, Warlord Vermek Skab, arrived. And that was not going to happen. Thanquol had prepared a little surprise for the warlord. Skab would never reach this place alive. The thought made his tail rigid. And yet...

Yet, despite all this power under his control, he could not get this one dwarf killed.

Anger and fear bit at the base of his stomach. Gotrek Gurnisson and his worthless human henchman were still alive. It beggared belief! How could this be?

It was almost as if he, the great Thanquol, was under a curse. He shuddered at the very thought. Surely the Horned Rat would not withdraw his favour from one of his chosen? No, he told himself sternly, that was not the real reason why the dwarf was still alive. The real reason was the worthlessness of his underlings.

Thanquol bared his fangs and allowed his rage to show. The accursed gutter runners had failed him. By their sheer incompetence, they had let the dwarf and the manling escape. Thanquol had a good mind to have Chang Squik hung up by his tail and flayed alive. Only his fear of possible reprisals by Clan Eshin kept him from ordering his bodyguards to seize the gutter runner.

Rumour had it that Squik was a favoured pupil of Deathmaster Snikch himself. That being the case, such straightforward vengeance was out of the question. But, Thanquol thought, there was more than one way to skin a rat. Someday he would make Chang Squik pay for this monstrous failure. Thanquol's problem right now, however, was to find a way to safely vent the killing rage that was on him, without making powerful enemies in the process. He lashed his tail in frustration.

Thanquol glared at Izak Grottle. The monstrously obese skaven lounged on a palanquin born by rat-ogres. The Clan Moulder packmaster had arrived this very morning, keen to take part in the triumph that was sure to follow this great offensive. He and his retinue had scuttled along the

Underways from the skaven secret base at Night Crag in the Grey Mountains.

Grottle tried to hold Thanquol's burning gaze but could not. He looked away and ran a paw over the largest of his body-guard of rat-ogres, a creature so massive that it made the late and unlamented Boneripper look small. The creature bellowed its pleasure as Grottle fed it a tasty titbit of human fingers. Behind Grottle, other packmasters and their beasts stood wait-ing. Thanquol decided that he would spare Grottle. He did not doubt he could destroy the fat one. He was not so sure that he could survive an attack by the outraged beasts if they got out of control. Anyway he could not blame the recently arrived pack-master for the failure of last week's attack.

He turned his attention to the rotting form of Vilebroth Null, low abbot of the plague monks of Clan Pestilens, who stood alone, well apart from any other skaven. From within the abbot's cowl, pus-filled fearless green eyes met his own. Thanquol instantly dismissed the idea of venting his rage on the diseased one. Like every skaven, he knew that the plague monks were quite mad. It was useless to antagonise them. Thanquol let his gaze slide slowly aside. The plague monk triumphantly blew his nose on the sleeve of his mouldering robe. A huge bubble of foul green snot swelled on his wrist and then burst.

Next in line was the armoured form of Heskit One Eye, mas-ter warp engineer of Clan Skryre. One Eye was small by skaven standards, dwarfed by his retinue of jezzail-armed bodyguards. Thanquol was still angry with him for the explosion of the farsqueaker. He suspected some sort of assassination attempt there, though, in truth, it seemed unlikely that Clan Skryre would be behind it. Intentionally blowing up one of their own precious devices to kill an enemy was not their style. Thanquol decided to spare Heskit. He was not in the slightest bit influ-enced by the fact that the bodyguard's long-barrelled rifles could shoot the wings off a fly at this range. No, not in the slightest.

He knew he couldn't punish these ones. They were too pow-erful. Their clans were too influential and he needed them to spearhead the attack on the mancity. Still, he had to kill some-one, both to re-establish his own authority and for his own pleasure. It wouldn't do just to let them all off. It was not the skaven way. An example had to be made.

One by one he turned his gaze on the Clan Skab warleaders. They were all present now, save for Warlord Vermek Skab himself. All wore the red and black livery of their clan. Each also had the single scar running from their left ear to their left cheek which was the badge of their clan. Each of them was as proud as a skaven could be, the unchallenged master of a host of vicious warriors, yet each of them hurriedly looked away when the grey seer met their eyes. They knew of his foul temper by reputation. Even Tzerkual, the gigantic leader of the stormvermin would not face his wrath. He studied his feet like a small runt facing discipline from his elders.

Good, thought Thanquol. They were cowed. He took a pinch of warpstone snuff and watched them quake. Bright mad visions of horror and carnage skittered through his brain. He puffed with self-confidence, convinced that at this moment he could face one of the Council of Thirteen and triumph. As always, the drug-induced confidence receded after a heart-stopping moment, leaving the afterglow of pure, Chaos-induced power searing through his veins. Quickly, before the heat could fade, he selected a victim. He stabbed out a pointing talon at Lurk Snitchtongue, the weakest of the warleaders and, not coincidentally, the one with least allies both here and back in Skavenblight.

'You find something amusing, Snitchtongue?' Thanquol demanded in his most intimidating high-pitched chitter. 'You think something is very funny, perhaps?'

Snitchtongue licked his snout nervously. He bobbed his head ingratiatingly and held up his empty paws. 'No! No, great one.'

'Don't lie. If humour there is in the abject failure of the mighty gutter runners, please share it. Your insight may prove most useful. Come! Speak! Speak!'

The skaven on either side of Lurk backed away, cautiously putting as much distance as they could between themselves and their doomed fellow. In moments Lurk found himself standing in an open space twenty feet across. He glanced over his shoulder, seeking some way to escape, but there was none. Not even his personal bodyguard would stand near him with the grey seer staring angrily down. Lurk shrugged, lashed his tail and put his hand on the hilt of his blade. He had obviously decided to brazen it out.

'If gutter runners failed it was because they were too subtle,' Lurk said. 'They should have attacked head on, in a massed rush, blades bared. That is the skaven way. That is the Clan Skab way.'

Chang Squik glared across at the skaven warrior. If looks could kill, Lurk would have left the chamber in a casket. Thanquol was suddenly intrigued by the situation. Here was an opportunity to twist the assassin's tail with no possibility of reprisals against himself. The grey seer decided that he would let Lurk live for a few moments longer.

'You are saying that you could have handled the situation better than your brothers of Clan Eshin? You are saying you could succeed where trained gutter runners of mighty Eshin failed?'

Lurk's jaws snapped shut. He stood for a moment, considering the implications of that last statement, seeing the trap that the grey seer had prepared for him. If he openly criticised Squik, he would make an enemy of the powerful gutter runner, and doubtless take a knife in his belly as he slept. On the other paw, he also obviously realised that he had been singled out to face the grey seer's wrath no matter what. He knew it was a choice between immediate and inevitable death – or possible doom in the future. He rose to the occasion like a true skaven warrior.

'Maybe,' he said.

Thanquol giggled. The after effects of the warpsnuff still dizzied him. The rest of the skaven present echoed their leader's amusement with great roars of false chittering laughter.

'Then perhaps you should take your warriors to the mancity above and prove it, yes.'

'Indeed, great one,' the warleader replied. His voice sounded relieved. He had a slim chance of living after all. 'Your enemies are as good as dead.'

Somehow Thanquol doubted it, but he did not say so. Then he cursed himself for his leniency. He had allowed Snitchtongue to wriggle out from under his paw and not blasted him into a thousand pieces as an example.

At that moment, a runner entered, puffing breathlessly. In the traditional cleft thighbone of a human he carried, he held a message. Seeing Thanquol he immediately abased himself before the grey seer and prodded the bone forward.

Thanquol was tempted to blast him for his insolence. There was a fine old skaven tradition of killing the messenger who brought bad news to be kept up, but at this moment Thanquol did not even know that the news was bad. Curiosity got the better of him and he pulled the parchment from the stick. He noted that the corners were creased and it had obviously been well-pawed.

No surprises there, then. Doubtless every spy between here and Skavenblight had bribed the messenger so that he could look at what he carried. That, too, was the skaven way. Thanquol did not care. He had established his own codes, cunningly concealed within deceptively innocuous messages, in order to keep his communications secret.

He looked down at the blocky runes scrawled in a strong skaven paw. The message read simply: The package has been delivered. A sense of triumph filled Thanquol and dispelled his earlier anger. He fought to control his sense of exultation and keep his pleasure from his face. He looked down at the messenger and sneered, knowing above all that appearances must be kept up and an example must be made.

'This message has been opened, traitor-thing!' he snarled and raised his paw. A sphere of greenish light sprang into being around Thanquol's clenched fist. The messenger cringed and tried to beg for mercy but it was too late. Tentacles of hideous dark magical energy leapt downwards from Thanquol's paw to encircle the doomed skaven's body. The bands separated themselves and flowed around the messenger, swimming through the air in the way that eels swim through water, with a horrible sinuous wriggling. After a few moments, the bands of energy lunged inwards, stabbing through the skaven's body, boring through the flesh and emerging darker on the other side.

Again and again they stabbed inwards, stripping away flesh and muscle and sinew. Again and again the messenger let out high pitched, agonising screams. The smell of the musk of fear mingled with the scent of blood and the ozone taint of the spell. In a matter of seconds only a stripped skeleton stood before Thanquol. After a heartbeat it collapsed into a pile of bone. The ribbons of magical energy flowed together, somehow consuming each other as they did so, until there was nothing left of them. The whole assembled skaven host let out a great sigh of wonder and disbelief at seeing their grey seer demonstrating his power in this satisfying manner.

Thanquol raised his paw and gestured for silence. In a moment all was calm, save for a few coughs from the back rows.

'Lament, skaven! Tragic news!' Thanquol said, and even the coughing stopped. 'Mighty Warlord Vermek Skab is dead, killed in a terrible accident involving a loaded crossbow and an exploding donkey. We will have the traditional ten heartbeats of silence to mark the return of his soul to the Horned Rat.'

Immediately all the skaven started to talk among themselves. The chitter of conversation only fell silent when Thanquol raised his paw again and let the warning glow reappear around his talons. All of them sensed the menace in the gesture and went quiet. None of them wanted to be the next to be consumed by those terrible wiggling bands of energy.

'Now we will prepare for the next phase of the master plan,' Thanquol said. 'In the sad absence of Lord Skab, I must reassume control of the army of conquest.'

'With great respectfulness, Grey Seer Thanquol such is not the case. As senior skaven here, my duty it is to assume command.' The booming voice of Izak Grottle filled the chamber. 'Clan Moulder had provided many warptokens to finance this expedition and I must see that they are spent wisely.'

'What nonsense is this?' Vilebroth Null inquired. The words bubbled phlegmishly from his ruined throat. 'If any is to command here, it should be me. To Clan Pestilens will go the honour of overthrowing the mancity. We have great plans! Great plans! It is our secret weapon that will destroy the human city!'

'No! No! I disagree,' chittered the reedy, high-pitched voice of Heskit One Eye. 'The siege machines of Skryre will make victory possible and so to Skryre should fall the leadership. Naturally, as the ranking representative of Clan Skryre I will now assume my duties as supreme commander.'

'This is a vile usurpation of Clan Moulder's privileges,' Izak Grottle roared. The rat-ogres, hearing the anger in his voice, bellowed with barely suppressed fury. The sound of their wrath echoed around the cavern. 'Mutinous behaviour cannot be tolerated! No! For the good of the force, warn you I must that one more word of such treachery and my warriors will execute you instantaneously.'

The jezzail teams around Heskit swiftly brought their weapons to bear on Izak Grottle. 'Your warriors? Your warriors?

There speaks a mad skaven. By what right do you name the warriors of my command your troops?'

'Both of you are trying my patience,' Vilebroth Null burbled. 'Seeing my two senior lackeys bickering in such a runtish manner cannot help but demoralise my army. Cease such treacherous behaviour at once or face the hideous and inevitably fatal consequences.'

Null flexed his paws menacingly and suddenly there was a package of filthy stuff in his hands. No one present could doubt that it was dangerous. The plagues of Clan Pestilens were famously deadly.

Grey Seer Thanquol looked on in baffled rage and barely concealed glee. He half hoped that the various leaders would come to blows, that violence would erupt and that these upstarts would slaughter each other. Unfortunately, until circumstances proved otherwise, he had to assume that he needed all of their help to overthrow the mancity. So it was time to put a stop to this nonsense.

'Brother skaven,' he said in his most diplomatic voice. 'Consider this. Until the coming of Vermek Skab, the Council of Thirteen placed me in command of this army. Since Vermek Skab is sadly no longer with us, the leader's place in the rear must still fall to me by edict of the council. Of course, if any of you wishes to challenge the council's ruling I will notify them of this at once.'

That quietened them, as Thanquol had known that it would. No skaven in his right mind would even hint at the possibility of disobeying a direct edict from the council. The dread rulers of the skaven race had a long reach and their punishments were swift and certain. By invoking the council's authority, Thanquol knew that he would ensure the obedience of all present until such a time as they could check back with their clan's rulers and representatives on the council. Hopefully in that time Thanquol would have brought the mancity to its knees.

'Of course, you are correct, Grey Seer Thanquol,' Heskit chittered. 'It is only that, as your second-in-command I felt that these others were overstepping the bounds of their authority.'

'I know not how Heskit can claim to be your second-in-command, grey seer, when all know my respect for you is boundless, and my devotion to your cause without limit,' Izak Grottle said.

Vilebroth Null merely coughed enigmatically and said: 'It pains me to see these overbearing oafs challenging your rightful authority, grey seer. Surely the power of my clan and my proven dedication to your person must mean that I rank second here.'

'I have yet to decide who the Underleader will be. I must retire to my burrow to contemplate strategy.' So saying, he descended from the bell carriage and the seething sea of skaven parted before him. Thanquol felt satisfied for the moment that he had the challenge to his leadership under control.

This was more like it, thought Thanquol. Let them bicker over who gets the scraps. The glory will belong to me.

As was only right.

Lurk Snitchtongue crouched down in his favourite hiding place, a small cave above a long narrow gallery far from the main Underways. He was worried as only a skaven of a naturally nervous disposition could be. He knew that he had only days to make good on his claim to be able to destroy the dwarf and the human who had humiliated Chang Squik, or else he would suffer the same fate as the messenger from Skavenblight.

He shuddered when he thought of that demonstration of the grey seer's awesome power. Truly, the warpstone magic that Thanquol wielded was to be feared. He knew that hiding would not help him, that the grey seer would find him no matter how deep he burrowed, but old instincts were hard to overcome. Even as a small runt, in times of trouble Lurk had always sought out the hidden places where he could spy on the bigger skaven and plan his revenge.

Somewhere in the back of his mind, rage skittered around on small, padded claws. He knew that Thanquol had picked on him and the instinctive need for vengeance made him want to bury his fangs in the grey seer's throat. The fact that he understood why he was Thanquol's chosen victim did not make it any easier to take. Basic skaven instinct told him the reason for Thanquol's decision. From an early age, every young rat-man learned to sense who it was unwise to antagonise and who it was possible to bully with impunity. Those who did not died in all manner of horrific ways and were usually eaten by those who killed them. On one level, he understood that Thanquol had victimised him for good, sound political reasons because he was the youngest of the skaven leaders, and the least secure in his position.

Lurk had risen to his current position as a junior warlord in Clan Skab by being the favourite of Vermek Skab, and by informing on those who had plotted against his distant cousin. He had a nose for ferreting out information that might be useful, a talent that was more than useful in a society so full of intrigue as that of a skaven clan. But now Vermek Skab himself was dead, and Lurk doubted that even his powerful kinrat would have been able to protect him against the wrath of a grey seer. No, he decided more realistically, Vermek would not have found him useful enough to be even bothered to try.

It was looking like his promising career was about to come to an end. He would either die at the axe of a maniacal dwarf whom, rumour had it, even Grey Seer Thanquol feared – or he would be blasted by the seer's mind-bogglingly potent sorcery. Neither prospect was particularly appealing to an ambitious young skaven. Still, at the moment, there didn't seem to be anything he could do about it.

Lurk heard voices coming from below him. He froze in place, realising that others had sought out this lonely place for their own purposes. He knew it was best to be quiet, for he was on his own and packs of skaven had been known to fall upon and devour solitary rat-men they found in remote tunnels. If truth be told, Lurk had done it himself. He listened carefully, his keen ears twitching, hoping to find out more about the approaching skaven.

'Curse Grey Seer Thanquol!' he heard a voice that he recognised as belonging to Heskit One Eye. 'He has denied me my rightful place at the head of this army, yes. Credit for victory over the humans should rightfully belong to me and, of course, to Clan Skryre.'

Lurk's whiskers twitched. This was treasonous talk and he was sure that Grey Seer Thanquol would like to hear about it. He listened now as if his life depended on it, thinking that he might have found a way out of his predicament, a path on which to creep back into the grey seer's good graces.

'Yes-yes, greatest of lords. A fool Thanquol is. Perhaps he too could have an accident like Vermek Skab!' Lurk recognised the fawning voice as belonging to Heskit's henchling, Squiksquik.

'Hush-hush! Speak not of such things. It has been tried before but somehow accidents always seem to happen to someone else, not to Grey Seer Thanquol. Perhaps it is true. Perhaps he does enjoy the favour of the Horned Rat!'

So even the mighty Heskit feared the grey seer. This did nothing to reassure Lurk about his own position. But still – what a patron the grey seer would make if Lurk could ingratiate himself. By clinging to Thanquol's tail, Lurk could rise very far indeed. The next thing he heard made his tail stand on end.

'The farsqueaker explosion should have worked but Thanquol has the luck of a daemon, most far-sighted of plotters.'

'Never, never refer to that again. The farsqueaker malfunctioned – that is all. Nothing more. If Grey Seer Thanquol was even to suspect that it was anything else, the consequences would be very bad, very bad. How goes the… other plan?'

'Well, greatest of warp engineers! We have located a hidden route into the manplace. Our warriors stand ready to grab the devices the moment you command it. Tonight is auspicious. The humans have all been summoned to a feast by their ruling breeder.'

Lurk felt the soles of his paws tingle. Here was something else to report back to Thanquol. A secret Clan Skryre scheme to acquire human treasures. Surely Grey Seer Thanquol would reward anyone who would report such a thing to him. He leaned forward stealthily so that so he could see what was going on below him. The movement dislodged some pebbles and sent them skittering to the floor. The noise disturbed the Clan Skryre skaven, he saw them jump into defensive stances and whip out their blades.

'What was that sound-noise?' Heskit demanded.

'I do not know bravest of leaders,' Squiksquik said. 'Quick! Quick! Go! Investigate.'

'A leader's place is in the rear. You go!'

Lurk cursed his bad luck. The noise had interrupted the Skryre's plotting and now he might never know what they were up to.

'Most likely it is nothing, wisest of warleaders. Subsidence merely. Tunnels are old.'

The two of them stood immobile in postures of listening. Lurk hoped they did not look up. He dared not even pull himself back into the shadows lest the movement attract the attention of their keen skaven senses. He felt sure that they would be able to hear the pounding of his heart. It was all he could do to keep from squirting the musk of fear.

Slowly the two nervous Clan Skryre rat-men relaxed, letting their breath come out slowly and easily. After a few more heartbeats, they returned to their plotting.

'What are your orders, most cunning of commanders?'

'We will attack the man-things' steamworks tonight during the dark of the moon. Their gun machines must be ours so that we can improve on them. Their steam-chariots must be examined to see how we may increase their effectiveness ten-thousand fold.'

'It will be as you wish, most superlative of technicians.'

'See that it is so!' Heskit barked and turned his back on Squiksquik to stalk away. Lurk could not help but notice that as soon as Heskit's back was turned, his lackey flicked his thumb against his protruding incisors in the traditional skaven gesture of disrespect. Heskit turned. By the time his leader's eye was upon him, Squiksquik had once again adopted a posture of fawning adoration.

'Do not stand there all day. Come! Come! Quick! Quick! There is much work to be done.'

In the darkness Lurk smiled. He had learned many useful things here, and it was time to visit the grey seer.

'What do you want?' Grey Seer Thanquol inquired, looking up from the scroll which he had been reading. 'I thought you went to the surface. To kill the dwarf!'

'No, most potent of sorcerers,' Lurk replied, adopting the form of address that worked so well for Squiksquik. He understood now its power. Thanquol seemed to swell visibly at the flattery and began to preen his fur. 'While rushing to obey your most clever command, I stumbled upon evidence of plotting and knew that only the great Thanquol himself would have the intelligence to know how to deal with it.'

'Plotting? Explain yourself! Hurry-hurry!'

Quickly, and leaving out only the details of how he came to be there, Lurk outlined what he had overheard. Thanquol tilted his head to one side and bared his fangs at the news. As he listened his tail began to lash backwards and forwards, a sure sign that a skaven was agitated. When Lurk was finished Thanquol glared at him for so long and with such an expression of piercing intelligence that Lurk feared his time had come and that he was about to be blasted. But the grey seer merely licked his lips, stroked his imposing horned head with one paw, and said: 'You have done well, Lurk Snitchtongue. I must consider what you have told me. Hold yourself ready to instantly obey my commands.'

'Yes, most shrewd of supreme commanders.'

'And Snitchtongue–'

'Yes, mightiest of sorcerers?'

'Say nothing of what you have told me, to anyone. On pain of instant and most painful annihilation.'

'Yes! Yes! To hear is to obey, most merciful of potentates.'

THANQUOL LOLLED BACK on the throne he had installed in this makeshift command cave. He scratched his itching back against the wood of the throne's back, then leaned his horned head forward on his paw. That fawning sluggard Lurk had given him something to consider indeed. So, as he had suspected, the farsqueaker explosion had been no accident. When he thought how close he had come to death on that day, rage and fear warred in the pit of Thanquol's stomach. Had Heskit stood before him at this moment, Thanquol would have blasted him into a thousand fragments, and let the Horned Rat take the consequences.

And this news of Heskit's treachery gnawed at his bowels. He fought to bring himself under control, knowing that such thinking was dangerous, that to give way to his rage would lead to eventual certain destruction. He had not reached his high position in skavendom by giving way to such impulses. He told himself that he would find other more subtle ways of gratifying his thirst for righteous revenge. He would find other ways to pay back the treacherous filth for his attempt on Thanquol's life.

And this new scheme of Heskit's – it was exactly the sort of thing he would have expected from those machine-obsessed traitors at Clan Skryre. Always lusting after new technologies and new machines. Always willing to betray the skaven cause for their own advancement. Always looking for ways to cheat their rightful leader out of his well-deserved share of the credit.

But wait! Was it possible that Lurk Snitchtongue had concocted this whole thing simply to ingratiate himself with Thanquol? The grey seer immediately discounted this possibility. Lurk was simply too stupid and unimaginative to come up with such a tale. Furthermore, it fitted with reports which Thanquol's other spies had brought him, of secret massing of elite Clan Skryre troops, of secretive comings and goings in the burrows that Heskit had commandeered for his forces.

Thanquol considered the possible outcomes. The warp engineers were planning on attacking the new College of Engineering, that was obvious. They wanted to acquire steamtanks and organ guns for themselves. The grey seer did not doubt that Heskit could make good on his boast of improving these human weapons a million-fold. He knew that no other race could match skaven genius when it came to constructing machines, and unfortunately, Clan Skryre were the most brilliant mechanicians of a brilliant race.

These new weapons would doubtless increase Clan Skryre's power and with that power would come increased influence on the Council. Just the news that Heskit had succeeded in acquiring the human weapons would bring a consequent increase in Clan Skryre's prestige, perhaps even enough to have Thanquol called back to Skavenblight and Heskit awarded the supreme leadership of this army. Such an outcome was unthinkable. A clod like Heskit could only lead this mighty force to disaster. It needed the titanic intellect of Thanquol to ensure crushing victory over the human scum. It was Thanquol's duty to his people to ensure that he stayed in charge.

But what were his options? He had already decided that Heskit was too powerful and too useful to be destroyed out of hand. So what could he do? He could confront Heskit with the knowledge of his treachery. Not good enough. The warp engineer could simply deny it and it would be Lurk's word against his. And doubtless he would simply find another way forward with his plans to steal the human machines when Thanquol's back was turned and his mind occupied with more pressing affairs.

Thanquol cursed Heskit and all his treacherous, ill-natured brood! Why did this have to happen now? He should be using his towering intellect to deal with more pressing matters than treacherous underlings. He should be planning the inevitable conquest of the mancity of Nuln and the destruction of Gotrek Gurnisson and Felix Jaeger.

But wait! Perhaps this was the key. Perhaps the Horned Rat had sent him the means to kill two babies with one bludgeon. A brilliant idea started to percolate into Thanquol's mind. What if he used his two enemies as a weapon against Heskit? What if he simply informed them of where and when the warp engineer's attack was to take place. Doubtless they would take steps to thwart the attack.

Yes! Yes! The Slayer's foolish quest for glory, and the fact that the pair were already discredited, would keep them from informing the stupid human authorities. Doubtless they would be moved to interfere in their usual blundering fashion, and would seek to stop Heskit's plan. They were too stupid ever to work out that they were Thanquol's pawns, and even if they suspected a trap it would not matter. The Slayer's own pride and his desire for a heroic death would ensure his interest even in the face of overwhelming odds. No! No! Particularly in the face of overwhelming odds.

And this way, if anything went wrong Thanquol's hands were clean. No one would ever trace the Slayer's intervention back to him, he could ensure that. The idea of using the pair to thwart his other enemies' schemes was too good to resist.

He turned the scheme over from all sides, examining the possible outcomes and finding it foolproof. Either the dwarf and the manling would foil the plot in their usual, brutally inept manner or they would be killed trying to do so. Either outcome suited Thanquol. If they foiled Heskit's plan, the warp engineer would be discredited. If they died, Thanquol would have lost two potent enemies and could still organise some nasty surprises for the Clan Skryre warlocks on their return. In the best of all possible worlds, the two sides would eliminate each other. Thanquol helped himself to some warpstone snuff and consumed it with glee. What a scheme! So intricate! So cunning! So truly skaven! Here once more was proof of his own incredible genius.

Now all he had to do was think of a way of letting the dwarf and his henchman know about Heskit's plan. It would have to be complex, subtle and ingenuous. Those half-witted fools would never suspect that they were aiding their mightiest enemy.

* * *

'MESSAGE FOR YOU, SIR,' said the small, grubby faced boy, holding out his hand for payment. In his other hand, he clutched a piece of coarse parchment.

Felix looked down at him and wondered if this was some sort of trick. The beggar lads of Nuln were particularly known for their ingenuity in parting fools from their money. Still he might as well pay attention. The lanterns had just been lit. It was early yet and the Blind Pig had not even started to look like it would fill up this evening.

'What's this? You do not look like a courier.'

'I dunno, sir. This funny looking gentleman handed me this scrap of paper and a copper penny and told I would get the same again if I delivered it to the tall blond-furred bouncer at the Blind Pig.'

'Blond-furred?'

'He spoke kind of funny, sir. Looked kind of funny, too. To tell the truth, he smelled kind of funny an' all.'

'What do you mean?'

'Well his voice wasn't exactly normal. It was kind of high pitched and squeaky. And he was wearing a monk's robe with a cowl that covered his face. I thought his robes hadn't been washed for a long time. They smelled like a dog or some furry animal had been sleeping in them. I know, 'cause my dog, Uffie, used to–'

'Never mind Uffie right now. Was there anything else you noticed about him?'

'Well, sir, he walked funny, all hunched forward…'

'Like an old man?'

'No, sir, he moved too quick for an old man. More like one of the crippled beggars you see down on Cheap Street 'cept he moved too quick to be crippled and… well, there's one more thing but I was scared to tell you in case you thought I had been at the weirdroot.'

'And what was that?'

'Well, as he was moving away, I thought he had a snake under his robes. I could see something long and snaky moving around.'

'Could it have been a tail? Like the tail of a rat?'

'It could have been, sir. It could have been. Do you think it could have been a mutant, sir? One of the changed?' A note of wonder and horror had entered the child's voice. He was obviously thinking that he might just have had a close call.

'Perhaps. Now, where did you see this beggar?'

'Down Blind Alley. Not five minutes ago. I rushed over here thinking I'd get myself a nice bit of pie with the copper piece you was going to give me.'

Felix tossed the kid a copper and snatched the piece of paper from his hand. He glanced across the bar to see if Gotrek was about. The Slayer sat at a side table, his massive shoulders hunched, clutching an ale in one brawny fist and his monstrous axe in the other. Felix beckoned him over.

'What is it, manling?'

'I'll tell you on the way.'

'No sign of anything here now, manling,' Gotrek said, peering down the alley. He shook his head and ran a brawny hand through his huge dyed crest of hair. 'No scent either.'

Felix could not tell how the Slayer could smell anything over the stench of the trash that filled Blind Alley, but he did not doubt that Gotrek was telling the truth. He had seen too much evidence of the keenness of the dwarf's senses in the past to doubt him now. Felix kept his hand on the hilt of his sword and was ready to shout for the watch at a moment's notice. Since the child had brought the note, he had suspected an ambush. But there was no sign of one. The skaven, if skaven it had been, had timed things well. It had given itself plenty of time to get away.

Felix took another glance down the alley. There was not much to see. Some light filtered in from the shop lanterns and tavern windows of Cheap Street but not enough for him to make out more than the outlines of rubbish, and the cracked and weather-eroded walls of the buildings on either side of the alley.

'This leads down into the Maze,' Gotrek said. 'There's a dozen entries to the sewers down there. Our scuttling little friend has got clean away by now.'

Felix considered the winding labyrinth of alleys which comprised the Maze. It was a haunt of the city's poorest and most desperate wretches. He did not relish the prospect of visiting during broad daylight, let alone trying to find a skaven there in the darkness of this overcast and moonless evening. Gotrek was probably right anyway: if it was a skaven, it was in the sewers by now.

Felix backed out into the street and moved under the lantern that illuminated an all-night pawnbroker's sign. He unfolded the coarse paper and inspected the note. The handwriting was odd. The letters were formed with jagged edges, more like dwarf runes than the Imperial alphabet, but the language was definitely Reikspiel, although poorly composed and spelled. It read:

> *Frends – be warned! Evil ratmen of the trecherus skaven klan Skryre – may they be poxed forever, espeshully that wicked feend Heskit Wan Eye – plan to attak the Colledge of Ingineering this nite during the dark of the moon. They wish to steel your secrets for their own nefare-i-us porpoises. You must stop them or they will be wan step closer to conquering the surface world,*
> *Yoor frend.*

Felix handed the letter to Gotrek. The Trollslayer read it and crumpled it up in one brawny fist. He snorted derisively. 'A trap, manling!'

'Maybe – but if so, why not simply lure us here and attack us?'

'Who can tell how the rats' minds work?'

'Maybe not all skaven are hostile. Maybe some of them want to help us.'

'Maybe my grandmother was an elf.'

'All right. Maybe one faction has a grudge against another faction and want us to settle it for them?'

'Why not settle it themselves?'

'I don't know. I'm just thinking aloud. Tonight is the Feast of Verena. There will only be a few people in the college. All the others will be at the Countess Emmanuelle's Feast for the Guild. Perhaps we should warn the watch.'

'And tell them what, manling? That a skaven sent us a note warning us his brother was going to burgle the Elector Countess's special arsenal. Perhaps you've forgotten what happened the last time we tried to warn anybody about the skaven.'

'So you're saying we should do nothing?'

'I'm not saying anything of the sort. I'm saying that we should look into this ourselves and not count on getting any help from anyone else.'

'What if it's a trap?'

'If it is, it is. A lot of skaven will die.'

'So might we.'

'Then it will be a heroic death.'

'We'd best get back to the Blind Pig first. Heinz will be wondering where we've got to.'

'YOU DELIVERED THE note as instructed?' Grey Seer Thanquol asked.

'Yes! Yes, most ingenuous of masters,' Lurk said.

'Good. You are dismissed. Hold yourself ready for further instructions. If anyone asks you what you were doing on the surface, tell them you were spying on the dwarf in preparation for killing him. In a way, it will be the truth.'

'Yes, yes, cleverest of councillors.'

Thanquol rubbed his paws together with glee. He did not doubt that the stupid dwarf and the hairless ape would fall into his cunningly woven trap. His beautifully composed and lovingly crafted message would see to that. Now all he had to do was wait and make sure that, whatever happened, Heskit's warriors failed in their task. And he knew just the way to do that.

HESKIT SURVEYED HIS corps of warp engineers with pride. He watched a team of warpfire throwers check their bulky and dangerous weapon, showing all the care of well-trained skaven engineers. The smaller of the two lovingly banged the firebarrel with a spanner to make sure it was full, while the other kept the dangerous nozzle pointed at the ceiling most of the time, in case of accidents.

Bands of sweating slaves rested for a moment, their breath coming in gasps, their tongues lolling out after long exertion. They had laboured long and lovingly to prepare the way for this night's work. They had spent many hours luring the sewer watch away from this place, and days working with muffled picks to finish these structures. Now the ramps were all in place, and they were ready to broach the surface and swarm out through the manburrow.

Heskit inspected their work with a well-trained professional eye. During his apprenticeships, he had overseen the construction of scaffolding around the great skaven warships. Scaffolding that almost never collapsed killing those upon it, Heskit thought with pride. It had been the wonder of his burrow. Well, after tonight, his fellow engineers would have even more to wonder about. He would surpass Mekrit's invention of the farsqueaker, and do more to advance the skaven cause than Ik had done with his invention of the portable tormenting machine. After tonight he would possess all the proudest secrets of the race of man. And then he would improve them in a thousand ways.

Heskit knew that he had picked his time well. Today was the Feast of Verena. The human guards were but a skeleton watch compared to their usual numbers, and doubtless were all drunk. Even now Clan Eshin assassins were moving above, picking off the few sentries which remained on duty. Soon it would be time to go forward with the plan.

A Poison Wind globadier hurried past, his face obscured by his metallic gas-mask. Only the globadier's nervous darting eyes were visible through the quartz lenses. He clasped his glass sphere of chemical death to his chest, protecting it against accidents the way a mother bird might protect a precious egg.

Heskit's chronometer chimed thirteen times. He tugged its chain and pulled the ornate brass device out of his fob pocket. He held it to his ear, and was rewarded by the sound of loud ticking from the lovingly crafted mechanism within. He flicked the chronometer open and glanced at the face. It showed a little running skaven. Its feet moved back and forth every heartbeat. Its long tail pointed to the thirteenth hour, and so did the short stabbing sword it clutched. It was exactly thirteen o' clock, to the hour, to the minute. Heskit turned and gave the sign for the operation to begin.

FELIX LOOKED AT the outside of the new College of Engineering. It was a most impressive building, more like a fortress than any University College he had ever been in. The tall, broad towers at each corner would have been more at home on a castle than on a place of study. All the windows at ground level were barred. There was only one way in, through a massive archway, large enough for a horse-drawn carriage.

A soft thud behind him told him that Gotrek had arrived and most likely fallen into one of the flower beds. He heard the dwarf curse in his harsh guttural tongue.

'Best be quiet!' Felix whispered. 'We really should not be here.'

It was true. Only authorised members of the Guild of Engineers and Mechanics, their apprentices and members of the Imperial military were allowed into this highly secret place, on pain of death or at least a long stay in the dungeons of the Countess Emmanuelle's infamous prison.

'The sentries are all too drunk to notice anything, manling. It's a disgrace but it's what you expect from humans.'

Felix reached up and tugged his new cloak off the low wall. It was ripped where the broken glass and nails set on top of the wall had pierced it. Still, Felix thought sourly, better a ripped cloak than a ripped hand. He glanced over at the sentry boxes beside the locked iron gates and was forced to agree with Gotrek. It was a disgrace.

One of the sentries was so drunk that he was simply lying asleep beside his post. Then Felix saw that there was something odd in the man's posture and he stepped over cautiously to have a look. As he did so, he saw more recumbent figures. Was it possible that all of the sentries were drunk and asleep? He crept up for a closer look, then ripped his sword from its scabbard.

The sentries were not drunk. They were dead. Each lay in a pool of blood. One of them still had a knife sticking from his back. Felix bent and examined it and immediately recognised the workmanship from his own encounter with the skaven assassins at the Blind Pig.

'It looks like our friend was telling the truth,' he said to Gotrek, who had joined him.

'Then let us go take a look inside.'

'I was afraid you were going to say that.'

HESKIT STALKED THE corridors of the college, surrounded by his bodyguards. In a way this was a comforting place for him. He was surrounded by familiar things: forges and benches and lathes and braces, and all the tools familiar to engineers the world over, whatever their race. The smell of charcoal and metal wafted through the place on the night breeze. Skaven seethed through the corridors like an invading army, ransacking the place as they went. He hoped that his lackey, Squiksquik, had managed to get into position in the central armouries, otherwise all the choicest of loot would have vanished.

To his right, he could see a rack of long muskets of a novel design. He immediately rushed over and pulled one down. It had the half-complete look of a new prototype. Its barrel was bound with copper wire, and a small telescope had been mounted above it. Nothing to get excited about, Heskit thought, simply an inferior attempt at the jezzails his own bodyguard already carried. Without access to warpstone for their powder mixes, the humans would never be able to get the same range and hitting power. He hoped that the other stuff here was more worthy of his consideration, or it was going to be a wasted night.

'Most perspicuous of lords, this way,' he heard Squiksquik call. Heskit strode down the long hall and found himself in another machine shop. This was more like it, he thought, when he saw the round stubby mass of the organ gun. This was worth having. He strode over and ran his paws over the cold metal of one of the barrels. Yes, indeed, this was worth having.

He looked down and saw the mechanism that would cause the barrels to rotate and the striker which ignited the fuses at the same time. Very clever! He wondered whether the tolerances of the metal could withstand the use of warpstone powder. Most likely not but then again, some of those new lead-warpstone alloys he had been experimenting with might just do the trick. He had not had any accidents with them since the last automated cannon had exploded and killed ten of his assistants.

'Quick! Quick! Take it!' he instructed Squiksquik. His lackey chittered a few commands and a party of Skryre slaves rushed forward. There was a slight squeaking as they wheeled the gun away. This did not bother Heskit. In fact, he found it quite relaxing.

He pushed on deeper into the halls, wondering what new toys he would find in this strange and exciting place.

FELIX FUMBLED WITH the door handle. He had been half-hoping to find it locked but it was already open, and he suspected he knew why. There was a very familiar smell in the air, a combined scent of musk and wet fur and sewer reek. No doubt about it, the skaven were here.

'Perhaps we should go and inform the watch,' he whispered to Gotrek.

'And tell them what? We just broke in to your armoury and discovered some skaven there. We weren't trying to steal anything honestly. We just wanted to look. Being hung as a thief is not my idea of a mighty doom, manling.'

'Then maybe we shouldn't have come here,' Felix muttered. He was already regretting that he had agreed to this harebrained scheme. In the heat of the moment, carried along by the momentum of events, it had seemed to possess a certain logic, but now he could see that it was nothing but pure madness. They were in a place where they had no business being, and most likely surrounded by fierce skaven warriors. By the time any help could get to them, they would in all probability be dead, and even in the unlikely event they survived until help came, their rescuers would, as Gotrek had suggested, most likely hang them as spies. How did he get himself into these situations, Felix wondered?

'Are you going to stand there all night – or are you going to open that door?'

Half expecting to feel a blade being thrust into his face, Felix slowly and cautiously pushed the door open. Ahead of him a long corridor loomed. It was dark save for the light that filtered in from outside. Felix wished that he had a lantern with him. There must be lights here, he thought –then realised that all they would do was draw unwelcome attention.

Gotrek pushed past and stomped off down the corridor, massive axe held ready to deal death. There was nothing for it but to follow him. Felix did not relish the prospect of being left in this vast and echoing building on his own.

'THERE IS A PROBLEM, most decisive and responsible of leaders,' Squiksquik said quietly. Heskit turned and glared at his lieutenant petulantly.

'Problem? What problem could there be, Squiksquik? Explain! Quick! Quick!'

'Overseer Quee thinks that, now he has seen the steam-tank, there might be some problems. He thinks that the supports might not be strong enough to take the weight. It might be unwise to take it down into the sewers.'

'Tell Overseer Quee to solve this problem quickly, otherwise he will have to be replaced by someone more competent. We must have this steam-tank! We must study the engines!

We must see how it works! Clan Skryre must possess this weapon.'

Heskit clambered up on top of the steam-tank. His followers had lit the place with the green glow of warpstone lamps, the better to see what they were doing. Just being on top of this mighty machine made Heskit's tail stiffen. He put his paws on his hips, struck a commanding posture and looked down on the chamber.

He looked around at this, the largest of halls, the place where steam-tanks were built. It was impressive. All the parts, lovingly hand-crafted, lay on workbenches nearby. Huge schematics had been pinned to a board on the wall for the guidance of apprentices. Overhead were all manner of pulleys, and wires and guy ropes for lowering all the pieces into place. It was a tangled and intricate enough web to cheer the heart of any skaven.

Nearby sat a partially assembled steam-tank, looking for all the world like the half-devoured carcass of some Leviathan. Above him were the galleries from where the masters could survey the work of their labourers and see that everything was done properly. Yes, there were definitely some ideas here which could be adapted to the skaven cause.

Heskit turned back and was soon lost in contemplation of the huge mechanical monster, overwhelmed by the possibilities hinted at in its design. Truly, the steam-tank was a most awesome concept. He ran a paw over the riveted metal and felt his heartbeat quicken. He could just see himself driving around in one of these, only his would be bigger and better, with a warpstone-powered engine and a warpfire thrower instead of a cannon. Bullets would ping off the armour of the hull. Arrows would be turned aside by the thickness of the walls. His foes would be crushed to bloody pulp under him. He would have a periscope to look out through so he wouldn't have to expose his head to enemy fire, and he would have tracks instead of these silly wheels so that he could pass over the roughest of terrain with ease.

It was a design with which the skaven could conquer the world, and he, Heskit One Eye, would be responsible for it.

AHEAD FELIX COULD see a huge open courtyard. In the centre of the courtyard was a massive gaping pit, from which emerged the

familiar stench of the sewers. The courtyard was lit by eerie flickering green lights. In their glow, Felix could see a horde of
rat-men scampering backwards and forwards between the pit
and the building proper. Each had a chest or a piece of machin-
ery over his shoulder. It looked like they were looting the whole
building. Felix wasn't sure what they were going to do. There
were simply too many of the skaven for them to overcome.

HESKIT CLAMBERED DOWN into the steam-tank and looked at the
controls. There was a small seat moulded to fit a human driver,
but the bulk of the chamber was taken up by a monstrous cannon and a huge boiler. Doubtless the boiler provided power.
The controls were simplicity itself for a skaven of Heskit's intelligence to figure out. This lever was forward; that lever was
reverse. The whistle could be used to make terrifying noises
and to relieve pressure on the boiler. This small wheel would
let you guide the steam-tank right and left, and this one would
aim the cannon. It was all too easy.

Suddenly Heskit knew exactly what he wanted to do, and
since he was a master warp engineer there was no one here who
could stop him. He was going to take this vehicle for a test
drive, just to make sure it worked. It would also save all the
effort of carrying it to the pit mouth and down into the sewers.
He barked instructions to summon two slaves and he soon had
them loading up the boiler with wood. Within minutes he had
the engine under pressure and was ready to go.

Heskit pulled the lever and the steam-tank lurched forward.

IN THE DISTANCE Felix heard a rumble like a dragon clearing its
throat. 'Sounds like a monster,' he whispered to Gotrek.

'Sounds like a steam engine more like, manling. We'd better
investigate.'

They hurried up the stairs and around the gallery above the
courtyard. Here and there lay the bodies of sentries, killed by
the same skaven blades as they had encountered earlier. Felix
flinched and kept his sword ready. At any moment, he expected
to run into a pack of fierce killers like those which had attacked
him and Elissa in his room the other night.

THE SENSATION OF speed and power was awesome. Heskit had
never experienced anything like it. He felt like he could crush

anything that got in his way, smash through any obstacle. With this one tank, he could overcome any foe. Visions of huge armies, spearheaded by warpstone-powered steam-tanks danced through his head. With such a force manned by fierce skaven warriors, Clan Skryre could conquer the world. And, of course, he, Heskit One Eye, would be suitably rewarded for his genius in coming up with the plan. He would see to that.

Heskit looked up to see where he was going. What was that foolish Poison Wind globadier doing standing in front of him with a look of panic on his face, Heskit wondered?

FELIX EMERGED ONTO a gallery above a huge hall which seethed with skaven. In the middle of the hall stood a gleaming new steam-tank. Smoke billowed from its chimneys and even as he watched, Felix saw that the vehicle was starting to move. It picked up speed fast and ran over a small skaven who stood clutching something in front of it. The skaven fell and something like a glass sphere rolled from its hands. The sphere fell and shattered into a million pieces. As it did so, a horrible cloud of greenish gas emerged. All of the rat-men down below who were caught in the cloud clutched their throats and fell coughing blood. They lay on the floor, tails lashing, feet kicking the ground. In a way they looked as if they were drowning.

He remembered Gotrek's tales of skaven gas weapons. He remembered that awful moment during his fight with the skaven in the sewers when he thought he had been gassed. He also remembered that the Slayer had suggested the solution was a handkerchief soaked in piss and placed over your mouth. He currently didn't have the time or the inclination to test that theory. Felix noticed gratefully that the gas appeared to be heavier than the surrounding air, and did not rise far. Indeed, it was already starting to disperse.

WAS HE DYING, Heskit wondered? Or had he managed to hold his breath in time? He did not know. His eyes watered from the gas which had seeped in through the open hatch. The two skaven slaves lay gurgling and gasping in front of him. Heskit knew he did not feel any pain. Perhaps the heartbeat of warning he had got when he saw the globadier had been enough. He had just enough time to snatch a lungful of air and hold his breath. He had certainly not wasted it on shouting a warning to the others. As a consequence of his own quick thinking, he had managed to save himself.

Heskit peered out through the green murk with watering eyes, and tried to guide the tank into the clear. Something bumped and squished under the wheels and he thought he heard a howl of agony. He ignored it and concentrated on staying alive. That was the most important thing.

His lungs felt like they were bursting. His heart beat at three times its usual rate. He had already squirted the musk of fear and soiled his fine armour. He did not care. All that mattered now was that he did not breathe until he saw clear air, and that he kept himself alive, in spite of the treacherous attack of the foolish globadier.

All around him he heard sounds of confusion, of skaven shouting orders, of barked commands, and weapons being brought to bear.

'We're under attack!' he heard Squiksquik shout. It wasn't until the jezzail shots started thumping of the side of the tank that he realised that the idiots thought that he was attacking them.

FELIX WATCHED IN mounting confusion at the scene of carnage. The gas had killed dozens of the skaven. The rest of the rat-men had turned on the steam-tank. Several teams of skaven equipped with long rifles had started taking pot-shots at the tank. Two weirdly equipped skaven were manhandling a huge and very unwieldy looking weapon into a position where it could fire at the tank.

Was there still a human alive down there and had he somehow managed to get the war-engine to work? Was he even now fighting for his life and in desperate need of help? Felix turned to consult with the Slayer – and only then realised that Gotrek had gone. Felix could guess where.

The skaven had manoeuvred their odd-looking weapon into position. One of them crouched down with a barrel braced on its back, the other wielding the connected gun. Suddenly a jet of greenish flame gouted forth and sprayed towards the tank. It clung to the metallic side panels, burning intensely, the flare illuminating the whole chamber and making Felix stand out in stark relief on the balcony. He knew this because a whole group of skaven were suddenly pointing at him and chittering.

He had a terrible feeling that he knew what was going to happen next.

HESKIT CLOSED HIS eyes and hoped that he would still be able to see when he opened them. The heat was intense and the warpflames of the fire thrower licked through the viewing slit of the steam-tank. Heskit screamed and squirted the musk of fear again, soiling the seat below him.

'Stop! Stop! Fools!' he shrieked. 'It is I, Heskit, your leader!'

If anyone heard him over the roar of the steam-tank, they gave no sign. All was confusion and madness. It was possible that his ratkin had lost sight of him in the confusion and thought he was a human attacker. It was equally possible that some vilely ambitious underling knew full well that he was in here and was taking this opportunity to try and assassinate his superior.

In fact, the more Heskit thought of this second option, the more likely it seemed to him. Those firethrower bearers, for example, were not stopping their assault, despite his express command. They might claim they could not hear him over the roar of the engine but Heskit knew better. He could see it all so clearly now. It was all part of a devilish plot to remove him from his rightful office. He would not be in the least bit surprised if Grey Seer Thanquol was behind the whole thing.

Filled with righteous vindictive anger, Heskit bared his fangs in rage and steered the steam-tank directly at the warpfire throwers. Too late, the treacherous vermin realised their peril and attempted to scuttle aside. Heskit was rewarded by the crunch of their bones under his wheels. Then there was a hideous crump as the barrel of phosphorescent chemicals exploded.

FELIX WAS TRAPPED. Skaven were flowing out onto the balcony on which he stood in a grim furry tide. There were dozens of them, far more than he could fight. He did not doubt that he could take out one or two of them on the narrow walkway but while he was doing so others would come rushing up behind him and drive their nasty little blades into his backs. Damn Gotrek! Where was the Slayer when he was needed?

As if in answer to his unspoken query, he heard a thunderous bellow from below him. Risking a quick glance, Felix saw that the Slayer had emerged into the room below, leaving a trail of dead and dying rat-men behind him. A dripping wet rag was wrapped round his face. Evidently the Slayer was taking no chances of being gassed before he achieved his heroic death.

Also below him, Felix could see the steam-tank as it careened onward. Blazing green flames raged around its wheels and along its belly. It bumped and bounced through the workspace leaving a comet trail behind it, crushing everything that got in its way. Then it slewed around, coming almost to a stop, its front end facing in the direction of the Slayer. Gotrek stood his ground, confronting the massive machine, for all the world like an Estalian matador facing a bull. All around the dwarf, panicked skaven scuttled for cover.

That was all that Felix had time to see, as the seething mass of skaven bore down on him. He knew that if he stayed where he was, he was dead. Seeing nothing else for it, he scabbarded his sword, leapt up onto the banister and reached up to grab one of the overhead lines. Swiftly he swung himself hand over hand until he was out over the middle of the courtyard. Felix hung there for a moment, getting his breath back.

Suddenly he felt the line begin to falter under his weight. He risked a glance backwards and saw an evilly grinning skaven sawing at the rope with his blade.

Oh no, thought Felix, as the line gave way with a snap.

HESKIT COULD NOT believe his eyes. Was that a dwarf standing in front of him brandishing a huge axe? How could there be a dwarf here, in the middle of this manburrow? Had he accidentally taken a whiff of the globadier's gas? Was he hallucinating? The whole tank was getting warm, and not just from the boiler. Heskit was certain he could smell warpfire burning somewhere. And where had all his lackeys gone? Surely the dwarf and the gas could not have killed them all. Well, one thing was certain: no dwarf could survive a face-to-face encounter with this steam-tank. Heskit upped the acceleration and raced directly at Gotrek.

THE LINE PARTED and Felix arced down towards the ground. He saw that Gotrek was almost directly below him and that the steam-tank was almost upon him. It looked like the Slayer was about to be crushed to a bloody pulp beneath the wheels of the blazing steam-tank. But at the last second, he stepped to one side and his axe struck the side of the vehicle with a deep, resonant clang like the tolling of a great bell.

Felix braced himself for a painful impact with the ground. Then at the last second he realised that the arc of his trajectory was taking him directly into the path of the steam-tank. It seemed all too likely that he was going to end up beneath its wheels.

HESKIT'S HEAD ACHED from the fumes and from the great ringing echo inside the tank. And what had that second bump been against the tank's side? He was beginning to regret that he had ever allowed his lackeys to persuade him to get into this accursed death-trap. Heads would roll once he brought the thing to a stop, that was certain!

He tugged hard on the braking lever and it came away in his hands. Ahead of him, the wall of the building loomed. It approached with appalling speed.

ALL THE BREATH was knocked out of Felix's lungs as he slammed into the top of the steam-tank. He felt himself start to slip. he could feel the heat beginning to scorch the soles of his boots. He reached out and grabbed for something to hold onto. His fingers caught the edge of the open hatch. Using the leverage this gave him, he pulled himself up and crouched on top of the speeding tank. He could see the wall approaching quickly. He tried to throw himself clear but it was too late. The force of the impact sent him tumbling headfirst through the hatch and down into the interior of the burning steam-tank.

THERE WAS A huge roar and a grinding sound as the steam-tank went right through the brick wall. The whole tank shook and the smell of burning intensified. Suddenly a heavy weight dropped on Heskit and he found human hands scrabbling against his fur.

FELIX FLINCHED AS the skaven bared huge jaws full of needle-sharp teeth and snapped at him. This was a nightmare, thought Felix. He was trapped, hanging upside down, in a tiny enclosed space, aboard a speeding vehicle, with a hideous mutant monster trying to tear out his throat. He pulled his head aside and lashed out with a fist, catching the skaven on the snout. All around he noticed that steam had started to billow and sparks had started to fly from the boiler.

The skaven lashed out at him. Razor-sharp claws tore his cheek. Felix had a moment to be glad that the space was too confined for the skaven to use its weapons. He let himself drop the whole way into the cabin and landed with his full weight on the rat-man. The two of them grappled and rolled around the cabin, hitting the control levers and sending the steam-tank skidding uncontrollably first left and then right. Through the viewing slit, Felix caught sight of terrified skaven running for cover. The steam engine was making weird snorting sounds. The heat and humidity were appalling.

It was a ferocious brawl. Felix was much bigger and heavier but the skaven had a horrible wiry strength and the advantage of possessing long sharp teeth. Pain flared through Felix as it sank them into his shoulder. He felt hot blood as it spurted through his shirt. With the pain and fear came a terrible anger.

'Right, that's it!' Felix spat, getting his hands around the skaven's throat and starting to squeeze. At the same time, he shoved the skaven's head away from him and started to smash it into the side of the steam-tank.

THIS WAS NOT a good night, Heskit One Eye thought, as the maniacal human bashed his head against the steel wall for the third time. The skaven could feel the strength draining out of him. There was no air in his lungs and no way to breathe with those iron-strong human hands around his throat. It was like being stuck in the gas once more, only a hundred times worse. If only he hadn't been betrayed by his worthless underlings, this would never have happened.

Over his attacker's shoulder, through the viewing slit, Heskit could see the open mouth of the pit leading down into the sewers. A mass of skaven were diving into it, fleeing from the scene of the battle. The steam-tank, too, was heading right for it.

FELIX HAD AN awful sinking sensation in the pit of his stomach as the steam-tank lurched and tumbled. They must have hit an obstruction or fallen into a pit, he thought, as he was thrown about the cabin. This is it, he thought, I'm going to die.

Suddenly the steam-tank came to rest with a horrid gurgling splash, and the familiar stink of the sewers filled Felix's nostrils.

His grip on the skaven's throat loosened and the thing took the opportunity to break free. It scampered up and out of the hatch like a ferret up a drainpipe. Judging by the flames comes from the boiler, Felix thought he'd better do the same. Painfully he reached up and pulled his battered frame up through the open hatch. He stood perched on top of the steam-tank for a moment, glaring at the skaven he had just fought.

As he had thought, the vehicle had fallen through the pit the skaven had dug in the courtyard and was now sinking into the sewers. Smoke and steam and flames flickered through the hatch below him, scorching his boots and setting his trousers to smouldering. The whole steam-tank bucked and shuddered in the mire. All around him, Felix could see a host of red eyes glittering in the dark. He was surrounded by skaven.

Out of the frying pan, into the fire, he thought.

WHERE HAD ALL these warriors come from, Heskit wondered dazedly? They should be up above fighting with the dwarf and his human ally, not cowering down here away from the fight. Not that it mattered right at this very moment. As a highly skilled warp engineer, Heskit recognised all the signs of a very serious malfunction in the steam-tank. He did not doubt that he had mere moments to get clear before it exploded.

Fear lent his feet wings. He sprang out into the tightly packed mass of skaven. Before they could react, he skittered across their shoulders, trampling on their heads as he went. Even so, he knew that he was not going to get clear in time. There was only one thing for it.

Holding his snout, Heskit dived headlong into the sewer.

JUDGING BY THE speed with which the terrified skaven took off over the heads of its fellows, Felix knew that something terrible was about to happen. He had to act, right now. He sprang upwards, grabbed the lip of the pit and pulled himself clear, just as the mass of skaven swarmed forward over the steam-tank.

He felt claws rip the leg of his britches as one of the pack leaders made a grab for him. Frantically he kicked out with his other foot, and felt something break as his boot connected with teeth.

Looking out into the greenly lit courtyard, he saw the Slayer jogging towards him.

Felix pulled himself upright and raced for the dwarf, shouting: 'Get down! It's going to ex–'

Behind him there was an enormous thunderous roar and a mighty flash like a lightning strike. A huge cloud of stinking smoke billowed forth. The shockwave threw Felix onto the ground hard. He was vaguely aware of a number of skaven forms tumbling headlong through the gloom around him. Then his head smacked into the ground and consciousness left him.

WHEN FELIX PULLED himself upright, Gotrek was standing nearby, peering down into the mouth of the pit. All around them were hideously mangled skaven corpses. Felix could not guess whether they were the products of the explosion or Gotrek's efforts. Not that it mattered. The result was the same in the end.

Behind him there was a sudden, mighty crash. Felix looked back to see that the whole wall of the college had collapsed. Indeed, peculiar greenish flames were lapping through the entire building. Something told him that no amount of effort by fire-fighters was going to extinguish that blaze until its sorcerous fury was spent.

He turned to look back at the Slayer, noticing for the first time the huge splashes of blood which painted the dwarf's body and dripped from his axe. Gotrek grinned and showed his missing teeth.

'Got most of them. The rest ran away,' he said in disgust. 'They seemed to lose heart after I killed the first fifty.'

'Yes, but at what a price! We've burned the college to the ground! Think of all that knowledge lost.'

'Colleges can be rebuilt, manling.' The Slayer tapped his head with one brawny finger. 'Knowledge is in here. The masters and apprentices survived. Things will go on.'

'We'd better go on and get out of here. The guard will be coming soon.'

Wearily, they made their departure. Somewhere in the distance the alarm bells were already tolling.

* * *

HESKIT RAISED HIS head above the brown sludgy mass and spat out a mouthful of rank sewer water. That had been too close for comfort, he thought. Only the fact that the jelly-like consistency of this part of the flow had absorbed the shock of the blast had enabled him to survive, he was sure. It looked like all the others were dead.

Still, he was alive, that was the main thing, he thought as he padded along through the water with strokes of his paws and lashes of his tail. Now all he had to do was find an explanation for this fiasco which the cursed grey seer would accept. Because somehow he was sure that Thanquol would know all about this night's work.

PLAGUE MONKS OF PESTILENS

'Having shed some light on the disaster which befell the College of Engineering in that accursed year, I feel that I can move on to cover another topic. It was during this period of my life that I acquired more knowledge of the foul breed of rat-men known as skaven than I ever wished or deemed advisable. Even the possession of such knowledge as I had would have been considered cause enough for burning at the stake by our more fanatically dedicated witch hunters. I have often thought that if such people showed half the zeal in persecuting the real enemies of our society as they do in pursuing innocent scholars, our world would be a safer and happier place. Of course, the real enemies of our society are a far more dangerous breed than innocent scholars and have allies in far higher places. I leave my readers to draw their own conclusions from that.'

— From *My Travels With Gotrek, Vol. III*,
by Herr Felix Jaeger (Altdorf Press, 2505)

THE MAN CLUTCHED his throat, gave a gurgling moan and keeled over, froth pouring from his lips, vile green stuff oozing from his nostrils. He lay on his back in a midden heap and frantically beat the muddy pavement with his fists, then all the strength seemed to leave him. His limbs twitched feebly in a final spasm of motion, then he gave a last long groan and lay still.

The people in the street all around looked at each other in fright, then raced away from the body as fast as they could. Beggars crawled away from their resting places. The one-legged man hopped away, almost dropping his crutch in his haste. Peddlers abandoned their stalls; goodwives ducked back into their buildings and locked their doors. Rich merchants urged their palanquin bearers to greater speed. Within moments, the street was all but deserted. Throughout the hubbub of the departing crowd ran one word – plague!

Felix Jaeger glanced around the suddenly empty street. It didn't look like anyone else was going to help the poor devil so it seemed the job fell to him. He covered his mouth with his tattered cloak and knelt beside the body. He laid a hand on the man's chest, searching for a pulse. It was too late. The man was beyond any help: he was dead. Felix had enough experience of death to know.

'Felix, come away. I'm frightened.' Felix looked up. Elissa stood nearby, her face pale and her eyes wide. She ran a hand through her curly black hair, then brought it back to her mouth.

'Nothing to be frightened of,' Felix said. 'The man is dead.'

'It's what killed him that scares me. It looks like he died of the new plague.'

Felix stood up, superstitious fear filling his mind. For the first time he was forced to consider the death he had just witnessed and the reason why everyone else had fled.

Plagues were terrible things. They could strike anywhere, kill anyone, rich or poor. No one knew what caused them. Some said the dark influence of Chaos. Some said they were the wrath of the gods on sinful humanity. The only certainty with plague was that there was very little that you could do to save yourself once you caught it, save pray. Such virulent diseases could baffle the best of physicians and the most potent of mages. Felix stepped away from the body quickly and moved to put his arm around Elissa reassuringly. She shied away, as if he carried the contagion.

'I don't have the plague,' he said, hurt.

'You never know.'

Felix glanced down at the body and shivered.

'It certainly wasn't that poor soul's lucky day,' Elissa said.

'What do you mean?'

'Take a look. There's a black rose on his tunic. He'd just been to a funeral.'

'Well now he's going to his own,' Felix said softly.

'THAT'S THE FOURTH death today from the plague that I've heard of,' Heinz said when Felix told him the news. 'The lads in the bar are talking about nothing else. They've a sweepstake going on how many it will be by nightfall.'

In a way, Felix was glad of this news. For the past few days, the citizens had talked of nothing but the burning down of the College of Engineering. Most claimed it was sabotage perpetrated by Chaos worshippers or the Bretonnians. Felix continually felt spasms of guilt as he was reminded of his own participation in the event.

'What do you think?' Felix asked, looking around at how many people were present. The bar was packed to capacity, and the inevitable jostling was already causing friction. Felix felt certain there would be trouble this evening.

'I put my money on it being ten. Last year, when the Red Pox came, there were twenty people gone by noon. But then the Red Pox was a nasty one. Worst in twenty years. Still, you never know – this one might be worse before it's done.'

'I meant, what do you think caused it?' Felix said. 'How do you think it spreads?'

'I'm not a physician, Felix, I'm a bartender. I guess that it's spread by tinkers and witches. That's what my old wife Lotte used to say.'

'Do you think I could have caught it from that poor man?'

'Maybe. I wouldn't worry. When Old Man Morr pulls your name out of his big black hat, there's nothing you can do about it, that's what I think. One thing's for sure though.'

'What's that?'

'It's good for business. Soon as plague comes, people hit the taverns. They want to forget about it as quick as they can.'

'Maybe they want to die drunk.'

'There's worse ways to die, young Felix.'

'That there is.'

'Well, you'd better get over there and stop those Tileans drawing knives on each other, or we'll soon have a graphic demonstration of just that.'

'I'll deal with it.'

Felix moved to hastily intervene in the dispute. In a few seconds he had far more immediate dangers to worry about than catching the plague.

'SO YOU'RE NOT worried about the plague?' Felix said, ducking a swing from a drunken mercenary.

'Never catch the things, manling,' Gotrek Gurnisson replied, grabbing the mercenary's ear, pulling his head down level with the dwarf's own and then dropping the man with a headbutt which sent blood from the man's bleeding nose spraying outwards to add a new and brighter tint to the Slayer's great crest of red-dyed hair. 'Been right through a dozen sieges. Humans dropped like flies; I was fine. Dwarfs don't usually get the plague. We leave that to less hardy races like elves and men.'

Felix caught two of the mercenary's squabbling comrades by the scruffs of their necks and hauled them upright. Gotrek grabbed one, Felix grabbed the other and they ran them out through the swinging doors into the muddy streets.

'Worst thing I've ever had was a bad hangover,' Gotrek said. 'And don't come back!' he bellowed out into the street.

Felix turned to survey the bar. As Heinz had predicted it was full. Slumming nobles mingled with half the cut-throats and rakehells of the city. A big gang of mercenaries fresh in from the Middenheim caravan route were spending their money like there was going to be no tomorrow.

Maybe they were right, Felix thought; maybe there wouldn't be a tomorrow. Maybe all the street corner seers were right. Maybe the end of the world was coming. Certainly the world had ended today, as far as that man who had died in the street was concerned.

In the far corner, he could see that Elissa was talking to a brawny young man garbed in the rough tunic and leggings of a peasant. Their conversation became animated for a moment, then Elissa turned to leave. As she did so, the youth reached out and grabbed her wrist. Felix began to move over to intervene. Being pawed was an occupational hazard for the serving wenches but he didn't like it happening to Elissa. She turned and said something to the youth. His hand opened and he let go immediately, a look of something like shock on his face. Elissa left him there, his mouth hanging open and a pained look in his eyes.

Elissa hurried past, chin up, carrying a tray full of empty tankards. Felix caught her by the arm, turned her around, kissed her cheek.

'I don't have the plague,' he said, but she still wriggled away.

Felix could hear the word plague being discussed at every table. It was as if there were no other topic of conversation in the whole blasted city.

'Really, I don't,' Felix added softly. He turned around and noticed that the youth who had been talking to Elissa was staring at him with a look of anger in his eyes. Felix was tempted to go over and talk to him but before he could, the young peasant got up and stalked none too steadily to the door.

'I KNOW YOU don't have the plague,' Elissa said, snuggling closer to Felix on the pallet they shared. She picked up a piece of straw which had burst out of the hole in the mattress and began to tickle him under the nose with it. 'You don't have to keep telling me. Really, I wish you'd just shut up about it.'

'Maybe I'm trying to reassure myself,' he said, grabbing her wrist and immobilising her hand. He reached over with his other hand and began to tickle her. 'Who was that you were talking to earlier?' he asked.

'When?'

'Down in the bar. A young man. Looked straight off the farm.'

'Oh, you saw him then?' she asked, her voice all feigned innocence.

'Apparently so.'

'That was Hans.'

'And who is Hans?' Felix said levelly.

'He's just a friend.'

'He didn't seem to think so, judging by the look he gave me.'

'We used to go out together back in my village but he was very jealous and he had a terrible temper.'

'He hit you?'

'No, he hit any man who looked at me in what he thought was the wrong way. The village elders got fed up with it and put him in the stocks. After that he ran away to the city, to look for his fortune, he said.'

'Is that why you came here, to find him?'

'Maybe. It was a long time ago and Nuln's a big place. I never saw him again, until tonight, when he came into the Pig. He hasn't changed much.'

'You were close?'

'Once.'

'Not now?'

'No.' Elissa looked at him seriously. 'You ask a lot of questions, Felix Jaeger.'

'Then stop me asking,' he said and began to kiss her hungrily. But in his mind, he was still wondering about Elissa and Hans and what had gone between them.

GREY SEER THANQUOL helped himself to another pinch of warpstone snuff. The brain-blastingly potent drug sent a charge of pure energy through his body, and his tail stiffened in ecstatic joy. He basked in the warm glow of triumph.

His intricately woven scheme had succeeded and his rival Heskit One Eye's plan to seize all of the technological secrets of the human College of Engineering had been thwarted. Thanquol bared his fangs in a death's head grin when he considered Heskit's discomfiture. He had made the proud warp engineer grovel in the dirt before his whole army while he explained what he had been doing. He had berated Heskit for almost jeopardising the whole glorious campaign to assault Nuln by his ill-considered actions, and sent him slinking off with his tail between his legs.

Now Heskit had retired to his chambers to sulk, while he waited reinforcements to arrive from Skavenblight to replace the warriors he had lost on the surface. With any luck no new warriors would come. Heskit might even be recalled to Skavenblight to explain his actions to his superiors. Perhaps, Thanquol thought, with a word in the right ear this course of action could be encouraged.

The curtain which separated Thanquol's private burrow from the rest of the Underways was wrenched open and a small skaven entered the chamber.

Reflexively Thanquol sprang back behind his throne. The eerie glow of dark magic surrounded his paw as he summoned the energy to blast the interloper to atoms, but then he saw that it was only Lurk Snitchtongue, and he stayed his spell for a moment.

'Grave news, most potent of potentates!' Lurk chittered, then fell silent as he noticed the aura of magic which surrounded the grey seer. 'No! No! Most merciful of masters, don't kill me! Don't! Don't!'

'Never, on pain of death most excruciating, ever burst into my chambers unannounced again,' Thanquol said, not relaxing his vigilance for a moment. After all, you could never tell when an assassination attempt might happen. Jealous rivals were everywhere.

'Yes! Yes, most perceptive of seers. Never again shall it happen. Only…'

'Only what?'

'Only I bring most important tidings, great one.'

'What would those be?'

'I have heard rumours–'

'Rumours? Do not barge into my sacred chambers and talk to me about rumours!'

'Rumours from a usually reliable source, greatest of authorities.'

Thanquol nodded. That was different. Over the past few days Thanquol had come to have a certain respect for Lurk's host of informants. The little skaven had a talent for ferreting out information that rivalled even Thanquol's… almost. 'Go on. Speak! Speak! Waste not my precious time!'

'Yes! Yes! I have heard rumours that Vilebroth Null and his chief acolytes have left the Underways and went surfacewards to the mancity of Nuln, there to establish a secret burrow.'

What could the Clan Pestilens abbot be up to, thought Thanquol, his mind reeling? What did this signify? It inevitably meant some sort of treachery to the sacred skaven cause, some scheme to grab the glory that was rightfully Thanquol's. 'Go on!'

'It may be that they took with them the Cauldron of a Thousand Poxes!'

Oh no, thought Thanquol. The cauldron was one of the most hideously powerful artefacts that Clan Pestilens was thought to possess. Since early runthood, Thanquol had heard dire tales of its powers. It was said to be the means of infallibly brewing terrible diseases, an artefact stolen from a temple of the Plague God, Nurgle, back when the world was young, and reconsecrated to the service of the Horned Rat.

If the cauldron was on the surface somewhere, that could only mean Vilebroth Null meant to start a plague among the humans. Under normal circumstances, Thanquol would have been only too pleased by such an eventuality – just as long as he was a thousand leagues away! Clan Pestilens plagues had a habit of running out of control, of afflicting skaven as well as their intended victims. Only the plague monks themselves seemed immune. Many seemingly assured skaven triumphs had been undermined by just this occurrence. Now Clan Pestilens were only supposed to unleash their creations by special authorisation of the Council of Thirteen.

The last thing Thanquol wanted at this moment was his army destroyed by a runaway plague. He considered the implications still more. Of course, the council did not argue with success. Perhaps the plague might succeed in weakening the humans without afflicting the skaven horde. But if it succeeded, the Council of Thirteen might extend its favour to Vilebroth Null, and withdraw its patronage from Thanquol. Null might even be rewarded with the leadership of the invasion force.

Thanquol considered. What else could be going on here? If the scheme was an honest effort to help the invasion, why had Thanquol not been informed? He, after all, was supreme commander. No – this had to be some sinister scheme of Null's to seize power. Something would have to be done about this treachery and this blatant defiance of the Council of Thirteen's edicts.

Then another thought struck Thanquol. His agents on the surface had already reported tales of some new and dreadful disease spreading among the human burrows. Undoubtedly Vilebroth Null had already begun to implement his wicked plan. There was no time to waste!

'Quick! Quick! Where did those treacherous vermin go?'

'I know not, most lordly of lords. My agents could not say!'

'Run! Quick! Quick! Scuttle off and find out.'

'At once, most decisive of leaders!'

'Wait! Wait! Before you go, bring me parchment and pen. I have an idea.'

* * *

'YOU SNEEZED!' Elissa said.

'Did not!' Felix said, well aware that he was lying. His eyes felt puffy and his nose was dripping. He was sweating a little too. And was that the first faint tickle of a sore throat he felt?

Elissa began to cough hackingly. She covered her mouth with one hand but her whole body shook.

'You coughed,' Felix said, and wished that he had not. Tears had started to appear in the corner of the girl's eyes.

'Oh Felix,' she said. 'Do you think we have the plague?'

'No. Absolutely not,' Felix replied, but in his heart of hearts he was far from certain. Cold dread clutched at him. 'Get dressed,' he said. 'We'll go and see a physician.'

THE DOCTOR WAS a busy man today; that much was obvious, thought Felix. There had been a queue stretching halfway around the block from his small and dingy office. It seemed like half the city was there, coughing and wheezing and hawking and spitting into the street. There was an air of barely suppressed panic. Once or twice Felix had seen people come to blows.

This was useless, Felix decided. They would never see a physician today under these conditions, and the aisles of the Temple of Shallya were full of supplicants. There had to be a better way.

'Come on. I have an idea,' he said, grabbing Elissa by her hand and pulling her from the queue.

'No, Felix, I want to see the doctor.'

'You will – don't worry.'

'FELIX! WHAT ARE you doing here?' Otto did not look pleased. In fact, he had not looked pleased since Felix had refused his offer of returning to the family business and, instead, started work in the Blind Pig. Felix looked at his brother keenly. Otto was dressed particularly richly today in a gown of purple brocade trimmed with ermine, and Felix felt his own ragged appearance keenly. It had taken him nearly ten minutes to convince the clerks to let him in and see his brother.

'I thought you might be able to help me.' Felix sniffed. There was a strange scent in the room, of spices and the sort of flowers that one usually only smelled at funerals. Felix wondered where it had come from.

'I'll do what I can, of course.' Otto regarded him warily.

Ever the merchant, thought Felix, waiting to see what price
was going to be asked.

'I need to see a doctor.'

Otto's eyes darted from Felix to Elissa and back to Felix again.
Felix could almost see the thoughts forming behind his brow.

'You haven't… got this girl into trouble, have you?'

Felix laughed for the first time that day. 'No.'

'Then what's the problem?'

Quickly Felix told his brother about the man who had died in
the streets, about his own symptoms and the huge queues at the
doctor's and the Temple of Shallya. Otto steepled his fingers and
listened attentively, occasionally fumbling with a brass pomander which he lifted to his nose and breathed deeply from. At
once Felix identified the source of the smell in the chamber.

'What's that?' he asked.

'A pomander of wildroot and silverspice from Far Cathay.
The vapours are a sovereign remedy for all airborne fluxes and
evil humours, or so Doctor Drexler assures me. Perhaps you'd
like to try it?'

He unhooked the chain from around his neck and extended
the small perforated sphere to Felix. The smell was very strong.
He politely handed it to Elissa. She placed it beneath her nostrils inhaled deeply and began to cough.

'It certainly clears the nostrils,' she gasped, eyes watering.

Felix took the pomander and breathed deeply. He immediately understood what Elissa had meant. The vapours cut
through the air like a knife. They had a sharp, minty tang and
almost at once a feeling of warmth spread through his head
and chest. His nose felt clearer and his breathing came easier.

'Very good,' he gasped, returning the device. 'But can you
help us see a physician.'

Otto pursed his lips primly. 'Of course, Felix. You are my
brother.'

'And Elissa?'

'Her too.'

IT'S AMAZING HOW money smoothes all paths, Felix thought,
looking around Doctor Drexler's chambers. Without the use of
Otto's name, he doubted the servant would have let him
through the doors of the doctor's luxuriously appointed townhouse. Felix had to admit that it was quite a place.

On the oak-panelled walls were framed certificates from the Universities of Nuln, Altdorf and Marienberg, as well as hand-written testimonials from maybe half the crowned heads of the Empire. A massive portrait of the good doctor painted by the famous Kleinmann beamed down impressively from the middle of them all. Of course, for the fees that he charged, Drexler could certainly afford the services of the great portrait artist.

Felix glanced over the doorway. The doctor and Elissa were in his consulting room. Felix had been left outside for the moment. He rose from the comfortable leather armchair and looked around.

Along one wall were a collection of large glass jars which would not have been out of place in an alchemist's shop. The bookshelves were lined with musty leather bound tomes. Felix picked one up. It was Johannes Voorman's *Der Natur Malorum*. A first edition, no less. The pages had been cut, which meant that someone around here had read it. It wasn't just window-dressing, straight from the bookbinders. Felix examined the other titles and was surprised to discover that only half of them were medical or alchemical in nature. The rest dealt with a variety of subjects, from natural history to the motion of the Spheres. It seemed that the doctor was indeed a well-read man.

'You are a scholar, Herr Jaeger?'

Felix turned to find Drexler had emerged from the consulting room. He was a short, slender man with a narrow, friendly face and a short, well-trimmed beard. He looked more like a successful merchant than a doctor. His robes were as rich as Otto's and there was not a sign of blood stains anywhere. Felix could not even see the traditional pot of leeches.

'I've read a little,' he admitted.

'That is good. A man should always improve his mind whenever there is an opportunity.'

'How is Elissa?'

Drexler took off his glasses breathed on them, then polished them on the hem of his robe. He beamed reassuringly. 'She is fine. She has a summer cold. That is all.'

Felix understood why the rich were so willing to pay for the services of this man. There was something hugely reassuring about his quiet soft-spoken voice and his calm certain smile. 'Not... not the plague then?'

'No. Not the plague. No buboes. No lesions. No suppurating ulcers of the skin. None of the usual symptoms of any of the greater plagues. Of that I am sure.'

Elissa emerged from the consulting room. She smiled at Felix. He forced himself to smile back. 'I understand that you were exposed to a plague bearer yesterday, Herr Jaeger,' the doctor said, suddenly all seriousness.

'Yes.'

'Best have a look at you then. Let me see your arm.'

For the next few minutes the doctor performed all manner of arcane rituals the like of which Felix had never seen. He touched his wrist and counted, while keeping track of a chronometer on the wall. He tapped Felix's chest painfully. He looked into Felix's eyes with a magnifying glass.

This was not what Felix had expected. Where were the scalpels, and unguents, and leeches? Was this man some sort of charlatan? He was certainly most unlike any doctor or barber Felix had ever encountered. His robes were not filthy and crusted with dried blood, for one thing. And the man was tanned, unusually so for a man who spent most of his life indoors. Felix mentioned this fact and Drexler looked at him sharply.

'I have spent time in Araby,' Drexler said. 'I studied medicine at the great School at Kah Sabar.'

Felix looked at the wall. There was no diploma there from any Arabic university. Drexler obviously understood his train of thought, for he laughed. 'They do not give degrees in Kah Sabar! By the time you leave you are either a healer or you are not. If you are not, no piece of paper will make you one.'

'A fair point. But what did you learn there that you could not learn here in the Empire?'

Like all of its citizens Felix considered the Empire to be the most advanced and enlightened human nation on the face of the planet. He could not conceive that there was anything the Arabs had to teach one of its people. The elves and dwarfs, certainly – but not the Arabs.

'Many things, my friend. Including the fact that we have no monopoly on wisdom and that much of what our doctors teach is simply wrong.'

'For example?'

'Well… I do not bleed my patients. It does more harm than good.'

Felix was at once relieved and shocked. Relieved because like most people he dreaded the physicians scalpel. Shocked because the man was obviously a charlatan! Everybody knew that bleeding was essential to release the foul humours in the blood and speed the patients recovery. And yet, Otto had claimed that this man was the best doctor in Nuln and had cured more people than all the other surgeon-barbers put together. Furthermore, Drexler did seem like a profoundly civilised and educated man.

'Do you think I have the plague?' Felix asked suddenly, surprised at the fear and anticipation that filled him as he waited for Drexler's reply.

'No, Herr Jaeger, I do not. I think you have a slight cold, nothing more. I think most of the people in this city who think they have the plague probably have the same, and I think that the panic such beliefs cause will be more harmful than the plague itself.'

'You don't think the plague is real, then?'

'Oh I certainly believe it's real. I think many people will die from it, as the summer heat comes on, and more people come in from the country. But I know you do not have it, nor do any of the wealthy people who come to see me. If you did, you would already be dead or dying.'

'That would make it easy to diagnose,' Felix said dryly. Drexler laughed again.

'I will give you and Fraulein Elissa the same herbal pomanders as I gave your brother and his family. The herbs are a protection against plague emanations, and I have cast a few spells on them as well.'

'You are a magician as well as a doctor then?'

'I am a healer, Herr Jaeger, and I use whatever means best help my patients. I dabble in enchantments of a protective sort. I cannot utterly guarantee their effectiveness, you understand, but they should help if you are exposed to the plague.'

'I thank you for that.'

'Don't thank me, Herr Jaeger. Thank your brother, after all he is paying my bill.'

Just as Felix turned to go, he noticed that Drexler was staring at him hard. His face had turned pale and his eyes hard.

'What is it?' Felix asked.

'The… the sword you carry. Would you mind telling me where you got it?'

'Not at all. It belonged to a friend, a Templar of the Fiery Heart named Aldred. He died and I took it, hoping one day to return it to his order. Why do you ask?'

'You were a friend of Aldred's?'

'We travelled together in the Border Princes. He was on a quest when he died.'

'I knew Aldred. We were friends for a long time. We studied in the Sigmarite Seminary together. I had not heard word of him in a long time.'

'Then I am sorry to be the bearer of such bad news to you.'

'He died well?'

'He died like a hero.'

'It is what he would have wanted. I'm sorry to have bothered you with this, Herr Jaeger.'

'No, I am sorry to be the bearer of such bad tidings.'

'HE SEEMED LIKE a very nice man,' Elissa said. 'And so wise. Very reassuring.'

'What did you say?'

Felix looked up at her. He was disturbed by the coincidence that Drexler had known the dead Templar, and he felt vaguely guilty about not having made a greater effort to return the blade. Still it was a very fine weapon, and it had saved his life on more than one occasion.

'I said, he was very reassuring.'

'Very.' Felix looked at her sourly. She had been singing the doctor's praises all the way back to the Blind Pig and her hand had never strayed very far from the herbal pomander. Felix wondered if it was possible that he was jealous. He actually agreed with the woman but admitting it was difficult for some reason. Elissa seemed to sense this. She looked up at him and smiled teasingly.

'Why Felix, are you jealous?'

Why did women seem to have such an uncanny instinct for these things, he wondered – even as he muttered his denials.

GOTREK LOOKED UP as they entered the tavern. He held a rolled tube in one massive fist. He tossed it straight at Felix.

'Catch,' he said.

Felix snatched the tube out of the air and recognised it at once for what it was. The parchment was of the same crude weave as the earlier message they had received, the one which had warned them of the skaven attack on the College of Engineering. He hastily unrolled it, and was not at all surprised to find that it had been written in the same semi-literate scrawl.

Frends – be warned!! The evil trechrus ratmen of Klan Pestilens do plot to spred playgue in yoor city, may the Horned Rat gnaw there entrails. I dont no wher or how they plan to do this. I kan only tell yoo to be ware of the Kaldrun of a thousand poxes. – Yoor frend.

'It was delivered when you were out,' Gotrek said.

'Same messenger?'

'No, another beggar. Claims it was given to him by a monk.'

'You believe him?'

'I saw no reason not to, manling. I got him to show me the place where he had met this monk. It was close to spot where the last message was delivered.'

'What are you talking about, Felix?' Elissa asked.

'Skaven,' Gotrek said ferociously, and the girl's face went pale.

'Not those creatures which attacked the inn the other night?'

'The same.'

'What do they have to do with you and Felix?'

'I do not know, girl. I wish I did. It seems like we have become involved in some feud among them.'

'I wish you had not told me that.'

'I wish you had not told her that,' Felix said.

'Do you think they will attack the Pig again?' Elissa asked, glancing at the doors and windows as if she expected an attack at any second.

'I doubt it,' Gotrek said. 'And if they do, we'll just slaughter them again.'

Elissa sat down in a chair near to the Slayer. He cocked his head to one side and smiled, showing several missing teeth. 'Do not worry, girl. Nothing will harm you.'

Gotrek was not normally what Felix would consider a reassuring sight, but his words seemed to calm Elissa.

'Do you think the skaven could have anything to do with this new plague?' Felix whispered, hoping that no one could overhear him.

'Our ratty friend would like us to believe this.'

'Then why hasn't he told us any more?'

'Perhaps he does not know any more himself, manling.'

THANQUOL STARED INTO his divining crystal. It was no use. He had no luck locating the plague monks and their accursed cauldron, and that in itself was not reassuring. A seer of his prowess, having invoked the proper rituals and made obeisance in the correct way to the Horned Rat, should have been able to detect an artefact of its power easily. Instead he had found no trace of it or its bearers anywhere. It suggested to Thanquol's keen mind that they were using magic of their own to cover their tracks. He knew that Vilebroth Null was a powerful sorcerer in his own right, and must have invoked spells of bafflement. Further proof of his treachery – as if any were needed!

Of course the traitor would claim that he had used the magic to escape detection by the human authorities, but Thanquol could see through such transparent ruses. He had not been born yesterday. The plague monks were simply trying to keep themselves hidden from their rightful leader until they could implement their plan and claim unwarranted glory.

Thanquol knew he must prevent this eventuality at all costs – as well as enforce the Council of Thirteen's edict, of course. He would simply have to find another way of locating his prey. He wondered if the dwarf and his human ally had taken any action yet. Or were they too stupid to do anything without prompting from Thanquol?

FELIX HURRIED THROUGH the darkness, his cloak wrapped around him. He stopped to cast a glance over his shoulder and to fumble at the pomander full of herbs at his throat. The smell of some fresh night soil which had been cast from the windows high above assaulted his nostrils. He dreaded putting his foot in it as much as he dreaded stumbling into one of the heaps of rubbish that lay decomposing in the street.

Why were all the houses not connected to the sewers, he wondered? Why did people still insist on dropping their rubbish and filth into the streets? He realised that his long trek through the wilderness with Gotrek had changed him. Until then he had been a lifelong city dweller and would never even have noticed the trash which packed the city streets. He paused for a moment to listen.

Was that the distant echo of footsteps? Was he being followed? He strained his ears for any noise but heard nothing.

He was not reassured by the silence. This was the wealthiest quarter of Nuln but not even the rich went abroad in the darkness without a full quota of bodyguards. Robbers and footpads were everywhere. It was not just the prospect of normal everyday robbery that bothered Felix. Ever since the night of the skaven attack he had dreaded another ambush by the rat-men assassins. He felt certain that he had survived their last assault by pure luck alone, and he was all too aware how quickly someone's luck could change.

Still he felt the potential gravity of the situation warranted risking these benighted streets. He needed help and he knew of only one source that might be able to provide the sort of aid he required. The door he sought was directly ahead of him. Drexler was an expert on diseases and he might be able to tell Felix something useful, if the skaven really were behind the current outbreak of plague. He knew that the man would most likely think him mad but he was prepared to take that chance. He was out of his depth, dealing with an enemy that could wield noxious plagues the way a man might wield a sword. What he needed was knowledge and Drexler impressed him as the man who might have it.

He reached up and pulled the handle of the doorbell. He noticed that it was moulded in the shape of a grinning gargoyle's head. In and of itself this was not unusual but the appearance was disturbing here and now amid the night and fog. He heard footsteps from within the building and a peephole within the door rattled open. A faint glimmer of light appeared, level with Felix's eye.

'Who is it?' asked a voice. Felix recognised it as belonging to Drexler's servant.

'Felix Jaeger. I need to see Doctor Drexler.'

'Is it an emergency?'

Felix considered for a moment before replying, 'Yes!'

'Stand away from the door and be warned. We have firearms within.'

Felix did as he was told. He heard huge bolts being thrown and the barking of very large dogs. It was apparent that the physician took no chances with his own safety, and Felix in no way blamed him for this. Such precautions were only sensible in the great cities of the Empire.

'Throw back your cowl and stand where I can see you.'

Felix did as he was told and the beam of a lantern was shone full on his face. He saw that the old man had recognised him.

'Sorry, Herr Jaeger,' the manservant said. 'You can't be too careful these days.'

'I quite agree,' Felix said. 'Now please take me to your master. I have urgent business with him.'

DREXLER SAT BY the fire in a huge study. The flicker of the flames underlit his face and made it look vaguely daemonic. He leaned forward with a poker and prodded the glowing coals until they collapsed, then added more from the bucket beside the fireplace. When he looked up the flames were reflected in his glasses. The effect was eerie.

'Now how can I help you, Herr Jaeger?' he said calmly, then smiled. 'You do not appear to be ill. Is it the girl?'

Felix glanced around the room. The servant had already retreated, the thick Arabian rugs absorbing his footsteps. It was an impressive chamber, even larger than his father's library in Altdorf and with a far greater selection of books. Felix's keen eyes sought out dark corners as if he half-expected to find enemies there, then he turned and looked directly at Drexler.

'What do you know of the skaven?' he asked bluntly.

Drexler stiffened for a moment and then carefully placed his poker back in the stand. He took off his glasses, polished them on the cuff of his robe and gave every appearance of serious consideration to Felix's question.

'They are a race of rat-men, considered to be extinct by many scholars. Spengler thinks they were a sub-breed of human mutant. Leiber theorised that they might be the product of ancient sorcery. It is said that in ancient times they warred with the dwarfs but...'

'I know they are not extinct.'

Drexler looked at Felix sharply. 'You know?'

'Yes. I have fought with them. They are here. In Nuln.'

Drexler sat back in his chair, placed his spectacles on the bridge of his nose and gripped an arm of the chair with each hand. 'Please be seated. You interest me.'

Felix allowed himself to slump down in the chair facing Drexler's. The heat from the fire had warmed one arm of it and made him uncomfortable. He pushed it away from the hearth slightly before he started to speak. He told Drexler of his time in the sewer watch and their encounter with the rat-men in the tunnels beneath the city. He omitted only the fact that they had broken into the house of Fritz von Halstadt and killed him. He spoke of the skaven attack on the Blind Pig which he presumed was some sort of revenge attempt by the rat-men. He left out any mention that he and Gotrek had also fought with the rat-men within the College of Engineering on the night it had been burned to the ground. Drexler watched him with increasing astonishment. When Felix had finished he spoke.

'Herr Jaeger if all this is true why have I not heard more of it. Why haven't the authorities acted?'

'I do not know. Perhaps the skaven have allies in high places.' He was thinking of von Halstadt now. How many more like him occupied positions of power in Nuln and the rest of the Empire? 'I sometimes think that there is a conspiracy within our society to cover up the effects of Chaos and all its works.'

He noticed that Drexler flinched slightly at the word conspiracy, but that the mention of Chaos did not seem to disturb him at all.

'If you were not so obviously sane, I would suspect you of being a lunatic,' Drexler added. 'Certainly, some of what you are saying sound like the ravings of a madman.'

'I know it,' Felix said. 'Unfortunately, it is all true.'

'That is certainly a possibility. In Arabia they do not consider the rat-men legendary and I have spoken with several dwarfs who have claimed to have encountered them. The elf seafarers also tell tales of the rat-men's power. But I fail to see why you have come to me other than to confide your tale.'

Felix handed over the letter that Gotrek had received. Drexler unrolled it and read it calmly.

'Clan Pestilens,' he said eventually. 'Yes, I have read of them.'

'What?'

'Clan Pestilens. Certain of the old tomes, most notably Leiber's *The Loathsome Ratmen And All Their Vile Kin*, claim that the skaven are divided into many different clans, each with its own role in skaven society, and its own unique brand of sorcery. Leiber claims that Clan Pestilens were plague makers. He goes so far as to state that they were responsible for the Great Plague of the year 1111. If whoever sent you this letter is a hoaxer, he is certainly an erudite one. I doubt that there are more than twenty people in the Empire who now own a copy of Leiber's book.'

'Do you?'

'Yes. I came across references to Leiber's theory about the Great Plague in Moravec's work and sought it out. I have what you might call a professional interest in these things.'

'May I see it?'

'Of course. But first, you must answer a few of my questions.'

'Certainly. Ask away!'

'Do you really seriously believe that the skaven may be behind this new outbreak of plague in the city.'

'Yes. From what I've seen of them it would suit their method of warfare. I believe that perhaps they are undergoing a resurgence and that soon our world will no longer doubt their existence.'

'Such would accord with Leiber's own theories.'

'What do you mean?' Felix looked up.

'Leiber claims that the skaven have a very high birth-rate and that when the conditions are right their population grows explosively. At such times they devour all the food in their own realms and must seek food and resources elsewhere. At such times, they explode onto the surface world in huge hungry hordes. And they keep fighting until either they conquer, or so many of them are killed that they can once more subsist in their own realm.'

'I must read this book.'

'Yes. It is very interesting. He makes other claims that are difficult to verify.'

'Such as?'

'He claims these eruptions usually correlate with strange disturbances and erratic behaviour from Morrslieb, the lesser moon.'

'Such as the one which preceded the Great Plague in 1111?'

'You are a learned man, Herr Jaeger. Yes, such as that occurrence and the one which preceded the great Chaos Incursion two hundred years ago. I believe that another may be due to occur in our own time.'

'So all the soothsayers and astrologers claim.'

'There may be truth in it.'

'Do you have any other questions?'

'Yes but they can wait. I can see you are anxious to get at Leiber's work and far be it from me to stand between a fellow scholar and his books.'

Drexler brought a small set of steps and a lantern and they proceeded through the rows of bookcases to the furthest corner of the room. From the highest shelf Drexler dragged down a musty leather-bound tome, handling it reverently with both hands. He blew the fine patina of dust off its cover and handed it to Felix.

'There is a table and a reading lamp over there. I will leave you for a few minutes. I have some tasks to perform.' Felix nodded, now totally wrapped up in his excitement over finding this volume.

It was heavy. The title and author's name embossed in gold leaf on the spine had been almost rubbed away. Two massive hinges of brass held the covers in place and helped them swing outwards. Felix sat down at the table and lit the reading lamp from a candle, turning the tiny handle at the base to extend the wick to its fullest length then placing the shade back over the flame. The pungent smell of aromatic oil filled the air as he began to read.

The book's title page said it had been printed by Altdorf Press over one hundred and eighty years ago. That meant that Leiber had most likely been around during the last great incursion of Chaos, or had at least known people who had been. It was possible that he might even have had first-hand experience of the rat-men.

As he read, Felix discovered that this was exactly what the author claimed. In the introduction he stated that he had encountered a horde of rat-men during the Great Chaos War. Unlike his fellows, Leiber had been convinced that they were not simply a new form of beastman but a completely separate race, and he had devoted the next ten years of his life to uncovering all manner of information about them. He referred to various scholarly sources, such as Schtutt, van Hal and Krueger, which Felix made a mental note to consult later.

His book was divided into short chapters, each dealing with an aspect of the structure of skaven society and its various clans. Felix read horrified as Leiber dwelled on Clan Moulder's vile experiments with living creatures, changing them into all manner of foul mutant monsters. He recognised the artificers of Clan Skryre as the creatures he and Gotrek had encountered at the College of Engineering. The thing which had set the monster on them in Fritz von Halstadt's mansion was a grey seer, some sort of verminous priest. Leiber may have written like a ranting maniac but everything he wrote tallied with Felix's own hard won experience. Even if the scholar was discredited, he was also correct.

Felix paid particular attention to the section on Clan Pestilens, and about how they created diseases and used all manner of foul devices to spread their filthy plagues. The descriptions of the Boil Lurgy and the Flea Buboes made his skin crawl. There were horrors here that went beyond any he had previously imagined.

A shadow fell on him and he looked up to see Drexler standing over him. He realised that he must have been reading for hours in the gloom, and that his eyes hurt from the strain.

'Have you found what you were looking for?' Drexler asked.

'More than I ever wanted to know.'

'Good. Come and see me tomorrow and I may be able to help you. You may take the book with you if you wish. '

'Help me. How?'

'We will visit the city morgue.'

'How will that help?'

'You will see tomorrow, Herr Jaeger. Now go home and sleep.'

GOTREK LOOKED UP from his plate as Felix entered the Blind Pig. 'Look what the cat dragged in,' he said, and stuffed a hunk of black bread into his mouth.

Elissa looked up from her place beside him. 'Oh Felix, I was so worried. You said you'd be back in a couple of hours and its almost dawn. I thought the rat-men might have got you.'

Felix laid the book down on the table and hugged her tight. 'I'm fine. I just had to find out a few things.'

'*The Loathsome Ratmen And All Their Vile Kin,*' Gotrek read, tilting his head and reading the spine of the book.

Elissa looked at him in astonishment. 'I didn't know you could read,' she said.

Gotrek grinned, showing the blackened stumps of his teeth. He flicked the book open with one greasy finger and began turning pages until he found the one bookmarked at Clan Pestilens.

'He knows his stuff, this Leiber. Must have consulted dwarfish sources.'

'Yes, yes,' Felix said tetchily. 'Must have.'

'Where did you get this, manling?'

'Doctor Drexler.'

'He's a man of many interests, your friend Drexler, if he owns books like this one.'

'You'll get a chance to find out for yourself.'

'Will I indeed? How so?'

'Because we're going with him to the morgue.'

GREY SEER THANQUOL scurried backwards and forwards, pacing the floor of his lair like one of the captured humans he kept working the treadmills back in Skavenblight. His mind raced faster under the pressure of all the warpstone snuff he had consumed.

Still those verminous Clan Pestilens traitors had conspired to elude him. Their sorcery had proved effective, even against his most subtle and potent divinations. His spies had not been able to uncover another word about their location no matter how deep they dug. It was all very frustrating. Somewhere deep in his bowels, Thanquol could sense with ominous certainty that the hour when the plague monks' plan would be implemented was drawing very close. He knew that he must be correct in this for in the past such premonitions had never been wrong. He was a grey seer, after all.

A terrible sense of impending doom filled Thanquol's mind. He wanted to run for cover, to scurry to a hiding place but right at this moment he could think of nowhere to go.

Plague, he kept thinking. Plague was coming.

'GOOD MORNING, Doctor Drexler,' the priest of Morr said and coughed. He looked up from his table set in an alcove at the entrance to the city morgue. His black cowl hid his face, making him seem as sinister as the god he served. The air was filled with the smell of black roses, fresh-plucked from the Gardens of Morr. 'What is it you require?'

'I would like to see the corpses of the latest plague victims.'

Felix was astonished at the calm manner in which the doctor made his request. Most of the people in the city would rather run a thousand miles than do what the doctor wanted to do. The priest obviously thought so too. He threw back the cowl of his robes to reveal a pallid, bony face framed by a stringy black beard.

'That is a most unusual request,' he said. 'I will have to consult with my superiors.'

'As you wish,' Drexler said. 'Tell them I simply want to ascertain whether all the victims died of the same disease or whether we're going to have a variety of plagues to deal with this summer.'

The priest nodded and retreated within the shadowy depths of the temple. Somewhere off in the distance a great bell tolled gloomily. Somewhere, Felix knew, another funeral service was about to begin.

The priest returned presently. 'The arch-lector says you may proceed,' he said. 'However, he also asked me to tell you that most of the bodies have already been sent to the Gardens of Morr for internment. We only have the four who came in last night.'

'That should be sufficient,' Drexler said. 'I hope.'

FELIX, GOTREK AND Doctor Drexler all paid the ceremonial copper piece and donned the black robes and headpieces of Morr. This was sacred ground the priest told them and it was needful that they do so. The robes had obviously been made for humans and the hems of Gotrek's dragged along the floor. Without another word they set off into the gloomy interior of the mortuary.

It was cool and it was dark. The floors were clean, washed with some sacred unguents. The smell of attar of black roses was everywhere. It was not what Felix had expected. He had expected rot and the smell of spoiled meat. He had expected the scent of death.

The central chamber of the Death God's house was arrayed with marble slabs. Upon each slab lay a corpse. Felix averted his eyes. The bodies belonged to people who had died under unusual circumstances and who needed special rites said over them to ensure their soul's easy passage into the afterlife. Many of them were not pretty. On one slab lay the blue and bloated corpse of a fisherman which had obviously recently been dragged from the Reik. On another lay the body of a woman who had been hideously cut up and mutilated by some mad man. They passed the body of a child which, Felix saw when he looked closer, had had its head separated from the body. He looked away swiftly.

Here the smell overcame the scent of incense and unguents. Felix understood with a start why their cowls had a special flap of cloth which could be drawn over the mouth and nostrils. He adjusted his to cut down on the stink and moved on to the section where the plague victims lay. Nearby stood two priests, eyes closed, censers held in their hands. They muttered prayers for the dead and showed no fear of what had killed them.

Perhaps they were simply inured to fear by their long exposure to death, Felix thought. Or perhaps they simply did not fear to die? They were, after all, priests of the Death God and were assured of preferential treatment in the hereafter. He decided that if he ever encountered one of the priests later he would ask them about this. He was curious how they had become so hardened.

Drexler advanced cautiously to the slabs and exchanged words and coins with the priests. They nodded, ceased their muttering and withdrew. Without fuss, Drexler drew back a sheet from the nearest body. It was the body of a short man, a trader, dressed in his best. A black rose was set in the lapel of his tunic. He looked oddly exposed and defenceless in death. He had been cleaned up since he died.

'Some bruising on the hands and knees as well as on the forehead,' Drexler pointed out. 'Most likely from where the man fell over in the last extremities of his anguish.'

Felix thought of the spasming of the man he had seen in the street and understood how this could have happened.

'Notice the swollen areas on the chest and throat and the slight crust of greenish stuff on the upper lip and nostrils.'

Drexler pushed the eyelids back with his fingers and there were faint traces of green around the eye rims as well. 'I am sure that if I performed a dissection, something which our priestly friends here would object to, we would find the lungs filled with a green viscous fluid. It is this which eventually kills the victim. They literally drown in it.'

'A horrible way to die,' Felix said.

'In my experience few diseases kill pleasantly, Herr Jaeger,' Drexler said. He moved on to the next body and drew back the sheet. This was the corpse of a middle aged woman, dressed in black. Her eyes were open and stared at the ceiling in horror. There was trace of rouge on her cheeks and of kohl around her eyes. Felix found that there was something rather pathetic about this attempt to improve the appearance of one who was now dead.

'At least she's dressed in the right colours,' Gotrek said – somewhat tactlessly, Felix thought.

Drexler shrugged. 'Widow's robes. Her husband must have died within the last year or so. She'll be joining him now.'

He moved along to the next slab and studied the body of a small child. There was a family resemblance to the dead widow. Drexler looked at the piece of parchment that was around her neck. 'Daughter. An unlucky family it seems.'

He turned and looked at Felix. 'Nothing unusual unfortunately. It is quite common for plagues and other diseases to spread among families and those who live together generally. It seems this plague can shift like a summer cold.'

Felix sniffed. 'What exactly are we looking for here, Herr Drexler.'

'A pattern. Something out of the ordinary. Something that would tell us whether there was any common factor that all of these poor victim's shared.'

'How would that help us?' asked Gotrek.

Felix already knew the answer. 'If we could find that we might find out how the disease is spreading. We might be able to take steps to isolate it. Or if it's really coming from the skaven we might be able to trace it back to its source.'

'Very good, Herr Jaeger. In a way, its like solving a murder or a mystery. You need to be able to see the clues, that way you'll find the culprit.'

'And have you seen any clues?' Gotrek asked.

Drexler removed the last sheet from the last body. It was a young man, barely out of his twenties. Felix felt a sudden shocking sense of his own mortality. The plague's victims could not be much older than he.

'Anything?' Felix asked, his mouth suddenly dry.

'Unfortunately not,' Drexler said, and turned to leave.

AFTER THE GLOOM of the mortuary, the daylight seemed impossibly bright. After the quiet of the halls of the dead, the cacophony of the street seemed impossibly loud. After the perfumed smell of the vaults, the stench of the city was nearly overwhelming. Felix's nose was runny and there was a slight pain in his joints. Not the plague, he told himself, fingering the pomander, just a summer cold. His earlier unanswered question returned to him.

'Why don't the priests of Morr get all the plagues and diseases that kill their... clients? Does their lord extend them some special protection?'

'I do not know. Their mausoleum is clean and well washed, and in my experience that helps stop the spread of disease. They are priests and thus well fed and well-rested; that helps too.'

'Really?'

'Oh yes. Grief, stress, poor living conditions, dirt, bad food – all contribute to the spread of disease, and sometimes help decide who will survive it.'

'Why's that?'

'I do not know. I can only say I have observed it to be true.'

'So you think these things help make the priests of Morr immune to disease?'

'I never said they were immune, Herr Jaeger. Every now and again, one of them falls ill.'

'What then?'

'He goes to his god, with no doubt a special dispensation in the afterlife due to the strength of his faith.'

'That's not very reassuring,' Felix said.

'If you want reassurance, Herr Jaeger, talk to a priest. I am a physician, and unfortunately, I must now return to making my living. I am sorry I could not have been of more help.'

Felix bowed to him. 'You've already been a great help, Herr Doctor. Thank you for your time.'

Drexler bowed back and turned to go. At the last moment, he turned and spoke. 'Let me know of there are any new developments,' he said. 'Look for a pattern.'

'I will,' Felix said.

'I'm going to look for a beer,' Gotrek said.

'I think that might be a good idea,' Felix said, suddenly wanting desperately to get the taste of the mortuary out of his mouth.

FELIX STARED DOWN into his third beer and considered what they had seen. His head ached a little from what he kept having to tell himself was a summer cold, but the beer was helping take away that pain. Gotrek sat slumped beside the fire staring into the flames. Heinz was standing by the bar, getting things ready for the evening rush. The other bouncers nursed their drinks and played hook-knife at the next table.

Felix was troubled. He felt baffled and stupid. He knew that there must be a pattern here but he just could not see it. It looked like something invisible and deadly was killing the people of Nuln and there was nothing he could do to stop it. It was frustrating. He almost wished for another raid by the gutter runners, or another attack by skaven warriors. What he could see, he could fight. Or to be absolutely specific what he could see the Slayer could fight and most likely beat. Thinking, Felix realised, was not their strong suit.

Once he had prided himself on being a clever and well-educated man, a scholar and a poet. But things had changed in his wanderings. He could not remember the last time he had put pen to paper, and last night was the first night in a long, long time when he had opened a book with any pretensions to scholarship. He had fallen right into the role of wandering mercenary adventurer, and his brain appeared to have fallen dormant.

He was out of his depth, he knew. He was not a razor-witted investigator of the sort which featured in the plays of Detlef Sierck. And to be honest, he did not believe that in real life things worked quite the way they did in the theatre, with clues arranged in neat chains of logic, pointing towards an inevitable solution. Life was messier than that. Things were rarely simple, and if there were really clues, doubtless they could be given far more than one neat and logical interpretation.

He thought about Drexler. So far the doctor had done nothing but help them, but it would be easy to put a sinister interpretation on his work and his motives. He possessed too much knowledge of the sort that was frowned on in the Empire, and that in itself was suspicious. In the more superstitious parts of the human realms, just the possession of the books that Drexler owned would be cause for burning at the stake. The reading of them would cause a witch hunter to execute him without trial.

And yet Felix himself had read one of those books, and he knew he was no friend to Chaos. Could not Drexler be in the same boat? Could he simply be what he appeared to be, a man who was concerned with acquiring any knowledge that would help him in his vocation of curing people, no matter what the source? It was all too difficult, Felix thought. The beer was starting to make his head spin.

Ultimately he knew in his heart of hearts that there had to be a link between the deaths of all the people. He was certain, in fact, that he had already seen evidence of it but was just too foolish to know what it was. So far the only link he could think of was that they had all ended up in the Halls of the Dead, in the temple of Morr, and that was no link at all. Eventually every man and every woman would end up there en route to burial in the Gardens of Morr. Every citizen of Nuln would end up in that huge cemetery one day.

He wanted to laugh bitterly at that, but then a thought struck him. Wait! There was a link between most of the people he knew had died of the plague. The man he had seen in the street two days ago had worn a black rose. Another victim, the one in the mortuary, had also worn a black rose, the traditional symbol of mourning. The woman and her child had been widow and orphan. Only the last one had not shown any connection, but perhaps if he dug deeply enough he would find one.

What could it mean? Was the Temple of Morr itself involved in the spread of the plague? Did the corruption run so deep? Somehow Felix doubted it. The first man he had seen had just been to a funeral. Had any of the others? The one wearing the rose was virtually a certainty. The mother and child? He did not know, but he knew a way to find out. He pulled himself up out of the chair and tapped Gotrek on the shoulder.

'We need to go back to the Temple of Morr,' he said.

'Are you developing a morbid attachment to the place?'

'No. I think it may hold the key to this plague.'

IT WAS DARK when they arrived at the temple. It did not matter. The gates were open. Lanterns were lit. As the priests never tired of pointing out, the gates to Morr's kingdom were always open, and a man could never tell when he might pass through them.

Felix asked to talk with the priest who he had spoken to earlier. He was in luck. The man was still on duty. The offer of some silver procured the information that he was always willing to talk. Felix and the Slayer were shown into a small, spartan antechamber. The walls were lined with books. They reminded him of the ledgers which lined the walls of his father's office. In a way, that was what they were. They contained the names and descriptions of the dead. Felix did not doubt they contained records of donations for funeral services and prayers to be offered in the temple. He had had dealings with the priests of Morr before.

'So you are Doctor Drexler's assistants?' the priest asked.

'Yes. In a manner of speaking.'

'In a manner of speaking?'

'We are helping with his researches into the plagues. We're trying to find a way to stop them.'

The priest showed a slow, sad smile. 'Then I don't know if I should help you.'

'Why?'

'They're good for business.'

Seeing Felix's shocked look, he gave a small, polite cough. 'Just a small attempt at humour,' he said eventually.

'You look tired,' Felix said to break the silence. The priest gave a long hacking cough. 'And ill.'

'In truth, I do not feel so well and it's been a long day. The brother who should have replaced me has himself fallen sick and is cloistered in his cell. He's not been well since he presided over the inhumations yesterday.'

Felix and Gotrek exchanged looks.

Felix nodded politely. Gotrek growled.

'Your, errm, associate does not look much like a physician, Herr Jaeger,' the priest said.

'He helps with the heavy work.'

'Of course. Well, how can I help you?'

'I need to know more about those people Doctor Drexler looked at this morning.'

'Not a problem.' He tapped the leather bound book in front of him. 'All the appropriate details will be in the current libram. What exactly do you need to know?'

'Had any of the deceased attended any funeral services just recently.'

'Frau Koch and her daughter had. I officiated at the inhumation of Herr Koch myself last week at the Gardens.'

'And the other gentleman.'

'No, I do not think so. He is not a man who we would allow to attend any of our services. Except his own inhumation, of course.'

'What do you mean? I thought anyone could enter the Gardens of Morr.'

'Not quite. Herr Gruenwald belonged to that noxious class of criminals who make their living by robbing family crypts and stealing corpses to sell to dissectionists and necromancers. He was under interdict. He would never be allowed within the gates of the garden on pain of supreme chastisement.'

'Death, you mean.'

'Precisely.'

'And the man wearing the black rose?'

'I will check the records. I suspect that given the nature of his adornment we will find that he too had attended an inhumation recently. You are not from Nuln, are you, Herr Jaeger? I can tell from your accent.'

'You are correct. I come from Altdorf originally.'

'Then perhaps you did not know it is a local custom to pick one of the black roses from the Death God's Garden when you attend a ceremony there.'

'I thought people bought them from the flower sellers.'

'No. The roses grow only in the Gardens and it is forbidden to sell them for profit.'

There was silence for a few minutes as the priest studied the records. 'Ah, yes. His sister passed away last week. Inhumed in the Gardens of Morr. Is there anything else I can do for you?' he asked brightly.

'No. I think you've told us enough.'

'Can you tell me what all this is about?'

'Not at the moment. I'm sure Doctor Drexler will inform you when he has completely formulated his theory.'

'Please ask him to do so, Herr Jaeger.' As they left, the priest was bent almost double in a fit of coughing.

'TELL ME WHAT all of this is about, manling,' Gotrek said as they entered the street. Felix glanced around to make sure that there was no one close enough to overhear them.

'All of the people who we know have died of the new plague have visited the Gardens of Morr recently. The tomb robber as well, most likely.'

'So?'

'That's the only connection I've been able to see and Drexler told us to look for connections.'

'It seems unlikely, manling.'

'Do you have any better ideas?' Felix asked allowing a measure of his frustration to show in his voice. The Slayer
considered for a moment then shook his head.

'You think we'll find our little scuttling friends brewing
plagues up in the city cemetery?'

'Possibly.'

'There's only one way to find out.'

'I know.'

'When?'

'Tonight. After work. It will be quiet then and we can take a
look around.'

Felix shuddered. He could think of many places he would
rather be than crawling around the city's main cemetery after
midnight with a bunch of skaven in attendance, but what else
was he going to do? If they took their tale to the authorities
they would most likely not be believed. Perhaps the skaven
would get wind of their presence and move their operation. At
least he felt sure that there could not be too many of the rat-
men up there. A small army camped in the graveyard would be
noticed. Hopefully they would be few enough for the Slayer's
axe to take care off.

Felix certainly hoped so.

THE GATES OF the Gardens of Morr were not open. Steel bars
filled the archway, padlocked by heavy chains. A small postern
gate was occupied by a night-watchman who sat warming his
hands at a brazier. Spikes covered the high wall which surrounded the city graveyard. Felix wondered at that. In some
ways the cemetery resembled a fortress but he was unsure as to
whether the walls were intended to keep grave robbers out or
the dead in. There had been times in history, he reflected, when
the dead had not slept easily in their graves.

There was a basic primal fear at work here, he thought.
Something intended to separate the dead from the living. In its
way, the physical barrier was reassuring. Except, of course, when
you intended to broach it, as he and the Slayer did tonight.

What was he doing here, Felix wondered. He should be at
home, back in the inn, sharing his pallet with Elissa now that
the night's work was done. Not skulking around in the
shadows, preparing to break into the city graveyard, a crime for

which the penalty was several years imprisonment, and interdiction by the Temple of Morr.

Surely there had to be an easier way than this. Surely somebody else could deal with the problem. But he knew this was not true. If he and Gotrek did not hunt down the skaven, who else was interested? They were the only people crazy enough to involve themselves in these affairs. If they did not do it, no one else would.

The authorities seemed to want to turn a blind eye to the evil which was happening in their midst. The best possible interpretation Felix could put on it, was that they were ignorant or afraid. The worst possible interpretation was that they were in collusion with the Powers of Darkness. How many more Fritz von Halstadts occupied positions of trust throughout the Empire? Most likely he would never know. All he could really do was act out his part. Perform the share of the actions which seemed to be allocated to himself and the Slayer, and hope things turned out for the best.

What else could he do? If he left the city, it was possible the plague would spread, and that it would wipe out Heinz and Otto and Elissa and the others that he knew and cared about here. It was possible that thousands might die, if he and the Slayer failed to solve this riddle.

And, if he was honest with himself, he had to admit that the thought of the responsibility thrilled as well as frightened him. In a way it was like being the hero of one of the stories he had read when he was a child. He was involved in intrigue and danger and the stakes were high.

Unfortunately, unlike the stories he had read when he was a child, the stakes were also all too real. It was easily possible that he and the Slayer might fail, and that death would be their reward. It was that thought, not the cold night air, which made him shiver.

THEY MADE THEIR way round the walls of the cemetery until they found a conveniently dark place. Felix made sure the lantern he carried was securely attached to the clip on his sword belt then vaulted up, caught one of the metal spikes and used it for leverage to pull himself to the top of the wall. Perhaps the spikes were mere ornaments after all, he told himself, and served no other purpose.

The moon broke through the cloud and he found himself looking out over the graveyard. It was an eerie sight in the silvered light. Mist was rising. Gravestones loomed out of it, like islands rising from some dismal sea. Trees leaned like enormous ogres, raising branched arms in worship to the Dark Gods. Somewhere in the distance, the lantern of a night-watchman flickered and then vanished, whether because its bearer had returned to the watch-house or for some other darker reason, Felix hoped never to find out. It was still. He was not sure whether it was sweat or mist that beaded his forehead.

The thought that this excursion would do nothing to help his cold struck him, and the incongruity made him want to laugh. He flinched as the beak of Gotrek's great axe curved over the stone beside him, and the Slayer used it to pull himself up the wall. The dwarf was swift and surprisingly nimble when he wanted to be – and when he was reasonably sober, Felix thought.

'Let's get on with it,' he muttered, and they dropped down into the silent graveyard.

ALL AROUND THEM loomed the gravestones. Some were tumbled. Others were overgrown with weeds and black rose bushes. Here and there an engraved inscription was almost visible in the moonlight. The graves were laid out in long rows, like streets of the dead. Old gnarled trees overshadowed them in places. Everywhere the mist drifted spectrally, sometimes becoming so thickly cloudy that vision was obscured. The smell of black roses filled the air. During the day it was possible that the Gardens of Morr was a pleasant place but at night, Felix found his mind turning all too quickly to thoughts of ghosts.

It was easy to envision the countless bodies decomposing under the ground, worms burrowing through rotting flesh and the empty eye sockets of corpses. From there it was but a short leap of the imagination to picture those corpses emerging from beneath the ground, skeletal hands reaching upward through the soil, like the fingers of drowning swimmers emerging from beneath the sea.

He tried to push the thoughts from his mind, but it was hard. He had seen stranger things happen, had encountered the walking dead before, in the hills of the Border Princes on his cursed trip across those empty lands with the exiled von Diehl family. He knew that old dark magic was capable of stirring the dead into an unholy semblance of life, and filling them with a terrible hunger for the flesh and the blood of the living.

He tried telling himself that this was holy ground, consecrated to Morr, and that the Death God protected his charges from such awful happenings. But these were strange times, and he had heard dire rumours that the powers of the Old Gods were waning as the power of Chaos increased. He tried telling himself that perhaps such things happened in far-off lands like Kislev which bordered the Chaos Wastes, but this was Nuln, the heart of the Empire, the core of human civilisation. But part of him whispered that Chaos was here too, that all of the human lands were rotten to the core.

To reassure himself he glanced down at Gotrek. The Slayer seemed unafraid. A look of grim determination was engraved on his face. His axe was held ready to strike and he stood immobile, nose twitching, head cocked, listening to the night.

'Many strange scents tonight,' the dwarf said. 'Many strange noises. This is a busy place for a boneyard.'

'What do you mean?'

'Things moving. A bad feeling in the air. A lot of rats in the undergrowth. You were right about this place, manling.'

'Wonderful,' Felix said, wondering why he was usually right when he least wanted to be. 'Let's get moving. We want to find the area where there are fresh graves. That's where the funerals will take place. And that's where the plagues are coming from, I think.'

THEY MOVED ALONG the thoroughfares between the graves, and Felix slowly realised that the Gardens of Morr were truly a necropolis, a city of the dead. It had its districts and its palaces just like the city outside. Here was the poor quarter, the area where paupers were thrown into unmarked communal graves. There were the neatly tended gravestones where the prosperous middle classes were buried. They competed with each other in the ornateness of their headstones, the way jealous neighbours might compete in life. Winged saints armed with stone swords held aloft books inscribed with the names and occupations of the dead. Stone dragons hunched over the last resting places of merchants like dogs protecting bones. Cowled, scythe-wielding figures of Morr stood guard over stones of black marble. In the distance Felix could see the large marble mausoleums of the rich nobles. They occupied palaces in death as they had in life.

Here and there black roses had been placed in bowers. Their sickly sweet perfume assaulted Felix's nostrils. Sometimes there were letters, or gifts or other mementoes from the living to the dead. An overwhelming feeling of sadness started to mingle with Felix's earlier feelings of fear. These things were some indicators of the futility of human life. It did not matter how rich or successful the men who lay in those graves had been. They were gone now. Just as one day Felix would be. He could understand in some ways the Slayer's desire to be remembered.

Life is written on sand, he thought, and the wind is blowing the grains away.

They chose a place near the open graves and concealed themselves behind some toppled tombstones. The smell of fresh turned earth filled Felix's nostrils. The chill of the mist bit through his clothing. He felt patches of dampness on his britches where they touched dew-bedecked plants. He pulled his cloak tight against the cold, and then they settled down to wait.

FELIX GLANCED UP at the sky. The moon had more than half-completed its passage and still nothing had happened. All that he had heard in that time was the scrabbling of ordinary rats. All they had seen were some vicious, mad-eyed vermin. There was no sign of the skaven.

Perhaps, he thought, half disappointed and half relieved he had been wrong. Maybe they had best consider going home. Now would be a good time to leave. The streets would be deserted. Most every honest person would be safely asleep. He wiped his nose with the edge of his cloak. It was running and he knew this night outside would do nothing for his cold. He stretched his legs, trying to work the stiffness and numbness out of them when he felt Gotrek's hand on his shoulder.

'Be still,' the Slayer whispered. 'Something comes.'

Felix froze and glared out into the darkness, wishing that he possessed the dwarf's keen senses and penetrating night vision. He heard his heart beat loudly within his chest. His muscles, locked in their unnatural position, began to protest against the strain, but still he held himself immobile, hardly daring to breathe, hoping that whatever was coming would not notice him before he saw it.

Suddenly he scented a foul and loathsome taint in the air. It smelled of rotting flesh and weeping sores, like the body of a sick man left unwashed in a hospice for weeks or years. If disease had a smell, it would be like this, Felix thought. He knew in an instant that his suspicions had been correct. In order to keep from gagging, he held the pomander close to his nose, and prayed that its spells would make him proof against whatever was coming.

A hideous figure limped into view. It resembled a skaven, but it was like no rat-man Felix had ever seen before. Here and there great boils erupted from its mangy fur, and something hideous dripped from its weeping skin. Most of its body was wrapped round with soiled bandages encrusted with pus and filth. It was emaciated and its eyes glowed with a mad, feverish light. Its movements were almost drunken; it reeled as if in the grip of a disease which interfered with its sense of balance. And yet, when it moved it sometimes did so with bursts of obscene speed, with the unholy energy of a sick man mustering the last of his strength for some hideous task.

It tittered loathesomely as it moved and talked to itself in its strange tongue. As it did all this, Felix noticed it held a cage in one palsied hand, and in that cage seethed rats. It stopped for a moment, hopped on one stringy leg. Then it opened the cage and took out a rat. Others burst free of the open door and dropped to the ground into the graves. As they fell, they leaked urine and foul excrement. When it touched the earth, for a brief moment there was a hideous, overwhelming stink that threatened to make Felix gag, and which only slowly subsided. The rats pulled themselves from the graves and dragged themselves feebly into cover. Felix could see that they left a trail of noxious slime in their wake, and it was obvious they were dying. What foul thing was going on here, Felix wondered?

The skaven capered past. Felix was surprised and appalled when the Slayer did not immediately strike it down, but instead gestured for Felix to follow and then set off on its track. It took Felix but a few moments to understand Gotrek's plan. They were going to follow the plague monk of Clan Pestilens – for such Felix guessed it to be – back to its lair. They were seeking a path into the very heart of corruption in the Gardens of Morr.

* * *

AS THEY FOLLOWED the capering plague monk through the mist-enshrouded cemetery, Felix noticed that there were other skaven present. Judging by the empty cages they carried they had all been on the same evil errand and were now returning to their lair. Some limped along, born down by the weight of rotting corpses – recently exhumed, judging by the earth which still clung to their grave clothes.

He and the Slayer were forced to move cautiously, lurking behind tombstones, taking refuge in the shadows beneath the trees, moving from patch of cover to patch of cover. In some ways, Felix thought it was unnecessary. The plague monks did not seem as alert as normal skaven. They seemed quite mad, and often oblivious to their surroundings. Maybe their brains were as rotted as their bodies by the diseases they carried.

Sometimes they would stop for minutes and scratch themselves until they bled, or their festering scabs broke and then they would taste the pus which stained their claws. Sometimes they would pause and stare into space for no reason. At times foul excrement would belch forth from beneath their tails and they would lie down and writhe in it, tittering insanely. Felix felt his flesh crawl. These creatures were not sane even by the crazed standards of skaven.

Now at last they were making their way towards a vast mausoleum deep in the noble quarter of the Gardens. They were walking along paved pathways, between well-tended gardens. Here and there statues loomed over sundials that were useless at this hour. More and more plague monks were becoming visible, and more than once Felix and the Slayer hid themselves within the arched entrances to the tomb of some noble clan. Only when the skaven had passed did they rejoin the nightmare procession making its way deeper into the old part of the cemetery, where the largest and most tumbledown of the tombs were.

They paused at a corner and Felix noticed the skaven disappearing into the mouth of the largest and most ancient of the mausoleums. The building was built almost like a temple, in the old Tilean style with pillars supporting the roof of the entrance hall and statues of what Felix assumed were the builder's families held in niches between the columns. Only after the last skaven had disappeared did he and Gotrek advance to the stairs leading up to the entrance.

In the moonlight Felix could see that the mausoleum was in a state of great disrepair. The stonework had crumbled, the friezes had been eaten away by the effects of centuries of wind and rain, the faces had crumbled of the statues to be replaced by lichen. It looked like the stone itself was suffering from some terrible disease. The gardens around it were wild and overgrown. Felix could not be sure but he guessed that the family who had built this place had died out. The place had an uncared-for look, as if no one had visited the place in years. By day this would be a forbidding enough place. On this night, Felix felt no great urge to look within.

Gotrek, however, bounded up the stairs as fast as his short legs could carry him. The runes on his axe gleamed in the moonlight. He grinned at the prospect of confronting the skaven in their lair. Briefly it struck Felix that the dwarf was just as mad in his own way as the skaven were in theirs – and perhaps the best thing he could do was scuttle off and leave them all to their own devices. Felix fought to bring this urge under control as they reached the doorway. He was surprised to find that there was no way in, only a blank stone wall. Gotrek stood before it, puzzled for a minute, scratched his tattooed head with one blunt finger and then reached out to touch one of the stone faces on the side of the arch. As he did so, the wall in front of them slowly and silently rotated to reveal an entranceway.

'Shoddy work,' Gotrek muttered. 'Dwarf work would not be so easy to detect.'

'Yes, yes,' Felix mumbled uneasily and then followed Gotrek through the open entrance of the tomb.

The door slid silently closed behind them.

THE STENCH WAS worse within. The walls were thoroughly caked with filth. Felix could feel it squelch under his hands as he fumbled his way forward through the darkness. Remembering the foul acts he had witnessed the plague monks perform made him want to vomit. Instead, though, he forced himself to follow the faint glow of the runes on the Slayer's axe ahead of him.

Gotrek moved quickly and surely, as if he had no difficulty seeing even in the absence of light. Felix suspected that this might be the case, and that the Slayer's vision might be as good in the gloom as it was in the daylight. He had followed the dwarf through dark places before and was certain that the Slayer knew what he was doing. All the same, he wished that he could light the lantern he carried.

From somewhere off in the distance, he heard a faint scratching sound, and he revised that thought. Perhaps a lantern would not be such a good idea after all. It would certainly warn the skaven of their presence, and Felix felt sure that their one chance of survival in the face of the rat-men's greater numbers was to attack swiftly with the advantage of surprise. Still if he was going to fight he was going to need light at some point, he thought. He prayed he had a chance to light his lamp before moving into battle.

He almost lost his balance as he put his weight forward and there was nothing there. Recovering himself, he realised that he was on a stair heading down. This was indeed a large mausoleum. Whoever had built this place had certainly spent a lot of money he thought. And why not? They were going to spend eternity here, or so they had thought.

Ahead of them now he could hear a loud chittering. It sounded like the skaven were involved in some obscene ritual. A faint glow of greenish, sickly light illuminated the corridor ahead. It looked like they were about to confront the rat-men in their lair.

VILEBROTH NULL CACKLED as one of his leprous fingers broke off and fell into the bubbling cauldron. It was a good sign. His own plague-eaten flesh would help feed the spirit which lurked there and strengthen the brew that would soon bring death to his enemies. The Cauldron of a Thousand Poxes was at once a sacred relic and a weapon for Clan Pestilens, and he intended that it would fulfil both purposes at once.

From his pouch he took out a thick handful of warpstone dust and threw it into the great vat. His remaining fingers tingled from the warpstone's touch and he licked them clean, feeling the tingling transfer itself to his tongue as he did so. He licked his gums so that some of the dust would contaminate the abscesses and ulcers there and perhaps make their contents even more contagious.

Null hawked a huge gob of phlegm into his mouth and then spat it into the thick soupy mixture for good measure, all the while stirring with the great ladle carved from the thigh bone of a dragon. He could sense the pestilential power rising from the cauldron the way an ordinary skaven might feel the heat from a fire. It was as if he stood in front of a mighty conflagration of toxic energies.

He breathed deeply, pulling the heady vapours that rose from the mixture into his lungs, and instantly was rewarded with a thick, treacly cough. He could almost feel his lungs clogging with fluid as the corruption brewed there. It was a just reward, he thought. His plans were going well. The tests were almost complete.

The new plague was as virulent as could be hoped, but most importantly it was his. He had used an old recipe but had added the new secret ingredient himself. Forever afterwards among the faithful of Clan Pestilens it would be known as Null's Pox. His name would be inscribed in the great *Liber Bubonicus*. He would be long remembered as the originator of a new disease, one that would ravage the furless ones like a ferocious beast of prey.

With every night, the brew grew thicker. With every new plague corpse added to the mix, the disease grew stronger. Soon, he judged, it would be ready. Already bodies suffering from the symptoms of the plague had been returned to the cemetery. He gave humble thanks to the Horned Rat for the inspiration which had made him seek out a hiding place where he could observe the results of handiwork. And where else could he find such a rich source of contaminated bodies to drop into the brew!

Tomorrow night, he would dispatch his agents to drop contaminated rats into the wells, and through the roofs of the great abattoirs where the humans slaughtered their meat. After that, the plague would spread most swiftly.

He added more of the corpse roses to the mixture. These were his final secret ingredients to the brew. There were no finer and no stronger ones to be found. They grew on plants whose roots dug through the flesh of corpses. They were ripe and strong with accumulated death energies.

He breathed deeply of the scent of corruption and peered out with his filmed eyes at his followers. They lay sprawled across the ancient human death-chamber, twitching and scratching, coughing and hawking like the true members of Clan Pestilens

they were. He knew that each and every one of them was united
in their sincere dedication to the cause of the clan. They were
filled with the sort of brotherhood which few other skaven
could understand. Not for them the endless intrigues and the
constant scrabble for advantage. They had sought and found
abnegation of self in true worship of the Horned Rat in his most
concrete form: the Bringer of Disease, the Spreader of Plague.

For each and every member of the clan knew that their body
was a temple which harboured the countless blessings of their
god. Their rotted nerve endings no longer felt the pain, save
occasionally when they felt ghostly echoes of their suffering,
like someone hearing the tolling of a distant bell while drowning in deep water. He knew that other skaven thought them
mad and avoided them, but that was because other skaven
lacked their purity of purpose, their total commitment to serving their god. Each and every plague monk present was
prepared to pay any price, make any sacrifice to reach the goals
of clan and deity. It was this commitment that made them the
most worthy of all the Horned Rat's servants, and the most suitable leaders of the entire skaven people.

Soon all the other clans would realise this. Soon this new
plague would bring the human city of Nuln to its knees, even
before the mighty verminous hordes entered its precincts. Soon
all would bear witness that the triumph belonged to Clan
Pestilens, to the Horned Rat, and to Vilebroth Null, the humblest of the great horned lord's chosen servants. Soon he would
be established as the only vessel suitable to bear the Horned
Rat's word. It would be fitting, for although he was but the
humblest of the Horned Rat's servants, he knew where his duty
lay, and that was not true of all skaven in this devolved age.

He knew that many of his fellow rat-men had lost sight of
their race's great goals, and had lost themselves in the pursuit
of self-aggrandisement. Grey Seer Thanquol was an example of
just such a tendency. He cared more for himself and his status
than he did for the overthrowing of the Horned Rat's enemies.
It was disgusting behaviour for one who should have been
among the most dedicated of the great god's servants, and
Vilebroth Null humbly prayed that he would never fall into
similar error.

He felt sure that, had Thanquol known about this experiment, he would have forbidden it, simply out of envy of one

who possessed knowledge of powers beyond his limited imagination. That was why they had to scurry to the surface in secret and perform their rituals without the grey seer's knowledge. The great work must progress despite the machinations of those who would prevent it. After the success of this plague, the foolish edicts of the Council of Thirteen would be repealed, and Clan Pestilens could show its true power to the world. And those like Grey Seer Thanquol who would seek to prevent this most sacred of the Horned Rat's works would be made to grovel in the dust.

Perhaps it was true, as some whispered, that Thanquol was a traitor to the great skaven cause, and should be replaced by one more humbly dedicated to the advancement of his people. It was an idea that certainly deserved the scrutiny of lowly but devoted minds.

Null opened the cage which lay close at hand, reached in and pulled out one of the large grey rats. It bit him viciously, drawing some of his black blood, but Vilebroth Null hardly felt the sharp teeth cleave his flesh. Pain was a near-meaningless concept to him. He closed the cage and left the other rats scrabbling within.

Taking the subject by the tail and ignoring its frantic struggling, he lowered it into the brew. The creature struggled as its head entered the foul liquid. Its eyes gleamed madly and it scrabbled frantically with its claws to try to keep itself above the surface. The abbot of plague monks took his other hand and pushed it down until its squeals were drowned out by the liquid entering its open mouth. He held it under for so long that its struggles almost ceased and then he drew it up again, still dripping, and set it down on the floor of the vault.

The rat sat there for a moment, blinking in the light, as if unable to believe that it had been reprieved. Null scooped it up and threw it into the second cage, where the newly treated rats were. It sniffed and vomited. Vilebroth Null scooped up some of the warm sickness and tossed it back into the cauldron. Soon the cage would be full and he would dispatch one of the brothers to release them in the cemetery, there to begin the spread of the new plague. And tomorrow, they would be sent far and wide through the city.

From somewhere Vilebroth Null heard coughing. In itself that was not unusual. His followers were all blessed with the symptoms of many diseases. No there was something about the tone of the coughing. It was different from that of a skaven. Deeper, slower, almost human-like…

FELIX CURSED AND tried to stop coughing but it was no use. His lungs were rebelling against the foul stench from within the vault. Tears streamed from his eyes. He had never smelled anything quite so foul in all his life. It was as if the combined essences of all stinks in all the sickrooms he had ever smelled were assaulting his nostrils. He felt ill just breathing it, and he had to fight down the urge simply to run off and vomit.

The sight of what was going on in the burial vault had not helped settle his stomach either. He had glanced into a chamber illuminated by the eerie glow of warpstone lanterns. In one long chamber, a dozen or so of the foulest and most leprous looking skaven he had ever seen lolled amidst the opened sarcophagi of long dead nobles. Great stone coffins lay flat on the chamber's floor. Their lids had been removed and their contents scattered. Skulls and bones lay everywhere. Among them lay skaven, enervated and ill-looking, sprawled in pools of their own pus and vomit and excrement, gnawing at the bones of the dead. At the far end of the room, the sickest and most evil looking skaven Felix had ever seen stirred a vast cauldron which rested upon a blazing fire, pausing now and again only to spit in it or add some foul rotting meat torn from a worm-eaten corpse.

Even as Felix had watched one of the thing's own fingers had dropped into the bubbling evil brew and the creature had not even blinked. It had paused only for a breath and added a glowing dust that could only be warpstone and then continued to stir. Then he had witnessed the strange ritual by which a living rat had been lowered into the foul brew and then recovered. Even the Slayer stood rooted to the spot by horrified fascination, watching every move made by the skaven as if trying to fix it forever in his mind.

Felix knew that what he was witnessing had something to do with the spreading of the plague. He did not understand quite how or why, but he was certain that it was so. These vile degenerate rats and their hideous rune-inscribed cauldron had to be involved in the creation of the disease. One look at their vile appearance told him that it just had to be so. Then he had felt the uncontrollable urge to cough. He had tried to hold it in, but the more he did so, the more the inside of his lungs tickled and threatened to explode. Eventually, the cough had burst out of him. Unfortunately, it did so during one of the rare moments of silence in the burial chamber.

Now the chief skaven stood frozen, its nose twitching, almost as if it sensed Felix's presence – although how it could do so over the cacophony of coughs, fruity farts and rasping breathing that filled the chamber Felix could not deduce.

All doubts vanished, however, when it gestured in his direction with one rotting paw. Felix breathed a prayer to Sigmar for protection and brought his sword to the ready position. Beside him Gotrek stirred from his frozen horror, raised his axe and bellowed his war cry.

INTERLOPERS, VILEBROTH NULL thought! Humans had found their way to this sacred place consecrated to the most holy manifestation of the Horned Rat by his most humble servants. Had some vile treachery brought them here, he wondered? Not that it mattered. The fools would soon pay for their folly with their lives, for the plague monks of Clan Pestilens were among the most deadly of all skaven warriors when roused to righteous frenzy. And if that failed, he could call on the mighty mystical powers loaned to him by his foul god.

AS FELIX WATCHED, the plague priest raised its staff high above its head and threw back its head. It barked a series of incantations in the skaven's high-pitched chittering language. The words seemed to be wrenched from deep within it, forming into figures of fire on its tongue. As it spat them out they became flaming runes which burned on the retina, bending and flickering forth before leaping out and touching each of its followers in turn. As they did so, a great halo of sickly light surrounded the skaven's flesh and then seemed to be absorbed into their bodies. The skaven's mangy fur stood on end, their tails stiffened and an eerie glow entered their eyes. They leapt to their feet with an electric grace and energy. High keening cries of challenge were torn from their throats.

Gotrek charged into the warm, misty chamber, Felix following him. The rat-men scuttled to their feet, picking up their loathsome, crusted weapons. Gotrek struck right and left, killing as he went. Nothing could stand in the way of his axe. No one sane or sensible would have tried to resist it.

And yet these skaven did not turn and flee as other skaven might have. They did not even hold their ground. Instead they attacked with an insane frenzy which matched the Slayer's own. They sprang forward, foam pouring from their mouths, their eyes rolling and wild. For a moment, the Slayer was halted by the sheer force of their rush and then they swarmed all over him, biting and clawing and stabbing as they came.

Felix lashed out at the nearest and it turned, swift and sinuous as a serpent to face him, air hissing from between its teeth, madness evident in its eyes. He could see yellow pus stained the bandages around the creature's chest. He poked the area with his sword and it sank in with a hideous slurping sound, almost as if Felix had struck into jelly.

The pain did not stop the rat-man. It came straight at him, pushing forward against Felix's blade, driving it deeper into its own chest. If it felt any pain, it gave no sign. Felix watched in horror as it opened its mouth to reveal yellowish fangs and a white, leprously furred tongue. He knew then that of all the bad things that might happen here, letting the creature bite him was the worst.

He lashed out with his left fist, catching the plague monk on the side of its snout, knocking its jaws to one side. The force of the blow sent several rotting teeth flying out of the creature's mouth to skitter across the dirty floor. It turned to glare at him with wide, evil eyes. Felix took the opportunity to shift his weight, hook his leg around the creature's own leg and send it toppling to the floor. He turned his blade in the plague monk's chest as he pulled it free but still the creature would not die. It beat at the stone flagstones around it with its fist, in a spasm of horrid nervous energy. Felix knew that evil sorcery was at work here, when creatures so weak and sickly could prove so hard to kill.

He brought his boot crashing down on the creature's throat, crushing its wind pipe and pinning it in place while he hacked repeatedly at it, and still the creature took a long time to die.

Felix looked around to see how Gotrek was doing. The Slayer was holding his own against the crazed skaven, but no more. He held one at bay with his huge hand but others swarmed over him, immobilising his deadly axe arm. It was an enormous ruck, a wrestling match between the Slayer's enormous strength and the horde of sorcerously enhanced plague monks.

Felix glanced around desperately, knowing that if the Slayer fell he would have mere moments to live. The sound of padding footsteps behind him told him that more skaven were arriving, returning from whatever insidious mission they had been on. Runes of fire still leapt from the lips of the chanting priest. They rushed over his head and Felix turned to see the eerie glow settle on the fur of two more plague monks, and the awful transformation overcome them. Things were not looking good, Felix thought. Unless something was done about the priest, it was all over. Sick at heart, he knew he was the only one in a position to do anything.

Without giving himself time to think, he vaulted on top of the nearest sarcophagus. He leapt to the next one, passing over the melee between Gotrek and the skaven, and kept moving towards the chanting priest. More and more fiery runes sprang up between the priest and its supporters and Felix knew for certain that the chanting leader was the source of its followers strength. His leaps brought him ever closer to the bubbling cauldron and its hideous master. He paused at the last, frozen for a moment by fear and indecision.

His next leap was going to have to carry him over the cauldron and into combat with the priest. It was an awful prospect. One slip, or a single misjudgement of the distance and he would find himself in that bubbling brew. He did not even want to consider the consequences of what would happen if he did that.

He heard Gotrek's war cry ring out and, turning, he saw the Slayer struggling with the new arrivals. It looked like he had mere moments in which to act. Offering up a silent prayer to Sigmar, Felix leapt. He felt heat below him, and the foul vapours of the cauldron caressed his face as he passed through them, then his feet connected with the plague priest's face and they both tumbled to the ground.

The skaven's chanting stopped but it reacted with surprising speed for one so decrepit, bounding to its feet as if on springs. Felix lashed out with his sword but the skaven leapt back and brought its bone staff down in a blurring arc which would have crushed Felix's skull had he not leapt aside.

Felix hastily pulled himself to his feet and circled warily, looking for an opening. From behind the cauldron, out of his sight, came the sounds of hideous carnage, which he could only hope was Gotrek piling into the plague monks. To his surprise, and unlike most solitary skaven Felix had ever fought, the one in front of him attacked swiftly and viciously. Felix parried another blow from the staff with his sword, and was surprised by its speed and power. The shock of the impact almost drove the sword from his hand. Another blow rapped his knuckles and this time he let go of his blade. A loathsome, oily tittering escaped from the skaven's lips as it saw the look of shock on his face.

'Die! Die! Stupid man-thing!' it screeched in badly accented Reikspiel. Once more the staff descended. This time Felix managed to move aside, and it thudded into the ground where he had stood mere moments before. Before the skaven could raise its staff again, Felix made a grab for it. In a heartbeat he found himself wrestling with the skaven for possession of the weapon. Its wiry strength was far greater than Felix would have guessed. Its fetid jaws snapped shut a hairsbreadth from his face. The sight of the diseased saliva drooling from those broken fangs made Felix quiver, but he continued to grapple with a strength born of terror.

Now he had the advantage of weight. He was taller and far heavier than the emaciated creature, and he used that advantage to spin around on the spot, all the while continuing to tug at the creature. When he had it facing in the right direction, he stopped pulling at the staff and pushed instead. The surprised skaven went tumbling backwards. It let out a shriek as its backside impacted on the hot metal sides of the cauldron. Felix ducked down, grabbed its feet and picked them up. With a mighty wrench he sent the skaven leader tumbling into its own cauldron.

It vanished from sight for a moment beneath the surface of the bubbling brew and then erupted from the surface, gasping for air, horrid liquid dribbling from its jaws. Desperately it tried to climb out of the cauldron. Felix picked up the staff and whacked it over the head, forcing it back under. Then, prodding down with the staff, he felt the struggling skaven move. Swiftly he pinned it firmly with the staff and leaned forward with all his weight. The writhing skaven tried to push back against him but Felix was too heavy to be moved.

Slowly its struggles ceased. Eventually Felix relaxed his weight and breathed easily. Looking down from the dais he saw the Slayer lash out with his axe and behead the last of the plague monks. The corpses of the others lay in various stages of dismemberment at his feet. He looked up at Felix and seemed almost disappointed to find out that he was still alive. Felix grinned and gave him the thumbs up sign.

At that moment, something horrible emerged from the cauldron before him.

VILEBROTH NULL FELT DREADFUL. He had swallowed so much of his own brew that he felt like he was going to explode. He had taken such a beating at the hands of that accursed human that even he could feel the pain. Worse yet, he had almost been drowned like a rat, yes, like a rat. It seemed like an eternity before that cruel human had taken his weight off Null's own staff and given him a chance to break the surface.

A quick glance around told him that all was lost. His acolytes lay dead on the flagstones and the ferocious looking dwarf with the huge axe was racing towards him. Null felt that he had barely been able to hold his own with the human. Against the two of them he would have no chance whatsoever.

Now the surprised looking human was recovering himself and stooping for his sword. Null knew he had only one chance to act. He threw up his arms, summoned all of his power and called up the Horned Rat to save him. For a moment, nothing happened, and Null knew that it was all over. The sword arced closer. He kept his eyes open and forced himself to watch his own death approach. Then he felt a faint tingling surround his body and knew that the Horned Rat had answered his prayer.

FELIX SLASHED WITH his sword, determined that this time there would be no mistake. This time, the foul plague priest was going to die, and Felix was going to chop it into little pieces just to be certain. The skaven shrieked what Felix hoped was a plea for mercy – and something strange happened.

An eerie glow surrounded the skaven. Felix tried to stop his blow, fearing some more noxious sorcery but it was too late. Even as he watched the blade connected but an odd thing happened. Space seemed to fold in around the priest, and it shimmered and vanished with a pop like a bubble bursting. Felix almost overbalanced as his sword passed through the empty air where the rat-man had been.

'Damn,' he muttered and spat in frustration.

'I hate it when that happens,' Gotrek muttered, looking woefully at the space where the skaven had stood. Felix cursed again and muttered venomously as if by sheer force of his imprecations he could make the skaven reappear for execution. He vaulted down from the dais and kicked the severed head of a plague monk just to relieve his frustrations. Then he glanced up at the Slayer. To his surprise, the dwarf was looking almost thoughtfully at the cauldron.

'Well, manling,' he said, 'what are we going to do about this?'

Felix studied their surroundings. The place was strewn with corpses. The tombs were broken open and the huge cauldron full of its foul and contagious brew continued to bubble. The cages which had held the rats had been broken at some point in the struggle and a few of the beasts lurked in the shadows of the room. Others had disappeared.

Felix himself was a mess. His clothes were covered in blood and pus and the foul substances that the rat-men had exuded as they died. His hair felt filthy and matted. The Trollslayer did not look any better. He was bleeding from a dozen small cuts and gore smeared his entire body. Some instinct told Felix that they needed to get clean as soon as possible and that all those bites and wounds should be treated by Drexler. Otherwise they might well go bad.

The main problem though was the great cauldron. If what Felix suspected was true, it represented as big a threat to the city as an army of skaven, perhaps more so, for at least an army could be fought against. Unfortunately, Felix was even less of an expert on dark sorcery than he was on loathsome diseases. It seemed obvious that the brew needed to be destroyed in some manner that rendered it harmless, but how?

Pouring it into the river might do more harm than good. Simply leaving it here would mean that the skaven might come back and collect it at their leisure. They obviously had their own secret ways into the Gardens of Morr and could come and go as they pleased. Not to mention their sorcery apparently allowed them to vanish at will. There did not appear to be any way they could set fire to the tomb.

As Felix considered all this, he realised that the Slayer had his own ideas. While Felix thought, the dwarf was already busy levering the cauldron over with the blade of his axe. The contagious brew spilled off the dais and onto the floor, covering the festering corpses of the rat-men in a nasty viscous pool. Eventually, the cauldron tipped over and lay there upside down.

'What are you doing?' Felix asked.

'Destroying this foul thing!' Gotrek took his axe and brought the blade down on the cauldron. Sparks flashed and a hollow booming sound echoed round the mausoleum chamber as the starmetal blade connected with the sorcerously forged iron. The runes flared along the axe blade and across the side of the skaven artefact. Gotrek's blade smashed through the side of the cauldron. There was a huge spark, followed by a mighty explosion of mystical energy, as the cauldron shattered into a thousand pieces. Felix covered his eyes with his arm as bits of shrapnel flew everywhere, adding to his mass of cuts.

The swirling surge of power stormed through the chamber. Sparks flickered, corpses began to burn. Felix was surprised to see that the dwarf still stood seemingly shocked by the result of his actions. Felix saw felt something burning against his chest, and realised that it was the talisman given to him by Drexler, apparently overheated by its efforts to protect Felix from the force that had been unleashed.

'Let's get out of here!' Felix yelled and they dived for the entrance through a blazing curtain of mystical energy.

FELIX WATCHED HIS old clothes burn. He had scrubbed himself clean with coarse lye soap a dozen times and still he wasn't sure he had removed the entire taint of the mortuary from himself. He clutched the protective pomander tight and hoped that it would prove efficacious against the plague. At least it seemed to have cooled down. He pushed the memory of the previous nights events aside. It had been a long trudge back from the Gardens of Morr, helping the reeling Slayer to Drexler's door.

Gotrek stomped into the courtyard. His scratches had been treated with some sort of ointment. He too carried one of Drexler's amulets.

'Well what did you expect?' he asked sourly. 'Dying of plague is no death for a Slayer.'

VILEBROTH NULL LOOKED around him. It was dark and gloomy, but somehow he knew he was back in the Underways. The

Horned Rat had heard his prayer and his invocation of escape had worked. It seemed obvious to Vilebroth Null that his lord had preserved his most humble servant for a reason. And that reason was most likely to uncover the vile traitor to the deity's cause who had betrayed the abbot's scheme to that accursed meddling twosome.

On careful consideration, it seemed likely, even to an intellect as lowly as his that those two could never have found their carefully concealed lair without help. It had been carefully chosen, well concealed and ringed round with spells to baffle all scrying. No, those two interfering fools must have had help from somewhere. It seemed unlikely that they could have simply stumbled across the lair. Vilebroth Null swore that he would uncover the traitor if it took him the rest of his life, and that when he found him, the treacherous rat-man would enjoy a slow and excruciating death.

And, thought Vilebroth Null as he began the long, limping trudge back to the skaven army, he suspected that he had a good idea where to start looking. As he hobbled back into the skaven camp, he paid no attention to the number of warriors who started to cough and sneeze as he passed.

BEASTS OF MOULDER

'The plague had come to Nuln. Fear stalked the streets. Not even the corrupt authorities could keep a lid on all the rumours that flew back and forth. On every street corner one began to hear tales of mutants and rat-men and huge wild-eyed rats which brought death and disease to all they encountered. I can now reveal some of the sinister truths behind those rumours...'

— From *My Travels With Gotrek, Vol. III,*
by Herr Felix Jaeger (Altdorf Press, 2505)

'You're moving in high society these days, Felix,' Heinz the landlord said, giving Felix Jaeger an uneasy grin.

'What do you mean?' the younger man asked.

'This came for you when you were out.' He handed Felix a sealed letter. ''Twas delivered by a footman in the tabard of Her Highness, the Countess Emmanuelle no less. He had a couple of the city guard to keep him company too.'

A sudden sick feeling grabbed Felix in the pit of his stomach. His eyes flickered towards the door, making sure he had a clear way out. It looked like his past had caught up with him at last. Quickly he reviewed all the things the authorities might want him for.

Well, there was a standing bounty on his and Gotrek's heads posted by the authorities in Altdorf for their involvement in the Window Tax riots. There was the fact that he had murdered the Countess's chief of secret police, Fritz von Halstadt. Not to mention the fact that they had been involved in burning her new College of Engineering to the ground.

How had they found him? Had they been recognised by one of the hundreds of informers who swarmed through the city? Or was it something else entirely? Where was Gotrek? Perhaps if they moved quickly enough they could still escape the jaws of the trap.

'Aren't you going to read it then?' Heinz asked, naked curiosity showing in his eyes. Felix shook his head, his reverie broken. He realised that his heart was pounding and his palms were sweating. Noting the way Heinz was looking at him, he realised that he must look guilty as sin. He forced a sickly grin onto his face.

'Read what?'

'The bloody letter, idiot. You must be able to tell we're all dying of curiosity here.'

Felix glanced around, and saw that Elissa, Heinz, and the rest of the staff were all staring at him quite openly, keen to know what business the ruler of their great city-state might have with him.

'Of course, of course,' Felix said, forcing himself to remain calm, to make his hands stop shaking. He walked over to his customary chair by the fire and sat down. The horde of curious onlookers followed him over and scrutinised his face intently. Felix glared at them meaningfully until they all backed off, then gave his consideration to the letter.

It was inscribed on the very finest vellum, and his name was written in good quality ink. There were no blots or smudges and whoever the scribe was possessed a fine hand indeed. The wax seal had not been broken and it showed the crest of the Elector Countess.

A measure of calm returned to Felix. You did not write letters to men you were going to arrest. If you were a stickler for formalities, you read them the warrant and then clapped them in irons. If you were the Elector Countess Emmanuelle, your thugs bashed them over the head with a club and they woke up in chains in the Iron Tower. Perhaps he told himself things were not going to be so bad after all. Still, he doubted this. In his experience, in this life whatever could go bad did go bad.

With nervous fingers he broke the seal and studied the message within. It was written in the same beautiful and courtly hand as the address, and was as simple as it was enigmatic:

Herr Jaeger,
   You are commanded to present yourself at the palace of Her Serene Highness, the Countess Emmanuelle, at the evening bell on this day.
   Yours in faith,
   Hieronymous Ostwald, Secretary to Her Serene Highness

How very curious, thought Felix, turning the letter over and over in his hands, as if by doing so he would find some clue as to why he was being summoned. There was none. He was left to wonder what the ruler of one of the greatest fiefdoms of the Empire might want with a penniless mercenary wanderer, and no answers were forthcoming. He realised that everybody was still staring at him. He stood up and smiled.

'It's all right. I've just been invited to visit the countess,' he said eventually.

ELISSA STILL LOOKED impressed and a little shocked, as if she could not quite believe there wasn't some mistake.

'It's a great honour,' she told him as they sat together by the fire. He reached out and took her hand.

'I'm sure it's nothing. It's probably for my brother, Otto, and was sent here by mistake.' He reached out and took her hand. She pulled it away quickly. She had been doing that a lot recently.

'You will go, won't you?' she said and smiled.

'Of course. I cannot refuse a command from the local ruler.'

'Then what will you wear?' He was going to say my own clothes, of course, but immediately saw her point. His tunic was stained and soiled in a hundred places from all the brawling and fights he had been in. His cloak was ragged and ripped at the hems where strips had been torn from it to make bandages. His boots were holed and cracked. His britches were patched and filthy. He looked more like a beggar than a

warrior. He doubted that he would be able to get past the front
gate of the palace looking like he did. They were more likely to
throw him a bone and send him on his way with kicks.

'Don't worry,' he said. 'I'll think of something.'

'Best do it quickly then. You've only got eight hours till the
evening bell.'

FELIX LOOKED ACROSS the desk at his brother. Newly bathed and
with his tattered clothes hastily washed and dried in front of
the fire, he felt self-conscious. His hands toyed idly with the silvered pomander which dangled from his neck. He wished he'd
never come to the warehouse where Otto's office was located.

Otto got up from behind his heavy oaken desk and lumbered
over to the window. He put his hands behind his back. Felix
noticed that his right hand was clutching his left wrist. It was
an old habit of Otto's. He had always done that when called
upon to answer difficult questions by their tutors.

'Why do I only see you when you want something, Felix?' he
asked eventually.

Felix felt a surge of guilt. Otto had a point. The only times he
had been near his brother recently was when he had needed a
favour. Like he did now. He considered the question. It wasn't
that he disliked Otto. It was just that they had nothing much
in common anymore. And perhaps, Felix feared that he would
ask him to join the business again, and he would have to refuse
again.

'I've been busy,' he said.

'Doing what?'

Crawling through graveyards, burning scholarly institutions
to the ground, fighting monsters, killing things, Felix thought,
wondering how much, if any, of this he would ever be able to
tell his brother. Fortunately Otto did not give him a chance to
reply, as he had some suggestions of his own.

'Brawling, I suppose. Hanging about with tavern wenches
and rakes. Frittering away that expensive education father paid
for. When you should be here, helping run the business, following in the family tradition, helping to make...'

Felix could not tell whether Otto was angry or simply hurt.
He fought to keep his own feelings under control. He stretched
his legs out, pushing the chair back until it rested on its two
rear legs. A huge portrait of his father glared down at him from

behind Otto's desk. Even from up there, the old man managed to look somehow disapproving.

'Do you know the Countess Emmanuelle?' The question interrupted the flow of Otto's ranting, as Felix had intended it to. His brother stopped, turned around and looked sharply at his younger brother.

'I met her on the last high feast day of Verena, when I was presented at court. She seemed a spirited and somewhat flighty young woman.'

Otto paused and turned away from the window. He slumped back into his comfortable chair again and opened a huge ledger. He had marked his place with a quill pen. It was a gesture so reminiscent of his father that Felix smiled. For a moment Otto's brow furrowed in concentration. He dipped the pen in the inkwell and inscribed something in the ledger. Without looking at Felix, he said: 'I've heard some rumours about her.'

Felix leaned forward until he almost touched Otto's neatly arranged desk. The front legs of his chair clunked back onto the stone floor. 'Rumours?'

Otto cleared his throat and smiled in embarrassment. 'She's supposed to be somewhat wild. More than somewhat, actually. It's not uncommon at Emmanuelle's court. They are all, shall we say, a little less than moral.'

'Wild?' Felix enquired. His interest was piqued. 'In what way?'

'She's said to be the mistress of half the young nobles of the Empire. Has a particular fondness for rakes and duellists. There have been a number of scandals, apparently. Only rumours, of course, and I don't pay any attention to gossip,' he added hastily, like a man who fears that what he is saying might suddenly be overheard. 'Why do you ask?'

Felix placed the letter on top of the ledger which Otto had been studying. His brother picked it up and turned it over in his hands. He studied the broken seal then slid the parchment from out of the envelope and read it. Otto smiled the same cold and calculating smile that their father showed in the portrait above.

'So you're moving among the nobility now. I won't ask how this has come about.'

It had been their father's ambition to buy the family's way into the nobility for as long as he could remember. So far he had not succeeded but Felix reckoned that it was only a matter of time. The old man was both wealthy and persistent. Otto continued to give him that long measuring look. He ran his eyes over Felix's old and tattered clothing.

'Of course, you need money,' he said eventually. Felix looked back considering his options. He didn't really want to take his family's money but under the circumstances it seemed advisable. He would certainly need better clothing for his visit to the court.

'Yes, brother,' he said.

FELIX WALKED OUT through the warehouse door feeling slightly sick of himself. The pouch of gold jingling within his jerkin was like a badge of his betrayal of his own ideals. The letter from Otto instructing any of the Jaeger businesses to give him what he required seemed tainted with his own greed. After so much time spent shunning his family, the generosity seemed almost excessive.

Felix shook his head and strode across to the river wharves. He looked down into the grey, misty murk of the Reik and studied the great barges which had come all the way from Altdorf carrying their cargoes of Bretonnian wines and Estalian silks. They lay at rest along the piers, like whales momentarily surfaced, bobbing in the river flow. He watched the sweating dockhands lifting the casks from the holds with hooked knives, and saw them roll heavy barrels up long gangplanks towards the warehouse. And he heard loud coughs and saw men holding handkerchiefs over their mouths. The plague had claimed hundreds over the past few weeks.

It seemed that his and Gotrek's efforts in the Gardens of Morr had at best slowed its spread, and at worst had no effect at all. He wondered how it was spread, and in his mind, he pictured the rats that the plague monk had been dipping into that vile cauldron. Somehow he just knew they had something to with it.

One of the men, older than the rest, remembered Felix from his younger days. He raised his hand and waved at him. Felix waved back. He could not even remember the man's name, but he was shocked to find him still labouring away after all these years. The dock worker had not been young even then.

Here, Felix thought, was the difference between the nobility of the Empire and those they ruled. That docker would continue to work for the pittance which the Jaeger family paid him until he keeled over and died. The nobles would lounge in their palaces, collecting the revenues of their estates and never raise their hands in honest toil in all their lives. There were times when Felix found himself in agreement with the revolutionists who preached rebellion across the Empire.

He smiled ironically. Fine words, he told himself, for a man who had just taken a hefty handout from his own rich family. Well, he had not made this world, he just had to live in it. He turned and walked along the bank of the river, losing himself in the sounds and smells and sights of the dockside.

The smell of fish assaulted his nostrils. Felix gagged and held the pomander he had acquired from Doctor Drexler under his nose. Its perfumed scent was starting to fade but it was still enough to sweeten the tainted air. Felix noticed that the smells of the street and other people seemed keener now that he'd had his first bath in weeks.

The rumble of huge drayage carts competed with the shouts of the dock workers. An armed guard in the black tabard of the city state stopped to take a pear from the cart of a small trader. A child pickpocket made a daring rush for the purse of an old trader too poor to afford bodyguards. It was all very much as Felix remembered it from his childhood visits to Nuln with his father and brothers. He headed onwards, making for the better part of town.

He had a niggling feeling that someone was following him, but when he turned around to look no one was there.

FELIX STUDIED HIS reflection in the mirror. Very nice, he thought. He knew he cut a fine figure. At the best of times he was tall, athletic and quite good-looking, if he said so himself. Now he was dressed to make the most of it. He took a deep breath, revelling in the smell of luxury, of oak panelling and fine old leather. This discrete tailor's shop, catering only to the highest category of nobles, was one of the Jaeger family's less well-known businesses. It had not even existed when Felix had last been in Nuln. It had been set up by Otto, using introductions passed on by the late Fritz von Halstadt. For once Felix was glad of Otto's corrupt association with the man he had killed.

His fine new clothes felt strange. The high leather boots pinched. The tunic felt a little stiff, the padded lining felt too soft. The white linen shirt smelled too fresh. He realised how used he had become to the harsh life on the road, when he had not changed his clothes for months. Only the new cloak of red Sudenland wool felt familiar. It resembled his old one, ruined by skaven blood during the attack on the Blind Pig. The sword he had taken from the Templar, Aldred, was encased in a fine new sheath of plain black leather.

'Would sir like any alterations made?' the assistant asked obsequiously.

Felix studied the bald-headed, sour faced fellow. Only an hour ago, when Felix had entered the shop, the assistant had inspected him as if he were a particularly large and repulsive cockroach. In a way Felix could not blame him. He had been dressed like a beggar. Of course, the assistant's attitude had changed within seconds of reading Otto's hastily scrawled note. When Otto Jaeger himself told his minions to give this client anything he wanted, fawning courtesy was thrown in as part of the bargain.

Felix gave the man his best condescending smile. 'No. I would like several copies of these garments delivered to my residence within the day. And have my old clothing packed and returned immediately.'

'Of course, sir. And where would sir's residence be?'

'At the sign of the Blind Pig, in the New Quarter. Have the clothes delivered to Felix Jaeger.'

Felix enjoyed looking at the man's face when he gave the address. He looked as if he had just swallowed that large and particularly nasty cockroach.

'The Blind Pig, sir? Isn't that a–'

'Where I stay is my own business, don't you think?'

'Of course, sir. It is simply that sir took one rather by surprise for a moment. A thousand apologies.'

'No need. Just make sure my clothes are delivered on time.'

'I will see to it personally, sir.'

Felix wondered if the man would have the nerve to come to the New Quarter himself. Maybe he would. He was obviously paid enough to make it worth his while to stay in Felix's favour.

'Will that be all, sir?'

'For the moment, yes.'

* * *

FELIX EMERGED FROM the tailors into the late afternoon gloom. He glanced around. No pursuers were visible. If there had actually been any, perhaps they had grown bored with waiting while Felix was in the tailors. He hoped so at least.

He noticed he was standing taller and he felt more poised than he had before. He carried himself like a different man from the weary wanderer who had presented himself at Otto Jaeger's warehouse earlier. It was amazing the difference a bath and a change of clothes could make in a man.

A feeling of nervous anticipation had been gathering in his stomach all day. It was not quite fear. It was more like a vague uneasiness about what he would encounter within Elector Countess Emmanuelle's palace. He was forced to admit that he prayed he would not embarrass himself in front of the nobility.

He considered that thought for a moment, then forced a smile. His manners were good. He was well-spoken and well-dressed. There was nothing to be afraid of. Yet he knew this was not true. The nobility did not like upstart newcomers from the merchant class. During his time at university he had endured many snubs by young nobles who had taken pains to communicate this to him. At the same time, he had always resented being looked down on by people who were often stupider and less well-educated than he, whose only qualification was that they happened to be born into the right inbred bloodline. Now he could not help but laugh at himself. He was certainly not working himself into the correct frame of mind for this interview.

He thanked Sigmar for small mercies: at least, Gotrek had not been summoned as well. He could just picture a confrontation between the local high-born and the sullen Trollslayer. It would be an encounter fated to end in disaster. Felix had never known the Slayer show deference to anything or anyone, and he doubted that the countess or her minions would appreciate his independence of spirit.

Suddenly a new problem presented itself, and one that he had not even bothered to consider earlier. The streets were muddy and full of rubbish. The gutters were overflowing. The crowds were unwashed and tightly pressed. He could not get to the palace without some of the dirt of the streets transferring itself to his superb new clothes. He knew it would never do to appear at the palace looking less than immaculate. He glanced around, hoping that a solution would present itself.

He gestured with his arm, summoning a passing palanquin. The litter's curtain's were open, showing it was for hire. The two burly bearers approached him deferentially. Felix was startled for a moment. Normally two such bravoes would have cursed him or exchanged coarse jibes, but now they were all attentive respect. Of course, he realised, it was the clothes. They saw him as a rich noble and a potentially lucrative fare. It was an impression which was in no way diminished when he said: 'The palace, and swiftly.'

He clambered into the plushly upholstered seat and the bearers set off at a fast striding pace. Felix pulled open the curtains at the back of the palanquin, checking to see if he was being followed once more. Was it just his imagination or had someone just ducked back into the mouth of that alley?

THE WAY TO THE palace was steep and winding. The townhouses of the nobility arrayed themselves around the highest hill in the city. From where Felix sat he could see a fine view of the roofs of the merchants below, and the great curve of the River Reik. He could see the spires of the temples and the great building site where workmen laboured to rebuild the College of Engineering.

Horses hooves clattered on the cobbled streets. Coaches swept past. Servants in the liveries of a dozen famous families swarmed everywhere, carrying messages, leading beasts, holding great satchels full of provisions. The lowest of them were better dressed than some of the city's merchants, and the highest ranking wore uniforms scarcely less ornate than a mercenary captain's. Everyone looked cleaner and better fed than the commoners down below.

Here and there nobles garbed in splendid raiment walked with their retainers and bodyguards, the crowd parting as if under the influence of some mysterious force before them. Felix studied their haughtiness, thinking that he recognised a few of the younger ones who played at being poor in the Blind Pig of an evening. He doubted that any of them would recognise him now.

Ahead of them loomed the walls of the palace. It dwarfed the stately townhouses around it. Even now, with its walls replastered and ornate statuary lining the approach, it looked far more like a fortress than a palace. The great arch of the gateway was huge, and the heavy oaken gates were shod with bronze and looked like they could resist a hundred battering rams. Sentries barred the entrance and scrutinised all who attempted to pass. Some were recognised immediately and allowed to go in unhindered. Others were stopped and challenged, and Felix guessed he would be in the latter category.

He tapped on the canopy of the palanquin to indicate that they should stop, paid the footmen the two silver shillings and added another shilling for a tip, then watched them depart. He patted his tunic to make sure his summons was still there, then strode as confidently as he could manage in the direction of the gate.

When one of the guards asked him his business, he showed them the letter and the seal and was surprised when a tall, lean man garbed all in black emerged from within the gatehouse. He looked at Felix with cold grey eyes.

'Herr Jaeger,' he said in a calm, emotionless voice. 'If you would be so good as to accompany me? I will explain the nature of this business on the way.'

Filled with sudden trepidation Felix fell into step beside him. He could not help but notice that two armed guards dogged their steps. They moved down long corridors, passed through a series of galleries and an enormous ballroom, before going down some steps into the dungeons below.

Somewhere in the distance, the evening bell tolled.

FELIX STUDIED THE office warily. It was large and sumptuously furnished, not at all what he had expected. He had expected a torture chamber or a cell, but not this. Nevertheless, the two men-at-arms had followed them in and positioned themselves against the far wall where they stood, immobile. As Felix watched, a lamplighter in the livery of the palace entered, carrying a small ladder. Another bearing only a lit taper clambered up the ladder and lit the candles set in the massive chandelier. Its light dimmed the rays of the setting sun that filtered in through the narrow window.

The tall man gestured to the massive leather armchair which sat in front of his equally enormous desk. 'Please, Herr Jaeger, be seated.'

Felix allowed himself to sink into the chair. The tall man wandered over to the window and stared out for a moment, before pulling the heavy brocade drapes closed. He considered the window as if he were looking at it for the first time. It was narrow, obviously designed as an arrow slit.

'This place was a fortress before it was a palace,' he said.

His words hung in the air. Felix turned them over wondering if there was some hidden meaning. He did not respond but waited for the man to continue, to amplify his statement if he was going to. The man considered this and smiled for the first time. His teeth were a brilliant white and made even his pale skin look sallow.

'Forgive me, Herr Jaeger; you are not quite what I expected.'

'And what did you expect, Herr…?'

The man bowed as one would to an opponent who had just scored a point in a fencing match. 'Forgive me, once more. It had been a long and harrowing day and I quite forget my manners. I am Heironymous Ostwald. I am personal secretary to Her Serenity.'

Felix was not sure whether he should rise and bow back. He was not given the chance. Ostwald moved swiftly behind his desk and sat down. Felix noticed that even in that comfortable chair he sat with his back straight, like someone used to the iron discipline of a soldier.

'In answer to your question, from the description I had of you, I expected someone less… polished than yourself. Serves me right, I suppose.' He opened a small leather book in front of him. 'You are a member of the Jaeger family, I see. Good. Very good.'

'Why am I here?'

'Dieter! Johan! You may wait outside.' Ostwald gestured to the men-at-arms. They opened the door and quietly and discretely vacated the room. Once they had gone, Ostwald steepled his fingers and started again.

'Tell me, Herr Jaeger, are you familiar with the skaven?'

Felix felt like his heart was about to stop. His mouth felt suddenly dry. He considered his words very carefully indeed. 'I know of them. I am not personally acquainted with any.'

Ostwald laughed again. It was a cold, mechanical laugh and there was no humour in it. 'Very good. I had understood that this was not the case.'

'What are you getting at?' Felix's nervousness made him sound snappish. He did not know the way this conversation was going but he could imagine several possible outcomes, none of them pleasant.

'Merely that you have served in the sewer watch and you claimed to your superiors there that you had encountered them. Is that not the case?'

'You know it is.'

'Yes. I do.' Again Ostwald smiled. 'You do not seem to me like a typical sewerjack, Herr Jaeger. The sons of rich merchants rarely leap at the chance to hunt goblins in our sewers.'

Felix was getting used to this now. He was not as surprised as he might have been by the unexpected nature of the statement. He could see that this was all part of Ostwald's technique. He liked to keep the people he was dealing with off-balance. It was like getting the measure of your opponent in a duel. Felix smiled back at him.

'I am the black sheep of my family.'

'Indeed. How interesting. You must explain to me how that came about some time.'

'I suspect you already know.'

'Perhaps. Perhaps. Let us return to the skaven, Herr Jaeger. How many times have you encountered them?'

'On several occasions.'

'How many precisely?'

Felix counted the number of times he was prepared to admit to. There was the encounter in the sewer. There was the attack on the Blind Pig. There was his fight in the Gardens of Morr. He decided that under the circumstances it might be undiplomatic to mention his meeting with the rat-ogre in von Halstadt's house and his battle with the warlocks of Skryre in the College of Engineering.

'Three.'

Ostwald consulted his book again. Another piece of the puzzle fitted into place, Felix thought to himself. He doesn't really know anything. He's just fishing. His style is to intimidate people and then see what they let slip. Of course, thought Felix, this knowledge will do you no good, if he orders you taken down into the dungeons and tortured. He decided to try a few questions himself.

'On whose authority are you doing this?' he asked.

'The Elector Countess Emmanuelle's,' Ostwald said with absolute certainty. 'Why do you ask?'

'I am just trying to work out what is going on here.'

Ostwald gave him a long cold chilling smile. 'I can explain that to you quite easily, Herr Jaeger. What do you know of Fritz von Halstadt?'

Once again, Felix felt his heart leap into his mouth. He fought to keep his guilt and his surprise off his face. A slight amused flicker in Ostwald's eyes told him that the man had noticed something.

'It's a familiar name,' he said. 'I think I saw him once at my brother's club.'

'Very good, Herr Jaeger. Allow me to share something with you – on the understanding on your word as a gentleman, that nothing I tell you goes beyond the confines of this room.'

The tone in which the words were said told Felix that Ostwald was not simply counting on his word as a gentlemen. Felix did not doubt that there would be serious and violent reprisals if he betrayed the man's confidence.

'Please go ahead. You have my word I will tell no one.'

'Fritz von Halstadt was murdered.'

Felix thought he was going to be struck down on the spot. He felt sure that his guilt was written all over his face and that Ostwald was going to summon the guard to have him thrown into the dungeon.

'By the skaven.'

Felix let out a long, rushing sigh of relief.

'I can see you are appalled, Herr Jaeger.'

'Am I?' Felix collected his scattered wits. 'I mean – aren't I just?'

'Yes. It's a terrifying thought, isn't it? I will tell you something else. Fritz von Halstadt was no ordinary servant of the crown. He was the chief of Her Serenity's secret police. We think he must have discovered some skaven plot and been murdered because of it.'

If you'd used the word 'joined' instead of 'uncovered', I would have to agree with you, Felix thought. What he said instead was: 'What makes you think this?'

'In the burned out remains of his home we found the skeleton of a creature that was not human. We suspect that it was some monster conjured by the skaven to assassinate Von Halstadt. He must have fought with it and killed it then died of his wounds. The house was probably set on fire during their struggle.'

'Go on.'

'Interestingly enough, soon after that there was an attempt on your life. As far as I know, you and your associate, the dwarf Gurnisson, were the only people who had then claimed to have seen the skaven. Perhaps this was an effort to cover their tracks.'

'I think I see what you mean.'

'There are other things you may not know, Herr Jaeger, and I tell you them now only so you will realise the seriousness of the situation. You may have heard that there was a fire at the College of Engineering?'

'Yes.'

'What you may not be aware off is that the fire was the work of the skaven too. I assure you, Herr Jaeger, this is nothing to smile about. The gods were against those rat-man devils in one way. There seems to have been some sort of accident, for we found many skaven corpses at the scene.'

'Why have I not heard more of this?' Felix said.

'You would have, except that Her Serenity deemed it wise to avoid a panic, and panic there would surely be if the common herd were to find out that our city is under siege by the skaven!'

Felix was astonished. After many fruitless attempts by himself to get someone to take the skaven threat seriously, someone was now trying to convince him of it! He did not know whether to laugh or be angry. He decided to play the part allotted to him, for on consideration he realised that showing more knowledge than Ostwald believed him to have could easily prove dangerous.

'I am not joking, Herr Jaeger. Since you and Gurnisson reported the presence of skaven war parties in the sewers, there have been other sightings, skirmishes even. And bands of the rat-men have even raided our docks by night, stealing food and even a grain barge. I tell you, we are under siege.'

'Siege? Isn't that a little strong? Where are the armies, the war engines, the chittering hordes?'

'They are strong words, Herr Jaeger, and in truth the situation calls for them. The chief of secret police assassinated. Citizens assaulted. A great Imperial armoury destroyed – and now the threat of plague!'

'I–'

'Now, Herr Jaeger. I know you take this seriously. I know you have some knowledge of this. We have a mutual acquaintance and he has told me all about your actions in this matter.'

'Mutual acquaintance?'

Ostwald produced a pomander similar to the one that hung about Felix's neck. He held it beneath his nose and breathed deeply from it before setting it down upon the desk.

'I refer, of course, to Herr Doctor Drexler. He has told me about your visit to the Gardens of Morr and what you found there. He treated your henchman, after all.'

'How do you know Doctor Drexler?' Felix asked to buy some time. He fervently hoped Ostwald never referred to Gotrek as his henchman within the Slayer's hearing.

'As a patient and as a friend. He is the physician to many noble families.'

'But—'

'I see that you are aware of another and deeper connection. I suspected a man of your resources might.'

Felix had being going to ask 'But why did Drexler tell you all this?' but he decided to keep his mouth shut and see what coldly clever explanation this cold and clever man came up with.

'I tell you this only because the situation is truly desperate, Herr Jaeger, and we badly need your help.'

Things must be desperate indeed, thought Felix, if you need my help. Particularly when I haven't a clue about what you're talking about.

'Drexler and I are both initiates of the Order of the Hammer.' As he said this, he made a peculiar variation of the sign of the hammer over his heart, reversing the normal order, of left, right, centre, down. 'You have heard of us?'

'Some sort of Sigmarite secret society,' Felix guessed. It was not a difficult guess to make. The hammer was the sign of the Imperial Cult, and there were many strange hidden societies with their own signs and passwords.

'That is correct. An order of dedicated men sworn to protect our ancient civilisation from the threat of Chaos. We share many goals and much ancient knowledge. He tells me that Aldred himself chose you as his successor.'

'Successor?' Felix was bewildered.

'You bear his blade, Herr Jaeger. You knew the man.'

'Mmm…'

'I know Herr Aldred was a member of several secret orders as well as the one to which he nominally belonged. He was a devout and fearless man, Herr Jaeger. Much like yourself he dedicated himself to fighting the forces of Chaos wherever he found them.'

'I do not belong to his order.'

'I can understand that you would deny this, Herr Jaeger. Herr Aldred belonged to many orders with even stricter vows of secrecy than our own. I will not press you on this.'

Just as well, Felix thought wryly, otherwise you'd find out exactly the depth of my ignorance.

Ostwald paused for a moment and then spoke as if trying to change the subject: 'Drexler tells me that you possess a great deal of knowledge yourself.'

'I possess only a little.'

'It may be that the little you know is actually a great deal, Herr Jaeger. Tell me about this strange skaven who writes you the letters of warning. How did you meet it?'

So, Felix thought, this is where all this talk of secret societies and grave threats is leading. It is an attempt to get this information. He realised that Drexler must have reported their entire conversation to Ostwald, so he saw no sense in hiding anything about the letter.

'I have never met it,' Felix said honestly. 'In truth I have no idea why it has selected me to communicate with. Perhaps it hasn't. Perhaps it has chosen Gotrek.'

'That seems unlikely, Herr Jaeger, given the dwarf's avocation. No, I am convinced that you are the chosen one. Why?'

'Perhaps because I can read.'

'You can read skaven runes?'

'No, but I can read Imperial script.'

'So the letter was written in Imperial script?' Ostwald looked astonished.

'Of course. How else could I read it?'

'You have these letters on you?'

'No, they vanished in a puff of smoke five heartbeats after I read them,' Felix said ironically. He was going to add that he did not normally carry the letters on his person but Ostwald interrupted him.

'Powerful sorcery indeed! Herr Jaeger, you must understand something. I have taken over Fritz von Halstadt's duties. The

security of this great state of Nuln lies in my hands. Should this
skaven contact you again, well, you must inform me at once.'

'Nothing would please me more,' Felix said sincerely.

'No, please take me seriously, Herr Jaeger. I sense that you
know more than you are currently willing to tell me. That is
fair. We must all have our little secrets. But I must insist that
you let me know. I want no more midnight forays into the
graveyards. I know you are a brave and resourceful man, but
these things are best dealt with by the authorities.'

'I agree completely.'

'Good, Herr Jaeger. Do not attempt to deceive me in this. My
reach is long.'

'I would not dream of it. You have my word.'

'Good. Then you are free to go. Just remember–'

'Do not worry, Herr Ostwald. Rest assured I will inform you
as soon as I learn anything of the skaven's plans,' Felix said, fervently hoping against hope that he never ever came into the
possession of such information again.

IZAK GROTTLE PULLED himself from his palanquin and lumbered
over to the great barred window. His breathing was heavy and
already he felt hungry. It had been a long trudge through the
Underways to reach this secret burrow. Soon it would be time
to eat once more. He congratulated himself. It was amazing
from what simple sources the most brilliant of inspirations
sprang. The entire enormous effort of this secret research warren had sprung from his own hunger. He doubted that any
other skaven would ever have thought of something so simple
and yet so inspired. Let others come up with intricate and complex schemes, thought Grottle! Soon he would demonstrate to
all of them that the simplest plans were the best.

He looked down into the great warp vats and saw the monsters taking shape within their bubbling, glowing feeding
fluids. He inspected the massive warpstone orbs which fed
carefully measured jolts of mutating power into the vats when
the watching vatmasters deemed the conditions perfect. The
rank smell of ozone and strange chemicals wafted up and
made his nostrils twitch. It was a reassuring smell to him, the
smell of the warrens in which his clan had raised him, from
where he had begun to the long climb to the power that he
wielded today.

He smiled, showing his great yellow fangs and felt the pangs of his dreadful hunger once more. All skaven suffered from it from time to time, usually after combat or some other violent activity. They called it the Black Hunger and for most of them it was a sign of triumph and indicator that they could devour prey. Izak Grottle suffered from it all the time. He had long suspected that continual exposure to warpstone dust and mutagenic chemicals had done something to him. He would not be the first Clan Moulder packmaster to acquire the stigmata of some mutation, nor would he be the last. In his case he also suspected that the change had done something to his brain – stimulated it, made him much cleverer and more cunning than other skaven, rewarded him with fantastic insight. That was why he needed to eat so much, of course, to fuel his incredible mind.

He stuffed his own tail into his mouth to try to control the terrible hunger pangs. Great gobs of saliva drooled down the bulbous flesh. He had already devoured every last scrap of the huge mound of dried meat he had intended to see him through his visit. He knew there was nothing much edible in this alchemical laboratory except his own bearers, and, in fairness, they had done nothing today to displease him. The jars all around contained mostly toxic chemicals; nothing there for him. He breathed deeply and fought to bring his appetite back under control.

Skitch looked up at him nervously. Grottle could tell that the little hunchbacked skaven was uneasy. Perhaps he was thinking of all the other lackeys which rumour claimed that the packmaster had devoured. Grottle licked his lips with his long pink tongue. As he liked to tell all of his research vermin, those rumours were utterly true. The light of warpstone lanterns illuminated the pebble thick lenses that Skitch used to compensate for his bad eyesight. Grottle nodded his head and twitched his tail just for the pleasure of seeing Skitch leap back nervously.

Skitch was small and weak, and so near-sighted that he could hardly see one paw in front of his face without his glasses. In many other skaven clans, such weakness would soon have caused him to have been killed and eaten, but Clan Moulder had recognised his potential and kept him alive and for that, Grottle knew, the little runt was truly grateful. And he had proven useful to Clan Moulder. Skitch was quite possibly the best vatmaster in the long and glorious history of the clan. He was a genius when it came to breeding and moulding all manner of beasts. Now he held out the cage that contained what was most likely to be Clan Moulder's greatest triumph.

Izak Grottle took the cage and inspected its contents. It was a huge, sleek fat female rat, already pregnant by the looks of things. The untrained eye would detect very little different from an ordinary rat, Grottle thought. Perhaps they would think it a little larger, a bit more vicious. Perhaps they would even notice the wicked gleam of some abnormal emotion in its eye. But they would never suspect that they were looking at one of the most potent weapons the world had ever known.

'It doesn't look like much, does it?' Grottle said in his slow, deep rumbling voice. 'Does it?'

Grottle liked to repeat himself. He was proud of his voice so powerful and so unlike a normal skaven voice. Skitch knew a cue when he heard one.

'Perhaps not, master – but then appearances are deceptive.' The vatmaster's voice was unusually high for a skaven's, and his words had an odd insinuating quality. 'This beauty will lay waste to entire cities, will bring nations to their knees, will cause the world to bow before the genius of Clan Moulder!'

Grottle nodded in a slow, satisfied way. He knew this was true. He just liked to hear his lackey say it. 'You are sure there will be no problems, Skitch? Absolutely sure?'

'Yes, yes, master, I am certain. We have bred thousands of these creatures and we have tested many of them to destruction in the approved manner.'

'Good! Good! And what did you find?'

'They have a huge appetite for almost any material. They will eat wood and waste if nothing else is available, but mostly they seek out and devour grain, meat and other foodstuffs.'

'Excellent.'

'They can consume their own body weight in less than a hundred heartbeats and be ready to eat again in hours.'

'You have done splendidly, Skitch. Splendidly.'

The hunchback seemed almost to swell up with the effects of the praise. 'And they can breed in litters of up to a hundred.'

'They grow quickly, of course?'

'They reach full mature size within a day, providing they find enough to eat.'

'And the breeders?'

'Can bear a litter each and every day, as you specified, master.'

Grottle threw back his head and let his deep rumbling laughter pour forth. Such a simple idea, he thought. When these rats were released into the human city, they would consume all the food within days. All the stored crops from the harvest would be devoured. All the food in shops would vanish underneath a furry avalanche of hunger. They would eat and breed and eat and breed unstoppably. And when no other food was available, they would eat the humans and their animals. And when all other foodstocks were exhausted they would consume each other. Or die. Their lifespan was measured only in days. But before that happened, the humans would starve or flee from their city and the triumph would belong to Clan Moulder. Word would soon reach the Council of Thirteen and a suitable reward would be found for Izak Grottle.

'We are ready to begin?'

'Yes master, We have the captured grain barge almost ready. The conversion will be done in days. We will ship the specimens to where it is hidden. It can begin its journey any time you wish, after that.'

'Perfect. Perfect.' The human warehouses were near the docks. All they would have to do would be to take the boat into the harbour and open the cages. A few disposable house troops could see to that easily enough. Perhaps some rat-ogres just to be on the safe side. 'Do so as soon as preparations are complete.'

'Of course, master.'

'You say you have thousands more of these?' Grottle said, reaching into the cage to stroke the sleek fat rat.

'Yes, master. Why?'

'Because I'm feeling a little peckish.' With that, Izak Grottle grasped the somnolent rat and stuffed it, still living, into his salivating mouth. It was still struggling futilely as it went down his throat. It tasted good, thought Grottle.

Just like victory.

FELIX WALKED THROUGH the swing doors of the Blind Pig and every head in the place turned to look at him. At first, he wondered what for, but when Katka, one of the serving girls, came to take his order, he realised it was because no one recognised him. He smiled at her, and was rewarded with a look of confusion until she saw who he was.

'Why, Felix, I would never have guessed it was you. Did the countess give you some new clothes?'

'Something like that,' he murmured as he raced up the stairs to get to his room and change clothes. He was grateful to discover the package containing his old garments had come from the tailor's shop.

Thank Sigmar, he thought. It wouldn't do to go brawling in this fine suit. Then it dawned on him that simple possession of this new finery was changing him. This morning he would never even have given a thought to such matters. Probably because he didn't have to. And what was he going to do with the pouch full of gold that Otto had given him? To his brother, it probably seemed like little enough money, but it was more than Felix could earn in a whole season of working at the Blind Pig. Gently he pried up a loose floorboard and dropped it into place there.

As he changed for work, he considered his encounter with Herr Ostwald. It seemed that, at long last, the authorities were taking the skaven threat seriously. At the same time, Ostwald appeared to have made some very strange assumptions about Felix. He seemed to assume that Felix was far cleverer and more involved with all of this than he actually was. He guessed that Ostwald was simply projecting his own reasoning and perceptions onto what he knew of Felix. Well, as long as he asked no questions about the death of Fritz von Halstadt and the burning of the college, Felix was not going to disappoint him. The fact that Ostwald had deduced a vast and well-organised skaven conspiracy from several random acts that Felix and the Slayer had perpetrated themselves might have been amusing – except for one thing.

It was quite evident that there was indeed a vast and well-organised skaven conspiracy. Even though he himself had killed von Halstadt, there had been powerful rat-men present. Clan Eshin assassins had nearly burned down the Blind Pig, and monsters had been sighted just before the blaze which destroyed much of the Poor Quarter. Even though he and Gotrek had interrupted them, the warlocks of Skryre had been robbing the college. Even though they had stopped the plague monks' ritual, the skaven had managed to infiltrate the Gardens of Morr and the plague was still spreading through the city like wildfire.

Hastily Felix put the enchanted pomander around his neck and breathed deeply of the herbs. Ostwald had made no secret of the fact that rat-men patrols had been sighted in the sewers and other areas around the city; scouting parties, most likely.

Felix knew that one of the creatures Gotrek had seen in von Halstadt's house was a grey seer, one of the rarest and most powerful of all the rat-men magicians according to Leiber's book. A being, in fact, usually only sighted when the skaven had great plans afoot.

A chill struck Felix and it was not just caused by his tattered clothes. He was forced to concede that, wrong though many of his facts had been, Ostwald's basic conclusion was most likely correct. The skaven planned something big here in Nuln. But what?

GREY SEER THANQUOL took another pinch of warpstone snuff and stroked his whiskers. Things were going well. He inspected the mass of papers that lay before him and revelled in the messages they contained. Almost ten thousand crack skaven troops would soon be in position in the Underways beneath and around the city of Nuln.

So large a host had not been mustered since the time of the Great Chaos Incursion. It was the largest force the Council of Thirteen had dispatched to assault a human city since the time of the Great Plague, when the entire human Empire had briefly lay under the iron paw of skaven rule. And it was his to command. When he gave the word, it would attack and in a frenzy of overwhelming ferocity would overwhelm the pitiful humans above.

For a brief instant the warpstone conjured up delightful visions of destruction and death before Thanquol's reddened eyes. He could picture the burning buildings, the humans hacked to pieces or led off in great slave trains. He saw himself striding through the ruins triumphant. The very thought made his tail stiffen.

Things were going very well indeed. Even Thanquol's enemies were aiding his plans. That vile twosome Gurnisson and Jaeger had, guided by Thanquol's brilliant insight, uncovered the lair of Vilebroth Null and stopped his plans in their tracks. The abbot had returned from the surface world alone, and no trace could be found of the Cauldron of a Thousand Poxes. Null had spent the last few days limping around the Underways muttering darkly about traitors. Thanquol tittered. There was a certain poetic justice in it all: it had been the abbot's intended treachery to the cause of Thanquol, and of course the entire skaven nation, which had been the cause of his undoing.

It even appeared that the abbot might have done the invasion force a favour, for Thanquol's agents on the surface reported some dire disease was dropping the humans in their tracks. Of course, potentially this meant that there would be less slaves once the conquest of Nuln had been effected so perhaps then would be the time to have the abbot punished. He could trump up the charges for the council and let them deal with Null. Yes, it was true, Thanquol thought: every cess-pit has a warpstone dropping in it, if only you know how to look.

He studied the plans of the city before him. The various invasion routes were well marked in red, blue and green warpstone ink. They glowed in front of his eyes in a bright tangle and snarl of lines. Here and there circles indicated breakout points where the army would erupt onto the surface. The sheer labyrinthine complexity of it all filled Thanquol's brain with pleasure. But the most pleasure came from his contemplation of what would happen afterwards.

The city would be garrisoned against human attempts to retake it. He would set up labour camps and make the captured human slaves build a big ditch around the city. Then they could dam the river with a great waterwheel which would provide power for the skaven's machines and sweatshop factories. At some point they would erect a huge one hundred tail length high statue of their conquerors, and it seemed only fair to Thanquol that he should be the model for it, for truly he would personify the skaven spirit of conquest to them. It would be a glorious time, and the first of many victories that would end with all the human lands permanently and utterly under skaven rule.

He heard a not very discreet hacking cough outside the curtains of his sanctum. A hoarse voice said: 'Greatest of generals, it is I, Lurk Snitchtongue, and I bring news most urgent.'

Disturbed from his reverie, Thanquol was inclined to be snappish but Lurk had proven to be an invaluable lackey just recently, and his sources of information had been excellent. At this moment, he seemed a little ill but Thanquol was sure that would pass.

'Enter! Enter! Quick! Quick!'

'Yes! Yes! Swiftest of thinkers!'

'What is this urgent news?'

Lurk twitched his tail. It seemed obvious to Thanquol that the little skaven had indeed come with interesting information, and intended to savour his moment of triumph.

'I once blasted a lackey who kept me waiting a moment too long. Stripped his flesh to the bones.'

'A moment, most patient of masters, while I gather my thoughts. Some explanation is needed.'

'Then explain!'

'My birthkin Ruzlik serves Clan Moulder.'

'Indeed. And you think this information is worthy of the consideration of a grey seer?'

'No! No, most perceptive of potentates! It's just that he has a habit of gossiping when he has consumed fungal winebroth?'

'I see. And you, of course, are often sharing a flask or two with him.'

'Yes! Yes! Only this morning in fact. He has told me that his master, Izak Grottle, has a great plan afoot. One that will bring the human city to its knees, and I hesitate to mention this, most understanding of skaven...'

'Hesitate no more. Quick! Quick!'

'He claims that Grottle's plan will bring him great glory, will make him more famous even – his words, not mine, master – than Grey Seer Thanquol.'

News of this treacherous claim came as no surprise to Thanquol. It was ever the fate of great skaven to be undermined by jealous lackeys. Doubtless Grottle sought to win esteem in the eyes of the Council of Thirteen at the expense of Thanquol. Well, the grey seer knew ways of dealing with that.

'And what is this plan? Speak! Speak!'

'Alas, the fool could not say. He has merely heard the Moulders chitter among themselves. He knows it has something to do with a grain boat, for he himself led the raid to steal one from the humans. He has no other hard details.'

'Then go and find some. Now!'

'I may need to spend warptokens, most generous of masters.'

'What you need will be provided – within reason.'

'I go, master.' Lurk bowed and scraped as he retreated back through the drapes. Thanquol slumped down in his throne. Certain things were starting to make sense. He had heard reports that one of the human grain barges had been stolen. He had merely put it down to some claw leaders exceeding their orders, and doing some private plundering. Now it seemed that there was another ulterior and sinister motive. Thanquol knew that his position would not be safe until he found out what that was.

'I DON'T LIKE YOU,' the man said, slumping down in his chair. 'I really don't like you.'

'You're drunk,' Felix said. 'Go home!'

'This is a tavern! My copper's as good as anyone's. I'll go home when I please. I don't take orders from the likes of you.'

'Fair enough!' Felix said. 'Stay, then.'

'Don't try and smooth-talk me. I'll go if I like.'

Felix was getting tired of this. He had seen drunks like this before: belligerent, full of self-pity, just looking for trouble. Unfortunately, Felix was usually the candidate they chose for it. They always picked him for an easy mark. He supposed they were all too scared of Gotrek and the other bouncers. There was something familiar about this one though. His coarse features and squat muscular form looked familiar even in the shadowy gloom of this corner of the tavern. He had been in several times over the past few days since Felix had returned from his interview with Herr Ostwald.

'Elissa's my girl,' the drunk said. 'You just leave her alone.'

Oh, of course; it was the peasant lad who used to go out with Elissa. He'd come back.

'Elissa can make up her own mind about who she wants to see.'

'No she can't. She's too sweet. Too easily led. Any city slicker with a smooth tongue and a nice cloak can turn her head.'

Felix saw the part he was being cast for. He was the heartless seducer leading the poor peasant girl astray.

'You've seen too many Detlef Sierck plays,' he said.

'What? What did you call me?'

'I didn't call you anything!'

'Yes, you did. I heard you.'

Felix saw the punch coming a league away. The man was drunk and slow. He raised his hand to block it. His forearm stung from the force of the blow. The man was strong.

'Bastard!' Hans shouted. 'I'll show you.'

He lashed out with a kick that caught Felix in the shin. Sharp pain stabbed through Felix. By reflex, he lashed out with his right hand and caught Hans under the jaw. It was quite possibly the best punch he had ever thrown against a man who was in no state to do anything about it. Hans dropped like a pole-axed ox. The surrounding crowd applauded. Felix turned around to bow ironically and he saw Elissa looking at him with a look of horror in her eyes.

'Felix, you brute!' she said, moving past him to nurse Hans's head in her lap.

'Oh Hans, what did that heathen do to you?'

Just looking at her, Felix could tell that any explanation of what had happened would be useless.

'You HAVE FOUND out more of the Moulder's schemes, I hope?' Thanquol allowed some of his anger and impatience to show in his voice. Over the past few days Lurk had spent considerable sums from the grey seer's treasure chest but still had not produced any results. The little skaven gave a wheezing cough.

'Yes, yes, most perspicacious of masters. I have.'

'Good! Good! Tell me – quick, quick!'

'It's not good, most forgiving of masters.'

'What? What?' Thanquol leaned forward to glare down at the little rat-man and watched him flinch. Few could endure the grey seer red-eyed stare when it suited him to use it.

'Regretfully, the wicked Moulders may already have implemented their plan.'

Cold fury clutched Thanquol's heart. 'Go on!'

'My birthkin overheard the packmaster gloating. It seems a grainship bearing Clan Moulder's secret weapon will arrive in the man-city tonight. Once it arrives, the city will fall. He knows that it has something to do with the city's grain supply but he's not sure what. Clan Moulder are very technical and have their own words for many things.'

'May the Horned Rat gnaw your birthkin's entrails! Is he hearing any more?'

'Just that the barge has been painted black to conceal it from human eyes and that it will arrive this very night. It may even have done so already, most magnificent of masters.'

Thanquol's fur bristled. What could he do? He could mobilise his troops and interfere but that would mean moving openly against Clan Moulder and every instinct the grey seer possessed rebelled against that. What if he summoned his troops, and they failed to find the ship. Thanquol would be a laughing stock and could not endure that. There was no time to waste. He knew that this called for urgent and desperate measures.

Swiftly he reached for pen and parchment, and inscribed a hasty message. 'Take this to the burrow where the dwarf and the man Jaeger dwell. Make sure they get it – and quickly! Deliver it personally!'

'P-p-personally, most revered of rat-men?'

'Personally.' Thanquol made it clear from his tone that he would brook no argument. 'Go. Quick! Quick! Hurry-scurry! No time there is to waste!'

'At once, mightiest of masters!'

VILEBROTH NULL looked up with rheumy hate-filled eyes. He coughed but the sound of his coughing was lost amid the hacking coughs of other skaven in the corridors. At last his patience had been rewarded. His long hours of lying in wait near Thanquol's lair had finally paid off. Somehow Vilebroth Null knew the grey seer had been behind the failure of his carefully contrived plan. So where was that little sneak Lurk Snitchtongue going at his hour? The abbot knew there was only one way to find out.

'HE STARTED IT!' Felix said, all too aware that he sounded like he was whining. He looked around the room they shared, his eyes caught by the package of clothes the tailor had delivered. He had still not unwrapped them.

'So you say,' said Elissa inflexibly. 'I think you're just a bully. You like hitting people like poor Hans.'

'Poor Hans put a bruise the size of a steak on my shin!' Felix said angrily.

'Serves you right for hitting him,' Elissa said. Felix shook his head in frustration. He was just about to get himself in deeper water when suddenly the window crashed in. Felix threw himself over Elissa to cover her as broken glass rained down. Fortunately, not too much landed on them. Felix rolled to his feet and scanned the chamber in the lantern light. Something dark and bulky lay on the floor.

Swiftly he drew his sword and prodded it. Nothing happened.

'What is it?' Elissa said, getting to her feet fearfully and pulling her nightgown tight around herself.

'Don't know,' Felix said, bending over to inspect it more closely. As he did so he recognised the shape and he thought he recognised the thing wrapped round it. 'It's a brick, and it's wrapped in paper.'

'What? It'll be young Count Sternhelm again. He and his cronies are always breaking windows when they get drunk!'

'I don't think so,' Felix said, gingerly unwrapping the paper. It was the same thick coarse parchment all the other skaven messages had come on. He unfolded it and read:

> *Frends – the Black Ship brings doom to yoor city! It comes tonite and carries certin deth! It is a grane barge loded wiv bad! Yoo must stop it! Go QUIK! QUIK! Yoo do not hav much time! They wil destroy yoor grane!*

Felix pulled himself to his feet and started to pull on his clothes.

'Run and get me some paper! I need to send a message to the palace. Move! Quickly!'

The urgency in his voice compelled Elissa from the room without asking any more questions.

LURK RUBBED HIS paws together and offered up a prayer of thanks to the Horned Rat. His message was delivered and somehow he had managed to avoid being chopped up by the dwarf's fearsome axe. Mere minutes after he had lobbed the brick through what he had ascertained was Jaeger's window he saw all the lights in the inn go on, and shortly thereafter, the human and the dwarf raced from the building bearing weapons and lighted lanterns.

A job well done, he told himself with satisfaction and rose to go. He sniffed heavily, trying to clear his nose. He was not feeling too well, and had been feeling less than well for days. He wondered if he was going down with the strange new disease that, rumour had it, was going around the skaven camp... the disease so strangely similar to the plague which was felling the humans. Lurk fervently hoped not. He was still young and had many things to accomplish. It would not be fair for him to pass away without achieving them.

He almost fainted when a heavy hand fell on his shoulder and a hideous bubbling voice whispered in his ear: 'You will tell me what you have been doing! All of it! Quick! Quick!'

Even through the thick wad of snot that filled his nostrils, Lurk recognised the oppressive stench of Vilebroth Null.

'WHAT'S THE HURRY, manling?' Gotrek rumbled. 'We don't even know where we're going.'

'The river,' Felix said, feeling a strange sense of urgency. The note had said they did not have much time, and their skaven informant had never lied to them before. 'A ship must arrive by river.'

'I know, manling but it's a big river. We can't cover it all.'

'It's a barge! There are very few places where a barge can tie up, and it must follow navigable channels.'

Felix considered the possibilities. What certainty did he have that this 'Black Ship' was going to tie up, rather than say, explode? None, really; he was just hoping that this was the case. Then it came to him. The big grain warehouses were down by the wharves and the letter had mentioned grain. At least, he hoped it had.

'The granaries,' he muttered. 'The Northside docks are near the granaries.'

'The Northside docks would seem to be the best bet then,' Gotrek said, hefting his axe.

'Well, we need to start somewhere.' They jogged on. Felix hoped fervently that the tavern boy had managed to deliver his note to Count Ostwald.

SKITCH CURSED AS the barge shifted off course again. It was not a vessel the skaven were used to handling and the helmsman had had a lot of trouble with the tricky currents on their way down-river. Skitch hoped that they would arrive soon, for if they did not reach the manburrow during the hours of darkness the whole plan would be ruined. The barge painted black to be inconspicuous on this moonless night would stick out like a human baby in a litter of runts by day.

Well, he supposed the ship had been necessary. There was no other way such a huge number of specimens could have been carried through the Underways and released into the human city without arousing suspicion. He knew the last thing that his master wanted was for either Grey Seer Thanquol or the humans to have any inkling of what was going on. It was a well-known fact that the plans of Thanquol's rivals had a tendency to fail if he found out about them. Skitch shuddered at the thought of what would happen if the humans found out what was going on.

He shook his head and returned to inspecting his charges. They scrabbled at the bars of their cages, hungry and desperate to be free.

'Soon! Soon!' he told them, feeling a certain kinship for these short-lived vermin that his mighty intellect had created. He knew they were flawed, just like he was. They would live only days.

The ship moved on through the night, coming ever closer to the sleeping city.

THE DOCKS BY NIGHT were not a reassuring place, Felix thought. Lights spilled from many seedy taverns, and many red lights illumined the alleys. Armed patrols of watchmen moved between the warehouses, but were careful not to enter the areas where the sailors took their pleasure. They were more intent in protecting their employer's goods than stopping crime. Still Felix was reassured to know that there were armed men within call if things went horribly wrong.

He stood on the edge of the wharf and stared out into the river. The Reik was wide at this point, perhaps a league across, and navigable by ocean-going ships. Not that many of them came this far. Most traders chose to drop their cargoes in Marienberg and have it shipped upriver on barges.

From here he could see the running lights of both barges and the small skiffs which carried folk across the river at all hours. He assumed that there would be many more craft out there than lights. Not at all boats or their passengers wanted their businesses known. Felix assumed that the Black Ship would be among their number. Only instead of carrying a cargo of illegal goods it was carrying some awful skaven weapon. Felix shuddered to contemplate what it might be. The Cauldron of a Thousand Poxes and the weapons of Clan Skryre had been terrible enough for him.

The wind blew cold and he drew his old tattered cloak tight about his shoulders. What am I doing here, he wondered? I should be at home back in the Pig, trying to patch things up with Elissa. Or maybe not. Maybe that was what he was doing here, avoiding Elissa.

He wondered where things were going with the girl, and he had no real idea. It was just something he had drifted into, not something he ever imagined would have a future. He knew he did not love Elissa the way he had loved Kirsten. Recently, he would not even say they were friendly. He thought that for her, too, it was just a passing thing, something that had happened. Maybe she would be better off with her peasant boy. He shrugged and continued to peer out into the darkness, and listen to the waves slopping gently against the wooden supports of the wharf.

'Our scuttling little friends have picked a good night for it,' Gotrek muttered, taking a swig from the flask of schnapps.

Felix studied the sky. He could see what the Slayer meant. The sky was cloudy and the greater moon was a sliver. The lesser moon was not visible at all.

'Smugglers' moon,' Felix said.

'What?'

'My father used to call moons like this "smugglers' moons". I can see why. Dark. The excisemen would find it hard to see you on a night like this.'

'River patrols too,' Gotrek said. 'Not that humans can see worth a snotling's fart at night anyway.'

'I suppose,' Felix said, wanting to contradict the Slayer, but knowing that he was right in this case.

'Aye, well just be glad a dwarf was here, manling. Even though he has only one good eye.'

'Why?'

'Because there is your Black Ship! Look!'

Felix followed the dwarf's pointing finger and saw nothing. 'You've had too much schnapps,' he said.

'Your people have yet to brew a draft that could get a dwarf drunk,' Gotrek said.

'Only legless...' Felix muttered.

'At least I'm not blind.'

'Just blind drunk.'

'I'm telling you there's a ship there.' Felix squinted into the gloom and began to think the dwarf might be right. There was something large out there, a shadowy presence moving erratically in the deep water.

'I do believe your right,' Felix said. 'I apologise most sincerely.'

'Save your breath,' the Slayer said. 'There's killing to be done.'

'Faster!' Felix said, standing on the prow of the skiff and keeping his eyes fixed on the shadowy shape ahead.

'I'm going as fast as I can, master,' the boatman said, poling with all the energy of an arthritic hedgehog. He was a hefty man, slow-moving and ponderous.

'A one armed man could pole faster,' Gotrek said. 'In fact, I'll bet if I chopped off one of your arms, you could move quicker.'

Suddenly the boatman found a surge of new strength from somewhere and they picked up speed. Felix wasn't sure whether to be glad or not. He was nervous about approaching the skaven ship in this small craft. He wished they had summoned the watch but the Slayer had become overcome with battle frenzy and insisted there was no time to waste. He assured Felix that the commotion they would soon be generating would attract the river patrols. Felix did not doubt that he was right.

As they came closer, he could see that it was a black ship all right, a huge grain barge painted all black and moving swiftly down river. He wondered why the skaven had done this. Certainly black made the ship inconspicuous at night, but during the day the barge would be as noticeable as a hearse in a wedding parade. Maybe it had travelled down river unpainted and they had disguised it this very evening. Maybe they had a concealed base somewhere within a night's sailing upriver. Such a base could be quite some distance away, for a barge could cover a lot of water in one night, moving with the current as this one was.

Felix dismissed all such speculation as pointless. He knew he was only doing it to keep his mind occupied and distracted from fear of the coming encounter.

What were they up to on the barge, he wondered? If they weren't skaven then they were the worst sailors he had ever seen. The barge now appeared to drifting in a great half circle. He could hear a faint muffled drumbeat and the creaking and clashing of oars. It sounded like there was some difficulty in guiding the craft.

'It's them, all right,' Gotrek said. 'skaven are even worse sailors than I'd heard.'

Felix could hear the distant squeaking calls of the skaven now, and knew the Slayer was correct. Unfortunately, the boatman had heard him too.

'Did you say "skaven"?' he asked, superstition and fear engraved across his fat, sweat-sheened face.

'No,' Felix said.

'Yes,' Gotrek said.

'I'm not going anywhere near a barge if there are Chaos-worshipping monsters on board!' the boatman declared.

'My friend was only joking,' Felix said.

'No I wasn't,' Gotrek said.

The boatman stopped poling. Gotrek glared at him.

'I hate boats almost as much as I hate trees,' he said. 'And I hate trees almost as much as I hate elves. And what I particularly hate are people who keep me on boats longer than I have to be on them, when there are monsters to slay and fighting to be done.'

The boatman had become very pale and very still, and Felix was almost sure that he could hear his teeth chatter.

Gotrek continued to rant: 'You will pole this boat till we reach that rat-man barge or I will rip off your leg and beat you to death with it. Do I make myself clear?'

Felix had to concede that the sheer amount of menace the Slayer managed to get into his voice was impressive. The boatmen certainly thought so.

'Perfectly,' he said and began poling with redoubled speed.

AS THEY APPROACHED the black barge, Felix saw a new problem. Their skiff was low in the water but the barge had high sides. On level ground, it would have been a simple climb, but on two moving vessels bobbing on water it was an entirely different proposition. He mentioned this to Gotrek.

'Don't worry,' the Slayer said. 'I have a plan.'

'Now I am worried,' Felix muttered.

'What was that, manling?' The Slayer looked close to berserk rage.

'Nothing,' Felix said.

'Just grab that lantern and be ready to move when I tell you.'

THE SKIFF DRIFTED into contact with the ship. As it did so, Gotrek smashed his axe into the barge's side. It bit deep and held there and the Slayer used it to pull himself up until he reached a porthole.

'Very stealthy,' Felix said sourly. 'Why not give a hearty shout of welcome while you're at it.'

Another smashing stroke saw Gotrek over the ship's side. He stood there for a moment and then lowered the axe, blade first.

'Grab hold,' he roared. Felix leapt up and grabbed hold of the axe shaft with his right hand, while holding the lantern in the other. Gotrek raised the axe one-handed, lifting it up, apparently effortlessly, despite Felix's weight and the uncomfortable angle. He swung the axe inwards over the ship's side and brought Felix with it. Felix dropped to the deck, amazed by the awesome strength the dwarf had just displayed.

'Looks like we're expected,' he said, nodding at the mass of skaven swarming up onto the deck.

'Good,' Gotrek said. 'I need a bit of exercise.'

WHAT WAS THAT, Skitch wondered? He had heard an almighty crash and the sound of wood splintering. Had those buffoons managed to crash the barge onto a sandbar again? He would not have put it past them. They had claimed to be experienced sailors and that crewing a human ship would be no problem. So far that had not proved the case.

If they jeopardised this mission, Izak Grottle would tear them all limb from limb and devour their entrails before their dying eyes, but such thoughts brought Skitch no consolation. He knew he would be the first course at the packmaster's punishment feast.

When he heard the crew's squeaks of alarm, Skitch knew it was even worse than running aground. They had been discovered by a human patrol. He cursed the bad luck which had enabled the humans to discover them. It must have been a million-to-one chance. Now he wished he had brought some rat-ogres after all. He had not done so, for fear that their roars and bellows would give away the ship's position, but that did not seem to matter now.

Part of him wanted to squirt the musk of fear, but then again it was his responsibility to see to his charges. He raced from the cabin into the hold. All around him, massive rats thrashed in their cages, desperate to get free and to eat. Seeing the look of feral hunger in their eyes, Skitch was glad that he had doused himself in oil of swamptoad, a substance that he knew his creations found repellent.

Hearing the sounds of terrible carnage from above, Skitch swiftly began to throw open the cages. The rats swarmed hungrily up the gangplanks, moving towards their living, breathing food.

FELIX LASHED OUT with the lantern. Its flame flared bright as it rushed through the air. The dazzled skaven before him leapt back, momentarily blinded. Felix took advantage of its confusion to stab it through the throat with his sword.

The deck was already slippery underfoot with blood and brains. The Slayer had left an awful trail of destruction behind him. His axe had reduced a dozen skaven to limbless corpses. The others were fleeing backwards or jumping over the side of the barge to avoid him. Felix moved along behind, killing those who sought to outflank the dwarf and putting the dying out of their misery.

His heart beat loudly within his chest. His sword's hilt felt sweaty in his grip but he was not as afraid as he usually was in mortal combat. Compared to some of the fights he had been in, this one was relatively easy. Suspiciously so, in fact, considering there was supposed to be some terrible skaven weapon on board this vessel.

Not that the relative ease of the fight would make much difference, he told himself, springing aside to duck a knife cast by one of the skaven sailors, and lunging forward to take another rat-man through the heart. All it would take would be one lucky blow, and he would be just as dead, as if a rat-ogre had torn him into little pieces.

Concentrate, he ordered himself – and then stopped in horror as the tide of furry forms started swarming up from the hold.

* * *

SKITCH SNUCK UP the stairway and peered out at a scene of terrible violence. A monstrous squat dwarf wielding a flailing great axe had killed half the crew and seemed intent on massacring the other half. In this he was assisted by a tall, blond-furred human who held a lantern in one hand and wicked looking blade in the other. All around, the killer rats gnawed at the bodies of dead and dying skaven.

Skitch froze on the spot and squirted the musk of fear. His paws locked on the last cage, in which frantic rats struggled to get away from the stink of the oil on his fur. Skitch recognised the pair who had invaded the ship. They had become something of a dark legend amongst the skaven besieging Nuln. This was the fearsome pair whom even the gutter runners had failed to slay, who had routed the warlocks of Skryre, whom it was said even Grey Seer Thanquol feared to meet again. They were formidable killers of skaven – and they were here, on this very barge!

Skitch was no warrior and he knew he could be of no aid to the skaven in the battle above. It was possible that even the killer rats would fail to overcome this seemingly invincible twosome. It was plainly his duty, then to escape, carrying the last of the surviving rats, to preserve them for the future when they might be used again.

So thinking, he held the cage high above his head and leapt into the night-black waters.

FELIX WATCHED AS more and more of the huge rats poured from the hold. There was a hunger and madness in their eyes which frightened him, and he wondered could these be the skaven secret weapon? One large fierce brute threw itself at him. He felt the horrid scurry of its paws on his leg. He lashed out, sending the beast flying and stamped down, feeling the spine of another crack beneath the heel of his boot.

He looked around at Gotrek. The Slayer beheaded another of the skaven crew, sending a great fountain of black blood belching into the air. Before the skaven corpse hit the ground, more and more rats had swarmed over it.

Something dropped on to Felix from above. He felt paws scrabbling in his hair, and small sharp teeth nipping his ear. A foul animal stench filled his nostrils. He dropped the lantern and reached up, feeling muscles squirm beneath fur as he

plucked the rat free. Fangs nipped at his fingers as threw the
thing over the side and into the river.

More and more rats dropped from above or pounced from
the deck. He felt like he was in the centre of a swirling storm of
fur. Gotrek stamped and hacked and kicked but he was in the
same position. The rats were too numerous and too fierce to
overcome. If they stayed they would die a horrible death by a
thousand bites.

'Not a death for a Slayer, I would say!' Felix shouted.

'Torch this blasted floating rats' nest!'

'What?'

'Torch it and let's begone!'

Felix looked around and saw the lantern. He picked it up and
threw it with all his force onto the deck. Burning oil spilled
everywhere. Felix had often heard his father say what a danger
fire was on a ship. They were, after all, built of wood and sealed
with inflammable pitch. Felix had never thought he would be
grateful for that fact, but he certainly was now. Flames started
to flicker and dance all around him.

The smell of burning fur and flesh reached his nostrils.
Squeaking rats scurried everywhere, their fur smouldering and
blazing as they tried to escape the hot flames. Some leapt over-
board and plummeted into the water like small living meteors.
Others continued their attack with redoubled fury, as if determined to drag something else down in death with him.

Felix decided that this was their cue to depart.

'Time to go!' he shouted. A backwash of heat blazed towards
him, singeing his hair and eyebrows.

'Aye, manling, I think you are right.'

Felix sheathed his sword, turned and vaulted over the side.
He tumbled into the water, rats falling all around him. After the
heat of the burning ship it was almost a relief to feel the shock
of cold dark water closing over his head. He kicked out and up
and his head broke the surface.

He could see that there were boats all around, come to look
at the fire. Fighting the weight of his scabbard, he struck out for
the nearest vessel.

Sopping wet, Felix sat glumly on the wharf and kept his eyes
peeled. So far there was no sign of the Slayer. He had not seen
Gotrek since he plunged into the water. He wondered if the

dwarf could swim. Even if he could, was it not possible that he had drowned trying to hold on to his precious axe? It would not exactly have been the glorious death he craved.

His clothes were wet and his teeth were starting to chatter but still he sat, wishing that he had some of the schnapps Gotrek had been swigging earlier. Felix wondered about the skaven weapon that was meant to have been on board the Black Ship. He knew now that he would never find out what it was. The barge was a burned out hulk resting on the bottom of the river. The boatmen who had picked him up had held their position in mid-river and watched it burn, before accepting a handful of silver in payment for carrying Felix to the shore.

There was a wet, slapping sound nearby Felix looked warily to his right. One of the huge, hungry rats had made it off the ship then. It clambered up the side of the ladder from the landing stage, shook its fur dry like it was a dog and trotted off up the wharf. Felix watched it go.

Briefly Felix considered finding the boatmen again and going out to search the river for the Slayer. He knew it would be a futile effort; the Reik was too wide and the current too strong. If the Slayer had drowned, doubtless his corpse would eventually be recovered and put on display at the Old Bridge, waiting with all the others the river had taken for someone to come and claim it. Felix could check there tomorrow.

He stood up wearily from the mooring post on which he sat and prepared for the long trudge home. As he did so, he caught sight of a familiar figure, berating an equally familiar boatman who was poling towards the landing stage. Felix waved a welcome.

'Current carried me down river,' Gotrek called, hauling himself up onto the wharf. 'Ran into our old friend here. Took most of the night to get back.'

'Going against the current,' the weary boatman said. He looked as tired as any man Felix had ever seen, and deeply scared too. Felix could guess the nature of the threats which Gotrek had used to motivate him.

'Well,' he said, 'let's get back to the Pig and have some beer. I think we've earned it.'

'Forgive me if I don't join you,' the boatman said. 'And... and there's the small matter of my fee.'

* * *

COLD, WET AND bedraggled, Skitch finally scuttled into the Underways. It had been a truly dreadful night. He had swum through the chilly waters carrying the last cage of rats. After that, he had scuttled along the riverbanks until he found a sewer outflow, and then he had spent the rest of the night wandering through the tunnels until he had found the familiar scent of skaven. Dodging human patrols in the dark, the trail had finally led him here.

He was proud of himself. He had managed a long and difficult trek. He had lost his bifocals and could barely see but he had made it, and he had managed to preserve a cage full of his precious specimens. Better yet, in the cage were several pregnant females so he would easily be able to start all over again. The rats were healthy too. Even now they were showing signs of agitation. Skitch realised it was because they could smell food. He was close to the storage chambers where the supplies for the great invasion force were kept.

Now, he thought, all he needed was a cover story to tell the sentries to explain his business. Easy enough; he would just say that he was bringing food for Izak Grottle. Anybody who knew the packmaster would believe that.

The thought made him titter. He was still tittering when his near-blind eyes failed to pick out the stone in front of his feet and he tripped, sprawling clumsily into the dirt. The cage rolled free from his grip. The battered lock clicked and it sprang open. The killer rats bounded forth and raced off in the direction of the skaven stores.

Skitch groaned. He knew what the consequences of that were going to be. Soon it would not be just Izak Grottle who was hungry.

THE BATTLE FOR NULN

'The days grew darker. Fear and hunger were constant companions. The great skaven plot drew to its inevitable conclusion, and it seemed to be our lot to be drawn into it. And yet, along with terror and horror, there was hope and heroism. As well as loss there was honour. The hour of utmost danger arrived and I pride myself that my companion and I were not found wanting...'

— From *My Travels With Gotrek, Vol. III*,
by Herr Felix Jaeger (Altdorf Press, 2505)

THANQUOL SAT BROODING on his great throne. Around him was marked a pentacle, inscribed with the head of the Horned Rat and surrounded by a double circle of the most potent protective symbols. He had invoked all of the great defensive spells he knew to shield him from the dire forces gnawing at his destiny. These were runes sovereign against curses, diseases, ill-luck and all manner of death-bringing spells. They numbered among the most powerful wards the grey seer had learned in a long career pursuing the Darker Mysteries. It was a measure of how bad the situation had become that Thanquol thought it necessary to expend so much of his carefully hoarded mystical power to invoke them all.

Thanquol lowered his great horned head into his hands and beat a tattoo on his temples with his claws. He was worried. Things were not going according to plan. Events were starting to slip beyond his control, he could sense it. His highly trained grey seer's intuition could feel forces at work here that were sending matters spiralling beyond the ability of any skaven, no matter how clever, to predict.

He was not quite sure how it had all happened. At first everything had gone so well. His agents reported the destruction of the Black Ship and he knew that once more his unwitting pawns, Jaeger and Gurnisson, had done his work for him. Mere days later, the Council of Thirteen had authorised an increase in size of his invasion force. It looked like utter crushing victory over the humans was within his grasp. But then...

But then the accursed plague had started to spread among his own forces. Soon the Underways were full to bursting with sick and dying skaven warriors. As fast as the bodies could be burned, dozens more followed. Even the skaven slaves manning the funeral ovens were falling sick. The symptoms – a hacking snuffling cough, an evil pus filling the lungs and finally a sudden onset of fatal spasms – were remarkably similar to the disease striking down the humans on the surface. Perhaps it was the same plague. It would not be the first time a contagion had made the leap between the two races.

As if the plague were not bad enough, another menace had arisen. The corridors now swarmed with large, fierce hungry rats. They were everywhere, devouring the corpses, eating the food supplies, fighting over scraps, defecating and urinating everywhere, helping spread the cursed disease – and at the same time starving the army. Even now some of them lurked, beady eyed, in the corner of his chamber, avoiding his pentagram but gnawing the furnishings. He could hear some of them moving beneath his throne. They must have been there when he cast his spells. Now they were trapped inside with him.

It would not have been nearly so bad if the offending creatures had not been rats. It was almost a sign that the Horned Rat had turned his snout away from the great invasion force, and withdrawn his blessing from the army. Certainly some of the more superstitious warriors were starting to mutter such things, and none of Thanquol's pointed speeches and sermons had reassured them.

It did no good for him to point out that the humans were suffering just as much, if not more, from these twin catastrophes: their granaries were empty, their food supplies consumed by the verminous host. The skaven warriors simply did not believe him. They did not have access to Thanquol's extensive spy network on the surface. They saw only that they themselves were starving and that their comrades were falling ill, and that there was a good chance that they in turn would be the next to be smitten by the plague. Morale had suffered, and no one knew better than Thanquol that morale was always a chancy thing at best for a skaven army.

He had done his utmost to hunt down those shirkers who muttered disloyal and treacherous remarks. He had assigned elite units of stormvermin to execute deserters on the spot. He had blasted several traitors himself with his most spectacular and destructive spells – but it had all been to no avail. The rot had set in. The army was slowly starting to fall to pieces. And there did not seem to be anything he could do about it.

Thanquol kicked one of the rats from under his feet, where it was gnawing at the bones of the last messenger who had brought him bad news. It flew through the air and impacted on the curtain of spells surrounding the pentagram. Sparks flickered, smoke belched and the rat gave an eerie keening cry as it died. The air was full of the smell of burned fur and scorched flesh as the creature fried in its own body fat. Thanquol's whiskers twitched in appreciation and he gave a brief savage smirk of satisfaction before returning to his brooding.

Since word of the armies' misfortune had filtered back to Skavenblight, no more reinforcements had arrived. It was not quite the overwhelming mass of skaven warriors he had hoped for, but it would be enough, if Thanquol used all his resources of cunning and far-sighted planning. Something would have to be done to save the situation and soon, while there was still an army left that was capable of fighting. He did not doubt that he still had enough troops at his command to overwhelm the human city if they attacked swiftly and savagely and with the advantage of surprise. Even if the army then dissolved, he would have achieved his goal. Nuln would be conquered and Thanquol could report success to the Council of Thirteen. It would then be up to his masters to rush garrison troops here to hold the city. If they did not get here in time that would not be Thanquol's fault.

The more Thanquol thought of it, the more this plan made sense. He could still achieve his assigned mission. He could still grasp his share of glory. He could then shift the blame for anything that happened afterwards to where it belonged – upon his incompetent underlings, and those traitors to the skaven cause who deserted the army just before its hour of triumph.

He reviewed the forces under his control. He still had close to five thousand almost-healthy warriors drawn mostly from Clan Skab. He still had several teams of gutter runners and a cadre of Clan Eshin assassins. The various foolish adventures undertaken by their treacherous leaders had left him with only a token force from Clan Skryre and Clan Pestilens. Izak Grottle and his force of rat-ogres, though, were still a formidable presence.

He knew that a simple frontal assault was not necessarily the best of plans under the circumstances. What he needed was a bold stroke that would lead to certain and overwhelming victory. And he believed he knew how that could be achieved.

Soon, his spies told him, the breeder the humans called the Elector Countess would be giving a masked ball, in a futile effort to distract her court from their troubles. If the palace could be taken with all the human nobles inside, then the human army in Nuln would be left leaderless and easy prey to the skaven assault. If the raid could be timed so that the two attacks were combined, so much the better. On the night the skaven took the palace, the city would also fall in blood and terror. Perhaps, with their chief breeder in Thanquol's clutches, the humans could even be induced to surrender.

It would have to be done soon, if he was to have any hope of success, but at least here was a chance that he could snatch victory from the slavering jaws of defeat.

Before that, though, he had another slight problem. He would have to negate the protective spells surrounding him so he could leave his chamber and begin giving orders. With a long-suffering sigh, Grey Seer Thanquol began the incantations that would let him out from inside his own pentagram.

* * *

FELIX JAEGER KICKED a huge fat rat from underfoot, sending it flying through the air to land in a midden heap. It turned and immediately began to devour the foulness in which it lay. Felix watched in hopeless disgust and despair.

The rats were everywhere, eating anything that was edible and a lot that was not. There were thousands of them, possibly millions. At times, whole streets seemed to be nothing but a seething sea of vermin. His employer, Heinz, had heard tales that they had taken to devouring babies in cribs and small children who got too close to them. Huge packs of the vile beasts flowed across the city streets, and the cats and dogs were too terrified to stop them.

The only good thing was that the rats appeared to be mysteriously short-lived. It looked like they aged months within a few days. But when they died, the rats' corpses lay strewn like some hideous furry carpet across the cobbles. It was not natural. In fact, the whole thing stank of skaven sorcery and Felix wondered if there was some evil purpose to it.

The city of Nuln appeared to be under a curse, Felix thought. The air smelled of sickness and disease, and human flesh burned on great pyres in the square outside the Temple of Morr. Whole tenement buildings had been boarded up, and turned into tombs. Felix shuddered when he thought of the mouldering corpses of the dead within them. Even worse, though, were the thoughts of those who had been entrapped there alive, victims of the plague who no one wanted to help. There were hideous rumours circulating of people recovering from the plague, only to die of starvation There were worse tales of cannibalism and folk feasting on flesh from the corpses of their family and friends. It was a horrifying thought. And it made Felix think that Sigmar and Ulric had turned their gaze from this city.

Ahead of him he heard the rumble of wheels and the tolling of a bell. He stepped aside to let the plague cart pass. The driver was garbed all in black and his face was hidden by a skull mask and a great peaked cowl. On the back of the cart, an acolyte of Morr swung a censer of incense, supposedly to protect him from the plague. It was like watching Death himself ride through the doomed city, accompanied by his servants. Felix could see the rotting corpses piled high on the backboard of the vehicle. The bodies were naked, already stripped of their valuables by their families or bold scavengers. Rats gnawed at the bodies. As Felix watched he saw one tear out an eyeball, and devour it whole.

The plague carts moved constantly through the streets, bells tolling to announce their presence, summoning those still strong and healthy to dispose of the bodies of those who were not. But not even the plague carts were safe. If they stopped for a moment, the rats were upon them, fighting each other to feast upon the corpses.

Felix's belly grumbled, and he pulled his belt a notch tighter. He hoped the others were having more luck in their foraging for food than he was. He had found nothing to eat on sale that had not been contaminated by rat droppings, and even that was being sold for ten times its normal price. Some citizens were getting rich from the ruination of this mighty city. There were always those, he thought, who could find profit in even the most dire of situations.

He wished that Gotrek would give up his mad desire to remain in the city. He had already considered slipping away himself, joining those hosts of the poor and the lowly who had snatched up their few possessions and departed. He had not done so for several reasons. The first and best of them was that he would not desert his friends. The second was a desire to see this thing through to its end. He suspected that soon the dire events would reach their climax, and at least part of him wanted to find out what would happen.

The final reason was simple. He had heard tales that the local nobles had quarantined the city, and that archers were shooting those who tried to depart by the public highways. Many of the barges which had set sail from the docks in the past two desperate weeks had returned, reporting Imperial naval ships on the river sinking any vessel which tried to pass them.

Perhaps a small band moving by night could slip through, but Felix did not want to try it without Gotrek. The lawless lands around the city would be even more dangerous now with all the local soldiers and road wardens enforcing the quarantine and bands of armed men robbing any refugees.

Law and order had already broken down in parts of the city inside the walls. By night gangs of looters roamed the streets searching for food, helping themselves to anything that wasn't guarded by armed men. Only two nights ago a mob had broken into the city granary, despite the presence of several hundred soldiers. They had broken down the gates only to discover the place was empty, filled only with the skeletons of the rats which had gorged themselves on the grain and then died.

A group of feral children was watching him with hungry eyes. One of them was roasting a dead rat on a spit. Normally he would have tossed them a coin out of pity but twice in the past few days he had almost been assaulted by such gangs. They had only turned back, discouraged, when he had drawn his sword and whipped it through the air menacingly.

He remembered the words of Count Ostwald. The city was indeed under siege but it was a siege of a most horrifying type. There were no siege towers. No weapons had been brought to bear except hunger and disease. There was no enemy which could be sought out and battled. Despair was the foe here, and there was no sword with which it could be fought.

Ahead of him lay the Blind Pig. Outside it lolled several men-at-arms mercenaries who had billeted themselves in the inn because they knew it and its owner, and stuck there now in a mass for their own protection. Felix knew them all and they knew him, but even so they watched him warily as he came closer. They were hard men who had decided that since they could not outrun the plague, they might as well be comfortable while they waited for it to strike them down. The Elector Countess was offering double pay to those who helped keep the peace, by reinforcing her guards and the sadly depleted city watch. These men were earning their extra pay.

'Any news?' one of them asked, a burly Kislevite giant known as Big Boris. Felix shook his head.

'Any food?' asked the other, a sour-faced Bretonnian everyone called Hungry Stephan.

Felix shook his head again and stepped past them into the inn. Heinz sat at the table beside the fire, warming his hands. Gotrek sat with him glugging back an enormous stein of ale.

'Looks like it will be rat pie for supper again,' Heinz said. Felix was not quite sure if he was making a joke. 'Young Felix has come back empty handed.'

'At least you still have beer,' Felix said.

'If it were dwarf ale we could live on it and nothing else,' Gotrek said. 'Many a campaign I've fought with nothing in my belly save half a barrel of Bugman's.'

'Unfortunately, it's not Bugman's,' Felix said dryly. Since the food shortages began, the dwarf had taken to reminiscing constantly and in a most annoying manner about the nutrient powers of dwarf ale.

'More skaven have been seen,' Heinz said. The city guard clashed with them in the Middenplatz last night. They seemed to be foraging for food as well, or so the guard claimed.'

'Most likely want to make sure we're starving,' Felix said sourly.

'Whatever's going to happen is going to happen soon,' Gotrek said. 'There's something in the air. I can smell it.'

'It's beer you smell,' Felix said.

'I hear Countess Emmanuelle is throwing a big fancy dress ball,' Heinz said with a grin. 'Maybe you'll be invited.'

'Somehow I doubt it,' Felix said. He had not heard from the palace since he had been summoned by Ostwald two weeks ago to explain the burning of the Black Ship. Of course, since then, all those mansions on the hill had become fortified camps, as the rich and the blue-blooded isolated themselves in an effort to escape the plague. Rumour had it that any commoner even setting foot on those cobbled streets was shot on sight.

'Typical of your bloody human nobles,' Gotrek said and belched. 'The city is going to the dogs and what do they do? Throw a bloody party!'

'Maybe we should do the same,' Heinz said. 'There are worse ways to go?'

'Anybody seen Elissa?' Felix asked, wanting to change the gloomy direction this conversation was taking.

'She left earlier, went for a walk with that peasant lad... Hans, is it?'

Suddenly Felix wished he hadn't asked.

LURK SNITCHTONGUE glanced around the gloomy chamber and controlled the urge to squirt the musk of fear. It took a mighty effort for he could never in all his life recall being cornered by three such fearsome skaven. He stifled a cough and fought to back a sneeze in case either would draw attention to him, but it was no use. Those three sets of malevolent eyes were drawn to his shivering form like iron filings to a magnet. Vilebroth Null, Izak Grottle and Heskit One Eye all stared at him as if he were a tasty morsel. Particularly Izak Grottle.

Lurk wished his body would stop aching. He wished his paws would stop sweating. He wished the pain that threatened to split his skull would go away. He knew that they would not. He knew that he had the plague and he knew that he was going to die – unless Vilebroth Null did as he had promised and interceded for him with the Horned Rat.

Truly, Lurk thought, he was caught with his tail between the cleaver and the chopping block. The only way he could save his life was by doing what the terrifying plague monk leader said. Unfortunately, Vilebroth Null wanted him to betray his master, Grey Seer Thanquol. Lurk shuddered to think of the consequences should that formidable sorcerer find out what had happened. The wrath of Thanquol was not something any sane skaven cared to face.

The three skaven put their heads together once more and started to whisper. Lurk would have given anything to know what they were talking about. On second thoughts, considering they were probably discussing his fate, he might conceivably be able to live without the knowledge. Lurk cursed his own weakness. He had known he was in trouble when he saw who had been waiting in the chamber that Null had led him to. He knew then, all too well, that the weeks of negotiations the abbot had alluded to had paid off, and two of the most powerful factions of skavendom were arrayed alongside Clan Pestilens.

In that secret chamber, far from eavesdroppers and shielded by Null's potent sorcery, Heskit One Eye and Izak Grottle had been waiting. As soon as he saw them, Lurk had known the game was up. Under Null's prodding he had told them everything. He had explained that Thanquol had somehow learned of their schemes (leaving out only his own part in their discovery) and he had told them, too, of the messages Thanquol had sent to their arch enemies, the human Jaeger and the dwarf Gurnisson. It went without saying that these lordly skaven were outraged by what they saw as the grey seer's despicable treachery.

He had sensed their murderous rage in the air and done everything in his power to avoid being the focus of it. He had heard all about the gory details of Clan Skryre's Excruciation Engines, and many times he had shuddered at the tale of how Grottle liked to consume his enemies' entrails before their very eyes while they still lived.

In order to avoid this fate, he had wracked his mind for every little detail he could remember, to convince them that he was co-operating thoroughly. The prospect of immediate painful death overcame any reluctance caused by the thought of what Grey Seer Thanquol might do to him in the future. And, in one small, cunning and deeply hidden part of Lurk's mind, it occurred to him that if these three could be made angry enough to take vengeance on Grey Seer Thanquol, then Thanquol would be too dead to take any revenge on him in turn.

He was pretty sure now that he had succeeded. Heskit One Eye had gnawed his own tail in rage as Lurk explained how the grey seer had sent explicit details to their enemies concerning Clan Skryre's plan to invade the College of Engineering. He had even fabricated a few convincing details of how the grey seer had laughed and gloated about how his stupid enemies would soon fall into his trap. Well, thought Lurk, Thanquol most likely had.

Izak Grottle had become so outraged he even spluttered out a mouthful of food when Lurk explained how Thanquol had told him that the fat fool would never suspect his idiotic plan to smuggle a secret weapon into the city on a converted barge would be betrayed by Thanquol's cunning.

Vilebroth Null called down the curse of the Horned Rat on his rival when Lurk told him how Thanquol, jealous of the favour their god had shown the abbot, decided to remove a dangerous rival by revealing the whereabouts of his secret lair in the human cemetery to his two most trusty agents on the surface, Gurnisson and Jaeger.

'Are you certain the grey seer is in league with those two?' Grottle demanded. 'Absolutely, definitely certain?'

'Of course, mightiest of Moulders. He forced me, on pain of hideous death, to deliver notes to them and they always responded to his instructions, did they not? I can only conclude that either they are in Grey Seer Thanquol's pay or–'

'Or what?' Vilebroth Null burbled.

'No. The thought is too hideous. No true skaven would stoop to–'

'Stoop to what? To what?'

'Or he is in their pay!' Lurk said, amazed by his own powers of invention. This set off another burst of outraged chittering.

'No! No! Impossible,' Heskit One Eye said. 'Thanquol is a grey seer. He would never submit to taking orders from any but another skaven. The thought is ludicrous.'

'And yet…' Vilebroth Null said.

'And yet? And yet?' Izak Grottle said.

'And yet it is indisputable that Grey Seer Thanquol had been in touch with the surface dwellers, and had betrayed our plans to them!' Null said. 'How else could they have got wind of our schemes? How else could such magnificently cunning plans have failed?'

'Are you seriously suggesting that Grey Seer Thanquol is a traitor to the skaven cause? Seriously?' Izak Grottle asked, showing his terrifyingly huge fangs in a great snarl.

'It's possible,' Lurk dared to add.

'All too possible, I fear,' Heskit One Eye said. 'It is the only explanation for why the grey seer would interfere with our mighty machinations, when all we were attempting to do was further the skaven cause.'

'And yet the human and the dwarf are his enemies too. By all accounts they almost killed him in the lair of the human, von Halstadt.'

'And he sent the gutter runners against them,' Vilebroth Null added. 'That was a true contract. Chang Squik still spits when he thinks of his failure.'

'What if Grey Seer Thanquol is cunning enough to use his enemies against us?' Heskit One Eye said excitedly. 'He pits them against us. He cannot lose! He thwarts a rival or we kill his sworn enemies for him.'

There was a moment of silence in the chamber, and Lurk knew that whatever else his enemies thought of the grey seer, they had suddenly gained enormous respect for his cunning. On consideration, he had to admit that he had too. Whatever flaws he might possess, it was hard to dispute that Grey Seer Thanquol was possessed of all the qualities of a truly great skaven.

'Even so, even allowing that Grey Seer Thanquol possesses devilish cunning, he has still betrayed us to the enemy! That is beyond dispute. He has revealed our hidden plans, and the hidden plans of our great clans to the enemy,' Izak Grottle said. 'Grey Seer Thanquol is a traitor and an enemy of all our peoples.'

'I agree,' Heskit said. 'A traitor he most certainly is. And more – he is our personal enemy. He has acted against us all once and almost caused our deaths. Perhaps he will be more successful with his next attempt.'

All three of them shivered when they thought of the daemonically clever intelligence which worked against them. Lurk could see the fear written on their faces, and in the nervous twitching of their whiskers.

'I humbly suggest,' Null said, 'that it might be the will of the Horned Rat that we remove Grey Seer Thanquol from his command of the army, and send him to make his explanations to the Council of Thirteen.'

'I heartily agree with your sentiments. Heartily!' Izak Grottle said. 'But how are we to accomplish this? The traitor remains in command of almost five thousand Clan Skab warriors while our own forces are but a shadow of what they once were.'

'Doubtless as the traitor planned,' Heskit said.

'Doubtless,' the other two agreed simultaneously.

'There is always assassination,' Heskit suggested.

'Possibly! Possibly!' Grottle said. 'But who would take the chance that the Eshin might be deluded enough to report the request for such a thing to the traitor himself?'

'We could do it ourselves,' Vilebroth Null said.

'Grey Seer Thanquol, despite his known treachery, is a lamentably powerful sorcerer,' Heskit One Eye said. 'We might fail and we might die!'

All three shuddered and then, as one, all three pairs of eyes turned on Lurk. He quivered to the soles of his paws for he knew what they were thinking.

'No! No!' he said.

'No?' Heskit One Eye said menacingly, reaching for the butt of his pistol.

'No?' Izak Grottle rumbled hungrily, and licked his lips.

'No?' Vilebroth Null said, hawking a huge lump of green phlegm onto the floor beside Lurk's feet where it bubbled corruptly.

'No! No! Most merciful of masters, I am but a lowly skaven. I possess not your mighty intellects and awesome powers. Any of you might expect to best Grey Seer Thanquol in combat or cunning but not I.'

'Then why should we preserve your life?' Izak Grottle said silkily. 'Why? Speak! Quick! Quick! I am hungry.'

'Because... because...' Lurk floundered around frantically seeking a path out of this hideous maze. He cursed the day he had ever encountered Grey Seer Thanquol or bore his messages to the human and the dwarf. Wait! That might be the answer. Perhaps in the grey seer's own great example was the solution to his problem. 'Because... because there is a better way!'

'Is there?'

'Yes. Yes. One that holds fewer risks and is more certain!'

'You interest me, Lurk Snitchtongue,' Izak Grottle said. 'What is there that you can see that we cannot?'

'Yes! Yes! Go on! Explain!' Vilebroth Null said in his hideous bubbling voice.

'You could use the grey seer's own methods against him!'

'What?'

'He has used Jaeger and Gurnisson against you. Why not use them against him?'

There was another pause while the three great skaven exchanged glances.

'They are certainly formidable,' Vilebroth Null said. 'For non-skaven.'

'Perhaps! Perhaps they could do it!' chittered Heskit One Eye.

'Do you think so? They are not skaven and Thanquol is a grey seer. A grey seer!' Izak Grottle said and banged his fist on the table for emphasis.

'With every humble respect,' Vilebroth Null said, 'you have not encountered this pair. Heskit of Skryre and I have. A more wicked and dangerous set of opponents it is hard to imagine. Even I, with all my magical powers, barely eluded them.'

'They slaughtered well over half of my company,' Heskit said, leaving out his own part in the massacre.

'I defer to your greater experience,' Grottle said 'But the question remains: how will we get them to go after Grey Seer Thanquol?'

'A letter!' Lurk suggested, carried away by the sheer pleasure of plotting.

'Yes! Yes! A letter,' Vilebroth Null said.

'It is fitting that Grey Seer Thanquol should be undone by the device by which he sought to undo us.'

'But where and how will our two assassins get their chance at him?'

'We must wait for the opportunity to arise,' Null said.

'And how will we write this letter?' Grottle asked. 'I for one have no knowledge of these primitive human runes.'

'I have some knowledge of the human script,' Heskit One Eye said almost apologetically. 'I need it for reading human schematics.'

'We must use the exact paper and pen that the grey seer uses,' Grottle said.

'Our friend Lurk can acquire those,' Vilebroth Null said, smiling horribly to reveal rotting teeth.

'And he can deliver the message to, in his usual way,' Heskit said smugly.

'It appears that I won't be eating you today then, Lurk Snitchtongue,' Izak Grottle. said 'We need you alive. Of course, should you attempt to betray us…'

'That will change,' Heskit finished.

Lurk did not know whether to be glad or sorry. He appeared to have prolonged his life but only at the risk of incurring Grey Seer Thanquol's wrath. How did he get himself into these things?

'WE'RE LEAVING THE CITY,' Elissa said challengingly. She glared up at Felix as if expecting him to contradict her. 'Hans and I. We have decided to go.'

'I don't blame you,' Felix said. 'It's a bad place to be and it's going to get worse.'

'Is that all you have to say?'

Felix looked around at the room they had shared during their brief time together. It seemed small and empty, and soon it would seem emptier still, once she had gone. Was there anything more to say? He really could not blame her for wanting to leave and, to be honest, he could see no real future for them together. So why did it still hurt? Why did he have this feeling of hollowness within his chest? Why did he feel this urge to ask her to stay?

'You're going with Hans?' he asked, just to hear some words. She looked at him coldly and crossed her arms together under her breasts defensively.

'Yes,' she said. 'You're not going to try and stop us, are you?'

She seemed almost to want him to say yes, he thought. 'It's not very safe outside the city right now,' he said.

'We're only going back to our village. It's less than a morning's walk.'

'Will they take you? I hear that people from the city are being stoned and shot with arrows if they go near villages and farms. In case they have the plague.'

'We'll survive,' she said, but she sounded less sure of herself. 'Anyway, it can't be worse than it is here, with the plague and the gangs and the rats and all. At least back in the village they know us.'

'They certainly know Hans. I thought you said the elders hated him.'

'You would cast that up, wouldn't you? They'll take us back. I'll tell them we're going to be married. They'll understand.'

'Are you? Going to be married, I mean.'

'I suppose so.'

'You don't sound very enthusiastic.'

'Oh Felix, what else am I supposed to do? Spend the rest of my life being pawed by strangers in bars? Going about with footloose mercenaries? It's not what I want. I want to go home.'

'You need any money?' he asked.

Suddenly she looked a little shifty. 'No,' she said. 'I'd best be going. Hans is waiting.'

'Be careful,' he said and meant it. 'It's not a safe city out there.'

'You should know,' she said. Suddenly she leaned forward and kissed him passionately on the mouth. Just as he was about to take her in his arms, she broke free and made for the door.

'You look after yourself now,' she said, and he thought he detected a glimmer of tears in the corner of her eyes. Then she was gone.

It was only afterwards, when he checked the loose floorboard that he discovered the purse of money Otto had given him was gone. He lay on the bed, unsure whether to laugh or to cry. Well, he thought, let her have the money. The chances were he would not live long enough to spend it himself.

GREY SEER THANQUOL glanced around the chamber at the assembled skaven captains. His burning gaze seemed to defy anyone to speak out. No one did.

Lurk counted the commanders present. All of the Clan Skab leaders were here, plus Izak Grottle, Vilebroth Null and Heskit

One Eye. Chang Squik, the Clan Eshin assassin skulked in one corner, glaring occasionally at Lurk with hate-filled eyes. He had not forgotten what Lurk had said about him on that long ago day when the grey seer had humiliated them both in front of the whole army.

The grey seer threw his arms wide. Trails of fire followed his paws as he gathered magical power. That got everyone in the room's attention, Lurk thought. Suddenly all eyes were riveted on Thanquol as if, with a single gesture, he might choose to annihilate anyone who did not look at him. That was certainly a possibility, Lurk thought. If he recognised the signs correctly, the grey seer had consumed an awful lot of warpstone powder.

Lurk shivered and continued to chew on the foul herbs that Vilebroth Null had given him to abate the plague. He fought down the urge to check within his breastplate and make sure the parchment and quill he had stolen from Thanquol's private stock were not sliding into view. He knew that nothing would draw attention to him quicker. He reassured himself that they were there. He could feel the nib of the pen poking into the tender fur beneath his armpit.

'Tonight is the night you have all been waiting for!' Thanquol said. ' Tonight we will smash-crush the humans once and for all. Tonight we will invade the city and enslave all the occupants. Tonight we will strike a blow for the Under Empire and the skaven nation that will long be remembered!'

Thanquol paused impressively and glanced around the room once more, as if waiting for an interruption. No one dared to speak but Lurk saw Null, One Eye and Grottle exchange glances, before looking at him. He hoped for all their sakes that the grey seer had not noticed. He glanced nervously at Thanquol, but fortunately the grey seer seemed to be caught up in the flow of his own mad eloquence.

'We will grind the humans beneath the iron paw of our massed skaven army. We will carry them off into inevitable slavery. Their wealth will be ours. Their city will be ours. Their souls will be offered screaming to the Horned Rat.'

Thanquol paused once more and Izak Grottle found the courage to ask the question that Lurk could tell had been on everyone's mind.

'And how is this to be accomplished, great leader?'

'How? How indeed! By a plan at once simple and yet staggeringly cunning. By a use of force and sorcery which will be talked about down the ages. By overwhelming ferocity and superior skaven technology. By–'

'By what precise means, Grey Seer Thanquol?' Vilebroth Null interrupted. 'I humbly suggest that, like every skaven out of runthood, we are all familiar with the general methods of attack.'

For a moment Lurk could tell that Thanquol was weighing up the pros and cons of blasting the plague monk into his component atoms for his insolence. He was glad when prudent skaven caution won out and the grey seer continued to speak.

'I was just coming to that, as you would have discovered had you not interrupted me. We will attack through the sewers. Each of you will lead your assigned force to a point marked on the map.' With this, the grey seer indicated the complex mass of symbols inscribed on the large sheet of parchment hanging behind him. Many of the assembled leaders leaned forward to see where they would be sent.

'I do not see your rune on this plan,' Heskit One Eye said. 'What will you be doing, grey seer?'

Thanquol glared at him with burning red eyes. 'I will be where you would expect your leader to be, performing the most difficult and dangerous of tasks.'

Silence fell over the assembled skaven leaders. This was not in point of fact where they would have expected their leader to be at all. They would expect him to be safely in the rear directing operations. The warpstone Thanquol had consumed appeared to make him talkative. He spoke on, into the silence.

'I will be leading the crowning attack. I will lead the assault by our stormvermin which will seize the palace of the breeder, Emmanuelle, and capture all of the city's rulers. Tonight they are having a ball, one of their purposeless social events. I will fall on them by surprise and have them all in my paw. Leaderless, the humans will surely fall to our attack.'

There were more murmurings from the assembled skaven. It was a good plan, and a bold one. Lurk wondered if any of the others saw what he saw. The grey seer had chosen his place in the assault carefully. By managing this bold stroke, by capturing the human leaders, he would assure himself of the lion's share of the glory. Further, it would undoubtedly be a lot safer attacking a bunch of humans and their breeders dressed for a ball than fighting massed troops in the city.

'Such a position is too dangerous for a leader of your great cunning,' Heskit One Eye said. 'It would be a tragedy if the genius of Thanquol was to be lost to skavendom. To prevent such a tragedy, I will lead this assault. I will shoulder the terrible risks.'

Lurk covered his mouth with a paw to prevent a snigger escaping, at least one other skaven had realised what was going on.

'No! No!' Izak Grottle said. 'I and my rat-ogres are ideally suited for this task. We will overwhelm all–'

Grottle's words were drowned out by the shouts of all the other skaven volunteers. Thanquol let them call out for a few minutes before silencing them with a gesture.

'Unfortunately, it will require my potent sorcery to effect entrance to the palace. I must be present.'

'Then I will gladly lay down my life to guard you,' Izak Grottle said, obviously determined to be present to share in the triumph.

'And I,' Heskit One Eye said.

'And I,' shouted every other skaven present, save Lurk.

'No! No! I appreciate your concern, brother skaven, but your leadership will be required on other, no-less-critical parts of the battlefield.'

It was obvious that Thanquol intended to share his glorious triumph with no one. The assembled war leaders subsided into disappointed chittering.

'I have here a route map, and a schedule for each of you, inscribed with precise instructions. All of you, that is, except for Lurk Snitchtongue. I would have a word with Lurk in private.'

Lurk felt his heart start to race, and it was all he could do to prevent himself squirting the musk of fear. Had the grey seer found out about his plotting with the three clan representatives? Was he about to enact some terrible revenge? Was there any way Lurk could avoid this meeting?

He turned desperate eyes on his three co-conspirators and saw that they glared at him evilly. If looks could kill, Lurk knew, those three would have put him in a coffin. They feared he would betray them to save his own skin – and of course they were right.

As the war leaders trooped forward one by one to receive the grey seer's blessing and their final instructions, Lurk prayed to the Horned Rat to preserve him.

FELIX WANDERED AROUND until he arrived at his brother's town-house. He was not surprised to see that it was locked and guarded. He was surprised to find that Otto and his wife had not fled the city, and furthermore that the guards recognised him and allowed him to pass.

Otto waited in his study to greet him. He was still working, inscribing things in his ledgers and writing dispatches that might never be received intended for other branches of the Jaeger businesses. Felix was strangely proud of him at that moment. It took a great deal of courage to continue to work under these trying circumstances.

'What can I do for you, Felix?' Otto asked, without looking up.

'Nothing. I just came by to see how you were?'

'Fine!' Otto gave a wan smile. 'Business is booming.'

'Is it?'

'Of course not! Rats are eating the stock. The workers are stealing everything that isn't nailed down. The customers are dying of the plague.'

'Why haven't you left town?'

'Someone has to remain and look after our interests. This will all pass you know. Disturbances always do. Then there'll be the business of rebuilding. Folk will need wool and timber and building materials. They'll need luxury goods to replace what's been looted. They'll need credit to buy it all. And when they do, Jaegers of Altdorf will still be here.'

'I'll bet you will.'

'And what about you?' Otto asked, looking up at last.

'I'm waiting to see the end of this all. I'm waiting for the skaven to show themselves.'

'You think they will?'

'I'm sure of it. I'm certain that this is all their doing some-how.'

'How can you be so sure?'

Felix looked at his brother long and hard. 'Can you keep secrets?'

'You know I can.'

Felix decided that it was true. In his business Otto would need a great deal of discretion.

'What I'm going to tell you could get me hanged or burned at the stake.'

'What you and the dwarf did in Altdorf could get you that already. You're a long way from the capital, Felix, and I'm not going to turn you in.'

Felix guessed that was true, and somehow he felt a need to tell someone exactly what had happened. So he told Otto the full tale of his encounters with the skaven, from the first day in the sewer to the last battle on the barge. He omitted nothing, including his duel with von Halstadt. Otto looked at him with an expression that went from incredulity to seriousness to, finally, belief.

'You're not making this up, are you?'

'No.'

'You always did take those hero tales you read too seriously, little brother.'

Felix smiled and Otto smiled back. 'I did, didn't I?'

'What is it like, living in one?'

'Not what I expected. Not what I expected at all.' Felix decided it was time to say what he had come to say.

'Otto – I think you and your wife should leave the city. I think the skaven are going to come soon, and that things will not be pleasant.'

Otto laughed. 'We have armed servants here and this house is a fortress, Felix. We will be much safer here than in the country.'

Felix knew his brother well enough to understand that there would be no persuading him. 'You know your own business best,' he said.

Otto nodded. 'Now come eat, man. I can hear your stomach rumbling from here.'

'WHAT IS IT, mightiest of mages? What do you require?'

Lurk Snitchtongue bowed and scraped before Grey Seer Thanquol, searching for the words that would save him. He felt sure that the grey seer's supernatural powers had enabled him to see Lurk's treachery and that now he was going to be punished. The terrible glow of warpstone still filled Thanquol's eyes, and Lurk could almost sense the dark energies that seethed within him.

'It concerns Vilebroth Null,' Grey Seer Thanquol said with an evil smile.

Lurk felt his musk glands contract. He would have spoken then but his tongue was tied. It felt like it had suddenly stuck to the roof of his mouth. All he could do was nod his head in a guilty fashion.

'And Heskit One Eye,' Thanquol said, his malevolent grin stretching still further. A plea for mercy stuck in Lurk's throat. He tried to force it out but it just would not come.

'And Izak Grottle,' Thanquol added. His burning eyes held Lurk pinned to the spot. The smaller skaven felt like a bird paralysed before the gaze of a serpent. He nodded again and fell to his knees paws clutched before him in a gesture of abasement.

'Get up! Get up!' Thanquol said. 'They are not so fearsome. No! Not at all. Now is the time to be rid of them once and for all and you will help me do it!'

'Get rid of them, mightiest of masters?'

'Yes! Did you see the way they questioned me when I was giving orders to the army? Did you see the way they tried to steal the glory from my brilliant plan. My mind is made up! I will tolerate them no longer. This night they will die!'

'How? How, lord of seers? Will you blast them with magic?'

'No! No! Idiot! My hands must remain clean. No – we will use the tried and tested method. I will inform my two pawns of their whereabouts. This evening, when the battle comes, my enemies will meet with the dwarf's axe. Then, hopefully, the rest of their force will bring down that interfering twosome.'

'How will you engineer this, cleverest of conspirators?'

'I have assigned all three to one strike group. Its place of emergence is very close to the burrow where Jaeger and Gurnisson and a horde of mercenaries dwell. You are also assigned to that group. You will go through first, on pretext of scouting, and you will warn that horrid pair of what is about to occur!'

'Yes! Yes! Consider it done, most supreme of schemers!'

'Take this message and see that it is delivered. Then flee to my presence and I will see that you are…suitably rewarded for your loyalty!'

Lurk did not like the emphasis the grey seer put on that last phrase at all, but he took the letter and, still bowing, backed from Thanquol's presence.

* * *

FELIX RANG DREXLER'S doorbell more from hope than any real belief that the doctor would be there, so he was pleasantly surprised when the viewing slot was opened and a servant peered out.

'Oh, it's you, Herr Jaeger,' he said. 'Are you alone?'

'Yes, and I would speak with your master.'

'Best come in then.' Felix heard bolts being thrown and the door creak open. He glanced back over his shoulder to make sure that no bandits were poised to take advantage of the situation, then hurried through. The servant slammed the door behind him.

Felix strode through the corridors of the doctor's mansion. It felt like years since he had first come here with Elissa, though in fact it had only been weeks. How had things changed so quickly, he asked himself, suppressing a flash of loneliness and sadness at the thought the woman was gone. He shook his head and smiled sadly, knowing that her departure was one of the reasons why he was here. He was just moving around to keep himself busy and avoid thinking about things.

The servant showed him into Drexler's study. The doctor sat by his fire, looking drained and weary. Weeks of treating plague victims had obviously taken something out of him. There were lines on his face that had not been there when Felix had last seen him, and a hint of pallor beneath his tan.

'Herr Jaeger, what can I do for you?'

'I've brought back your book,' Felix said, producing the doctor's copy of Leiber's work. 'I would have returned it sooner but I have been very busy.'

The doctor smiled wanly. 'So Herr Ostwald has told me. It seems Aldred chose a worthy successor for ownership of his blade.'

'I'm not so convinced,' Felix said, gesturing vaguely in the direction of the city. 'All of my and Gotrek's efforts seem to have come to naught.'

'Do not be sure of that, Herr Jaeger. What man can tell of all the consequences of his actions? It may be that things would be a lot worse without your intervention.'

'I wish I could believe that but I do not think it is so.'

'Only Sigmar can judge a man's actions, Herr Jaeger, and I believe that in some ways he smiles upon you and your friend. You are still here, aren't you? How many others would be able to say the same if they had undergone your adventures? I know I could not.'

Felix looked at him, struck by the fact that there was some truth in the man's words. 'You are a good doctor, Herr Drexler. I feel better just for talking to you.'

'Perhaps you should wait until you see my bill before you thank me,' Drexler said. His smile showed that he was joking. 'You found what you wanted in the book?'

Felix set it down on the table. 'More than I ever wanted. I'm not sure that it helps knowing how evil and depraved the rat-men are.'

'Again, Herr Jaeger, who knows what knowledge might prove useful? Have some food. I have managed to preserve something from the afflictions of our city.'

Felix thought guiltily of the meal which he had already eaten at Otto's. His stomach felt full but, well, on the other hand he had no idea when he might eat again. If Gotrek's theory about the skaven's imminent onslaught was going to be correct, he was going to need all his strength. 'Why not?' he said. 'It may be the last meal I get!'

'Why do you say that?' Drexler asked, and Felix decided that now was the time to deliver his warning.

'Because I believe that the skaven will attack the city soon. I also think that you should leave. I say this as a friend.'

'I thank you for the warning, Herr Jaeger, but I cannot go today. You see, tonight I am attending a ball at the palace, in the presence of Elector Countess Emmanuelle herself.'

Somehow the thought sent a shiver running down Felix's spine.

LURK KNEW IT was going to be bad when he felt the heavy hand of one of Izak Grottle's troops on his shoulder and he was hustled unceremoniously into the fat skaven's palanquin. He found himself looking up into the folds of flesh beneath the chin of the gigantic Moulder packmaster. Grottle's huge belly virtually pressed him back against the cushions of the palanquin with a life of its own.

'Now where are you going?' Izak Grottle asked. 'Where indeed?'

Lurk thought fast. He did not like the hungry gleam that had appeared in the packmaster's eye. He thought of the letter that he bore for the grey seer. He thought of the disease that threatened to fill his lungs with pus, unless the abbot continued to intervene on his behalf with the Horned Rat. 'I was just on my way to see you, most majestic of Moulders.'

'Then it is fortunate I have found you. Tell me, what is it that you are carrying?'

Lurk told him everything. He had expected Izak Grottle to reach out with one podgy hand and snap his neck but the packmaster merely laughed a rich booming laugh. 'It would appear the grey seer has been too clever for his own good. You will deliver your message but it will be one I shall dictate and Heskit One Eye shall write down.'

'As you wish, most potent of all packmasters.'

FELIX TRUDGED BACK towards the Blind Pig, feeling almost too full to move. Over the past few weeks his stomach had shrunk and what once might have been a normal meal now left him feeling bloated. Two such meals in one day made him feel like he was going to explode.

He wore a new herbal talisman given to him by the doctor and he carried another within his pouch for Gotrek. It was a slight reassurance to him. So far, he had not caught the plague, but that might not signify anything. Nobody else he knew had either. Perhaps it was mere chance that had spared them, or perhaps it was the fact that Heinz insisted they kill every last rat they spotted around the Pig. Felix could not even begin to guess. He only knew that he was grateful to Drexler for the gift.

He looked around into the gathering gloom and shivered. The city looked like a mere ghost of the thriving metropolis it had been when he and Gotrek first arrived. Many buildings had burned down. More were empty. No lights shone in most of the tenements. The bustling life of the streets had been replaced by an aura of fear. The only ones likely to be abroad now were predators – and their victims.

He felt the flesh crawl between his shoulder blades, and was suddenly convinced that someone was watching him. He turned his head to look at the mouth of a nearby alley. The whoosh of air alerted him too late. Something hit him on the skull. He shook his head in response, half expecting a surge of pain. None came. He raised his fingers to his brow but felt no blood. He looked down to see what had hit him and saw that it was a rolled up piece of parchment, similar to all the others which had borne a warning concerning the skaven. He bent down to pick it up and glanced round at the same time. He heard the sound of scuttling down a nearby alley, and realised that it was most likely whoever had thrown the paper.

Without thinking, Felix scooped up the parchment and raced off in pursuit. He stretched his long legs to the maximum as he ran down the alley. Ahead of him he thought he caught sight of a cowled figure. Was it possible that that was a long rodent-like tail protruding out from under that monkish robe? All too possible, he decided.

The figure had reached the end of the alley and turned hastily down another of the winding maze of streets. Felix raced past open doorways, scattering amazed-looking beggars and tread-ing monstrous rats underfoot as he raced onwards. His heartbeat sounded loud in his chest and sweat poured down his face. He felt nauseous and wished that he had not eaten quite so much at Doctor Drexler's, particularly after the heavy meal at his brother's. He clutched the scroll tight in one hand and restrained the scabbard flapping on his belt with the other.

'Stop, skaven!' he shouted. His words had no effect on the fleeing rat-man. All the beggars leapt for cover within the near-est door. Felix raced on.

Why am I doing this, he asked himself? As far as he knew, the skaven ahead had done them nothing but favours by warning him of his brethren's plans. In that case, why was he fleeing, Felix asked himself – but he already had an answer. Who could tell why the rat-men did anything? Who could guess at the rea-sons of a creature that was not even human?

Felix's heart leapt as he saw the rat-man trip and fall. Perhaps he could overhaul it after all. Caught up in the fury of the chase, he desperately wanted to do so. He wanted to grab the rat-man and look into its eyes and question it. Not, he thought, that it would likely understand the human tongue. According to Leiber, the rat-men had their own languages including a number of specialised dialects used by the various clans. Still, at least this one knew enough Reikspiel to write its notes, Felix thought, so perhaps it could be interrogated. He ran faster, hope blazing in his breast that at last he might be able to get some answers to his questions about the skaven.

* * *

LURK GLANCED BACK over his shoulder and chittered a curse. It was no use. That foolish human was still following him! Why? What did it hope to achieve by persecuting him in this way? Why could it not leave him alone and read the message that Heskit One Eye had inscribed on the parchment? If it did that, it would surely realise that it had more urgent business this night – like heading to the palace and thwarting Grey Seer Thanquol's plan.

Life was so unfair, Lurk thought unhappily. Here he was, in poor health, brow-beaten by some of the most ferocious skaven who ever lived, about to make an enemy of one of the mightiest sorcerers of his race. His head hurt. His eyes burned with fever. His heart felt like it was going to give out from the strain of this race. His lungs felt like they were on fire.

And where was he? Not in some comfortable burrow back in Skavenblight, but being pursued through the horribly open streets of this human city by a large and terrifying warrior. It was like some dreadful nightmare. The sheer unfairness of it all galled Lurk. What had he ever done to deserve this?

He shot another backward glance and saw that his pursuer was starting to narrow the distance that separated them. Lurk prayed that night would come, or that mist would arise. He felt certain that in darkness and shadow, he could lose the human. Or if he could just reach the hidden entrance to the sewers where the bulk of the invasion force waited, he would find safety. He risked another look back – and cursed as he felt his feet go out from beneath him.

He knew he should have looked where he was going!

FELIX CLOSED THE gap quickly as he saw the skaven scrabble to its feet. He wondered briefly whether he should pause and draw his sword. He decided against it. He would lose ground again and the skaven did not appear to be armed. He could always produce his blade when he had the rat-man cornered. Breathing heavily, he ran on.

PRAISE THE HORNED RAT, thought Lurk! Ahead of him he could see the opening into the sewers. He knew that he merely had to leap down it and he would be safe in the comforting bosom of the skaven army. Down there waited Vilebroth Null, Izak Grottle, Heskit One Eye and all their soldiers. But as he gathered his legs beneath him in preparation for the mighty leap that would carry him to safety, he felt a powerful hand clamp onto his shoulder.

FELIX FELT THE skaven stiffen as he grabbed it. He pulled hard, spinning it around – and almost let go as the wicked-looking creature glared up at him with hate-filled eyes. Of all the rat-men he had ever encountered this was the most sly and nasty looking. It was smaller and thinner than most but had a wiry strength that made it difficult to hold.

'Now,' Felix panted. 'Tell me what you're doing here!'

A sudden pain flared in his left wrist as the rat-man bit it. Overcome by shock, Felix let go.

LURK BROKE FREE from his tormentor's grip and dropped gratefully into the sewer. Breaking the surface, he looked around and saw that the skaven assault force had already gathered. A horde of rat-men waited in attendance. He looked around and saw Izak Grottle and the others waiting in the leaders position at the rear. A stormvermin clawleader looked down at Lurk as he pulled himself out of the filth and shook his fur clean.

'What is it?' the clawleader asked.

'I am pursued...' Lurk gasped without thinking. Before he could expand on his statement the clawleader reacted, keen to grab some glory.

'Right!' the skaven shouted. 'Quick-quick! Charge!'

FELIX INSPECTED HIS bitten wrist. It did not look too bad, he thought. Then he glanced up in horror as he heard the first of the rat-men begin to swarm up the sewer access ladder. Only moments before he had debated whether to pursue the escaping skaven into the sewers. Now he saw that it would have been suicidal. Already the leering face and snapping jaws of a burly, black-armoured rat-man had emerged into the gloom. Felix wasted no time. He launched a heft kick that sent the furiously squeaking skaven tumbling back down among his fellows, and then turned and ran.

Moments later a mass of furiously chittering skaven warriors emerged into the alley. Somewhat ahead of schedule, the great invasion of Nuln had begun.

* * *

'No! No!' LURK squeaked as the tightly packed mass of skaven warriors surged past him. The press of furry bodies pushed him back into the foul waters of the sewer. For a horrible moment he felt like he was going to drown, but then he broke surface once more, just in time to see the last of the stormvermin clambering with unrestrained fury into the light. Above him, the mad face of Vilebroth Null leered down.

'Did you deliver the message?' burbled the low abbot of the plague monks.

'Yes! Yes!' Lurk chittered, thinking that now was possibly not the best time to tell Null that the skaven troops above were now doing their best to hunt down and kill the man to whom the message had been delivered.

FELIX COULD HEAR the shouts of his foul pursuers behind him, and the screams of the unfortunates who got in their way. A quick glance over his shoulder revealed that the skaven were putting anyone in their path to the sword. The sight of it sickened Felix but in a way he was also glad. Every little pause and hesitation enabled him to increase his lead over them.

His wrist throbbed where the little skaven has bit it. He noticed that the scroll it had thrown at him was crumpled in his hand. Briefly he toyed with throwing it away. Instead he thrust it inside his tunic and continued to sprint. At least he was not weighed down with heavy armour the way his pursuers were.

The thought trickled slowly into his mind that the skaven invasion must have started. The sight of so many heavily armed rat-men in the streets could only mean that they were ready to begin an all-out attack on the city and that they had no fear of the defenders. Right now, Felix guessed their confidence was justified. He could not see a single member of the city guard. Of course, most of them were probably up in the Noble Quarter around the palace, making sure all the guests at the countess's party were safe.

Felix slammed into a wall and rebounded again, turning quickly to hurtle down a connecting alley. This area or narrow lanes and alleys was a veritable maze and he was not at all sure he was heading in the right direction. He could only move as quickly as possible and listen to the noise of his pursuers, praying that he did not blunder round in a complete circle and run right into them again.

He searched his brain for a plan, but all he could come up with was to get back to the Blind Pig as quickly as possible and warn Gotrek and the others. At least there was a strong force of mercenaries and a potential rallying point for any human warriors. Now all he had to do was find a way out. His heart filled with fear, he continued to run.

LURK TRIED TO keep himself right in the middle of the teeming mass of warriors. He had endured enough excitement for one evening and did not need anymore. He focused his attention on keeping Izak Grottle in sight. The Moulder packmaster's bodyguard of huge rat-ogres represented his best hope of protection in the coming conflict. Lurk seriously doubted that anyone would want to attack the huge creatures.

So far, the assault appeared to be going well. The skaven force in this area had met with little resistance. He could smell burning and the distinctive oil-and-naphtha smell of warpfire throwers. From the backwash of light off to the south he realised that some of the Clan Skryre warpfire throwers were using their weapons on the buildings. Squinting through the shadows, Lurk could see jets of flame squirting out at the tenements. Fire licked and curled at the woodwork. Stone began to splinter and crack under the sheer heat generated by the awesome skaven weapons.

Lurk was not so certain that this was a good idea. He was not sure Grey Seer Thanquol would approve of such indiscriminate destruction of his future property. Of course, if the message Lurk had delivered achieved its goal, the grey seer would be in no position to voice his objections. He would be dead.

Lurk wondered whether the human, Jaeger had managed to escape. Part of him hoped not. He could still remember the wretched human's hand clamped on his shoulder, and the pain where the iron fingers had bit into his fur. There was no sign that he had been taken prisoner, nor any sign of his corpse. Not that that meant anything, Lurk thought. In these winding alleys, already crammed with skaven victims, a body could be lying almost anywhere. Already the skaven force had started to break up and fan out. Some of the warriors, meeting little resistance had already begin looting and eating.

Lurk was not sure that this was a good idea either. Surely things could not go so easily. Surely they would meet more resistance than this? Where were the accursed human warriors? His questions received no answers. All around, buildings were beginning to burn.

CHANG SQUIK CLAMBERED up the sheer face of the cliff leading to the palace of the human breeder, Emmanuelle. The line attached to his grapnel held firm. The heavy weight of the rune-encrusted seeing stone entrusted to him by Grey Seer Thanquol personally rested securely in the knapsack on his back. Chang Squik braced himself and scrabbled with the claws of his feet for purchase on the smooth stone of the cliff face. Things were going well. In a few more minutes he would be in position with the stone placed within the halls of the palace, ready for whatever mighty magic the grey seer had planned. He would have played his part in the skaven victory today – and gone some way towards mitigating the disgrace of his failure to kill the dwarf and his human henchman. Hopefully that painful memory was something which could be laid to rest before this night was over too.

Suddenly below him, in the distance, he heard the faint but distinct chittering of skaven war cries, and the answering screams of their human victims. Twisting on the rope he glanced back and saw the eerie glow of what could only be warpfire throwers being used in the distance. Surely the attack had not begun already? The fools were supposed to wait until he was within the palace and Grey Seer Thanquol's plan had been implemented!

He cursed and redoubled his efforts to climb. The noise and the sight of the fire would draw human sentries and other spectators to the battlements above him. Chang Squik could ill-afford to have his grapnel line discovered. All it would take would be one human with a knife to slice the black rope, and his long and honourable career would come to an end. Controlling his urge to squirt the musk of fear, the Clan Eshin assassin pulled himself upward.

THE STRANGE GREENISH light in the sky confirmed Felix's suspicions that the invasion had indeed begun. He recognised the colour of the flames as being the same as those produced by the strange weapons which had destroyed the College of Engineering. Looking back, he could see fire leaping from the rooftops of blazing tenements. The college had been a separate building isolated behind the walls of its own grounds. The buildings here in this part of the city, in contrast, were packed as tight together as drunks in a crowded tavern. Many of them leaned conspiratorially over alleyways. Some were linked by high bridges far above the ground, and by supporting arches in the alleys. Most had thatched roofs and wooden support beams. Felix shivered in spite of himself. The conflagration was going to spread quickly. The city was going to burn.

Still, at least for the moment he seemed to have lost his pursuers. There was not a rat-man in sight. Better yet, he recognised this street at last and knew that he was not too far from the Blind Pig. He paused, leaning forward with his hands braced on his knees, panting for breath and shaking his head to clear the sweat from his eyes. Once he reached the tavern he would be able to put together a plan with Gotrek and the others.

Suddenly from the mouth of a nearby alley he heard a shrieked war cry. Looking up, he saw a large group of skaven erupt out into the cobbled street. Gathering all his energy, Felix ran for his life.

GREY SEER THANQUOL led his elite force of stormvermin into position. His keen grey seer's intuition told him that directly above them was the palace. He could sense its presence. He trampled the corpse of the sewer watchman beneath his paw and allowed himself to gloat. So far the Clan Eshin assassins had done their work. Every human in the sewers who might have given away their presence was dead. By now, teams of gutter runners would be in position at the base of the cliff on which the castle rested. Hopefully, by now Chang Squik would be in position.

Thanquol produced the scrying stone from within his robes. He began to mutter the incantations which would link it to the twin carried by the leader of the Eshin forces. Now would be the time for a mighty feat of sorcery, one that would grant the skaven swift and inevitable victory. In order to perform it, Thanquol knew he would need vast amounts of power and therein lay the danger.

In order to acquire enough mystical energy to power the spells that he needed to perform, Thanquol would have to consume an enormous amount of warpstone, and that had its dangers. This was not the mild, refined stuff which made up his snuff. No, this was the pure product, the very essence of magic, concentrated and purified by skaven alchemists. It was a substance capable of providing its user with awesome power, but its use carried equally awesome dangers. Many grey seers had been driven over the edge into madness by the corrosive effects of the substance on their sanity. Others had been reduced to mindless, Chaos-spawn by its mutating effects. Taken in large enough doses by those of insufficiently strong will, warpstone could devolve its user into a formless amorphous thing.

But what was that to him, mightiest of grey seers? Thanquol was a practised user of warpstone, was capable of consuming it in gigantic quantities without ill effect. The things that happened to all those others could not happen to him. Definitely, positively not...

For a moment, brief niggling doubt flared in Thanquol's mind. What if there was something wrong with the warpstone? What if it were not pure but contaminated with other stuff? Such things had happened. What if Thanquol were not as strong as he believed? Mistakes in dosage were always possible. But only for a second did the grey seer hesitate, before his natural confidence in his own mighty abilities returned. He was not one to flinch from the dangers of warpstone. In fact, he admitted to himself, he rather enjoyed it. He reminded himself of this as he reached into his pouch and put the first luminous piece of warpstone onto his tongue. It tingled even as he consumed it. Now memories of his long-gone youth came back to him. He recalled his initiation into the use of warpstone.

No, thought Thanquol, there was nothing to fear here. So thinking, he began preparing himself, making himself ready for when the correct time came to cast the spell which would grant his forces victory.

Ahead Felix could see the lights of the Blind Pig. A wave of relief passed through him. If the tavern did not quite represent safety, at least it had to be better than this nightmare chase through the darkened streets with a horde of shrieking rat-men on his trail. He could see Boris and Stephan and a host of their companions standing in the street, shielding their eyes as they studied the distant fires.

'Beware! Skaven!' Felix shouted and saw them all reach for their weapons. In moments, swords glittered in the half-light of the burning city. From inside the tavern a number of armoured figures spilled out into the gloom. Felix was relieved to see the massive squat figure of Gotrek among them. There was something enormously reassuring under these circumstances about the massive axe clutched in his hands.

Felix raced up to the warriors as they braced themselves for the skaven attack. Behind him the skaven, unwilling or unable to give up the heady rush of the chase, came on like an avalanche of fur and fury.

Felix made his way through the throng to stand beside Gotrek. The Slayer had the usual look of mad joy in his one good eye that he always got before combat.

'I see you found our scuttling little friends, manling,' he said, running his thumb along the blade of his axe until a bright red bead of blood appeared.

'Yes,' Felix gasped, struggling to get his breath back before the combat began.

'Good. Let's get killing then!'

DOCTOR DREXLER LOOKED around him. Something was very wrong. Many of the warriors had gone to the battlements to look at the fires and not come back. Ostwald had already herded the women back into the ballroom. Messengers had been rushing to and fro between Ostwald, Countess Emmanuelle and those outside. Something was very definitely happening and he needed to find out what it was. If he had not known better, he would have sworn that Ostwald had ordered the orchestra to play louder to drown out the sounds of the disturbance.

That must be it, Drexler thought, knowing that he had guessed the truth. Something was happening and in order to forestall a panic, Hieronymous was covering it up. He glanced around at the others present, and adjusted his mask. Most of the people in the ballroom consisted of ladies of rank, together with a sprinkling of hangers on, toadies and those simply too drunk to leave the hall. Of course there were footmen present, and a few guards too, but the situation was not very reassuring. He glanced across at Ostwald, not wanting to divulge the connection between them but filled with curiosity about what was going on. The secretary was garbed as a wood elf warrior, complete with bow. Drexler walked up to him, still nibbling at a savoury.

'What has happened?' he asked.

'Some disturbance in the town, Herr Doctor. Arson and possibly worse. With Her Serenity's permission, I have ordered troops from the barracks to quell the problem.'

'Nothing wrong in the palace then?'

'Not as far as I know, but I have ordered the guards to double-check.'

'Let us pray to Sigmar that it is only some looters. Things have been dreadful recently.'

'I fear the worst,' Ostwald said, looking up as another courier approached. Drexler agreed. Somewhere nearby his sorcerously trained senses told him that powerful magic was gathering.

CHANG SQUIK CURSED and ducked for cover. The placed smelled like a reeking midden. Looking around with his dark-accustomed eyes, he could tell this was, in truth, a human privy. Well, there were worse places to hide, he told himself but this was not going to help his mission.

He knew it was no use. He was not going to make it to the great chamber above the ballroom that he and the grey seer had agreed on. All of the stolen maps of the palace he had studied and still carried in his head told him this. He just did not have the time to get there and, even with his supreme skills at sneaking and skulking he doubted that he could find his way, unseen, through the mass of humans crowding the palace corridors and heading to the battlements in search of a view of what was going on below. This place was just going to have to do.

He took the knapsack from his back and reached within. The heat and the glow produced by the seeing stone told him that he was only just in time. Perhaps even a little late. He wondered how long the grey seer had already spent glaring out into the darkness of the inside of his pack. He shuddered when he thought of the wrath of Thanquol, as he squatted down, pressed his nose to the side of the stone, and gave the thumbs-up sign.

FELIX DUCKED THE swipe of a jagged scimitar and lashed out with his sword. His blow took the skaven beneath the ribs, and cleaved upwards in search of its heart. The skaven gave an eerie high-pitched shriek, clutched its chest and died. It fell to the ground even as Felix withdrew his blade from its chest.

Felix glanced around at the swirling melee. To his right he saw Heinz dash out the brains of a skaven leader with the cosh he held in his left hand, while he fended off the attack of another skaven with the blade he held in his right. Boris and Stephan fought back-to-back in the teeth of the tide of rat-men. Somewhere in the distance he could hear Gotrek's bellowed war cry.

Right at this moment, it was difficult to tell how the fight was going. The mercenaries seemed to be holding their own against the skaven, and the battle seemed to have attracted the attention of others. Humans were pouring out of the nearby tenements. Some clutched bedpans and pokers and other improvised weapons. Others carried swords and blunderbusses and other, rather more useful looking instruments of destruction. It seemed that the citizens had decided that they would rather meet their end in battle with their foes than be burned to death in their homes. That was good, thought Felix, for the mercenaries needed all the help they could get as more and more skaven were being drawn through the blazing streets to the sound of battle.

Even as he stood there, a severed head came flying out of the gloom, spinning, spilling blood from disconnected arteries, spraying all those below it with a shower of black raindrops. It aimed straight toward Felix and he batted it aside with his sword. Salty black fluid splattered his face and he fought the urge to lick his lips to clean them. Looking down he saw that the head belonged to a huge skaven warrior.

He wiped his face with his cloak quickly, worried that something might take advantage of his blindness and stab him. Shaking his head he moved forward cautiously to where he could hear Gotrek shouting. Ahead of him he could see an enormous ruck. The Slayer stood poised atop what first Felix took to be an enormous mound of bodies but swiftly realised was a plague cart. A wave of furious skaven scrabbled to reach him but were being hewn down by the awesome power of the Slayer's axe.

In the distance, looming over the great mass of lesser skaven, Felix could see a huge wedge of creatures he had come to think of as rat-ogres. Gotrek obviously saw them too, for he dived from the top of the plague cart into the seething sea of skaven. Within moments, his flickering axe had left a wall of broken and dying bodies all around him as he thrust his way towards the giant monsters that were his goal. Felix debated for only a moment whether to follow him and then pushed forward, shouting: 'Follow me, lads! Let's kill some bloody rat-men.'

As he hacked to left and right, he hoped the mercenaries were listening and following, otherwise he and Gotrek were in for a hard time when they closed with the rat-ogres.

THANQUOL GLARED INTO his scrying crystal. His head swam. His brain felt aflame. The power of the warpstone flowed through his veins like a drug. It made him feel dizzy and wonderful at the same time. At this moment, he felt sure he could perceive the underlying pattern of mystical forces focused on the crystal. He concentrated harder on making the thing work.

At last the darkness had cleared. At last he could see the leering face of Chang Squik. It appeared that the Clan Eshin assassin had reached his objective. Good, Thanquol thought. About time. He could barely contain the enormous mass of warpstone-fuelled mystical energy which boiled within him. He felt so saturated with power that it seemed that at any minute he might explode. His head swam and his vision blurred; everything seemed to swim around him. Frantically he tried to remember the syllables of the spell he had memorised so long ago in that great black book in the Accursed Library.

For a long moment the words eluded him, squirming and sliding just out of reach of his thought processes. Thanquol bit the insides of his cheek until he tasted blood. The pain seemed to sharpen his wits, for eventually the words came to him. He opened his lips and the syllables of his ancient language seemed to vomit forth from his mouth, ejecting with them a roiling cloud of dark, magical energy.

Thanquol's heartbeat accelerated to levels he would not have believed were endurable. His heart thumped wildly in his chest and his breathing was ragged and choked. He knew he was losing control of his spell and fought to rein in the flow of power before it destroyed him. Brain-blasting visions danced through his mind, and he knew that his seer's gifts had been driven to incredible new heights by the unprecedented amounts of warpstone he had consumed. Briefly his consciousness seemed to leave his body and scenes flickered through his mind in swift succession.

For a moment his spirit hovered over the city and he had a panoramic view of all that was happening. Below him the streets blazed with fire and violence. A river of skaven raced through the city, killing all that were in their path. Here and there they had encountered pockets of armed resistance where human garrisons or just the mobs of citizens had taken to the streets in defence of their homes. He saw swift, savage scuffles and giant rats devouring the corpses of man and skaven alike. He saw burning buildings and broken bodies. He saw the whole of the great ancient mancity of Nuln in flames.

Thanquol's attention was drawn to one particular struggle which suddenly leapt into focus when he recognised two alarmingly familiar figures. The dwarf and the human, followed by a disciplined pack of human warriors, were hacking through the skaven warriors towards the hulking bodyguard of Izak Grottle. In his trance state, Thanquol could see the roaring rat-ogres – and the appalled look on the face of his henchling Lurk as he contemplated the prospect of imminent violence. He saw the mad eyes of Vilebroth Null glaring into space as if he sensed the presence of some disembodied watcher. It looked very much to the grey seer like his plan was working and the interfering twosome were about to destroy his bitterest rivals.

Good, he thought, let them! Thanquol would brook no others claiming an unfair portion of his glory.

He saw Heskit One Eye bark instructions to his jezzail-equipped bodyguards and saw the long-barrelled rifle swing to bear on the dwarf. No! No, Thanquol thought furiously. None of that! With an almost imperceptible flicker of his thoughts, he touched the sniper's mind. Its fingers curled on the trigger but its warpstone bullet went wild, smashing into the skull of a rat-ogre, almost killing the brainless beast. The thing roared and went wild, surging forward into the skaven troops from the rear, killing as it went.

Thanquol felt dizzy and realised that he was losing himself in his spell. His power was bleeding away and, if he intended to accomplish what he wanted, he had better do it soon. With a wrench he sent his spirit soaring back towards the castle. He funnelled it into the link with the scrying stone and looked out once more on Chang Squik. Suddenly, with a snap, he was back in his own body again and the words of the spell were tumbling from his mouth.

He concentrated with all his might, bringing to bear all the relentless discipline of his many years as a grey seer and the spell swiftly returned to his control. In the air before him, the dark cloud shimmered and parted, revealing a rift in space running from the point just in front of where Thanquol stood to the ground around Chang Squik's scrying crystal.

'Quick! Quick! Forward!' he shouted to his Stormvermin guard. They walked forward into the black cloud, shimmered and vanished to reappear – Thanquol most earnestly hoped! – in the very heart of the breeder Emmanuelle's palace.

AHEAD OF THEM, Felix could see the rat-ogres. They loomed head and shoulders above the crowd, monstrous creatures, man-shaped but with the heads of immense rabid rats. Vast boils erupted through their mangy fur. The stigmata of a variety of foul mutations marred their flesh. Each had paws the size of shovels which ended in claws like daggers. Huge tusk-like fangs dripping with saliva filled their mouths. Their bellows were audible even over the din of battle.

At the sight of them, Felix felt the urge to halt and flee. He could tell the mercenaries following him felt the same way. The momentum of their charge was dissipating as they contemplated the horrific appearance of their foes. Only Gotrek showed no fear. He ploughed onward, unwilling or unable to be bothered by the fearsome nature of his foes. The rat-ogres were no more troubled by the Trollslayer's arrival than he was by theirs. With an ear-shattering roar, they charged rabidly to meet him.

It seemed unlikely to Felix that anything could survive the mad rush of such huge creatures. It was like expecting someone to be able to withstand the charge of a herd of elephants. Nothing should have been able to withstand the onslaught of that huge mass of muscle and teeth and claws. For a moment, all heads turned and even the skaven stopped their relentless advance to watch.

Completely undaunted by the fact his opponents were twice his size, Gotrek came on. His axe flashed, glowing red in the lurid blaze of the burning buildings, and one of the rat-ogres tumbled backwards, its leg chopped off at the knee. As it fell the Slayer's axe slashed back again and severed its arm. Clutching at the bloody stump with its good paw, the creature rolled over on the ground, writhing and shrieking.

Another of the immense creatures reached out and made a grab for the dwarf. Its razor-like talons bit into his ruddy flesh. Bloody droplets appeared on Gotrek's shoulder as the mighty beast raised him high above its head. It opened its huge jaws to the fullest extension as if intending to drop the Slayer in and devour him in one bite. Gotrek brought his axe crashing down. Powered by all the awesome strength of the Slayer's mighty arm, it smashed the rat-ogre's head in two. Blood, brains and teeth exploded everywhere. The Slayer went flying backwards through the air, propelled skyward by the reflex action of the rat-ogre's death spasm.

Seeing the remaining rat-ogres begin their advance towards Gotrek's recumbent form, Felix mustered all his courage and shouted: 'Charge! Charge! Let's send these foul vermin back to the hell that spawned them.'

Not daring to look back over his shoulder to see if anyone was following him, he raced forward into the fray.

CHANG SQUIK WATCHED in amazement as the air in front of him shimmered. For a moment, it appeared like a small, bright hole had been punched in the very fabric of the world. Through that hole leaked a vile black gas which smelled of warpstone and dark magic. Even as the assassin watched, the cloud expanded and shimmered until it stood higher than any skaven. Then the cloud itself parted to reveal a gateway joining the privy in which Chang Squik stood to the place where the grey seer was.

Chang Squik heard a sudden noise behind him and span around to see an ornately garbed human enter the privy, fumbling with his codpiece as if he intended to make water. The human reeked of alcohol. He paused in amazement and looked at the skulking skaven, then shook his head as if to clear it.

'I say,' he said. 'That's a ruddy good costume!'

Then his eyes widened further as he noticed the ranks of stormvermin starting to pour through Thanquol's sorcerous gateway. He opened his mouth and had just time for one shriek of warning before Chang Squik's throwing knife buried itself in his heart.

More and more skaven warriors flowed into the chamber, bursting out from the privy and into the corridors of the palace.

FELIX DUCKED, THREW himself flat and rolled under a blow that would have taken his head off, had it connected. Up close the rat-ogres were, if anything, even more frightening to behold. Their muscles were like the cables used to moor ships and they looked as if they could smash through a stone wall with little effort. The creature's massive tail lashed through the air with a crack like a whip. Worse yet was the smell, an awful combination of animal reek, wet fur, and warpstone. It reminded Felix of old and very sour cheese but was infinitely stronger, and threatened to bring tears to his eyes.

He rolled to one side as a fist the size of his head smashed into the ground where he had been. He kicked out at the rat-ogre's leg, hoping to unbalance it, but he might as well have been kicking a tree trunk. Hot saliva dribbled from the thing's mouth and landed on his hand. Felix fought down the urge to flinch and kept moving, knowing that his life depended on it.

Mad triumph appeared in the monster's small beady eyes. It opened its jaws and bellowed so loudly that Felix thought he would go deaf. The creature reached for him and from his prone position Felix lashed out with his blade and caught it across the knuckles with the razor-sharp edge. The rat-ogre's eyes went wide in surprise at the pain. Whimpering like a child, it pulled its hand back to its mouth to lick the wound. Taking advantage of its distraction, Felix half rose and stabbed upwards, driving the point of the sword right into the rat-ogre's groin.

The creature gave a shriek like the whistle of a steam-tank and reached down to touch its severed nether parts. Felix drove the point of his blade into the thing's opened jaws, pushing it right through the roof of the mouth and into its tiny malformed brain. The light went out of its eyes as it died instantly. Felix felt a momentary surge of triumph – which faded almost instantly as he realised that the rat-ogre's corpse was going to topple on him.

Felix sprang hastily to one side as the monstrous form crashed to the ground like a felled tree. Pausing to catch his breath a moment, he looked around. The last of the rat-ogres was going down, the mercenaries swarming over it like rats over a terrier, but the victory had been won at awful cost. Many human corpses covered the ground for every rat-ogre which had fallen. It looked like only he and Gotrek had bested one of the beasts in single combat.

Still, briefly and temporarily though it might turn out to be, it looked like the tide of battle had turned in their favour. The skaven leaders, including the grossly fat monster which had ordered the rat-ogres to attack, were fleeing backwards to regroup.

More and more people were massing in the streets to fight off the invaders. In the distance, Felix could hear the sound of horns and drums as the small army which surrounded the Noble Quarter began to advance down into the city. He wished he had some idea of how the battle was going. In the raging maelstrom of conflict it was difficult to say. They had won a victory here but it was all too possible that the skaven were triumphant in every other part of the city. Perhaps now would be a good time to make a run for it, he thought.

Then he saw the Trollslayer. Gotrek marched through the crowd towards him. A terrible grin revealed his missing teeth. Mad battle lust filled his one good eye.

'You brought a good fight with you, manling,' he said.

Felix nodded – and then remembered how this had all started. He fumbled within his tunic to retrieve the scrap of parchment, then slowly unrolled it to read its message.

GREY SEER THANQUOL watched the last of his troops pass through the gateway and then stepped through himself. He felt a sense of relief as the mystic portal closed automatically behind him. Even for a grey seer of Thanquol's awesome powers holding it open while hundreds of stormvermin poured through had been a terrible strain.

Now he could relax and watch his plan unfold before him. His tail lashed in anticipation of his triumph. Victory was within reach! Soon he would hold the human rulers hostage and command them to order their troops to surrender on pain of most hideous death. If they refused – which Thanquol rather hoped they would – he would make an example of some of them until they did agree. He was looking forward to some sport. Then the twitching of his nostrils warned him that something odd was happening, and he squinted around the chamber to confirm his suspicions.

Yes, it was true. Even Thanquol's warpstone addled senses could tell that this room was the wrong size, and it did not smell like a great hallway. It smelled like a midden. Thanquol stuck his head through the door. He looked into a corridor in which stormvermin milled in confusion. This was not the hallway they had been told to expect. He could see their clawleader studying his map with a look of puzzlement on his face. The awful truth dawned on Thanquol: that incompetent buffoon Chang Squik had placed his scrying crystal in the wrong place!

Thanquol bared his fangs in a ferocious snarl. It was just as well for the Clan Eshin assassin that he was not in sight, thought Thanquol. The grey seer swore that when he found Squik he would flay his flesh from his bones using the darkest magic that he could command.

Warpstone-driven euphoria and drugged rage warred in Thanquol's mind as he stalked out into the corridor to search for his goal.

FELIX LOOKED DOWN at the parchment. It was hard to tell in the gloom but the writing looked somehow different, smaller, neater, more precise. Not that it mattered right now, as Felix read in horror what it had to say.

> *Hoomans! the traitur Grey Sere Thanquol will invade the palaz this nite and kapture the breeder Eeman-yoo-ell and all yore pack leeders! Yoo must stop him or yore city will fall.*
>
> *Also this Thanquol is a very powerful sorcerur and will yoose his eevil majik to stop yoo. He must die-die or no hooman in yore city wil be safe.*

Felix looked down at Gotrek then passed him the note. 'Well?' he said.

'Well what, manling?'

'Do we go to the palace and rescue our noble rulers from this skaven menace?'

'They're your rulers, manling, not mine!'

'I think this grey seer is the thing we encountered in von Halstadt's house. The rat-man which got away. I think it might be behind this whole invasion.'

'Then killing it would be a great deed – and dying in the attempt would be a mighty doom!' Gotrek rumbled.

'Only one problem, then: we're going to have to fight our way through the city to get there!'

'Where's the problem in that?'

'Who knows how many rat-men stand in our way?'

Felix wracked his brain for a way out of this dilemma. It would take an army to fight its way across the city.

In a flash of inspiration worthy of a Detlef Sierck hero, the answer came to him.

LURK SNITCHTONGUE cowered in the shadow of Izak Grottle. The huge Clan Moulder packmaster looked at him hungrily. He still seemed to be in a state of shock from watching the defeat of his prized rat-ogres.

'I thought you said the human and the dwarf had received the message and were on their way to… intercede with Grey Seer Thanquol.'

'The message was delivered, master of Moulders! I cannot be held responsible for what happens next. Maybe they were caught up in the fighting.'

'Maybe! Maybe! All of this has left us exposed, though. Very exposed. We must find another skaven force quickly or return to the safety of the sewers.'

'Yes, yes, most perceptive of planners.'

'Have you seen Heskit One Eye or Vilebroth Null?'

'Not since we were attacked, greatest of gorgers.'

'A pity. Well, let us be on our way!'

'At once.'

FILLED WITH warpstone-fuelled rage Thanquol stalked the corridors of the palace. The damnable place was huge and it was as much a maze as anything he made his pet humans run through. His carefully contrived plan had fallen apart because of the incompetence of Chang Squik. It had relied on speed, surprise and the fury of the skaven assault to overwhelm the defence. Now his stormvermin were reduced to racing through the corridors and fighting skirmishes with groups of sentries. It was only a matter of time before the humans realised what was going on, concentrated their forces and began to fight back. Thanquol still expected a victory under those circumstances.

His warriors were many and bold, but there was always the possibility that something might happen to tip the odds against them. Thanquol would have much preferred a sudden overwhelming victory, not this period of anger and doubt.

HESKIT ONE EYE chittered in excitement. Once again he watched the warpfire throwers sweep through the buildings. These huge human structures burned well. Their wooden supports caught fire easily, and the soft stone and brick from which they were made melted in the fierce heat of the warpflames.

Heskit had thought it politic to separate from the others when his jezzail team had accidentally shot one of Izak Grottle's rat-ogres. It was an accident, Heskit knew, but the skaven of Clan Moulder were insanely suspicious. Heskit had no desire to have Izak Grottle 'accidentally' stab him in the back so he had led his troops away from the main battle to continue spreading destruction.

And how glad he was that he had done so. There was something truly enthralling about watching the machineries of destruction at work, of feeling the heat and flames his warriors had caused warm his face and watching these giant structures tumble down.

Heskit stared upwards for a long time, watching the tenement collapse. It was only at the very last moment that he realised that tons of brick and blazing wood were crashing down right on top of him. And by then, it was far too late for him to escape.

FELIX LEAPT ON to the back of the plague cart. Bodies squelched under his feet. The stink was appalling. He really would have preferred to stand somewhere else but this was the only way he could get the attention of the crowd.

'Citizens of Nuln!' he bellowed in the orator's voice he had not used since the Window Tax riots. 'Listen to me!'

A few heads turned in his direction. Most of the others were too busy hacking at skaven corpses or shouting gleefully at their neighbours.

'Citizens of Nuln! Skaven slayers!' he shouted. A few more people looked at him. They began to tug their neighbour's arms and point in his direction. Slowly but surely Felix felt the attention of the crowd turn on him. Slowly but surely, the crowd fell silent. These people had seen him and Gotrek slay rat-ogres. They had also seen them lead the charge into battle. These people were leaderless and in need of direction. Felix thought he could provide them with both.

'Citizens of Nuln! The skaven have attacked your great city. They have burned your homes. They have killed your loved ones. They have brought madness and plague to your streets.'

Felix saw that he had them now. All eyes in the crowd were riveted to him. He could sense the crowds anger and hatred and fear, and he could sense that he had given it a focus. He felt a sudden thrill at the power he held. He wet his lips and continued to speak, knowing that he must sway them to the course he wanted now or he would lose them.

'You have killed many skaven. You have seen their monsters fall. You have seen their vile weapons fail. Victory is within your grasp. Are you ready to kill more skaven?'

'Yes!' cried a few of the crowd. Many still looked uncertain. For the most part they were not warriors, just ordinary people suddenly thrown into a situation they did not truly understand.

'Are you ready to drive the skaven from your city? For if you do not, they will return and carry you away as slaves! '

Felix had no idea whether this was true or not, but it was what they had done in the past and it sounded good. More to the point, it sounded frightening. More voices shouted: 'Yes.'

'Are you ready to slaughter these monsters without mercy? For rest assured, if you do not, they will slaughter you!'

'Yes!' roared the whole crowd in a frenzy of rage and fear.

'Then follow me! To the palace! Where the chief of all this foul breed even now threatens the life of your rightful ruler!'

Felix leapt down from the cart and landed on the cobbled street. Hands stretched out from the crowd to pat him on the back. More still shouted their support. He saw Heinz and the surviving mercenaries give him the thumbs up. He looked down at Gotrek; even the dwarf looked pleased. 'Let's go,' Felix said and they broke into a run.

As one, the crowd followed them through the burning streets of the city.

CHANG SQUIK DREW his long black cloak in front of his face and stalked forward, blade in hand. He kept to the shadows, moving quietly on the balls of his feet, ready to strike in any direction at the slightest provocation.

In the dim distance he could still hear the sound of fighting. From up ahead, he could hear the strange scraping noise that humans called 'music'. He emerged onto a balcony and blinked his eyes momentarily dazzled.

He stood, looking down upon a huge chamber. The vaulted ceiling above him was painted with an enormous picture of the human gods looking down benevolently. Enormous chandeliers, each holding hundreds of candles, provided dazzling illumination. Down below an orchestra played and many gowned breeders and a few costumed males stood at ease, drinking and eating happily. The smell of food made Squik's nostrils twitch and drew his attention to the tables below. They groaned beneath the weight of roasted fowl and pig. Platters of cheese and bread and all manner of savouries were there. So much for starving the city, thought the Eshin assassin! Then he realised that maybe the ordinary people were starving, but the rulers had preserved all these dainties for themselves. In this, then, the humans were not too different from skaven, he decided – then started at the sound of footsteps on the balcony behind him.

Two figures, a male and a breeder, had emerged onto the balcony behind him. Their clothing was in a state of disarray and it looked odd even for humans. The man was garbed as a shepherd in some sort of tunic. He carried pan pipes and a golden mask shaped to have small horns like a goat's covered his face. The woman, too was masked but she was dressed in some sort of dancer's costume, with diamond-patterned tights, a tricorned hat and a domino mask. They stared at him and to his surprise emitted the strange wheezing sound that humans called laughter. They stank of alcohol.

Chang Squik was so surprised that he paused in the middle of his death stroke. He had intended to strike them down and withdraw into the shadowy corridors. 'I say, what a super costume!' the man said.

'Absolutely wonderful,' the woman agreed. She bent over and tugged at Squik's tail. 'So realistic.'

Squik had no idea what they were saying. He understood no words of their odd rumbling language but it was starting to filter into his brain that these people were wearing some sort of costume, like high ranking skaven performing a religious rite. And they appeared to have mistaken him for one of them.

Was it possible that these people were so drunk and so uncaring that they did not realise that there was a skaven invasion going on outside? To his astonishment Chang Squik realised that it must be so. Worse, he could see that all eyes down below were on them. He considered pushing the pair off the balcony and ducking back into the shadows but that meant going back into corridors filled with fighting stormvermin and an angry Thanquol. Another plan struck him. Nodding politely to the two revellers, he put away his blade, walked down the stairs and into the crowds of masked and disguised humans.

He helped himself to a savoury from a tray carried by a passing waiter, picked up a goblet of wine and strolled through the hall, nodding left and right to those he passed. Perhaps if he could find the breeder, Emmanuelle, he might yet redeem himself in the eyes of Grey Seer Thanquol.

VILEBROTH NULL LOOKED up in astonishment at the onrushing horde of humans. Where had they all come from? How had they mustered such a huge force so suddenly? Had Grey Seer Thanquol underestimated their numbers? Certainly that was possible and, if so, just another example of the grey seer's incompetence. Not that it would make any difference if he did not get out of their way.

He had spent the night since the invasion force had erupted from the sewer wandering lost through the twisting maze of alleys and lanes, killing any humans he encountered, and trying to locate Izak Grottle and the others. He cursed the initial blind rush which had separated them all. Now he was left to face this horde of humans without any sort of bodyguard.

He looked up and realised that he recognised the leaders of the charge – and what was worse, they recognised him! It was the human and the dwarf who had interrupted his ritual and destroyed the Cauldron of a Thousand Poxes. For a moment, a vast righteous anger swept through Vilebroth Null. Almost without thinking, he summoned his powers and an eerie green light swept into being around his head and paws. He mumbled the chant that would summon destructive spirits of disease to smite his foes.

The humans did not even slow their headlong rush. Vilebroth Null realised that they could not. The ones at the back were pushing the ones at the front of the herd forward. If the leaders slowed they would be trampled. He kept chanting, desperate now to summon the powers which would protect him, knowing that most likely it was already too late. The humans were upon him.

The last thing Vilebroth Null saw was a huge axe descending towards his skull.

FELIX SHUDDERED. He had recognised the green-robed rat-man in the last seconds before the crowd had trampled it. It was the plague priest from the cemetery. And Felix was glad that it was dead.

He was warm now, sweating from exertion and the heat of the blazing buildings which surrounded them. He tried to ignore the screams of those trapped within and focus on taking vengeance on those responsible. Somewhere off in the distance he heard a crashing sound. A pillar of sparks rose skyward as a tenement collapsed. Felix knew that if anyone survived this, they would have their work cut out for them rebuilding the city. This was as bad as the Great Fire of Altdorf.

They hit the slopes around the palace, and Felix noticed that many of the buildings here were intact. They were like his brother's house, small fortresses as well as mansions. Ahead of them was a force clad in the black tabards of the Nuln city guard. They had their halberds raised to repel a charge but lowered them confused when they saw that the mob were human, rather than rat-men.

'Skaven!' he shouted. 'There are skaven in the palace!'

He did not know whether the captain of the guard believed him or not, but he did not have much choice. If his men stood there much longer they would either have to use their weapons on their fellow citizens or be trampled under foot. The captain made a snap decision: he barked an order and his men stood aside. Felix could see that the great gate of the palace was still open. It must have been left that way to allow the coaches of the guests to enter, Felix decided.

He rushed onwards, praying that they were in time to save Countess Emmanuelle.

* * *

DREXLER TURNED TO look in the direction of the scream. Suddenly the balcony seethed with huge, black armoured skaven. Those were not costumes, he could tell immediately. These were the real thing. Monstrous, man-sized, anthropomorphic rats armed with huge scimitars and bearing round shields inscribed with the sigil of their evil god.

He saw a few of the guards, elite troops, move to interpose themselves between the guests and the skaven. They were cut down swiftly by the disciplined phalanx as it poured down the stairs and into the room. Slowly the orchestra stopped playing. The notes faded out into discordant echoes. Screaming guests in fancy costumes were herded towards the great throne dais by massive snarling rat-men.

Drexler wondered if he should risk a spell, but decided against it. There were too many skaven for him to affect them all. Where were the guards, he wondered? Where were all the men who had gone to the battlements to look at the fire?

Then he sensed the presence of terrible magical energy. Looking up he saw a huge, horned, grey furred rat-man descending the stairs. It looked like an evil god come to bring doom to all mankind.

THANQUOL STRODE FORWARD across the corpses of the dead humans. At last, from up ahead he could here a gratifying number of screams. It seemed that his stormvermin had discovered the Great Hall at last, and that the human leaders were finally within his grasp. Filled with a tremendous sense of his inevitable righteous triumph, the grey seer advanced to victory!

FELIX LED THE charge into the courtyard. Looking up, he saw a struggle taking place on the battlements.

'Quick!' he shouted to Heinz. 'Scour the battlements! Kill any skaven you find!'

'Right-o, young Felix,' Heinz said, rushing towards the steps with the mercenaries in tow. 'Follow me, lads!'

Felix glanced around at the mob pouring into the courtyard. They looked ferocious, ready to kill anything they saw. A number of them began to race after Heinz.

'Where to now, manling?' Gotrek asked. 'I want to get to grips with that rat-man wizard. My axe thirsts for more blood!'

Good question, thought Felix, wishing he had an answer. Think, he urged himself. Where is the logical place to go? The grey seer wanted to capture Emmanuelle. Tonight he knew from Drexler a great ball was taking place. The logical place for the countess to be was the ballroom that Ostwald and he had passed through the first time he had visited the palace. Now, if only he could remember the way there!

'Follow me!' he shouted, trying to make his voice as confident as possible.

THANQUOL PAUSED AT the head of the stairs to survey the great ballroom. He wanted to give the pitiful humans the chance to appreciate the full awful majesty of their conquerors. He wanted to savour his moment of ultimate triumph.

All eyes turned to look at him. He could tell the humans were impressed by his dignity and his presence. They always were. The majestic form of a grey seer always inspired respect and admiration in equal parts from all who saw him. He glanced at the crowd and looked around to see if he could find his chosen prey.

In truth, he had expected to be able to tell her by the elaborate nature of her costume, and by the fact that she wore a crown, but he could see that all the humans present were garbed in strange disguises, almost as if they had intended to thwart him. Well, well, he thought, they would see that a grey seer was not so easily balked. He singled out one of the human males, a man garbed like some primitive tribesman.

'You, man-thing! Where is your chief breeder? Answer me! Quick! Quick! ' Thanquol asked in his best Reikspiel.

'I haven't the faintest idea what you're talking about, old man,' came the reply. Sweat dribbled down the man's face. Thanquol blasted him with a surge of pure magical power. Women's screams filled the air as the stripped and blackened skeleton of his victim fell to the floor. Thanquol selected another victim, a woman dressed like one of the humans' goddesses.

'You! Tell me where is the chief breeder? Answer! Now! Now!'

The woman looked at him blankly. 'What is a breeder?' she asked. Thanquol's answer was to blast her with magic as well. Another charred corpse tumbled to the floor. Thanquol selected a man very cunningly disguised as a Clan Eshin assassin.

'You! The chief breeder! Where?!' Thanquol bellowed. The disguised assassin turned, its tail twitching remarkably like a real skaven.

'No, master! Don't blast me!' it cried in fluent skaven. Remarkable, thought Thanquol. A human who speaks our language! Then he realised that this was no human. It was that damnable Chang Squik, hiding himself among the humans. Thanquol looked at the assassin and licked his lips, thinking of how the assassin's folly has almost cost Thanquol his triumph, remembering all the other failures Chang Squik had been responsible for.

This was perfect, thought Thanquol,. If anybody ever asked, he could claim that it was all a terrible error. He summoned all of his powers. Chang Squik screamed most satisfactorily as dark magic consumed his body.

Thanquol gloated for a brief but joyous moment, then picked out another human. 'You! Where is the chief breeder? Answer! Quick-quick! Or your miserable life is forfeit!'

'But I don't know what a breeder is,' whimpered the fat man garbed as a huge pink rabbit. Thanquol shrugged and blasted him. Yet more bones clattered onto the marble floor.

It began to occur to Thanquol, even through the haze of warpstone clouding his mind, that there was something wrong with his strategy. The humans did not quite seem to understand what he was getting at. What could it be? Where were their feeble minds going astray? He had asked for their chief breeder, after all. Perhaps if he asked for her by name? He signalled out a cringing breeder, and pointed one talon at her.

'You! You! Are you the chief breeder Emmanuelle?'

The breeder was obviously too overwhelmed by the sheer majesty of Thanquol's presence to speak. He blasted her as a lesson to the others that they should reply when he asked a question. He selected another male next, hoping that it would be slightly less witless than the breeder.

'You – where is the chief breeder Emmanuelle?' The male shook its head defiantly.

'I will never tell you. I have sworn to serve the Elector Countess wi–'

Thanquol yawned and unleashed another blast of dark magic before the human could finish its speech. He so hated it when they became contrary. His specimens back home in Skavenblight could be the same way sometimes, particularly after he took their breeders and runts away to experiment on. An amazing race in some ways certainly, he thought, but so stupid.

Out of the corner of his eye, Thanquol caught sight of two human breeders muttering to each other. Slowly he swung his burning gaze towards them. As one the breeders straightened and one of them strode towards him. She pulled off her mask to reveal a pale but determined face.

'I believe you are looking for me,' she said defiantly. 'I am Elector Countess Emmanuelle!'

Thanquol was almost disappointed. The warpstone power still surged within him, and he had been enjoying using it. There was nothing quite like the thrill of blasting lesser beings to bits, unless it was the sense of power doing just that gave one.

'Good! Good!' Thanquol said. 'You will order your troops to surrender immediately and I will let you live. Fail to do so and...'

DREXLER SHUDDERED AS he watched the monstrous horned skaven stride through the crowd. Just the sight of it filled him with fear. It wasn't the red, glowing eyes or the way its fur bristled that scared him. It was the power it so obviously carried within it.

Drexler's mystically attuned senses could see that the thing fairly bristled with dark magical energy. He was enough of a sorcerer himself to see that there was something deeply unnatural about it. No living creature should be able to wield or contain such power without suffering the consequences. At the very least, it should go mad. At most it might explode, blown apart by the vast energy roiling within its body.

Where could it have acquired such power, Drexler wondered? The only possible source of so much energy was said to be pure warpstone. Could the creature possibly be consuming the stuff? Such a supposition beggared belief.

Perhaps the creature had not escaped its use unscathed. Its slurred speech and stumbling, jerky movements certainly hinted that something was wrong with it. The way its whiskers quivered and its head twitched made it look as if it were in the terminal stage of some fatal addiction. Yes, the creature was mad. No doubt about it. The way it had so casually blasted apart anyone who did not answer its questions to its satisfaction stated that fact clearly. The question now was what was he, Drexler, going to do about it?

He was appalled by his own cowardice. Each time the creature had gathered its dark powers, he had sensed it. He could have at least tried to work a counter-spell but he had not. He had been to overcome by the horror of the thing's appearance and the thought of what might happen to him if he had intervened. He felt sure that he would lose any mystical duel with this rat-man and that attracting its attention would be fatal. Even if he could somehow hold the skaven mage in check, its black armoured lackeys filled the room. At a word from it, they would surely cut him down with those cruel swords.

So he had done nothing and half a dozen people had died. He was proud of what Baron Blucher had done, the way the man had defied the skaven before he died. Why could he not summon such courage? The healer in him was appalled that he had done nothing to prevent such loss of life. Now the countess herself stood in peril, willing to give her own life to spare her subjects. Drexler vowed that this time, he would intervene, if the skaven attacked.

There would be no more magical killings if he could help it.

'I WILL DO NO such thing,' Countess Emmanuelle said shakily. 'I would rather die than order my troops to surrender to you foul vermin.'

'Foolish breeder – that is just what you will do, if you defy me!' Thanquol said. He raised his paw and dark magical energy played around it menacingly. The breeder flinched slightly, but did not move or open her mouth. Thanquol wondered if there was some way around this impasse. Perhaps if he ordered some of the humans tortured before her eyes she would weaken. Thanquol's experiments had led him to believe such a course would often work. Yes, that was it!

Then from somewhere around him in the ballroom, he sensed the slow build-up of magical energies. They were not skaven magical energies either. He heard footsteps rushing closer too, even as he turned his head to seek their source.

'Well, well, what have we here?' a harsh grating voice said like two great boulders rubbing together, cutting like a knife to the very core of Thanquol's being. 'It looks like we're just in time to kill some rats.'

Thanquol quelled the urge to squirt the musk of fear. He recognised that harsh, flinty growl! The grey seer jerked his head to one side just to confirm his worst fears, and he saw that they were true. Standing in the entrance to the chamber were the dwarf Gurnisson and the human Jaeger, and behind them was a teeming mass of human troops.

Thanquol howled in frustration and rage. He reached deep into his corrupt soul and hurled all his lethal power at his enemies in one mighty blast.

FELIX PREPARED HIMSELF to spring to one side as he saw the midnight black thunderbolt gather around the grey seer's paw. The nimbus of evil mystical power around the rat-man's head was so bright that it was almost impossible to look at. Gotrek held his ground unflinchingly, seemingly totally unafraid as the enormous blast of destructive power was suddenly unleashed directly at him.

There was a mighty flash and a crackling, booming noise as of thunder unleashed directly overhead. The air was filled with the burnt-metal reek of ozone. Felix was vaguely aware that two bolts of energy had leapt from the grey seer's paws. One was aimed at him. One was aimed at Gotrek. He closed his eyes, fully expecting to die.

Instead of the anticipated blast of incredible pain, he felt nothing except a mild tingling on his flesh and his hair starting to stand on end. He opened his eyes and saw that both he and the Trollslayer were enveloped in a golden field of energy. Long golden lines raced from the aura that surrounded them back to the hands of Doctor Drexler. Felix could see the look of strain on the doctor's face. Grateful as he was to the physician for saving them, he knew that the doctor could not long stand against the storm of magical power which surrounded them.

'Is that the best you can do?' Gotrek bellowed. 'Rat-man, your life is over!'

The Slayer charged through the corona of coruscating energy. Felix charged right beside him.

* * *

NO! NO! GREY SEER Thanquol thought in panic as he saw his two enemies racing towards him. This was not happening! How could this be? How could this abominable pair appear to thwart him in his hour of triumph? What evil deity protected them, and kept them alive to interfere in his plans time after time? He bared his lips in a snarl and continued to unleash his destructive energies against the swirling golden shield which stood between the pair and destruction. He could feel it start to give way under the relentless pressure of his magical energies.

Unfortunately it was not giving way quickly enough. At the rate the human and the dwarf were closing the distance between them, they would reach Thanquol before he could shred their flesh from their bones. He snarled a curse, and reined in his spell, knowing that something other than magic was needed now.

'Quick! Quick!' he ordered his stormvermin. 'Kill them! Now! Now!'

With visible reluctance, the stormvermin moved to the attack. They had heard of this pair. Tales of the destruction they had wreaked among skaven were legend among the army assaulting Nuln. Their very presence was demoralising to Thanquol's troops. The way the dwarf decapitated the experienced clawleader as if he were a mere puppy did nothing to reassure the skaven. Nor did the vast howling tide of angry humans flowing into the ballroom. Thanquol sensed that the morale of his force was mere moments from breaking.

Swiftly he weighed the odds of victory, and saw that his moment had passed, and that triumph had slipped through his talons. Now it was a case of measuring his chances of survival. If he left now, while his troops still slowed down the pursuit, Thanquol realised he might reach the privy. Once there he could use the scrying stone to create a gate back to the sewers. Of course, now with his power at a low ebb, he would not have the strength to hold it open for all his warriors. In fact, he doubted that more than one solitary skaven would escape through it.

Still, he knew the genius of Thanquol must be preserved. On another day, he would return and take his revenge.

'Forward, my brave stormvermin, to inevitable victory!' Thanquol shouted, before he turned tail and ran with all his might. He did not need his grey seer's intuition to tell him that the slaughter behind him was going to be one-sided and merciless.

EPILOGUE

'So it was that the skaven were driven forth from the
city, although at great terrible cost in lives and damage
to property. I had thought to rest and catch my breath
after our exertions but it was not to be. The hand of
doom reached out for my companion. And so began a
journey that was to end at furthest and most gods
forsaken reaches of the world...'

— From *My Travels With Gotrek, Vol. III*,
by Herr Felix Jaeger (Altdorf Press, 2505)

FELIX SAT IN HIS favourite chair in the Blind Pig and finished
inscribing the notes in his journal. He would leave this book in
storage with Otto until such a time as he returned to claim it.
If ever he did get round to writing the tale of the Trollslayer's
heroic doom, it might prove invaluable.

From outside he could hear the sound of hammers. The
builders had been at work for weeks now, trying to restore the
battle-scarred city to its former glory. Felix knew that it would

be many years before Nuln recovered fully, if it ever did. Still, he was not hugely troubled. Things had ended well, more or less.

The countess had been grateful, but there was not much she could do to reward two criminals wanted by the authorities in Altdorf without antagonising the Emperor himself. There had been many protestations of gratitude and sweet smiles of thanks, but nothing more. Felix did not care. He was just glad to have avoided being thrown into prison, just as he was glad to have survived the night of conflict which had followed the storming of the palace.

He still shivered to think of the savage battles which had been fought in the streets between man and skaven. It had taken all night and most of the rest of the following day to clear the city, and even after it was done most people had remained awake the following night, not quite able to believe they were safe. It had taken many more days of hunting afterwards to winkle the skaven out of all their hiding places, and he was still not sure that the sewers were entirely free of them.

On the other hand, the plague had abated. Perhaps the great fire had cleansed the city – or maybe it had simply claimed all the lives it was capable of taking. Drexler claimed that this was often the way with plagues. It had vanished now. No more deaths were reported. No more people had been stricken.

And for a wonder, the great plague of rats had ended too. For days, more and more of them had appeared but they seemed weaker, and bore the stigma of mutations, as if something had gone wrong with them before even they were born. Many of the later generations had been still-born. It was as if they had been created with some deliberate flaw by the skaven. Perhaps they had been intended to scourge the city and then die out, leaving the skaven free to claim everything. It was an idea of such devilish cunning that it made Felix shiver. Were the rat-men really capable of such a thing? Or had it all been merely an accident?

Somewhere in the distance, temple bells rang. Of course, the priests were claiming that their particular gods had intervened to save Nuln. Such was their way. Felix had seen precious little evidence that the immortal ones had acted to preserve Nuln but who was he to say? Perhaps they had been there, invisibly shielding the folk, as Drexler claimed. Certainly Felix thought that Gotrek and himself had been very lucky, and perhaps that was the favour of the gods.

The gods had spared others. Otto and his wife were safe, prospering even. As his brother had predicted, there was a great demand for all manner of stuff for use in the reconstruction and Jaegers of Altdorf were helping provide it.

Drexler had recovered almost fully from his sorcerous battle with the grey seer. Felix had been to see him several times since the fateful night, and the man looked as calm and cheerful as ever. One time, he had even encountered Ostwald at the doctor's townhouse. The spymaster had treated Felix with a deference close to hero worship which Felix had found embarrassing.

Heinz and most of the mercenaries were well. The old innkeeper had taken a nasty knock on the head, and his head was swathed in so many bandages that he looked like an Arab, but he was still there behind the bar, pulling pints.

Felix had no idea where Elissa was. He had not seen her or Hans since the day before the battle, and no one he knew had any knowledge of her whereabouts. He sincerely hoped she was well and had escaped back to her home village. He still missed her.

They never found the skaven grey seer, despite searching the palace from top to bottom. All that the court magicians had found were some strange magical resonances in the privy. It was assumed that Thanquol had used magic to effect his escape.

For the most part, the citizens were happy. They had survived and were rebuilding. In any case life went on as usual and Felix was looking forward to a nice long rest.

Having avoiding meeting his heroic doom yet again, Gotrek had stomped around like a bear with a sore head in the days after the fighting finished before consoling himself with a three day long binge of boozing and brawling. Now he sat in the corner of the Blind Pig, nursing his hangover and bellowing for ale.

The saloon doors swung open and another dwarf came in. He was shorter than Gotrek and lighter in build. A circlet of bright red cloth was wrapped round his head and his beard was clipped short. The tunic he wore was divided into red and yellow squares of ungodly brightness. The newcomer looked around and his eyes widened when he saw Gotrek. He strode across to the Slayer with a purposeful step. Felix closed his journal, put down his pen and watched with interest.

'You are Gotrek, son of Gurni, a Slayer?' the newcomer said, speaking in Reikspiel as dwarfs often did when humans were listening. Felix knew they liked no one to hear their secret tongue.

'What if I am?' Gotrek said in his most brutish and surly fashion. 'Want to make something of it?'

'I am Nor Norrison, a bonded messenger to the clans. I have a message for you of great importance. I have come a thousand leagues to deliver it.'

'Well, get on with it then! I don't have all day,' Gotrek grumbled impatiently.

'It is not a verbal message. It is written in runescript. You can read, can't you?'

'About as well as I can punch out the teeth of messengers who cheek me.'

The messenger produced a parchment envelope with a great flourish. Gotrek took it and tore it open. He started to read – and as he did so all the colour left his face. His beard bristled and his eyes went wide.

'What is it?' Felix asked.

'A mighty doom, manling. A mighty doom indeed.' He rose from his chair and reached for his axe. 'Get your gear. We're leaving.'

'For where?'

'The ends of the earth, most likely,' Gotrek said, and could be prevailed upon to say nothing more.

Also from the Black Library

TROLLSLAYER
A Gotrek & Felix novel
by William King

HIGH ON THE HILL the scorched walled castle stood, a stone spider clutching the hilltop with blasted stone feet. Before the gaping maw of its broken gate hanged men dangled on gibbets, flies caught in its single-strand web.

'Time for some bloodletting,' Gotrek said. He ran his left hand through the massive red crest of hair that rose above his shaven tattooed skull. His nose chain tinkled gently, a strange counterpoint to his mad rumbling laughter.

'I am a slayer, manling. Born to die in battle. Fear has no place in my life.'

TROLLSLAYER IS THE first part of the death saga of Gotrek Gurnisson, as retold by his travelling companion Felix Jaeger. Set in the darkly gothic world of Warhammer, Trollslayer is an episodic novel featuring some of the most extraordinary adventures of this deadly pair of heroes. Monsters, daemons, sorcerers, mutants, orcs, beastmen and worse are to be found as Gotrek strives to achieve a noble death in battle. Felix, of course, only has to survive to tell the tale.

Also from the Black Library

DAEMONSLAYER
A Gotrek & Felix novel
by William King

THE ROAR WAS so loud and so terrifying that Felix almost dropped his blade. He looked up and fought the urge to soil his britches. The most frightening thing he had ever seen had entered the hall and behind it he could see the leering heads of beastmen.

As he gazed on the creature in wonder and terror, Felix thought: this is the incarnate nightmare which has bedevilled my people since time began.

'Just remember,' Gotrek said from beside him, 'the daemon is mine!'

FRESH FROM THEIR adventures battling the foul servants of the rat-god in Nuln, Gotrek and Felix are now ready to join an expedition northwards in search of the long-lost dwarf hall of Karag Dum. Setting forth for the hideous Realms of Chaos in an experimental dwarf zeppelin, Gotrek and Felix are sworn to succeed or die in the attempt. But greater and more sinister energies are coming into play, as a daemonic power is awoken to fulfil its ancient, deadly promise.

Also from the Black Library

FIRST & ONLY
A Gaunt's Ghosts novel
by Dan Abnett

'THE TANITH ARE strong fighters, general, so I have heard'.
The scar tissue of his cheek pinched and twitched slightly,
as it often did when he was tense. 'Gaunt is said to be a
resourceful leader.'

'You know him?' The general looked up, questioningly
'I know *of* him, sir. In the main by reputation'.

GAUNT GOT TO his feet, wet with blood and Chaos pus. His
Ghosts were moving up the ramp to secure the position.
Above them, at the top of the elevator shaft, were over a
million Shriven, secure in their bunker batteries. Gaunt's
expeditionary force was inside, right at the heart of the
enemy stronghold. Commissar Ibram Gaunt smiled.

*IT IS THE nightmare future of Warhammer 40,000, and
mankind teeters on the brink of extinction. The galaxy-span-
ning Imperium is riven with dangers, and in the
Chaos-infested Sabbat system, Imperial Commissar Gaunt
must lead his men through as much in-fighting amongst rival
regiments as against the forces of Chaos. First and Only is
an epic saga of planetary conquest, grand ambition, treachery
and honour.*

Also from the Black Library

EYE OF TERROR
A Warhammer 40,000 novel
by Barrington J. Bayley

Tell the truth only if a lie will not serve

'WHAT I HAVE to tell you,' Abaddas said, in slow measured tones, 'will be hard for you to accept or even comprehend. The rebellion led by Warmaster Horus succeeded. The Emperor is dead, killed by Horus himself in single combat, though Horus too died of his injuries.'

Magron groaned. He cursed himself for having gone into suspended animation. To be revived in a galaxy without the Emperor! Horrible! Unbelievable! Impossible to bear! Stricken, he looked into Abaddas's flinty grey eyes. 'Who is Emperor now?'

The first hint of an emotional reaction flickered on Abaddas's face. 'What need have we of an Emperor?' he roared. 'We have the Chaos gods!'

IN THE DARK and gothic future of Warhammer 40,000, mankind teeters on the brink of extinction. As the war-fleets of the Imperium prepare to launch themselves on a crusade into the very heart of Chaos, Rogue Trader Maynard Rugolo seeks power and riches on the fringe worlds of this insane and terrifying realm.

Also from the Black Library

INTO THE MAELSTROM

An anthology of Warhammer 40,000 stories, edited by Marc Gascoigne & Andy Jones

'THE CHAOS ARMY had travelled from every continent, every shattered city, every ruined sector of Illium to gather on this patch of desert that had once been the control centre of the Imperial Garrison. The sand beneath their feet had been scorched, melted and fused by a final, futile act of suicidal defiance: the detonation of the garrison's remaining nuclear stockpile.' – **Hell in a Bottle** *by Simon Jowett*

'HOARSE SCREAMS and the screech of tortured hot metal filled the air. Massive laser blasts were punching into the spaceship. They superheated the air that men breathed, set fire to everything that could burn and sent fireballs exploding through the crowded passageways.' – **Children of the Emperor** *by Barrington J. Bayley*

IN THE GRIM and gothic nightmare future of Warhammer 40,000, mankind teeters on the brink of extinction. INTO THE MAELSTROM is a storming collection of a dozen action-packed science fiction short stories set in this dark and brooding universe.